The War Between Us

ALSO BY MARGARET JAMES

THE DENHAM FAMILY SAGAS
Book 1: The War Between Us

STANDALONE
The Final Reckoning

The War Between Us

MARGARET JAMES

The Denham Family Sagas Book 1

Choc Lit
A JOFFE BOOKS COMPANY

Revised edition 2025
Choc Lit, London
A Joffe Books company
www.choc-lit.com

First published in Great Britain in 2005
as *The Morning Promise*
Also published as *The Silver Locket* in 2010

This paperback edition was first published
in Great Britain in 2025

Cover art by Jarmila Takač

ISBN: 978-1781898635

To Jan — the best of sisters

CHAPTER ONE

The view from the breakfast room at Charton Minster was of the most beautiful garden in the whole of Dorset, but on this bright March morning Rose Courtenay hated it.

The sight of golden daffodils in full flower beneath the spreading trees merely reminded her she was trapped, perhaps forever. She turned away and was about to go upstairs again when she heard her mother on the phone.

'Of course you must bring Alex,' Lady Courtenay was saying. 'Poor boy, it's not his fault Viola Denham was his mother. We should be glad she let him come to Henry. If she'd left him with that painter fellow, he'd probably have turned out very badly.'

Alexander Denham — that's all I need, thought Rose. She wondered if she'd dare to have a migraine which would get her out of going to her mother's evening party. She couldn't stand that silent, sullen boy who never seemed to do anything but scowl, but with whom she was expected to get on just because Henry Denham and her father were old friends.

Lady Courtenay's parties were tedious enough at any time, but if she had to talk to Alex Denham or — appalling prospect — dance with him, this one would be purgatorial.

'Well,' she said to Boris the black Labrador, who could smell the bacon in its silver dish and was looking at her hopefully, 'they can't *make* me dance.'

'What did you say, darling?' Frances Courtenay came into the room. Tiny, plump and blonde, beautifully dressed and always smelling like a lily, at fifty she was still a pretty woman, with eyes as blue as cornflowers that sparkled in a face unlined and flawless as a peach. She'd kept the lissom curves of youth in places where most women of her age had flab and bulges. She always made her tall and slender daughter feel like a giraffe.

'Nothing, Mummy,' Rose replied, and sighed.

'What do you plan to do today?'

'Oh, I don't know — be bored?'

'Rose, don't be ridiculous.' Lady Courtenay nodded to the maid to pour her coffee. 'I know it's not the fashion these days, but I think girls of your age should be married. Then you'd have no time to brood and mope about the place, or read those frightful novels, which can't be good for you.'

'If I were allowed to do something useful with my life, I shouldn't mope!' retorted Rose. 'You know how much I want to go to Oxford. Somerville has offered me a place, so why do you and Daddy insist I stay in Dorset?'

'Darling, we merely want the best for you.' Frances Courtenay shrugged expressively. 'If you went to Oxford, and did all that silly studying, how would you find a husband?'

'I don't want a husband.'

'You don't know what you want. That's why you need a husband, someone who'll look after you and correct your taste.' Lady Courtenay waved the maid away. 'But the right sort of men hate clever women. So although you did quite well at lessons, I'd keep it to yourself if I were you.'

Then she noticed Boris, who was chewing at the fringes of a priceless Persian rug. 'Rose, I wish you wouldn't bring that horrid dog in here. Where are you going, darling?'

'Only to my room.'

'Well, don't get your head stuck in a book. I promised we'd look in on Mrs Sefton, we must collect your dress from Dorchester, and there are a million other things to do today.'

Rose pulled a face behind her mother's back. She edged out of the breakfast room, swiping a rasher of bacon on the way.

'Here, good boy,' she whispered, winking conspiratorially at Boris, who lumbered after her with drooling jaws.

* * *

As Alex Denham washed and shaved that evening, he scowled at his reflection in the pitted, freckled glass. Why was he bothering, he wondered. Why was he going to so much trouble, when he knew what they all thought of him?

If he'd burst in wild and dishevelled, dressed in poacher's corduroys or the old tweed jacket he wore when he went hacking, they wouldn't be surprised. They'd merely nod their heads and whisper, 'Well, of course he's Viola's son. What can one expect?'

So he didn't want to go to Lady Courtenay's party. He'd always hated going to Charton Minster, the gracious honey-coloured mansion half a mile away, where the ghastly Courtenay family lived in regal splendour. He was going tonight to please his guardian, for Henry seemed determined that Alex should mix socially with the people who had snubbed his mother.

'Let bygones be bygones, turn the other cheek,' said Henry Denham. But Alex wasn't made like that, and he could not forgive.

He wiped the flecks of soap away and then reached for his shirt. He wondered if he'd see the heiress, if he'd have to watch as she was fawned over and courted by the flower of the county.

He'd rather liked her once — at least, as much as a boy of twelve could like a girl of ten. But since she'd left the schoolroom she had put her hair up, laced herself into a set of stays, and learned to look down her well-bred nose at him.

Perhaps, he thought, he shouldn't be surprised. She'd probably heard a version of events that had shocked and horrified a sheltered girl like Rose, especially if she hadn't suspected anything before.

Alex, on the other hand, had been collecting shreds and patches of the local gossip for almost twenty years. He'd stitched them all together to make his mother's shroud.

'She was always flighty from a girl.'

'It was grooms and gardeners first of all.'

'Then she had that artist chap, who was the boy's real father.'

She'd been dead for eighteen months, but still the gossip flowed. In rural Dorset, friends and neighbours usually let the dead rest in their graves, but in Viola Denham's case they made a rare exception.

'Ready then, my boy?' Henry Denham's kind but foolish face appeared at the door of Alex's dressing room. 'Come along, old fellow. We're going with Lizzie Sefton and her daughters. It doesn't do to keep the ladies waiting.'

'I'm coming now, sir,' Alex said.

Although he liked Henry Denham very much, Alex was secretly quite glad the old man wasn't his father. As well as a crumbling manor house and a decrepit, rabbit-bitten estate, he might have inherited those embarrassing jug ears, and that great, bulbous nose.

* * *

It has been a tedious process, being dressed and crimped and titivated by her mother's maid. But when she looked in the glass that evening, Rose could see the hours of pain and boredom had paid off.

The riot of unmanageable black curls had been subdued, cajoled then tamed with bandoline, and her unruly brows were plucked and arched. Two discreet spots of rouge were carefully smudged on her pale cheeks.

Now she was laced into a cruel whalebone corset, she had a woman's figure, not a gawky girl's, and her new gown became her very well. Simply cut and artfully draped in the elegant fashion of the spring of 1914, the dress was made of softest salmon-coloured taffeta. The style rounded out her slender figure, while the colour warmed her sallow skin. A scatter of tiny crystal beads was sewn across the bodice, catching the light and adding sparkle to her large grey eyes.

When she met her father on the landing, Sir Gerard stood back to look at her, then nodded his approval. 'You look enchanting, darling,' he began. 'That's an exquisite gown.'

'Thank you, Daddy.' Rose smiled back at him, reflecting that he hadn't yet seen the bill. But Sir Gerard might be worked on, she decided. She'd go to Oxford yet.

She walked down the great staircase, hung with portraits of the Courtenays going back to Elizabethan times. As she passed an earlier Rose Courtenay, dark-haired and grey-eyed just like herself, but formal and unsmiling in her starched white ruff and rich brocaded stomacher, she saw the Denham party coming in.

She knew she shouldn't be unkind, but she couldn't help noticing that poor Henry Denham looked his usual shuffling mess. Their neighbour Mrs Sefton's purple gown had obviously been made for someone half her ample size, and her two beaky daughters were trussed up like dowdy hens.

But Alex looked quite striking in the scarlet jacket and tight black trousers of the Royal Dorset Regiment.

Of course, it had had to be the Royal Dorsets, and even then they'd had to pull some strings to get him in. There wasn't the remotest chance they'd have him in the cavalry or the Guards, Rose had heard her mother whisper to Mrs Sefton, even if Henry had been rich enough — not with a family history like that.

She watched Alex moving through the crowd. He nodded to acquaintances, but hardly ever spoke and never smiled.

He'd grown up quite good looking, Rose decided. Those heavy eyebrows and that square, determined jaw, so unprepossessing in a child, were actually attractive in a man. As a boy, he'd scowled and frowned so much she had seldom felt the urge to go and talk to him. When she'd made the effort, he would grimace as she spoke, and rarely mutter more than a single syllable in reply. As Rose's nanny had often said, young Master Denham was neither use nor ornament.

But it seemed that these days he was not entirely without manners. As Rose joined her mother to welcome some new guests, he came up to speak to Lady Courtenay, who said she was delighted he had come.

Then Lady Courtenay drifted elegantly off to go and speak to someone else, leaving Rose and Alex to look at one another.

It soon became apparent to Rose that Alex wasn't going to speak, so she decided she must fill the silence. 'What a delightful day it's been,' she said, without expression. 'So warm and pleasant for the time of year.'

'Yes, indeed,' said Alex, who was fiddling with the braiding on his cuff.

'I dare say you've been riding, or walking on the headland?'

'No,' he muttered.

'Then perhaps you went to Dorchester?'

'I had some things to do at home.'

He didn't elaborate, and as Rose was thinking it would be much easier to swim through frozen treacle, the musicians hired for the night began to play. In a matter of minutes, almost everyone under thirty-five was up and dancing.

Alex had his back to them, and didn't seem to notice. He stared down at his highly-polished shoes and gnawed his lower lip. Finally, when even fat, absurd Georgina Sefton had been asked and led into the waltz, he found his voice. 'Miss Courtenay, if you mean to dance—'

He left the sentence hanging in the air.

Rose was mortified. If she said she did, she would look either forward or pathetic, and which was worse?

'No, Mr Denham,' she said, crisply. 'I'm afraid I have a headache. I shall not dance this evening.'

Alex seemed to think this meant he could make his escape. He bowed and walked away.

Glad to see the back of him, Rose became aware of the bustle and commotion of some late arrivals, but she was too annoyed to go and see who had turned up. She was sitting in the supper room, alone and irritably picking at a candied pear, when she heard a familiar, pleasant voice.

'Miss Courtenay?' Michael Easton smiled and bowed. 'I looked for you among the dancers, but then Mrs Sefton said she'd seen you come in here. I hope you're not unwell?'

'I had a headache earlier, but I'm much better now.' Rose looked at the vacant chair beside her, hoping Michael Easton might sit down.

He did, and then he glanced at Rose's plate. 'That pear looks rather good,' he said. 'Perhaps I'll have one, too.'

'I wouldn't bother if I were you.' Rose pushed her plate aside. 'They're much too sweet. In fact, they're quite disgusting.'

'Then I'll resist temptation.' Michael edged his chair a fraction closer. 'May I stay a while and talk to you?'

'Yes, of course,' smiled Rose. 'When did you get back from Cambridge?'

'Only yesterday, and on the train I happened to meet this most amazing fellow—'

Rose liked Michael Easton, an eldest son who had great expectations, if not much ready cash — his father's love of gambling saw to that — for Michael was always such good company.

He was handsome, too. Six feet tall, broad-shouldered and blue-eyed, he had a head of blond, leonine hair that made him look the image of a Viking warrior from a children's story book. Nowadays, to her embarrassment, Rose found she sometimes wondered what this modern Viking looked like without clothes. She realised she was wondering now, and blushed as pink as her new gown.

'Miss Courtenay, would you like to dance?' asked Michael.

Rose pulled herself out of her reverie. 'Yes, very much,' she said, 'but I can't this evening.'

'Why, because it's Lent and you're too holy?'

'I told Mr Denham I didn't intend to dance.'

'Mr Denham?' Michael frowned. 'Oh, you mean *Alex* Denham. Don't worry, he won't notice.'

'How do you know?'

'I saw him heading for the billiard room with Henry and my father. They'll be there all night. Come on, let's have some fun.'

So Rose danced with Michael, who told her all about what he'd been doing at Cambridge, and made her wish she had been born a boy.

'What's been happening here?' he asked.

'Nothing very interesting,' said Rose. 'Daddy sacked a gamekeeper for drinking and bawling *The Red Flag* under Mummy's window at four o'clock one morning. A maid has given notice, she's going to work in Dorchester, she means to learn stenography, and she—'

'My sister says you haven't been to see her for a month or more,' interrupted Michael suddenly.

'I haven't,' Rose agreed, but then decided he wouldn't want to hear about her progress in geometry, or her place at Oxford. 'I've been rather busy.'

'Well, you must come over soon.' He grinned. 'I promise you we'll make it worth your while.'

'How?' Rose smiled, intrigued.

'We've bought a gramophone.' Michael's blue eyes sparkled. 'It's tremendous fun! We've all the latest music — tango, ragtime. Of course, we have to keep the contraption in the butler's pantry. The parents don't approve.'

'Mummy wouldn't have one in the house.' Rose sighed wistfully. 'She hates that ragtime music. She says it's decadent.'

'Yes, it's frightful stuff.' Michael pulled her close, so she was crushed against his chest. 'It makes your heart beat like a drum, and your pulses pound.'

In Michael's warm embrace, inhaling the beguiling scents of shaving soap, cologne and clean, male perspiration, Rose felt fairly decadent already. The thought of being alone with Michael Easton, of dancing to that wonderful, intoxicating music, made the hot blood rush into her face.

* * *

The room grew warmer, noisier, and Rose was starting to enjoy herself, but as Michael whirled her round in yet another waltz, she suddenly had a feeling she was being watched. She turned to see Alex Denham standing by the open door.

His jacket was unbuttoned at the collar. A lock of jet black hair had fallen forward so it lay across his forehead. He'd obviously been drinking. An empty whisky glass hung in his hand, and he seemed to lean against the doorframe for support.

Then he began to make his way across the crowded floor, weaving unsteadily between the other dancing couples, avoiding some but ploughing into others, and making everybody stare at him.

The music stopped, and Alex stood in front of Rose and Michael. 'Your headache must have gone, Miss Courtenay,' he said pleasantly.

Rose was so surprised she couldn't speak.

Then Alex smiled at her, his dark eyes meeting hers, and to Rose's great embarrassment she couldn't look away. No, it was even worse than that — she didn't *want* to look away.

'When they begin to play again,' said Alex, 'will you dance with me?'

'Miss Courtenay is engaged for every dance,' said Michael, his blue eyes hard and cold.

'Every single one?' Alex frowned at Rose in disbelief. 'Miss Courtenay?'

'I'm sorry, Mr Denham,' Rose replied, more sharply than she'd meant, and horribly aware that she was blushing.

'I see.' Then Alex shrugged and smiled again. 'Well, never mind, Miss Courtenay,' he said softly, his dark brown gaze unfocused but intent. 'Maybe some other time?'

The music started, and somehow he managed to get himself across the ballroom floor.

'Denham can be very irritating,' muttered Michael, and Rose felt his hand become a fist, pressing hard between her shoulder blades. 'I suppose we shouldn't be surprised. We all know what he is and where he came from, after all. But maybe someone ought to teach the fellow courtesy.'

'It doesn't matter.' Rose became aware her feet were aching. The straps and laces of her undergarments were digging trenches in her flesh. The vile whalebone corset crushed her ribs.

She wanted to sit down. But Michael danced on, talked on, told her more amusing stories, and she felt obliged to smile, although she wasn't really listening to anything he said.

Michael finally noticed her abstraction. 'You must be getting tired,' he said, and before she could deny it he was leading her towards some chairs. 'You sit here, and I'll fetch you a cordial.'

As Michael walked away, Rose noticed several chaperones sitting together on a window seat, no doubt exchanging scandal. She didn't mean to eavesdrop, but the women were all deaf, their shrill, aristocratic voices carried, and she could hear very well what they were saying.

'Viola never had any shame,' rasped one. 'So we shouldn't be surprised if her son decides to make a foolish exhibition.'

'But he's such a very attractive boy.' A second woman sighed. 'So tall, so handsome. He has his mother's eyes, her charming smile, and there's a certain sort of girl who doesn't ask for more.'

'Well, Henry won't allow it, I shall see to that.' The first crone shook her head. 'One bastard at a time is quite enough for any family. If Alex thinks he can play fast and loose with Charlotte Stokeley — that child is just fifteen.'

'Your cordial, Miss Courtenay.' Michael handed Rose a glass, then sat down beside her and started telling her another story.

But Rose didn't hear Michael, didn't see him. She didn't know why she felt like this, she didn't understand it — after all, she didn't even like the man.

All she could hear right now was Alex asking her to dance with him. She could still see his smile.

CHAPTER TWO

'Come on, Phoebe sweetheart, that's enough. You know old Maisie wouldn't have wanted you to break your heart.' Maria Gower drew back the green plush curtains with a flourish, sending the brass rings rattling down the rails and letting the dusty light of the East End flood into the dark parlour.

She sat down by her sister and put a comforting arm round Phoebe's shoulders. 'I must admit I'm glad the funeral's over. I reckon they really did us proud, don't you?'

'Yeah, it was the business.' Phoebe Gower sniffed and gulped and rubbed her swollen eyes. 'People was impressed by that glass carriage an' all them black 'orses. But it must've cost a fair old bit?'

'I had some money saved, and Maisie deserved the best of everything.' Maria gazed round the little terraced house in which their foster mother had brought them up. 'If she hadn't taken us from the Spike, if she hadn't treated us like her own, God only knows how we'd have ended up.'

'You'd 'ave done all right, Maria,' said Phoebe. 'You got brains.'

'But you have looks. A lovely figure, pretty face and beautiful black hair.'

'The blokes all goes for blondes an' redheads these days,' muttered Phoebe, and Maria reflected that her own fair hair and clear grey eyes were such a striking contrast to Phoebe's gipsy colouring no one would have guessed they might be sisters.

'I got something to tell you,' added Phoebe. 'You ain't goin' to like it. But I've thought about it for a while an' now I've decided, so you won't change my mind. I'm goin' on the stage.'

'The stage?' Maria stared. 'But you've just started work at Mrs Rosenheim's, round at the corner shop.'

'I don't work there no more. I give me notice Monday.' Phoebe grimaced. 'I've 'ad enough of flippin' Nathan bumpin' up against me. I'm sick of Mrs R, always givin' me 'er dirty looks as if to say, don't you think you're goin' to catch my Nathan, you schemin' little *shiksa*. God, Maria — as if I'd want to go to bed with him!'

'But you had a place to live, a job—'

'I'll soon get another place, don't worry. As for a job, that Mr Harris down the Royalty says 'e'll find me somethin', maybe in the chorus line.'

'But you can't sing — or dance.'

'Maria, I could bloody learn!' Phoebe's full, red lips were pressed together, in fierce determination. 'It's all right for you,' she muttered, angrily. 'Anythin' you wanted — a scholarship to that fancy school, where you learned to talk like Lady Muck. Then you got the Board to let you train to be a nurse. You just 'ave to whistle, an' it all comes along.

'But it's never been like that for me. In any case, now Maisie's dead, you know we can't stay 'ere in Bethnal Green. It's not where we belong.'

'Where else could we go? Phoebe, we must—'

'Anybody 'ome?' The front door opened, and their next door neighbour poked her head into the parlour.

'Come in, Mrs Taylor,' said Maria, wearily.

'I ain't stoppin'.' Still resplendent in her funeral finery, Mrs Taylor dabbed her red-rimmed eyes. 'I just popped round to tell you some of us is goin' down the George, an' we'd like you girls to come along. We wants to see old Maisie off in style.'

Lady Courtenay's party had evidently been a huge success. The great pile of bread and butter letters lying on her breakfast table seemed to prove it. As she opened them and read, she smiled with satisfaction.

Even Alex Denham had sent her a short note, which she passed across the toast and coffee and invited Rose to read.

'Good God, his handwriting's atrocious,' muttered Rose, who didn't actually want to read the letter, or even touch the letter, come to that, because she wanted to forget him, or at any rate forget the strange, uncomfortable emotions he'd aroused.

'You're a fine one to talk, my dear,' said Lady Courtenay, tartly. 'All you young people scrawl. But he writes a very charming letter, don't you think?'

'Yes, if you say so,' murmured Rose. 'I'm taking Boris for a walk.'

'Be home by twelve,' called Lady Courtenay, after her departing back. 'Mrs Sefton is coming here for luncheon. You have a fitting with your dressmaker at two.'

* * *

Rose walked moodily along the headland, throwing sticks for Boris who was much too fat and lazy to chase them very far, and wondering if she might meet Michael Easton — he often rode this way.

If she did get married, should she marry Michael Easton? She liked him, she supposed. But marriage meant having babies, running households, having dismal, boring parties like the one last night.

Boris eventually caught a stick then sat down panting heavily. So Rose slumped down beside him. She could hear shouts and cries of laughter coming from the beach. So now she inched her way towards the cliff top, intending to look down and find out who was making all the noise.

Alex and Charlotte Stokeley, the eldest daughter of Henry Denham's bailiff, were running up and down the beach with Charlotte's dog, a much more energetic beast than Boris.

The dog was barking like a lunatic and going berserk with joy as Alex threw sticks into the surf for it to find and fetch, and Alex himself was laughing as the dog came charging up the beach, and shook itself all over him and Charlotte.

Then they had a race. Alex shouted *go*, and Charlotte and the dog shot forward. A few moments later, Alex started running, soon caught up with them, but then he stumbled, grabbed Charlotte by the arm, and they both fell over on the sand, rolling over and over and over as Charlotte squealed with laughter, and the dog went wild with joy again, and jumped all over them.

They were soon on their feet again, and started playing what looked like tag. Alex dodged and feinted, laughing as Charlotte ran and tried and failed to catch him, and was easily caught when it was his turn to chase Charlotte.

Rose could see quite well that all of this was merely horseplay, and nothing at all improper was going on. But she still felt her face grow hot, and wished *she* was down there on the beach, that Alex Denham had chased and caught Rose Courtenay, and — kissed her, maybe?

God, what was she thinking?

She shut her eyes and frowned, determined to put all thoughts of Alex Denham right away.

She was so wrapped up in contemplation she didn't hear Alex and Charlotte coming up the cliff path, and the first she knew of it was when Charlotte's spaniel came bouncing up to Boris to greet the older dog.

She felt very silly and at a disadvantage, sitting there all prim and solitary in her new spring coat and matching hat and gloves, while Alex and Charlotte laughed and gasped and panted as they climbed the last few steps that were cut into the cliff.

As they came into view, Rose wondered if she ought to speak to them. She supposed she'd better — it would be polite.

But what on earth was Alex wearing? It looked like one of Henry Denham's horrible old suits. She shuddered, waiting for a moth or several to fly out of it, and she was still wondering what to say when Charlotte beat her to it.

'It's Miss Courtenay,' she began, and ducked her head respectfully at Rose. 'Good morning, miss.'

'Good morning, Ch-ch-charlotte,' Rose choked out.

'Miss Courtenay.' Alex nodded too, and when at last Rose managed to meet his gaze, she saw his dark brown eyes were shining and he looked full of — mischief, devilment?

She'd been about to make some pointless comment about the weather, but now she changed her mind.

Alex just stood there, and now he was staring out across the English Channel, humming something to himself.

'My mother had a note from you this morning,' said Rose eventually, still looking up at Alex and wishing the sun would go behind a cloud, because at the moment it was in her eyes. 'She says you write a charming letter.'

'She gave a charming party. I enjoyed it very much. It was very kind of her to make me feel so welcome.' Rose didn't quite like the sound of that. Alex didn't sound at all sincere. But he was smiling, his actual smile seemed genuine enough, so she supposed perhaps he'd meant it.

'How long will you be staying in Dorset?' she asked him somewhat stiffly, aware she sounded like a dowager duchess speaking to a groom, but totally unable to do anything about it.

'I'm here until Friday, when I go to Ireland.'

'Mr Denham will miss you.'

'I'll miss him.'

'My mother will be wondering where I am.' Charlotte clicked her fingers at the dog. 'Dancer, heel,' she said. 'Miss Courtenay, Mr Denham.'

'I'm coming your way, too.' Alex nodded again to Rose, then he and Charlotte Stokeley turned inland and walked away, and Rose could hear them chattering and laughing.

As she sat there alone, she felt like crying.

* * *

The spring of 1914 kept its promise. Although the first weeks of May were cold and damp, and no one walked along the shingle beach that lay beyond the manor house — for there the grey-green sea rolled up the pebbles, foaming white and lashing the black rocks with salty, wind-whipped spray — the summer was a golden dream.

At Charton Minster, the sunny afternoons were filled with tennis tournaments, garden parties on the sloping lawns, and games of croquet. There were picnics on the headland, bathing parties on the beach, and drinks served on the terrace as the sun went down.

Rose was not to go to Somerville. Lady Courtenay was adamant, and Sir Gerard liked a quiet life, so when Rose asked him to intervene on her behalf, he'd refused to argue with her mother.

'I dare say you'll be getting married soon,' he'd added, smiling. 'That young Easton fellow — Mummy and I think very well of him.'

Rose hardly thought of him at all.

A year ago, before she'd dared to hope that she might go to Oxford, before she'd realised there was another world outside her social circle, becoming Mrs — and in due course, Lady — Easton would have been the height of her ambition. If Michael had proposed, she would have accepted him.

But nowadays she was restless. She was longing for adventure. In search of inspiration, she read all the newspapers the butler laid out every morning in the library. They predicted conflict, most probably in Ireland. But Austria was looking dangerous, too.

She saved up her allowance, and by the end of June she was quite rich. 'The papers seem to think there'll be a war,' she said to Boris, who was as usual chewing at a rug. 'So if the men go off to fight, women are going to have to do their work — *and* look after any who get hurt. I don't suppose they'd let me be a nurse . . .'

* * *

'Sir Thomas and Lady Easton will be motoring over here for luncheon,' Lady Courtenay said at breakfast, one hot morning in July. 'Michael and Celia are coming too. I was thinking you young people might like to take a picnic to the beach.'

'I'm going to the village.' Rose put down her fork. 'Polly said the church hall's being turned into a cottage hospital. The Red Cross is collecting sheets and blankets. Marjorie and Polly are going to wash the china that people have donated, and I'm going to help them.'

'I don't think so, Rose.' Lady Courtenay frowned. 'You would meet some very common people.'

'Mummy, I'd meet the people from the village. I've known them all my life!'

'Don't be silly, darling,' said her mother. 'We don't know them socially. In any case, I don't think you should do that sort of thing.'

'Why ever not?'

'You'd ruin your lovely hands. Now, what about this picnic?'

'It's far too hot,' said Rose. 'In any case, I have some things to do.'

'My dear, Michael and his sister—'

'May talk to you and Daddy, have a game of croquet, eat potted shrimps and strawberries — I'm sure they don't need me to entertain them.'

* * *

But when Michael Easton and his family arrived, Rose dutifully went downstairs to greet them.

'My dear child, you grow prettier every day,' said Lady Easton, as she offered Rose her cheek to kiss.

Rose couldn't say the same for Lady Easton, who was heavily pregnant once again, with her twelfth or possibly thirteenth child — Rose had long lost count. Michael was grown up, Celia would be coming out next year, but still at boarding school and in the nursery was a swarm of children, eating their parents out of their dilapidated home.

Rose knew Michael had some money left him by an uncle. But the other children would have nothing, or maybe less than nothing. As his farms and cottages decayed, as his fields grew crops of thistles and the equinoctial gales blew masonry from Easton Hall into the English Channel, Sir Thomas bought motor cars he couldn't drive and often crashed, and gambled his inheritance away.

But, reflected Rose, Sir Thomas was a baronet. The Courtenays might be rich and long-established in the district, but were mere country gentry all the same. Sir Gerard's knighthood, his reward for sitting as a magistrate for almost thirty years, was only six months old.

'Rose, what a lovely dress.' Celia Easton, plain and gangling in a faded cotton print, looked at Rose's pale green watered satin enviously.

'Green has always suited Rose.' Lady Easton smiled, and Rose saw she'd lost another tooth. 'She looks like a waternymph in green.'

'Yes, indeed she does.' Lady Courtenay smirked complacently. 'But that colour is quite hard to wear. It wouldn't do anything for Celia. She would look washed out.'

Rose blushed pink, embarrassed by her mother's tactlessness. Celia was too tall, too thin, too awkward, and she never had any pretty clothes.

'Have you done any of your lovely paintings recently?' Lady Easton gazed around the drawing room as if expecting to see Rose's latest watercolour hung in pride of place. 'You're such a talented little artist. I was saying to Michael yesterday, Rose is such a clever girl, she can paint and draw so beautifully—'

'It seems we're going picnicking,' interrupted Michael, who looked very handsome in comfortable flannels and a plain white shirt that set off his light tan. 'Celia, Miss Courtenay and I are going to walk along the beach, so you go round the headland.'

'Why can't I come with you?' asked Celia, pouting.

'We have things to talk about, that's why.' Michael Easton handed Rose her hat. 'We'll see you at the usual place, so now be a good fellow and buzz off. You could take the basket, actually.'

* * *

'You didn't have to be so mean to Celia,' said Rose, as she and Michael walked along the tide line, where the sand was firm.

'Actually, I did.' Michael skimmed a pebble and it bounced across the waves. 'She's so jolly nosy, and she couldn't keep a secret if she tried. I say, Miss Courtenay — may I call you Rose?'

'Yes, of course you may.' Rose smiled at him. 'You always did. I'm not sure why you stopped.'

'But you've come out now, so I thought it might seem disrespectful.'

'I don't think so, we're old friends,' said Rose. 'What's this secret Celia couldn't keep, and why do you want to talk to me?'

'Your father's been discussing things with mine.' Rose saw Michael flush beneath his tan. 'They talked about my trust fund, and the settlement Sir Gerard means to make on you.'

'Oh, I see.' Rose had always known that as her father's only child she would make her husband an extremely wealthy man. 'Michael, let's not spoil—'

'Please, Rose, hear me out!' Michael cleared his throat. 'We've known each other all our lives. I've always thought you were a splendid girl. We had a lot of fun together as children, and now we're both grown up we get on famously. The parents are all for it, so why don't we get engaged?'

* * *

The third battalion of the Royal Dorsets had almost finished its short tour of duty in Belfast. After some embarkation leave, it would be going to India, where Alex meant to make his fortune.

But just now he was lying on his bed, wishing it was not so hot and he was not so bored. He screwed the letter he'd been reading into a tight ball, then lobbed it at the bin.

He didn't intend to write to Charlotte Stokeley, who'd written in her childish schoolgirl's hand to confess undying love for him.

Charlotte was too young to know the first thing about love, and now he wished he'd never said hello, or passed the time of day with her when he'd been in Dorset, or played those games down on the beach.

He was sure he'd never encouraged Charlotte to think of him romantically, but now it seemed she'd needed no encouragement, and that she had a major crush on him.

He watched a puzzled wasp climb up the inside of the open window. He thought about the heiress, as he always called her, mainly to remind himself that even if she'd liked him — which of course she didn't — he wouldn't stand a chance.

It was four months since he'd seen her last, the day after her mother's awful party in the spring, when he had got so drunk he'd managed to ask her if she'd dance. It was just as well she had refused. She would have had to hold him up.

She'd grown so beautiful it had offended him to see her in that dress, run up by some provincial seamstress in the most hideous shade of giblet pink, and sewn all over with ridiculous glass beads.

If she married a man who had some taste, her dress sense might improve. But she'd probably marry Michael Easton and bury herself alive at Easton Hall, a decaying pile that made Henry Denham's shabby house look like a palace.

Men off duty dozed, others drilled or marched in perfect columns across the barrack square, and Alex wondered if there'd be a civil war in Ireland. He didn't like the thought of dying on the dirty streets of Londonderry or Belfast, just because the Ulster people didn't want home rule for a united Ireland.

Reaching for the silver case Henry had given him when he'd joined the army, he found that he was out of cigarettes. But his servant wasn't around, so if he wanted any he would have to go and buy his own.

He was crossing the parade ground when someone called his name, and so he stopped and turned to see who wanted him. 'Oh — hello, Chloe,' he began.

Chloe Jarman, the daughter of the quartermaster sergeant, looked pleased or possibly it was relieved to see him. 'W-where are you going?' she gasped, as she caught up with him.

'I need some cigarettes.'

'I'm going to buy some thread.' Chloe fell into step beside him, hopping and jumping now and then to match his longer stride. 'May I walk with you?'

'Yes, of course you may.'

Alex was quite fond of Chloe Jarman, who was a gawky, colourless blonde with sallow cheeks and staring, pale blue eyes. When he had first arrived in Ireland, still grieving for his mother, in a subaltern's uniform that was stiff and sharp and rubbed him raw, she had befriended him.

When he was not on duty, they'd gone walking, and he had found it easy to talk to Chloe Jarman. He'd never meant to let things go beyond the walking and the talking, but somehow it had happened.

They'd been out in the countryside one pleasant summer evening. Chloe had looked so pretty, she had seemed so fond of him and, although he had been very willing, she'd been willing, too. Afterwards, she'd said she'd been a virgin, but he hadn't confessed to Chloe that the same applied to him.

At first, he'd thought he was in love. But when a fellow officer had noticed he went missing now and then, and often came back looking like the cat who had not only got the cream but all the pilchards too, Freddie had prised a somewhat wry confession out of him.

Then Alex had learned that Chloe would go with anyone, provided he had pips or crowns upon his epaulettes.

'She's anybody's,' Freddie Lomax told him. 'Do be careful, Denham. You don't want the pox.'

Alex had left the sergeant's daughter to her own devices after that, and was both relieved and miffed that she had seemed quite anxious to avoid him, too.

'What's the matter, Chloe?' he asked now, as she hopped and skipped along beside him.

'What do you mean?'

'You don't have much to say for yourself today.'

'I — I'm rather tired,' she whispered. 'It must be the heat.' But then she gulped, and suddenly she was sobbing like a child.

Alex was astonished. 'Chloe, don't!' he cried.

'But I can't help it!' Chloe wailed.

'Of course you can.'

He took her arm, and then as good as marched her over to a small arcade where drill equipment was kept under cover.

'Please,' he begged, 'don't cry like this!' He found his pocket handkerchief, and dabbed at Chloe's face. 'What's happened?' he demanded. 'Who's upset you?'

'N-nobody.' She blew her nose, then rubbed two spots of colour into her white cheeks. 'I'll get this washed,' she added, pushing his handkerchief into her pocket. 'It's just that I — it's terrible! I'm going to have a baby!'

Alex stared, amazed. 'Chloe, are you sure?'

'I used to be so skinny, but I'm getting really fat. I'm having to let out all my clothes.' She looked at him in anguish. 'Alex, are you furious?'

'Furious?' he began and frowned, but then he understood. 'You mean the baby's mine?'

'Of course it's yours!' She burst into another storm of weeping. 'Whose else would it be?'

Alex was about to say it could be anybody's, half the officers here have been through you.

But then he realised this could not be so. Chloe's mother kept her busy with the younger children, and she was not allowed to come and go just as she pleased. She'd have had to lie about the time she'd spent with him.

As far as his fellow officers were concerned, Chloe was not a lady. She was therefore rubbish, to be slandered round the mess by the foul-mouthed likes of Freddie Lomax, whom Alex wouldn't have actually trusted with a penny piece.

'I'll be disgraced,' she sobbed. 'My mother will throw me out, I'll have the baby in the workhouse. They'll shave my head, they'll say I'm wicked, mad—'

'Hush, Chloe, it's all right.' Quickly glancing round, Alex saw the parade ground was deserted. He put his arms round Chloe's narrow shoulders and pressed her to his chest. 'I'll look after you.'

But Chloe's sobbing didn't abate, and soon he felt warm wetness seeping through his scarlet tunic.

He willed her to stop crying, wanted to tell her not to be so silly, but he didn't want to make things any worse. He stared across the empty square, focusing on the regimental emblems carved into an architrave. Lions, thistles, banners, roses—

Rose!

He felt his heart contracting painfully. But he mustn't think about Rose Courtenay — not here, and certainly not now. 'Chloe,' he said, 'I — well, listen, Chloe. I'll marry you.'

'You'll *what*?' Jerking away, she gaped at him. 'But Alex, you're a gentleman. You can't marry me!'

'Of course I can.' Alex felt as if he were being sucked down into a whirlpool. But he knew Chloe Jarman wasn't lying. She was getting fat, and she was carrying his baby, and he was determined no child of his should be a bastard.

'I'll marry you,' he said again, as much to convince himself of it as Chloe.

'I can tell my parents?' She stared at him in disbelieving joy. 'I can tell my father, Alex?'

'Yes, of course you may.'

'Oh, Alex!' She began to cry again, butting her small head against his shoulder.

He let her cling to him. But then he heard brisk footsteps coming closer, and prised her thin arms from round his neck. 'I'll come and see your father later on this evening,' he told Chloe. 'But now I have to go.'

When he reached his quarters, he realised he still had no cigarettes. Needing to do something, he poured water from a pitcher then began to wash his hands and face.

He knew he didn't love Chloe. He liked her well enough — there was nothing he could *dis*like about Chloe — but, ignorant, unworldly and provincial as she was, nowadays she bored him. He knew that if he had to live with her for any length of time, the empty chatter and mindless conversation which he had once found comforting would chafe and irritate him worse than a hair shirt or army vest.

He couldn't believe he'd just asked her to marry him.

As he was rubbing hard with a rough towel, a fellow subaltern walked in. 'Hello, Denham,' he said, breezily. 'Well, they say it will be war at last.'

'What, here?' muttered Alex.

'No, in Belgium.' The other officer grinned. 'At any rate, the Brass is getting twitchy. We're ordered back to Blighty right away.'

CHAPTER THREE

'It shouldn't take long to teach the Kaiser a lesson he won't forget.' Gerard Courtenay looked up from his newspaper and gave his wife and daughter his most reassuring smile. 'I don't suppose we'll need that little hospital they've set up in the village.'

'Let's hope not, Daddy.' Rose was afraid they would, and very soon. But she thought it wisest not to argue. She was in enough trouble with her mother, and didn't want to annoy her father, too.

'When is Michael coming, Rose?' demanded Lady Courtenay.

'After luncheon, Mummy,' Rose replied.

'I hope you will be civil to him today.'

'When have I been anything else?'

'Please don't be impertinent, my dear. It's very vulgar.' Frances Courtenay sighed and shook her elegant blonde head. 'I never thought my daughter would turn out to be a flirt.'

This remark was laughably unjust, but Rose thought it best not to reply.

When Michael had proposed, she'd said she needed time to think about it, and to her relief he'd said there wasn't any hurry. But it seemed their mothers had assumed they'd get engaged without delay. Three months later, Rose was still being silly, as her mother chose to put it. Lady Courtenay's temper grew more and more uncertain day by day.

'I shall be staying in my room this morning,' she announced, as she got up and dropped her napkin by her plate. 'Rose, I hope you don't mean to be difficult forever. What if Michael has to go and fight? Sir Thomas seems to think it's very likely. After all, the poor boy's in the Dorset Yeomanry.'

'I'm sure he won't be leaving yet. I know they're all on standby, but they haven't been called up for service overseas.' Rose met her mother's irritated gaze. 'I'm going to see Celia this morning.'

'I can't think why,' said Lady Courtenay. 'After all, you have no interest in the Easton family.'

'Mummy, that's unfair—'

'I don't think so.' Lady Courtenay shook her head again. 'You're such a disappointment to me, Rose.'

'I'm *so* sorry!' Rose's grey eyes flashed, her colour deepened. 'Of course, some people can't or won't accept that others might not wish to fall in with their schemes—'

'Rose!' Sir Gerard stared at her, amazed. 'I will not have you speaking to your mother in that fashion! Apologise at once!'

But Rose threw down her napkin, pushed her chair back, got up and left the room.

* * *

When she reached Easton Hall, she found that Michael had gone into Dorchester to see about a gun. But Celia was full of the latest gossip. 'Michael says it's just what he'd expect of Alex Denham,' she told Rose, as she unpacked the contents of a huge wooden crate.

Celia had joined the VAD and, as Mrs Sefton had observed to anyone who would listen, was doing vital war work while

Rose Courtenay shirked. This morning, Celia announced, she was going to roll a thousand bandages and make up first aid kits for the Red Cross.

'You were telling me about this Denham business,' prompted Rose.

'Oh, yes.' Celia grimaced. 'It's disgusting. Alex and this woman seem to be engaged. Mrs Sefton told us Mr Denham is frightfully upset. She wouldn't be at all surprised if he decides to make another will, leaving Alex out of it completely.'

'If the girl's respectable, I really can't see why.'

'Oh, but she's nothing of the sort! She's a sergeant's daughter, and she led him on quite shamelessly. Now it appears she's going to have a child.' Celia blushed pink. 'But as Mrs Sefton said to Mummy, whose is anybody's guess.'

Rose suddenly felt light-headed. As Michael's sister babbled on, she told herself that Alex wasn't anything to her, and his philandering was none of her concern. But she was still upset, and didn't know why.

She stared at Celia's busy hands, neatly wrapping dressings and swabs in oilskin packaging. 'I could help with that,' she offered.

'I don't think so, Rose.' Celia looked important. 'I have to initial every one I pack, so if it turns out anything is missing, I shall be in very serious trouble. I say, your face is awfully red.'

'It's quite warm in here.' Rose stood up. 'Well, if you don't want my help, I shall be on my way.'

Rose walked straight home again, and by the time she was back at Charton Minster she had come to a decision.

'I'll be out for the rest of the morning, Polly,' she told her maid, who was busy sorting out some linen.

'Very good, Miss Courtenay.' Polly Jackson pulled open a drawer. 'What shall I say to Lady Courtenay, if she asks for you?'

'I'm going to the village. I need to buy some — stamps.'

'Stamps, Miss Courtenay?' Polly frowned. 'I'm sure I saw plenty in your box.'

'One can never have too many stamps.' Rose picked up her bag. 'Polly, when you've finished that, I'd like you to look through my clothes. The mauve silk dress needs ironing, and the green skirt has buttons coming loose.'

* * *

It was agony waiting for the train. But to Rose's huge relief, nobody from Charton seemed to be going anywhere today.

She didn't want to arouse the suspicions of the booking clerk, so she bought a ticket to Stratton Lacey, the next stop down the line. When the inspector came along, she would apologise profusely. She'd say she'd had her mind on other things, and pay him the right fare.

At almost every station after Charton, men in khaki uniforms and carrying huge haversacks piled into the train. They crammed into the third-class carriages, waving from the windows to their wives and families, most of whom were trying to look brave, though some were weeping.

Five minutes after they left Wareham, a sergeant major of the Royal Dorsets came to ask if he could put some men in her compartment. 'Second and third are full,' he added, looking at her steadily as if daring her to say that yes, she did object. 'So the guard says if you wouldn't mind?'

'I don't mind at all,' said Rose.

So half a dozen shy, embarrassed Tommies shuffled into the first-class compartment. Straw-haired, raw-boned farm lads, they all wore stiff, new uniforms and had sore, red patches on their necks where their collars chafed.

They nudged each other, whispering and giggling like children on an outing, which Rose supposed they were, for most of them had probably never been any further afield than Dorchester, and now they were going on a great adventure.

The day dragged on and on. Rose's stomach frequently reminded her she hadn't eaten since morning. But it also promised her that if she tried to fill it, she'd be sick.

When she got to Paddington, it was dark. The blackened vaults and arches loomed threateningly overhead, and soot-stained pigeons flying home to roost flapped their dirty wings against her veil. The whole place stank of coal, hot iron and grease, and smuts danced everywhere, settling like black snow.

She didn't know where to go or what to do. She knew some parts of London very well, because when Lady Courtenay came up to go shopping, she and Rose always stayed at smart hotels. But now, her money had to last, and she dared not fritter it away. She pushed her way through the vast crowd of people on the concourse, and went to find a cab.

* * *

'Where to, miss?' the driver asked, as he released the hand brake.

'Chelsea,' Rose replied. She had a vague idea that poets and artists lived in Chelsea, so she hoped it might be cheap. 'I forget the name of the street. But if you drive around, I'm sure we'll find it.'

The glow from the gas lamps cast soft, golden pools along the dirty pavements, but everything else was sunk in foggy gloom.

'Miss,' began the cabman, as he drove back up a one way street, 'I dunno what you think you're playing at, but my old lady will be wonderin' where—'

'It's that house on your left!' interrupted Rose, in desperation. 'The one next to the dairy, that's the place!'

* * *

Rose signed the register of the small hotel in Hartland Row. It had looked respectable from the cab, and had a spruce new board outside that offered rooms to ladies.

'Where's your luggage, miss?' enquired the woman at the desk, as Rose gazed round the gloomy lobby.

'It — it's coming later.' Sick with nerves and faint from lack of food, Rose was sure that any minute Sir Gerard would burst out of a hidden cupboard, then drag her back to Dorset in disgrace. 'M-may I see my room?'

'This is a clean, respectable establishment, Miss — Jackson.' Eyeing Rose suspiciously, the woman pursed her lips. 'I don't make no assumptions, miss, so please don't be offended. But people without luggage—'

'I was in a hurry.' Rose prayed for inspiration and it came. 'My fiancé had to join his unit with hardly any notice. I'd like to see him off.'

'My dear, of course you would.' The woman looked ashamed. 'But you understand we must be careful.'

'Yes, of course.'

Rose didn't know what she meant, but on that cold October evening she was far too tired and too appalled by what she'd done to think of anything but sleep. She took her key, then followed a grinning boot boy up the dark and dusty stairs.

* * *

Alex, Freddie Lomax and the remains of their platoons crouched in a Belgian cellar, trying to forget they were afraid and to ignore the fearful racket going on outside.

As another shell exploded, Alex flinched and dug his dirty nails into the palms of both his hands. Terrified of letting anyone see that he was scared, he told himself the time to worry was when the barrage stopped, because this meant a new attack would soon be under way.

The battles of September and October had been fought and sometimes won. The British army had been decimated, but in spite of this the Germans had been pushed back to the Aisne. The Belgian army had then dug in north of Ypres, so for the time being the Channel ports were safe — and so was England.

Alex's own battalion was occupying a devastated village, holding it against the German troops who were a mere hundred yards away. In the course of a night spent on patrol, he'd killed a German sentry, and was still feeling nauseous at the memory of this. He'd never forget the sucking, gurgling sound the wound had made as he'd jerked his bayonet out of the twitching body.

Of course, he had as good as killed before — he'd lobbed grenades, he'd shot at German snipers and he'd fired at enemy emplacements. But he still couldn't quite believe he'd actually stuck a weapon into another human being.

Later, he and Freddie snatched some sleep, forced down a disgusting meal of turnips and boiled horse, then started to play cards.

Freddie dealt again, then he and Alex and a couple of NCOs began a game of whist. 'Denham, you're not concentrating, damn you.' Putting down his three of clubs, Freddie trumped Alex's ace of spades. 'You're thinking about the sergeant's lovely daughter.'

'Actually, Lomax, I was wondering when we'll get our orders to pull out, and how we'll get our casualties away.' Alex stared around the gloomy cellar, in which the battered remnants of the company slouched or lay.

Their captain had been killed the previous night, and lay unburied in the mud outside. They'd have to wait until it was dark before they had a chance to bring him in. Twenty or maybe thirty of the men were badly wounded, but it wasn't possible to get them to an aid post, or for any doctor to get out to them.

At first light that morning, the Germans had brought up heavy guns and begun to pound the village with artillery. The Royal Dorsets trying to defend it had only their rifles and a few grenades.

'We'll get our orders soon enough,' said Freddie grimly, as he dealt again, then cut for trumps. Alex saw the tremor in Freddie's hands, but it was no comfort to know the only other officer left alive was just as scared as him. 'Unless those st-stinking bastards back at base decide to leave us to our fate.'

'Captain Tucker said he was expecting a battalion of Black Watch.'

'As indeed he might have been, but I don't think we should count on it.' Freddie's grin made his face look like a skull. 'I saw some of those bonny Highland laddies in Boulogne. Peculiar little chaps in skirts and aprons, who don't speak any English, or not as we know it. Jesus, that was close!'

As another shell burst overhead, flakes of plaster floated down and coated everyone with fine, white dust.

Alex cowered and wondered if this was the end.

* * *

Since the third battalion had been in it right from the beginning, he had not had time to marry Chloe, as he'd promised and still intended. He'd spoken to her father, who had made him feel two inches tall, and on a twenty-four hour leave before he'd sailed for Belgium he'd confessed to Henry Denham.

Henry had been a brick, and at the old man's instigation Alex made his will, leaving everything he owned to Chloe and the child.

'Mr Denham, sir?' As the noise intensified and the cellar shook, a corporal came to bawl in Alex's ear. 'I think Private Patterson must 'ave snuffed it.'

Alex crawled across the broken floor towards the corner where the body lay. He felt the pulse and shook his head. They wrapped the soldier in his greatcoat, and Alex wrote the details in his notebook. He'd have to send a letter of condolence to the soldier's parents — if he lived long enough.

'Denham, I think we need to beat a tactical retreat!' yelled Freddie Lomax. 'We can't defend this stinking place, so if we don't get out, we're going to die!'

'But what about the wounded?' Alex shouted. 'We can't carry all of them, we don't have—'

'Listen, Denham! If you want to sit and wait until the place caves in, that's up to you. I'm going to take the able-bodied chaps, and make a run for it.'

'If you do so, Lomax, I'll make sure you're court-martialled!' Alex glared at Freddie Lomax. 'Look, we've all got rifles, there's loads of ammunition. When the Germans come, it'll be damned hard for them to shift us—'

'Denham, you're insane!' Freddie Lomax grabbed his rifle, then ran up the stairs. His hand was on the latch that held the flimsy wooden door when a huge explosion rocked the village, and the cellar walls came down.

* * *

'Do come in, Miss Courtenay.' The matron of the sixth or seventh hospital she'd called at offered Rose her hand. 'Please have a seat.'

Rose sat down gingerly.

'How old are you, my dear?' enquired the matron.

'I'm twenty-four,' lied Rose. At the first four hospitals she'd given her real age. But then she'd seen a poster for the VAD, and realised that at eighteen she was far too young to be a nurse.

'Do you have any experience of nursing?' asked the matron.

'Only in the home.' Rose had decided not to lie again — it wouldn't take very long to catch her out.

But there would have to be a little embroidery nonetheless. 'I'm a children's governess,' she fibbed. 'I've been with the same family for years. The youngest daughter went to school last month, so I shall need another situation. But I'd really like to do some war work. I make excellent water gruel,' she added, desperately.

'There's not very much demand for gruel on a ward full of soldiers,' said the matron. 'They prefer rather more substantial fare. I presume you're offering your services as a volunteer?'

'Yes, of course,' said Rose. 'I have some savings, and I could afford to work here for three months at least.'

'By which time let's hope this dreadful business will be over. You're living with your parents, I assume?'

'Yes, that's right, in Chelsea.'

'So you're not too far away.' The matron smiled. 'This is not a military hospital, but we've set aside half a dozen of our largest wards for wounded soldiers. We have trained nurses and male orderlies, but we do need extra people who could wash the men, feed those who cannot feed themselves, and shave them.'

'I could do all that!' beamed Rose, who'd never washed anyone but herself. She'd never seen a man without his clothes, never fed anybody water gruel or anything else, and never touched a razor in her life. 'When shall I begin?'

'As soon I have seen your references.'

'Of course,' said Rose. She hadn't thought of references. But she could forge a couple, it wouldn't be a problem.

'You'll need some proper working clothes.' The matron was writing on a sheet of paper. 'Get yourself some comfortable black boots, and always wear black woollen stockings, silk won't do at all. Go to this shop in Marshall Road and buy a plain blue dress, a plain white apron, and some caps and cuffs. I've written down exactly what you'll need.'

'W-when is the earliest I could start?'

'On Monday morning,' smiled the matron, standing up. 'At six o'clock.'

* * *

Rose bought her uniform and a pair of cheap black boots, which she knew would give her dreadful blisters until she broke them in, but she didn't dare squander her resources.

The hospital was in Victoria, near the railway station. The shops nearby had cards in all their windows, offering board and lodging. She knew she couldn't stay at the hotel. It was too expensive. But could she live in lodgings? Who would wash her clothes and cook her dinner? She realised she might have to learn.

Propping her parcel up against the window of a shop, she wrote down details of rooms to let to ladies.

The first two were in such foul-smelling courts that she didn't even ring the bell. But the third was in a terraced house that had a whitened step and smart brass knocker on the door.

'I've come about the room,' she told the woman in a floury apron.

The woman looked Rose up and down. 'It's fifteen shillin' a week, all washin' done and meals as taken,' she said briskly. 'You pays a month's deposit and there's references required.'

'May I see the room?'

'Come in.'

The woman led Rose up the stairs and showed her into a small, airless room that overlooked a dismal, brick-paved yard where chickens pecked and rabbits fretted in a wooden hutch.

But it wasn't dirty, it didn't smell of anything unpleasant, and there was a grate, so maybe she could have a fire?

'I'll take it,' Rose said, firmly. 'May I move in tomorrow?'

'If you pays me the deposit now.' The woman glanced at Rose's parcel. 'You a single lady, miss?'

'Yes, that's right,' said Rose. 'I've just come down from Dorset. I'm going to train to be a nurse, at St Benedict's in Walton Road.'

'Well, if this Belgian business carries on, I'm sure there'll be a lot for you to do.' The woman's heavy, jowly face was less unfriendly now. 'Put your parcel down and try the bed. It's got a new feather mattress, so it's soft and comfortable.'

'I'm sure it will be fine.'

'Then that'll be three pounds to pay — Miss?'

'Courtenay.'

'Mrs Pike.' The woman took Rose's money. 'I'll let you have a look around and make yourself at home. Remember to shut the door on your way out. The cat will get in else, and you don't want dead mice under your bed.'

When Rose walked down the stairs a minute later, she heard the woman talking to someone in the parlour.

'No, she ain't a tart,' said Mrs Pike. 'She reckons she's goin' to be a nurse. She puts it on a bit, talks all lah-di-dah an' seems to think she owns the place. But that don't matter if she pays her way.'

* * *

Rose's first shift at St Benedict's was a hideous nightmare into which she stumbled at six o'clock the following Monday morning. Bleary-eyed and terrified, having failed to sleep on Mrs Pike's new feather mattress, she was dreading what she might be asked to do or witness.

'Come along, Miss Courtenay,' said the sister who bustled into the lobby, then led Rose up endless stairs. 'We're so pleased you've joined us! You'll be helping out on Kingston Ward. I understand you were a governess?'

'Yes, that's right,' blushed Rose.

'You'll soon settle down. I'll show you where to put your things, then you can help the orderlies serve breakfast. After the boys have eaten or been fed, we do the round. None of our chaps can wash without assistance, and some need everything to be done for them, so we'll keep you busy.'

The sister glanced at Rose's feet. 'Those boots look rather flimsy. If you can afford it, I should get yourself a stronger pair, with higher lacing to protect your ankles.'

Rose put on her apron, cuffs and cap, jabbing hair pins awkwardly into her mass of thick, dark, curling hair. Then she left the safety of the locker room and walked into the ward.

Orderlies were already serving breakfast and seemed pleased to see her, so now she went scurrying round the beds, carrying loaded trays.

Private Benson told her that although he only had one arm, he could feed himself. But Corporal Keenan was still shaky, so she'd better help him with his bacon, or he'd get it everywhere.

'Chop it up all nice an' small for 'im,' he said to Rose, then grinned. 'I 'spect I'll see you later, Sister — when they does the washing. You mind you come to me!'

Rose was dreading this. She'd never seen a naked man. 'You start this side,' said a staff nurse crisply, pointing to the six beds on the left. 'Don't touch any of their dressings, mind — just top and tail them, and don't forget to comb their hair.'

'Do Private Bannerman first,' added the sister, who was walking past. 'But be very careful when you shave him, because he's got a mole on his cheek. If you happen to catch it with the razor, it bleeds like anything.'

Rose thought she'd cut and run.

But then she squared her shoulders and told herself she hadn't come all this way and tried so hard to fall at the first hurdle. She owed it to herself to see it through.

'Private Bannerman?' She poured out boiling water from a jug into a bowl. 'Good morning, I'm Miss Courtenay, the new volunteer. I'm going to wash and shave you.'

It can't be very difficult she thought, as she stropped the razor clumsily. After all, men do it every day.

Private Bannerman opened one dull eye. 'Mind me mole,' he said.

'Miss Courtenay?' As Rose wiped soap and blood from Private Bannerman's butchered face, a nurse came up. 'Goodness, you took ages with that shave! I need some help with Sergeant Fowler. It takes two to turn him and he's got nasty pressure sores, so come along with me.'

* * *

By the end of that first week, Rose thought she had died and gone to hell. She had constant backache, her hands were red and raw, she'd somehow hurt her shoulder, and although she did her best, the nurses criticised her all the time.

She had to admit she was no good. Even laying breakfast trays was far beyond her skill. She could not remember which of the patients needed cups or beakers, who liked scrambled egg, who wanted fried tomatoes or who had just toast.

'They'll be sacking you,' observed a sour-faced staff nurse, at the end of yet another awful, muddled and exhausting day.

'Girls like you are nothing but a nuisance. Sister Fraser nearly had a fit when she saw how you'd put away the linen, up on Bentley Ward.'

But Rose did not get sacked, for the wards were filling up with yet more wounded soldiers and she could see that even her haphazard help was needed desperately.

By copying the others and secretly consulting a notebook she kept in her apron pocket, she somehow got through those first awful weeks.

'You're doin' all right, Sister,' Private Benson told her, as she combed his hair one Friday morning. 'You ain't so nervous now, an' you got a lovely gentle touch, not like some people I could mention.' He glanced towards the staff nurse who was constantly berating Rose. 'Don't take no notice when certain people grumbles. They're only jealous 'cos you're a looker an' they ain't.'

Rose blushed, but was encouraged. She told herself she would stick it out.

Later that same day, towards the end of what had turned out to be a gruelling shift, she heard somebody call her name. She turned to see what she'd done wrong.

But Staff Nurse Gower wasn't glaring angrily, and Rose breathed again. She liked Maria Gower, who never nagged or scolded. The men all liked her too, for she was pretty. She had soft, fair hair and mild, grey eyes.

'I know you're due to go off duty soon,' said Staff Nurse Gower, 'but before you leave, I'd like some things brought up to Stafford Ward.' She pointed to a tray, piled high with kidney bowls and shaving mugs and a jugful of thermometers.

Rose picked it up, then followed Staff Nurse Gower. She was so very tired, and her feet and ankles ached so much she could have cried. But after she had taken up this tray, she could go home to Heston Terrace, where Mrs Pike would have her dinner waiting, and she tried to concentrate on that.

She turned the corner into Stafford Ward, and then disaster struck. She didn't know how it happened, for her boots had rubber soles and usually kept their grip, even on these highly-polished floors. But she had still lost her balance. The contents of the tray flew up like missiles, and she was sitting sobbing amidst a heap of broken glass and china.

The staff nurse was ahead of her, and when she heard the crash she came to help Rose to her feet. Then they began to gather up the broken crockery.

'Be careful with the glass, you'll cut your hands,' the staff nurse warned. 'Go and fetch a broom. There's one in the ward cupboard.'

'I'm so sorry!' Rose began to brush the mess into a dusty heap. 'I just seemed to slip—'

'Don't worry, these things happen. That wretched floor's a menace.' Staff Nurse Gower handed Rose a clean white handkerchief. 'Come along, dry your eyes.'

But Rose could not stop crying, even though the men could see her through the open doors of Stafford Ward, even though she knew she'd be sent home and told not to come back.

'Come in here, Miss Courtenay.' Staff Nurse Gower led Rose into the ward sister's office and shut the door behind them. 'Do sit down,' she said.

Rose sat on the edge of a hard chair.

Maria poured her a small brandy, then made her choke it down. When Rose was merely gulping as opposed to sobbing as if her heart was going to burst, she fixed her with grey eyes in which Rose could see a hint of steel.

'Let's have the truth,' she said.

'I beg your pardon?'

'You're no more a governess than I'm the Queen of England. So who and what *are* you? A German spy?'

CHAPTER FOUR

'I was only joking,' said Maria, as Rose stared in horror. 'But I've been watching you. It's obvious that before you came to work here at St Benedict's, you had never fed an invalid. You'd never washed anybody in your life. I don't suppose you'd even washed yourself. You had a maid to do it.'

'No, you're wrong!' Panic-stricken, Rose gaped at Maria with wide, scared eyes. 'I know I'm sometimes clumsy. But that's because I'm nervous. Some of the men have dreadful wounds, and I'm afraid of hurting them.'

'This kind of nursing is new to all of us. We're all seeing terrible things we've never seen before. But *you* can't slice the top off a boiled egg. So unless you've come from somewhere where they don't have eggs?'

Rose saw it was no use. She'd been found out. She hardly ever cried, but tonight she was so tired and so unhappy she couldn't help herself.

Maria let her sob for a minute, then offered her a fresh, clean handkerchief. 'Where's your home?' she asked.

'In Dorset,' Rose replied.

'What do your people do?'

'My father is a farmer.' This was true enough, thought Rose, for Sir Gerard's tenants did farm several thousand of the ancestral acres on his vast estate.

'Why did you run away?'

'I didn't run away!'

'Rose, I think you did.'

'They wouldn't let me breathe.' Rose looked at Maria helplessly. 'You can't imagine what my life was like. Every single move I made, they watched me. I wanted to go and help in a hospital they'd set up in the village. But it was no, you can't do that. You must stay at home, marry the man we choose for you, and bury yourself alive.'

'You must tell your parents you've come here,' Maria said, firmly. 'Poor things, they must be frantic. They probably think you've been abducted and sold as a white slave.'

'Perhaps, but I don't care.'

'Why, did they beat you, or hurt you in some way?'

'No, but — you wouldn't understand.'

'Rose, I'll keep your secret,' said Maria. 'But you must write a letter to your mother. You must do it now, and I'll post it when I leave tonight.'

'What if I refuse?'

'You won't do anything so cruel and foolish. Listen, you write that letter, and I'll get you transferred to Stafford Ward. We're not so rushed up here, the orderlies are helpful and the sister is a gem. We'll turn you into a real nurse — agreed?'

'You promise you won't tell Matron what I've done?'

'My God, I wouldn't dare.' Maria grinned. 'She took you on, and she'd have a heart attack if she ever found out you took her in! You'll find some writing paper in that drawer.'

So Rose wrote the letter. After she had sealed the envelope, she felt as if a burden had been lifted from her shoulders. Even though she expected to be summoned home to Dorset straight away, and threatened with all sorts of dire reprisals if she refused to go, she trudged back to her lodgings feeling almost happy.

She ate the meal of mutton stew and glutinous rice pudding Mrs Pike warmed up for her, then she had an undisturbed night's sleep, the first since she'd arrived in London.

She worked out a plan. She wouldn't leave the hospital, and if her parents tried to force or bribe her to return to Charton, she'd run away again.

So she was surprised and slightly hurt when she heard nothing. 'Do you think they got my letter?' she asked Maria, when a fortnight had gone by.

'I expect they did.' Maria shrugged. 'But if you're worried, why don't you write again?'

'It would look as if I minded, and I don't.' Rose picked up a tray of instruments needing to be washed then sterilised. 'Sister said to clean the sluice and then sort out the linen, but may I watch you do some dressings later?'

'You could do some yourself.'

'All on my own?' Rose stared, alarmed. 'It's not the actual bandaging,' she added. 'I can do that now, and I'm not squeamish, I don't mind the blood. But I'm just so scared of hurting them.'

'Then you might as well go back to Dorset.' Maria's mild grey eyes met Rose's dark ones. 'Private Coleman, Corporal Spink and Sergeant Major Logan. You watched me change their tubes and do their dressings yesterday, so today you'll do them by yourself. I'll be on the ward, so if you're stuck just ask me what to do. But if you're only playing at being a nurse?'

'I'll do the dressings.'

As Rose's confidence increased, her skill improved. The pace on Stafford Ward was not as hectic as on Kingston, so she had time to watch the other nurses, then try things on her own.

As she finished doing dressings one November morning, Sister Hall called Rose into her office. 'Staff Nurse Gower says you're doing well,' she told her, smiling. 'I know you came here as a volunteer, to help us out in this emergency. Matron says you were a governess. But I think you're the sort of person who would make a splendid nurse.'

* * *

Rose felt she had come home. 'Sister says she thinks I should apply to Bart's or Guy's,' she told Maria, as they did a round together later that same day.

'What do *you* think, Rose?'

'I'd love it!' Rose's eyes were shining. 'When the war is over, I shall ask my father if he'll let me train at one of the big London hospitals. I'd like to work with children, actually.'

'You've heard from your parents, then?'

'No, not yet.' Rose bit her lower lip. 'Maybe I should write again?'

'Yes, perhaps you should.' Maria rubbed her eyes and yawned. 'You talk about the war being over, but that isn't going to be for ages.'

'Why do you say that?'

'Rose, don't you ever listen to the men?' Maria sighed. 'The Germans dig their trenches and then sit down on their side of the wire. We sit on the other side, and nobody's prepared to give an inch. England's full of factories producing shells and rockets and grenades, and I dare say Germany's the same. So how's it going to end?'

'*I* don't know!' cried Rose. 'Anyway, it's up to the government to sort it out.'

'You trust the government?'

'I suppose I do.' Rose shrugged. 'Well, women can't do anything, anyway. We don't even have the vote, and my father says we never will.'

'I do hope he's wrong.' Maria smiled. 'You should come to a meeting where we discuss these things.'

'You mean to listen to Mrs Pankhurst?' Rose looked doubtful. 'Daddy says she's mad. They ought to put her in a mental home for hopeless cases.'

'Your father sounds a very decisive man,' observed Maria. 'You must take after him.'

* * *

'I thought you were dead.'

Chloe stood scowling on the station platform, dressed in old black boots, a wide-brimmed hat devoid of veiling or a single feather, and a shapeless coat of an unflattering mud brown.

She twisted a strand of colourless hair around one long, thin finger, while the other hand sat on her bulging pregnancy. 'Why didn't you write to me before?'

'I was in a coma.'

'But when you came out of your coma?' Chloe's tone was sharp and accusatory. 'Why didn't you write then?'

Alex merely shrugged. He knew he ought to touch her, kiss her, make some simple gesture of affection, but, although he wanted to feel something, and although he knew he ought to be considerate and kind, and take an interest in Chloe and the baby, he just stood there, feeling nothing.

Since he had woken in that army hospital, it had seemed a dead weight of indifference, to everyone and everything, had replaced his living, beating heart.

He didn't feel any pain or fear, but more than that he didn't feel any affection, any love for anything or anyone — except for one specific someone, and he couldn't allow himself to think of that, he would go mad. 'I wrote as soon as I could hold a pen,' he muttered, tersely.

'I'm sure I'm very honoured.' Chloe's pale blue eyes were chips of glass. 'What happened, anyway?'

'We were in a cellar that got shelled. Some bricks fell on my head and knocked me out. Or so the nurses said. I had some cuts and bruises, but they've healed.'

'So you weren't badly hurt at all — no broken bones or anything like that.' Chloe pursed her lips. 'The Royal Dorsets have taken quite a hammering. My father says they're down to half their strength.'

'Yes, so I've heard,' said Alex.

'My mother thought you'd washed your hands of me.' Chloe began to walk along the platform. 'She said your kind don't marry girls like me, so was she right?'

'No, she was wrong.'

'So we *will* be married?'

'Yes, of course.' Alex took her limp, white hand and tried to force a smile. 'We'll need to get a move on, though — I shan't be in England very long. How old are you, Chloe — twenty, twenty-one?'

'I'm twenty-two next Wednesday. So we wouldn't need to wait for anyone's consent, unless of course you're not—'

'I was twenty-one last May.' Alex led Chloe through the barrier, out on to the concourse. 'So we could get a special licence. Chloe, I have a fortnight's leave. We could go and stay in a hotel, as man and wife.'

'Stay in a hotel?' Chloe's pale face flushed. 'Alex, I don't think my mother—'

'Oh, for God's sake, Chloe, you're grown up! It doesn't matter about your mother! If you want to marry me—'

'You know I do. But my father said you'd have to get permission from the colonel.'

'I've spoken to the colonel.'

'Oh — I see.' Chloe squared her rounded shoulders, lifting the enormous mound of baby. 'Alex, I've been thinking about names. If it's a boy, I rather fancy Victor — or maybe Jack, or Frank? If it's a girl, the names of flowers are pretty. What do you think of Lily?'

'Let's wait until the baby's born.' Lily, Violet, Poppy — anything, thought Alex, provided it's not Rose.

* * *

Maria didn't take Rose to meet Mrs Pankhurst or her daughters, to be harangued by harridans who wanted to turn women into men and make them ride astride. There wasn't time to go to meetings. Everyone was working double shifts, and every day new casualties came in.

More wards at St Benedict's were cleared for wounded soldiers. The nurses were kept more than busy, learning on the job themselves as well as training volunteers.

But Rose did meet Maria's sister, who was waiting in the lobby as they came off shift one Wednesday night.

'Rose, this is Phoebe,' said Maria. 'Phoebe — Rose.'

'Hello, Miss Gower.' Rose held out her hand.

'Pleased to meet you, Rose.' Phoebe Gower grinned. 'I've 'eard all about you. Maria said you was a governess?'

'Yes, and now I'm going to be a nurse.' Rose looked at the other girl, and saw she was nothing like Maria. Phoebe had crudely-bleached blonde hair, glittering dark eyes and a knowing grin that was nothing like Maria's warm, engaging smile.

A short, tight hobble skirt revealed her slender, shapely ankles. A fitted jacket showed off her curvaceous bosom, and a tiny velvet hat sporting a feather at a jaunty angle drew attention to her heart-shaped face.

If she let her hair grow out into its natural brown, and wore clothes that enhanced her shape but didn't emphasise it, she wouldn't look half so common, Rose decided — then she blushed. I sound just like my mother she thought, embarrassed.

'Do *you* work in a hospital?' she asked.

'God in 'eaven, no!' said Phoebe, shuddering theatrically. 'No, I couldn't be doing with none of that. Anythin' to do with blood an' guts gives me the creeps.'

She smirked and preened. 'I'm in the Varieties,' she continued. 'I started small, I was in the chorus for a while, but then I 'ad me break. I got me own act now, up the Haggerston Palace Music Hall — ain't that right, Maria?'

'Yes, that's right.' Rose saw a spasm flicker across Maria's pretty face. 'Phoebe and her friends are doing wonders for recruitment.'

'Maria means I sings a song or two, shows the blokes me drawers, then they comes up on stage an' takes the shillin'.'

Phoebe grinned again. 'Yeah, I might not be much cop at bandagin' an' that, but I does me bit. Maria, I was wonderin'—'

'Yes, you told me.' Maria turned to Rose. 'Do you think you could excuse us for a moment? Family business—'

'Actually, I left my gloves upstairs.' Rose smiled diplomatically. 'I'll just run up and fetch them.'

* * *

When she walked back into the lobby, Phoebe and Maria were deep in conversation. 'You know I hate it when you take that stuff,' she heard Maria mutter. 'He shouldn't make you work so hard, and *you* should have more sense—'

Then Phoebe noticed Rose and motioned to her sister to be quiet. 'Got your gloves?' she chirped, her eyes unnaturally bright.

'Yes, thank you.' Rose was blushing, wondering if they'd think she had been trying to listen to what they said. 'Maria, I know we'd planned to have some supper, but I could go home by myself.'

'No, wait for me, I'm coming now.'

'But your sister—'

'I'm just off.' Phoebe dropped some coins into her bag. 'Some of us 'as got to work tonight. Rose, it was nice to meet you. If you're ever over Haggerston way—'

'I shall be sure to come and see you,' promised Rose.

'Over my dead body,' Rose thought she heard Maria say. 'Rose, we were going to have some supper.'

'Yes.' Rose watched Phoebe mince away, sashaying down the hospital steps and off into the night. 'Sister Hall was saying there's a nice place near the station, where lots of nurses go. She said the food's all right.'

Rose and Maria walked through the cold streets. These days they were full of men in khaki, officers and men. 'Good evening, Sisters,' said a captain, touching his hat to them as he walked by.

'It's strange how it takes a war to make men treat us with respect,' murmured Maria. 'If we'd met that man six months ago, he'd have thought we were a couple of tarts, looking for trade.'

'Even though we're nurses?'

'Especially since we're nurses,' said Maria. 'We're not ladies, so we must be whores.'

Rose bit her lip and wondered — was Phoebe Gower a whore? She looked like one, and even Rose knew actresses were women of easy virtue, who often lived with men they hadn't married.

Alex Denham's mother was supposed to have been a whore. So had she had her hair bleached brassy yellow to the texture of dry straw, had she worn tight skirts that showed her figure, had she had a saucy grin and glittering dark eyes?

Alex Denham. Rose knew she should forget him, or at least consign him to the vault of memory, sealed inside a box along with other things and people she couldn't think about, or she would cry.

'A penny for them?' said Maria.

'What?' Rose rubbed her eyes. 'I'm sorry, I'm just tired.'

'Do you want to go straight home?'

'No, I want my dinner.' Rose lengthened her stride. 'Look, Oldham's Supper Rooms — that must be the place.'

* * *

Rose was expecting trouble. But when she finally received a letter from her mother, there were no reproaches and no threats. Lady Courtenay didn't even ask if Rose was coming home. She did mention Boris was pining for his mistress, plodding round the Minster howling and keeping everyone awake at night.

Poor Boris, Rose thought guiltily. *He* hadn't tried to make her marry Michael or forbidden her to join the VAD.

She wrote back to her mother straight away, saying she was sorry for the anxiety she must have caused and promising to visit as soon as she could get away. But she also wondered why her mother wasn't angry — or didn't seem to be.

She found out soon enough. As she was doing dressings one morning, Sister Hall came up and said she had a visitor in the lobby.

'I'll see to Corporal Anderson,' she added, with a twinkle in her eye. 'Off you go, Miss Courtenay. You may have the rest of the morning off.'

Rose expected it to be her father, possibly with two policemen and a padded van. But when she walked into the lobby, determined to assert herself and resist arrest, she saw Michael Easton standing chatting to the porter. He was in the uniform of a second lieutenant in the Royal Dorsets, and looked very handsome.

'Hello, Rose,' he said. 'I thought I'd come and see you.'

'I hope you didn't make a special journey?' Rose hoped she looked braver than she felt.

'No, of course not.' Michael smiled urbanely. 'I had to see my tailor and do other things in town.'

* * *

They took a cab to Piccadilly. As they drove along, Michael didn't speak to Rose at all. He took her to a restaurant, where he ordered without asking what she wanted. He told the waiter that the lady would like a glass of wine.

'Well, what a pretty pickle,' he observed.

'I'd rather you didn't talk to me as if I were a child.'

'Why shouldn't I?' Michael's blue eyes sparkled. 'You've behaved like one.'

'Michael, I don't think—'

'No one's accusing you of thinking, Rose. Quite the reverse, in fact.'

Rose was about to answer back, but then she realised there was nothing to be gained from arguing with Michael. 'I hope you didn't worry,' she said placatingly.

'The woman I've asked to be my wife goes missing for a month, then sends a mysterious letter to her mother to say she's well and happy, but isn't coming home. Of course I didn't worry.'

'I'm sorry, Michael.' Rose looked down at the tablecloth. 'But you know they'd never have let me go, and I simply had to get away.'

'I understand.' Michael smiled, then nodded to the waiter. When he'd served their soup and backed away, Michael covered Rose's hand with his, and held her gaze. 'So is it what you'd expected?' he enquired. 'Do you find nursing interesting? Do you feel fulfilled?'

'I feel I'm doing a useful job.'

'As I'm sure you are — and having some experiences you wouldn't get in Dorset on the side.'

Rose didn't like the tone of that remark, but she was relieved to find he didn't seem inclined to make a scene. As she dipped her spoon into her soup, it was suddenly obvious Michael hadn't cared when she'd gone missing. She wondered if she ought to feel annoyed.

She waited for the ultimatum she was sure must come. She'd had her little adventure, he would say, and if she would go home with him tonight and resume the empty life she'd led before the war, they'd say no more about it.

But Michael didn't speak. When he'd finished his soup he merely sat back in his chair and lit a cigarette.

'Any news from Charton?' Rose enquired.

'No, not really.' Michael shrugged. 'Alex Denham married his — whatever she is, and he's gone back to France.'

Rose felt her heart begin to thump. 'I heard she was going to have a child,' she murmured casually, as the soup slid down her throat like slime.

'Yes, I believe that's right.' Michael's eyes were on her, and she couldn't look away. 'Denham got himself blown up,' he added, carelessly.

'What?' Rose gave up all pretence of eating. 'When was this?'

'Oh, months ago, long before he married whatsername.' Michael pushed his empty bowl aside. 'What's the matter, Rose? You've gone quite red.'

'It's very hot in here.' But she had to know. 'What happened to him? I mean—'

'He was in a cellar or something when the Germans bombed it and the walls caved in. Some fellows from the Norfolks dug him out. A few of his chaps were killed outright and most of them had injuries, but I believe our friend escaped intact.'

Michael's gaze roamed over Rose's face. 'Well — more or less intact. He had bad concussion, but he's still got his arms and legs and — things. He came home for a bit of leave and made an honest woman of his trollop, so now he's a married man.'

Rose's heart was hammering. She knew her face was scarlet. She tried to think of something innocent and conversational, some remark about the awful weather, but she couldn't find anything to say.

'They're talking of turning Charton Minster into a convalescent home for officers,' said Michael, suddenly. 'If you're still keen to do your bit, perhaps you could work there.'

Rose looked at him and saw it was a plot. But before she could say no, she meant to stay in London, the door of the restaurant opened and a gust of air blew in.

'Well, I don't believe it! 'Ello, Rose!' Phoebe Gower was looking like a fashion plate. She wore a light wool dress and matching fur-trimmed coat in a flattering shade of silver grey, which suited her and took the strident brassiness out of her dyed hair, most of which was hidden by a velvet hat today.

Sauntering behind her was a sallow but good-looking man. In his middle thirties, he wore a cashmere coat draped round his shoulders and a smart, dark suit.

As he snapped his fingers and the head waiter scurried over, Phoebe smirked at Michael. 'Well, you're a deep one, Rose,' she grinned. 'I never knew you 'ad a feller, 'specially an 'andsome one like this! You goin' to introduce us, then?'

CHAPTER FIVE

'What was her name again?' asked Michael, as he and Rose walked up the steps towards St Benedict's.

'Phoebe Gower,' said Rose.

'Phoebe, the chaste goddess of the moon. I doubt if it's appropriate.' Michael grinned sarcastically and shook his golden head. 'How did you meet somebody like that?'

'She's the sister of a nurse who works with me.'

'She was with a desperate-looking chap.'

'Yes, he did seem rather rough.' Rose hadn't liked the look of Phoebe's friend. Dark-haired, saturnine and heavily built, he had merely nodded when Phoebe introduced him as Mr Daniel Hanson, and proudly announced he was in property.

He had let Phoebe flirt and chatter for a minute or so, and brag about her spot at the Haggerston Palace Music Hall, then he'd stalked over to a private booth, and she had scuttled hastily after him.

* * *

'So you're not coming back to Dorset?' Michael asked, as they stood on the top step.

'No, I'm staying here.' Rose looked up at him beseechingly. 'Please, Michael, try to understand. *You'll* be going away.'

'Perhaps.'

'So you'll have your chance to see the world.'

'Rose, *I'll* be going to fight! It won't exactly be a holiday. I'll probably be wounded. I might even be killed.'

'I know.' Rose hung her head. 'But I'm not going back to Dorset, to be buried alive.'

'I see,' said Michael. He looked Rose up and down. She could see him taking in her scuffed and battered boots, cheap cotton uniform and the cloak she'd bought from Staff Nurse Pearson second hand. 'What are you doing for money?'

'I'm managing,' she said. 'I have most of my meals in the hospital canteen. My lodgings are quite cheap. I have some savings.'

'I don't know what's come over you. Everyone in Dorset thinks you're mad, and I'm beginning to agree with them.' Michael took out his watch and frowned at it. 'I have to go and see my tailor now.'

'I must get back to work. But, Michael?'

'Yes?'

'Please don't think I meant to hurt you. I—'

'I'm late already,' Michael interrupted. 'Goodbye, Rose.'

Rose watched as Michael strode off briskly down the busy London street. The city was full of men in uniform, and soon he was just another smudge of khaki, lost among the crowds.

As she walked through the lobby, she was mulling over what he'd said. He'd told her Lady Courtenay looked as if she'd suddenly aged ten years. Rose's father never mentioned her, or not in public anyway.

But still she couldn't regret what she had done.

She wondered about Michael. If he still wanted her to marry him, and if she *did* become his wife, how was she going to live with him, go to bed with him and have his children, when she didn't love him and hardly even liked him any more?

'I must be very wicked,' she told herself, as she went up the stairs to Stafford Ward. 'I have no conscience, I don't care whom I hurt. If my parents cut me off without a penny, it will serve me right.'

She walked in through the double doors and down the ward towards the sister's office.

'Excuse me, Sister Courtenay?' Corporal Anderson was grinning. 'What did I do, to make you run away from me like that?'

'You didn't do anything, as well you know.' Rose smiled back at him. 'Somebody came in to see me, and—'

'Yeah, so we heard,' said Private Floyd. 'Some young feller, wasn't it?'

'Some 'andsome captain, I'll be bound,' said Private Coleman. 'Look, lads — Sister Courtenay's blushing!'

'You mustn't call me sister,' Rose said sternly. 'I'm a volunteer, so you should address me as Miss Courtenay.'

'I'm a sick man, Sister.' Private Coleman shook his head. 'You can't expect me to remember guff like that.'

'Good afternoon, Miss Courtenay.' Maria came up and handed Rose a tray. 'I hope you had a pleasant outing? Sergeant Curtis, Private Floyd and Lance Corporal Townsend need their tubes and dressings changed, so if you wouldn't mind?'

'I'm glad it's you, Miss Courtenay,' Sergeant Curtis murmured, as Rose drew the curtains round his bed. 'You've got the gentlest hands of all the nurses on this ward.'

Rose blushed again, but this time with pride.

* * *

Alex's leave came to an end and he rejoined his company in France. The third battalion was in trenches near Arras, and his new platoon was in the actual front line, but the men who'd occupied these trenches last had made them almost cosy. The pumps worked properly, so when it rained the water didn't lie in muddy puddles, soaking everything.

The officers had a dugout roofed with corrugated iron and furnished with a table and some armchairs stolen from a nearby farmhouse that was now a ruin. There were crates of whisky, a new paraffin stove and piles of blankets, as well as several recent *Punches*, *Tatlers*, and other magazines.

'A little home from home,' observed the captain who showed Alex round. 'When it's quiet we all cram in, then get a decent fug up. You wouldn't know there was a blasted war going on outside.'

'It's all very snug, sir.' Alex put his pack down on a bunk. 'They told me back at base we'd only be here for another couple of weeks. Do you know where we'll be going next?'

'We hope there isn't going to *be* a next!' Captain Ford looked grim. 'I don't know what they're saying back home in Blighty, but the fellows here can't believe the Brass is going to let us sit and look at Jerry all the flipping winter. They promised we'd be home in time for Christmas, after all.'

Alex merely shrugged.

'Come and have a dekko at the saps,' the captain added, pointing to the entrance of a tunnel snaking under no-man's-land. 'We've packed them all with high explosive, so the Jerries opposite are going to get a nasty shock tonight. I understand you've done a course in mining?'

'Yes, that's right.'

'Then you could get in there and make sure everything's been set up as it ought to be. The last time we did this, we lost five men, and Colonel Parker wasn't pleased. So when you've had a gander, come and tell me what you think.'

* * *

Although his fellow officers were hoping to be home in time for Christmas, Alex didn't care where he went next, to England or Siam. He was relieved to get away from Chloe, who hadn't proved to be a blessing.

After their furtive hole and corner wedding in a register office, at which the guests had been a solemn Henry Denham and an embarrassed Mrs Jarman, the newly-married pair had gone to spend a couple of days in Dorset.

Chloe had waddled round Henry's cold, dark and dilapidated house complaining that it wasn't what she'd expected. The whole place smelled of mice, she grumbled, and there were rotten floorboards everywhere. The banisters were broken, and if she didn't watch it she would take a tumble down the stairs and break her flipping neck.

When it was time for Alex to go back, Chloe announced she couldn't stand the quiet of the country any more, and was going to stay with her Aunt Emily in Wolverhampton. 'So I must have some money,' she said sharply. 'Forty pounds at least.'

Alex gave her fifty.

Chloe put the money in her purse. 'It's not at all like I'd imagined,' she added, sniffing miserably.

'What's not as you'd imagined?'

'I'd have thought a gentleman like you would have a grand, imposing house, not a horrible, draughty barn like this. I thought there would be silver plate and lovely velvet curtains and servants everywhere.'

'You must have read too many novels. Most of the country houses hereabouts are just like this one.'

'But I don't want to live in an enormous, crumbling ruin!' Chloe sat on a dusty chair and wept. 'I want to live in a town, where there are shops and parks and buses! I want to wear nice clothes from Gamages. I want to have my friends and neighbours round for supper and a little sing-song now and then. I want a garden with herbaceous borders and a chicken coop, so we can have fresh eggs. I want a little house that's all my own!'

* * *

Alex crawled out of the sap, lit a cigarette and told himself that Chloe was very young. She would adapt to living in rural Dorset, and it would all work out. But even if it didn't, at least her child would be legitimate, and that was worth a lot.

He could still remember those first months at boarding school. Michael and he had gone down on the train, and

Michael had promised faithfully he wouldn't tell a soul. But the strain of secrecy had proved too much for him.

A few weeks into term, they'd had a scrap about some blackbird's eggs. Contrary to decent sporting practice, Michael destroyed the nest and pinched the lot. Alex had given Michael a black eye, and Michael had called Alex a stupid, pox-faced bastard.

'Language, Easton,' warned a junior master, who'd happened to be passing and had broken up the fight. 'If Dr Preston heard you calling other fellows bastards, he would have you flogged all round the cloister.'

'But Denham *is* a bastard, sir,' Michael had protested, '*and* his stinking mother is a whore.'

'Any comment, Denham?' The master had looked quizzically at Alex. 'If that's malicious slander, you can black his other eye. I'll hold him down for you.'

Alex had just stared at Mr Lewis in helpless misery.

One hour later, Michael's version of the story was all round the school. For the next three years — until he grew big and strong enough to beat up his tormentors — Alex was addressed as *bastard* with impunity. It was common knowledge that his mother was a harlot, who was anyone's for half a crown.

* * *

Alex threw his cigarette away. The saps were amateurish, but the explosive was packed in properly, the fuses looked all right, so they were as ready as they'd ever be.

He went to look for Captain Ford, who wasn't in the dugout. So he set off down the trench, stepping over men snatching a nap, and stores and boxes of equipment.

'Good morning, sir,' exclaimed a spruce young corporal, who was carrying a sack that wriggled. 'Rabbits, sir,' he grinned. 'A mother and her babies. My old man was a poacher down in Charmouth and I used to be a butcher's boy. It's rabbit stew tonight.'

'Well done, corporal.' Alex shuddered. 'Do you know where I'll find Captain Ford?'

'He's in Park Lane, sir. It's the new communication trench.' The corporal stroked his squirming sack. 'If you're going up there, sir, I'd keep your head well down. The Jerries are sending over all the heavy stuff today and they've got good marksmen. An officer who came out here from Blighty just a week ago got his brains blown out by a sniper only yesterday.'

Alex didn't care if there were half a dozen snipers, if all their sights were trained on him. He'd done his duty by Chloe, who would soon forget him. The child would probably be Henry's heir, and Chloe would get a pension from the army, so she'd be a fairly merry widow. She could have her little house in some dull, sprawling suburb — herbaceous borders, chicken coop and all.

He set off down Park Lane, hands in his pockets, whistling tunelessly.

* * *

'They're opening another ward for soldiers,' said Maria, as she and Rose made beds one gloomy morning in the middle of December. 'This one will be for amputees and other serious cases, like head injuries.'

'I'll be staying on Stafford, I suppose?'

'On the contrary.' Maria looked at Rose. 'I've asked to go on the new ward. I hope you'll come with me. We've four more volunteers starting Monday, and Stafford would be an ideal ward for them. You could handle much more challenging stuff.'

'But I'm not a proper nurse,' frowned Rose.

'You have a nurse's instincts. You've learned more these past few weeks than some people learn in four whole years of formal training. You get on with the other staff. The men adore you. Rose, you *are* a nurse.'

Rose went pink with pleasure.

The new ward was made ready and took its first twelve patients. 'Two gas gangrene cases, seven snipers' bullets in the head, and three blokes got too close to grenades,' intoned the RAMC orderly who'd come in with the men. 'Look out for that fellow with the ginger hair — he should be in a bin, if you ask me.'

Rose tried to look calm and confident, but she was horrified. On Stafford Ward, the men had all been wounded, but theirs had been straightforward injuries — broken legs and bullet wounds and gashes caused by shrapnel. They had been in hospitals in France before they'd come to England, and by the time they reached St Benedict's they were getting better.

But these twelve new patients had come straight from the front line. The three who had had amputations still had field dressings on their other injuries. The ones whose heads were bandaged still wore bloodstained uniforms. They all looked tired to death.

The red-haired man had wild, dark eyes, and as Rose went up to him he let out such an eldritch shriek of horror that she backed away.

'Shut it, Kingsley.' One of the men who'd had a sniper's bullet in his head scowled at the red-haired man, whose right arm was missing and whose khaki jacket was dark with blood. 'Be careful, Sister — he's a violent bugger.'

Maria and another staff nurse came to Rose's aid. 'Come along, Private Kingsley,' soothed Maria. 'Let's get you cleaned up and into bed. Dr Lane will be here in a minute. He'll give you something to help calm you down.'

The nurses cut off dirty uniforms, washed the men and got them into bed. Rose smoothed the blankets and smiled at a man whose left arm was a stump, and whose remaining hand had lost three fingers to a grenade.

'Thank you, Sister.' The wounded soldier — a middle-aged reservist, Rose supposed, called up and sent to France when it all started — glanced up at her and sighed. 'You look like you ought to be at school. If you don't mind my asking, just how old are you?'

'I'm eight — twenty-four,' lied Rose, and blushed.

'Eighteen, eh?' The soldier shook his head. 'So you're just a kid, but at least you had the sense to be a girl. There's boys of your age dying over there.'

'I know,' said Rose. 'But you're out of it now.'

'Yeah, I'm out of it.' The wounded soldier closed his eyes. 'I used to be a carpenter, you know. I made chests and cabinets and boxes, lovely things they were, inlaid with mother of pearl and ivory. But I won't be doin' that no more. Last week, I saw this lad just turned nineteen get blown to bits. I wish it had been me.'

* * *

'It's horrible!' cried Rose, as she and Maria snatched a coffee break later that day. 'Men are being mutilated, driven mad—'

'I know.' Maria stirred her coffee, round and round and round. 'Rose, if you can't deal with it, you only have to say.'

'*I* can deal with it!' Rose glared at Maria. '*I* can look at mangled limbs and bullet holes with all the flesh and muscle hanging out, *I* can deal with horrible, great wounds! But what about the men? What are they *doing* out there? Just sitting in their wretched trenches like a row of targets, waiting to be shot at, bombed or blown to smithereens?'

'You've heard what the men have been saying down on Stafford Ward,' Maria said gently. 'You know what must be happening over there.'

'But I didn't really think about it. I didn't understand how awful it must be until today.' Rose could not drink her coffee. 'It's wicked,' she continued. 'It's evil and it's cruel. It's not a war, it's just a pointless slaughter.'

'You sound like a pacifist.'

'I want to go to France.' Rose looked at Maria earnestly. 'I'm going to join the VAD, then volunteer for service overseas.'

'You can't, you're much too young.'

'I'll lie about my age.'

'If you go abroad, you'll need to forge a birth certificate — unless you plan to steal one?'

'But I can't stay here and do nothing!' Rose exclaimed.

'You're hardly doing *nothing.*' Maria met Rose's anguished gaze. 'Listen, spend the next few months here at St Benedict's, learning how to treat these dreadful wounds, and how to deal with your own emotions. Rose, you're very young. Let yourself grow up a bit.'

'Everybody treats me like a child,' muttered Rose.

'We wouldn't let a child see what you have seen today,' Maria said wryly. 'If you don't want that horrid coffee, let's get back. We've work to do.'

* * *

'Come along, my dear. It's nearly supper time, but you've still got lots of work to do.'

In the stuffy bedroom of a grimy house in Wolverhampton, the midwife wiped the expectant mother's face with a damp cloth. 'I know it's hurting, but you need to push. I can't do it for you.'

'I can't push any more.' Chloe was exhausted, for she'd been in labour all that day and half the previous night. 'I'm so tired, and it hurts so much! I'll never have another baby, ever!'

'That's what everybody says, but they all change their minds.' The midwife crouched to look between her patient's parted legs. 'You're nearly ready now. So if you can ride this next contraction, and then push really hard, your baby will be here. Come now, Mrs Denham, do your best. Just think how proud and happy Mr Denham's going to be.'

'My husband doesn't care about me or the baby.' Chloe bit her lip. She didn't want to think of Alex.

He didn't love her and he never had, for since he'd been in France he had never written a proper letter, saying that he missed her and was looking forward to seeing her again.

She felt another contraction coming, braced herself, but this one hit her with the force of a typhoon. She screamed in agony and terror. She'd thought she couldn't push any more, but now she heaved and grunted, straining like a man trying to lift a weight almost as heavy as himself.

'Stop a moment — Mrs Denham, please!' The calm, efficient midwife suddenly sounded frightened. 'Mrs Denham, wait, the cord is round your baby's neck!'

But Chloe didn't want to wait. She shut her ears to the midwife's warning. She pushed hard once again, then it was over, and she closed her eyes.

She could hear the midwife saying she was so sorry, so very, very sorry, and Aunt Emily crying. But she couldn't really take it in, because she was so tired — so very tired.

* * *

It was ten o'clock at night when Rose and Maria finally got away to have a meal in the canteen. Private Kingsley had been very difficult today, but Rose found she could soothe and comfort him. So she'd sat at his bedside for an hour or more, crooning the nursery rhymes and lullabies her nanny had once sung, and finally he'd drifted off to sleep.

Maria had had a little smile playing about her lips, and been looking as if she had a secret all that day, but Rose hadn't had a chance to ask what it might be.

They lined up for their plates of mince and vegetables, then sat down to wolf their soggy supper.

'Come on, then — spill the beans,' said Rose, as she pushed her empty plate away.

'Beans?' said Maria, looking blank.

'Staff Nurse Gower, don't be such a tease!'

'Oh, very well, I'll tell you. But it was Sister Hall's idea, not mine.' Maria started on her treacle pudding. 'You said you'd like to go to France.'

CHAPTER SIX

All over Christmas, Alex's company had manned a line of deep, dry trenches full of ammunition that they knew would blow them all to glory if the Germans bombed it.

They'd managed to have a fairly merry Christmas, all the same. They'd had plenty of whisky and food, and enough packs of cigarettes to supply a whole brigade.

The enemy had been quiet, even at night. Although there had been rumours of British front line troops and their German counterparts from the trenches opposite playing football in the mud and mess of no-man's-land, there hadn't been any of that sort of fun in Alex's sector of the line. An unofficial cease-fire was declared on Christmas Day, but only so burying parties could go out and dig some graves unscathed.

After stand to arms on New Year's Day, Alex took the letter from Chloe's mother from his pack and read it once again. He had not imagined it — there it was in Board School black and white, the news that the baby girl had been stillborn, that Chloe herself was very ill and would most likely die.

He knew he could have got compassionate leave. He could have gone to Wolverhampton, could have sat in Chloe's Aunt Emily's dark Victorian parlour while he waited for his wife to die, but what would have been the point?

The thought of facing Quartermaster Sergeant Jarman and his moon-faced wife, who he knew despised him for a vile seducer of their virgin daughter, made him feel sick.

He was sorry for Chloe, of course he was — he couldn't begin to imagine how upsetting it must be for a woman to lose her new-born child. But it didn't seem anything to do with him. He thought it would probably be much better if he didn't see any of them again.

The way things were going, he doubted if he would — for in this sector, an officer had a life expectancy of round about a fortnight.

He shoved the crumpled paper back into his pack and walked out of the dugout to breathe the frosty air.

On this first day of the brand new year, the sun was shining and the sky was blue. It had snowed a few hours earlier, and the broken, battered trees amongst which they had dug their lines of trenches looked almost pretty, white with rime.

The men who were busy shoring up some sections of the trench that had become unstable whistled as they worked. A lark or something similar — Alex didn't know the song of one bird from another — was singing overhead, its thin melody trickling through the unharmonious crumping of the heavy guns.

'Happy New Year, sir!' Corporal Brind, the happy poacher who had kept the company in festive fare throughout the festive season, even getting hold of a fat goose for Christmas Day, grinned cheerily at Alex.

'Thank you, Corporal Brind.'

'We never thought we'd be out 'ere this long — did we, sir?' The corporal shook his sleek, dark head. 'There's my old lady, thought she'd 'ave me 'ome for Christmas Eve. I 'ope she didn't let any other bugger get their leg over instead.'

'I'm sure she didn't,' murmured Alex, and rubbed his bleary eyes.

'Mr Denham sir, I 'ope you're right. If she's been playing fast and loose, she'll 'ave 'er teeth pushed so far down 'er throat she'll 'ave to eat 'er breakfast with 'er arse, pardon my French.

'Anyway sir, Captain Ford sent me to look for you. There's another gentleman joining us this lovely morning. I think you'll be showing 'im the ropes. Look, 'e's coming now.'

Alex looked, and Michael Easton's cold blue eyes bored into him, stopping his smile of welcome in its tracks.

He saw the new lieutenant looked hangdog, anxious — frightened? The artillery behind them had just opened up and missiles were flying through the air towards the enemy lines. So although it was fire from their own side and the inevitable counter-attack had yet to come, the noise was deafening.

Easton would soon get used to it, he thought. After a week or so, he'd actually miss it — on the rare occasions when it stopped. He was about to say as much when Captain Ford came stumping down the trench, scowling at a sheaf of papers flapping in his hand and kicking clods of frozen earth aside.

He glared at Michael Easton. 'You must be the new lieutenant,' he began, and grimaced. 'Mr Easton, isn't it? You're in time to have a bit of fun. What's the matter, man?'

Michael gulped and shuddered.

'God, don't say they've sent me yet another windy blighter?' Captain Ford brushed past his junior officers and went into the dugout. 'Come into the parlour, anyway. Mr Denham, you could come in, too. Where are Lomax and McCarthy?'

'They went out with a digging party, sir.' Alex looked along the trench. 'I think they're coming now.'

'About time, too.'

The other two lieutenants came in brushing snowflakes from their shoulders. Captain Ford began to dole out papers from his bundle.

'Sorry to burden you with all this skite, Lieutenant Easton,' he said insincerely, as he handed out the maps and notes and lists and plans. 'I'd have liked to let you find your feet, but there isn't time for that. If you get stuck, ask Mr Denham here.'

'So we're to be involved in a new show?' asked Freddie Lomax.

'Mr Lomax, you're a genius.' Captain Ford glared at him irritably. 'Yes, I'm afraid those buggers at HQ have noticed our boys haven't had much exercise of late, so we're going to a busier sector. By this time tomorrow, the London Irish will be in our cosy quarters here, minding all this ammunition, and we'll be sitting in some filthy hole five yards away from the front line.

'All right, get the lazy buggers moving. We're to be entrained by four o'clock this afternoon.'

* * *

'I suppose they must use trains?' asked Rose, as she and Maria sorted through all the forms to be completed, before they could be attached to the army as civilian nursing volunteers.

'They must do — how else would they get the men out of the battle zones?' Maria handed Rose another sheaf of documents to sign. 'Rose, are you sure you want to go to France?'

'Of course I'm sure.'

'If they find out you've lied about your age, they'll send you home again.'

'I'll have to take that chance.'

'What about your parents? I think you ought to visit them before you leave the country.'

'If I do, they'll try to stop me going.' Rose looked down at her ruined hands. Lady Courtenay would be appalled to see the rough and reddened skin, cracked and discoloured nails and ragged cuticles that were the inevitable result of having her hands in water all the time, of nursing men with gangrene, frostbite and infected wounds. 'I've written to them, of course.'

'Well, if you change your mind, Matron is sure to let you have some leave.' Maria grinned. 'You could say you have an ancient grandmother in Scotland, whom you'd like to see before she dies.'

'I don't think so, somehow. But what about you, Maria? You never talk about your family.'

'There's only Phoebe,' said Maria, shrugging. 'We never knew our parents. My first memory is of the orphanage in

Bethnal Green. Then they farmed us out, to be brought up by a foster mother. But she died last year, and Phoebe — well, she has her life, I have mine.'

'I met her in a restaurant once,' said Rose. 'I don't know if I mentioned it?'

'I don't believe you did.' Maria sniffed. 'I dare say she was with some man?'

'Yes, quite a young, good-looking one, in fact. She said he was in property.'

'He was probably a gangster, then.' Maria shuddered, then handed Rose another sheet of paper. 'All right, fill in this one next. What are you going to say? You're Miss Rose Helen Courtenay, formerly a governess, of 15 Heston Terrace, Chelsea Bridge. You're twenty-four years old. You cannot find your birth certificate, but you have a baptismal one from St James the Great in Alton Road — and various other documents that verify your age.'

Maria smiled ruefully. 'Rose, these forgeries are excellent. You've missed your vocation. You should have been a criminal or a fence.'

'I was always good at lettering and drawing,' murmured Rose. 'When I was a child, I loved making treasure maps. I used cold tea and coffee or soot from up the chimney to make them look authentic.' She glanced up from her forgeries. 'Do you think I'll pass for twenty-four?'

'I expect so,' said Maria. 'You look so self-assured, which always helps, and you're quite tall.'

'How old are you, Maria? You don't look more than twenty-one to me.'

'You obviously need spectacles.' Maria signed a form. 'I'm twenty-six. The men on Essex Ward are going to miss you.'

'They're going to miss you, too.'

'But you're their special sweetheart. You're the one they ask to write their letters, you're the one they tell about their wives and girls and children. You're the one they love.'

'I love them, too,' said Rose. 'Maria, they're so brave, so uncomplaining. I don't know how they stand it, when we have to change their dressings and clean their wounds with saline. It must be agony. But they never grumble or make any fuss.'

* * *

Rose, Maria and four more volunteers from St Benedict's crossed the storm-tossed Channel the following February, in a battered pre-war steamer now being used for ferrying troops to France.

As they went on board at ten o'clock that rainswept Wednesday evening, an officer directed them towards the first-class lounge. 'Make yourselves at home,' he told them, briskly. 'You won't be disturbed. This deck is out of bounds to officers and men.'

'A pity,' murmured Julia Neale, as the officer left them there to look at one another.

'We're not allowed to fraternise with soldiers,' said Amy Ward regretfully, as they watched the endless lines of khaki march aboard and pack into the lower decks. 'Sister Hall says discipline is very strict in France.'

'We're not to look at anyone directly, or speak to anybody from the army unless he speaks to us and it would be rude not to reply.' Lucy Wallis grimaced. 'Matron told me any nurse who so much as smiles at a soldier will be sent home straight away.'

'Do you think they'll give us any supper?' asked Katie Smead, as she stared round the empty lounge from which all the furniture and fittings and even the carpet had been stripped.

'I've got some ham rolls and bars of chocolate,' said Maria, and took them from her bag.

'I have a flask of coffee and some cakes,' said Amy Ward.

'I have biscuits and some home-made gingerbread.' Rose produced a grease-proof paper parcel, packed for her by Mrs Pike and presented as a parting gift.

The other nurses brought out half-sized bottles of medicinal brandy, slabs of fruit cake and brown paper bags of sausage rolls and meat paste sandwiches. 'Excellent,' Maria said, as she surveyed the contents of the heaped-together picnic. 'We can have a feast.'

* * *

'We're nearly there!' cried Lucy Wallis, shaking Rose's shoulder and rousing her from a brandy-sozzled slumber on the bare wood floor. 'Come and have a look.'

As Rose was stumbling over to a porthole, the troopship nosed into the ferry port. The first thing to catch her eye was a green hill rising in the distance. It was covered with rows of bell-shaped tents.

'We're going to have to live in those,' said Julia Neale, shuddering. 'Rose, I hope you've brought your woollen drawers?'

'But my cousin's living in a hut,' objected Katie. 'She's got a stove and running water, and a wardrobe — everything'.

'Then she's flipping lucky.' Amy grinned at Rose. 'We'll be living in those wigwam things they've pinched from the Boy Scouts, with buckets for the necessary, if you get my meaning.'

'Yes.' Rose sniffed the air that drifted through the open porthole. She could smell hot fat and frying crepes, the yeasty tang of beer, the sourer undertones of oil and sewage, and it all added up to something new, exciting, strange. She grinned and hugged herself. She'd made it — she had arrived in France.

* * *

'So remember, ladies. You're on active service now,' said the RAMC officer who'd met them at Le Havre.

He'd marched them to a tiny, cluttered room behind an officers-only Red Cross café. But he failed to offer them any breakfast and, while they were tormented by the smell of roasting coffee beans and hot, fresh bread, he lectured them for half an hour.

They should wear full uniform at all times, because civilian dress was not allowed. They should not fraternise or form associations with officers or men. They were not *in* the army, but they were attached to it. So if they committed any crimes they would be tried by military courts.

The officer looked down at his list. 'Miss Courtenay and Miss Gower?' he barked.

Rose and Maria stood up.

'You are to report to Colonel Streatham, the officer in charge of ambulance trains. He will explain your duties. I hope you ladies don't get travel sick?'

'You lucky things!' Katie Smead grinned up at Rose. 'You've fallen on your feet! I dare say I'll be living in a wigwam, peeing in a bucket, and—'

'Silence, ladies!' The officer glared angrily at Katie, asked for her name, then wrote it down. 'Miss Courtenay and Miss Gower, you are dismissed. Your driver is outside.'

But Colonel Streatham wasn't in his office. The adjutant said he had no orders for Maria or Rose — in fact, he didn't know anything about them. 'I'm sorry, ladies,' he continued, shrugging. 'It appears you don't exist.'

He sat down at his desk and had a riffle through some papers. Then at last he glanced up at the driver, and grinned as if inspired. 'I suggest you take these ladies to the CCS at Arlescourt. Then, when a train comes in — and if it turns out they *are* expected — they'll be on the spot.'

The journey to the casualty clearing station was through pretty countryside lightly dusted with a silver powdering of snow. But as they went further east, the landscape grew more desolate.

'Look,' whispered Rose, as they passed an ancient church whose tower lay in ruins.

'Over there, as well,' Maria murmured, as they drove through the village.

The inhabitants must have died or fled, thought Rose, leaving their burnt-out homes and packs of hungry dogs who howled at them mournfully as the car sped past.

The roads grew rutted, and the fields on either side were full of weeds and thistles. The land had not been ploughed in autumn, and would not be ready for the spring.

Then they heard the guns. At first the sound was muted, a series of dull thuds like distant thunder, as if a storm were breaking miles away. Then the noise intensified. It became continuous and much more threatening. A few miles later, a rocket screeched menacingly overhead, then exploded in a nearby wood.

'Blasted things,' the driver muttered, and Rose saw his knuckles were clenched and white upon the wheel. 'But don't worry, Sisters. They don't usually get this far behind the line. The CCS is just a couple more miles down this road. I dare say they're expecting you.'

The casualty clearing station was a clutch of wooden huts a mile behind the line. Sick or wounded soldiers walked or were carried there from first aid posts, either for further treatment or to await evacuation.

Rose saw the huge white crosses painted on the flimsy roofs. She hoped the German aeroplanes she'd seen flying overhead did not regard the crosses as so many targets.

The railhead was a hundred yards away and, as Rose and Maria got out of the car and dragged their luggage from its boot, a train came chugging down the track towards the wooden buffers.

'Miss Courtenay and Miss Gower?' A harassed-looking RAMC major came striding from the nearest hut. 'You're late. You should have been here yesterday.'

'But we only arrived in France this morning,' Rose began.

The major glared at her, then scowled down at his sheaf of papers. 'You will be Miss Courtenay — or Miss Gower?'

'Miss Courtenay, sir.'

'Well, Miss Courtenay, let's get one thing straight. We don't need nurses who give cheek to their superior officers. So if you can't keep a civil tongue, the best thing you can do is bugger off back to Blighty.'

As Rose blushed red, Maria spoke. 'Where will we be billeted, sir?' she asked the major calmly and politely.

'I beg your pardon?' The major looked as if he'd have a fit. 'You and your delightful friend have both been posted to the ambulance trains, God help us all. You will be escorting men from the clearing stations to the general hospital at base, and you'll be billeted on the bloody train.'

* * *

'That was Dr Callaghan, he's always rather irritable,' a young Queen Alexandra nurse told Rose and Maria. She took them on to the empty train and showed them where to stow their kit, in a sleeper carriage in the middle of the train. Here the nurses, orderlies and doctors had their cramped but warm and draught-proof quarters.

'You two are being thrown in at the deep end,' grinned an orderly, who was walking past with piles of blankets.

'So I hope you're fit.' The QA nurse shoved Rose's Gladstone bag into a luggage rack. 'We heard this sector's had a dreadful battering these past weeks, so I dare say the men we've come to fetch will be in quite a state.'

She glanced out of the window. 'Look, here come the stretcher bearers now.'

It took two hours to load the train with wounded, broken men. Some were clean and in the regulation blue pyjamas, but most still wore their mud and blood-streaked uniforms.

'We'll get them settled first,' the QA nurse told Rose. 'The stretcher cases can go on the floor, and we'll get the others into bunks. Pack the pillows and blankets round them, so they won't feel the jolting of the train.'

As the train moved off, the orderlies were lighting primus stoves to boil up water for hot drinks and to wash the men. Rose set to work, and soon she realised this would be no picnic.

St Benedict's had been a modern hospital where there'd been running water and every possible facility. But here she was working in a badly-lit and tiny space, trying to undress and wash exhausted, filthy men crammed into bunks like narrow bookshelves, and all the time the train was jolting, lurching, swaying from side to side.

'Thank you, Sister.' The corporal whose gashed and mangled arm she'd washed and bandaged awkwardly managed a feeble smile of gratitude. 'I know you're busy, but could I have a drink?'

'Of course.' Rose packed the blankets round him. 'I'll ask the orderly to bring you something.'

The soldier braced himself against the side of the couchette. 'Harry Liston, down there on the left,' he whispered, pointing. 'He's got a bullet in his brain, and they think he's going to lose his sight. So go and let him feast his eyes on you, and he'll die happy.'

* * *

It was dark and snowing heavily when at last the train came shuddering to its final halt. Now the staff would help the stretcher bearers get the wounded off, then strip all the bunks, clean up and get the train all ready to go off again.

Rose peered into the darkness and saw lights. Suddenly there were dozens of men in RAMC uniform, opening the doors and working with a calm, methodical efficiency as the sick and wounded were unloaded and taken to the waiting ambulances, to be driven to hospital or shipped home to England.

'Poor thing, you look all in.' The QA nurse who'd shown Rose where to put her luggage smiled. 'I dare say you're hungry?'

'Yes, I suppose I am.' Rose yawned and rubbed her aching, bloodshot eyes.

'When did you last eat?'

'When we were on the boat.'

'Last night?' The nurse looked horrified. 'Look, we'll be here for an hour or two at least, while they change the engine and we sort out the train. So fetch your friend, then go and have a decent meal in the Red Cross canteen. You'll find it at the end of Platform 2. Miss Courtenay?'

'Yes?'

'I kept my eye on you. I saw you were nervous, and occasionally you weren't sure what to do. But you didn't keep asking. Instead, you used your gumption. You did very well.'

'Thank you, Sister.' In spite of her fatigue, Rose smiled. She'd done very well, and it was going to be all right.

* * *

The spring came slowly to the blasted land, furtively clothing it with green and hiding all the wounds inflicted that appalling winter, but with the warmer weather came new military offensives. Maria and Rose spent March and April as relief staff on the ambulance trains, constantly being ordered from one sector to another, never knowing where they'd end up next.

They trudged along endless pot-holed country roads, hitching lifts in lorries or squashing into the back seats of military cars. They rode in London buses, half a dozen of which had been transported to the front to ferry troops around.

'I don't understand these orders.' One April morning, Rose pored over the long list of badly-typed instructions they'd received from the sister in charge a minute or two ago. 'It's the seventeenth. We were supposed to be in Aix-les-Givres yesterday.'

'Then we'd better shift ourselves.' Maria shoved the last few bits and pieces into her carpet bag.

Later that same evening, several lifts and lots of walking later, they were alone and stranded somewhere deep in rural France, having been assured their destination was a few yards up the road.

They started walking once again. Reaching the railhead, they picked their way across the tracks, dodging shunting engines and looking for their train.

'There you are at last!' The QA sister who let them on the train looked down at them and frowned. 'Why weren't you two here yesterday? We were so short-staffed, but we still had to fetch a crisis load, then take it back to Rouen.'

'But we've just come from Rouen,' Rose began.

'Then why didn't you wait for us?' The sister grimaced. 'You civilian girls don't ever seem to use your common sense.'

So it went on.

'It'll be a French train down to Herlancourt,' Maria said one May morning, as she and Rose dashed into a canteen to snatch some breakfast, before they went trundling off again. 'God, I hate French trains.'

'I prefer them,' smiled Rose — for French trains were exciting. English carriages, that had been shipped over to supplement the French, had corridors. So the train was one long ward, and nurses could walk safely from one end to the other.

But French trains had no corridors, so to get from coach to coach the nurses had to foot-board down the outside of the train, getting rained on, snowed on, and with their long skirts flapping in the wind.

They were supposed to get down from the train and walk along the track to the next carriage. But the tracks were muddy, and foot-boarding was fun.

'You shouldn't do this at night,' scolded Maria, as Rose appeared in the carriage one dark, rainy evening, breathless but with eyes aglow. 'You should wait until we reach the junction, not assume you have enough time when we've just stopped at points.'

'Everybody does it, even Sister Langford,' countered Rose, as she brushed the smuts off her white apron.

'You sisters are amazing,' said a corporal. 'They ought to put you all in the front line.'

'Yeah, they should.' A sergeant grinned. 'Jerry would take one look at Sister Courtenay and run back to Berlin.'

* * *

But after VAD Rose Courtenay hurt herself when foot-boarding along the carriage of a train that moved off suddenly, the nurses were forbidden to do this any more. In future, they'd have to wait until the train was at a junction, and the guard was watching. They'd have to jump down into all the muck and mud, then trudge along the track.

'A good thing too,' observed Maria, when she visited her friend in hospital in Boulogne. 'Rose, you're lucky to be alive. How is your arm today?'

'It's fine,' said Rose. Still embarrassed by what had happened, she stared down at the blanket on her knees. 'The doctor said the break was clean.'

'Rose, you're such an idiot,' said Maria. 'What possessed you, trying to change carriages in all that rain and darkness? I'm not surprised you slipped. What if that other driver hadn't seen you? What if he hadn't stopped in time?'

'As it turned out, he did.' Rose shrugged. 'I hear they've banned foot-boarding now?'

'Yes, and just as well.'

* * *

'You're going to a convalescent hospital for junior officers, in Marlancourt,' the matron told her, when Rose's cuts and bruises had all healed and she was passed fit again that July. 'You'll be on light duties until that arm is really strong again.'

Rose kept her eyes cast meekly down. 'Thank you, ma'am,' she whispered gratefully, for she'd been dreading being sent back to England.

'No more derring-do, Miss Courtenay,' said the matron crisply — but as Rose looked up, her blue eyes twinkled. 'You've been a model patient, but we don't wish to see you here again.'

* * *

'It's two in a tent,' announced the VAD who welcomed Rose to the new hospital, which turned out to be a huddle of wooden huts in a French forest. 'Come on, I'll show you round.'

Rose discovered all the nursing staff lived under canvas, and decided that in summer this ought to be pleasant — except for all the insects. Already she'd been bitten on her neck and ankles, and knew she would be scratching half the night.

'The boys are mostly mobile,' went on the VAD. 'So there's not much lifting to be done. We spend as much time playing whist and writing letters home for them as doing their dressings and handing out their pills.'

'So this place is a convalescent home for us, as well?'

'Yes, I suppose it must be.' The VAD grinned archly. 'We heard about your accident. *I'm* getting over scarlet fever.'

'But didn't you want to go back home and rest?' demanded Rose.

'God forbid!' exclaimed the VAD. 'My mother didn't want me to come and nurse in France. If I went home to convalesce, she'd put her foot down. I'd never be allowed to come back here again.'

* * *

'You'll be on Trafalgar Ward this week,' the matron said to Rose, when she'd been in the forest for a fortnight and had settled in. 'They're a very lively set of boys, so since you're new they're bound to rag you. But don't take any nonsense. We're in charge, although we mustn't be *too* hard on them.'

Rose went down the boardwalk that connected all the huts. In the sister's office, she found the list of patients and the day book. She began to read the latest notes.

Turning the page, she stared in disbelief. But then, she thought, she shouldn't be surprised. He was on active service here in France, and had as much chance as anyone of being wounded.

'Miss Courtenay?' A young VAD came in. 'I'm Belinda Cross. Sister Minton's busy on another ward just now, and she said I should show you round.'

'What happened to the man in the third bed?' asked Rose, as they went down the ward.

'Why, do you know him?' asked Belinda.

'Oh — no.' Rose blushed. 'I'd just begun to read his notes when you came in to fetch me.'

'He copped it when the Germans bombed a dugout,' said Belinda. 'It seems he spent last winter at the sharp end, doing night patrols, undermining German ammunition dumps, going out on raids — all very dangerous stuff, but he never got a scratch on him. Then his company went into support and bought it with a vengeance.'

Belinda smiled. 'But he's doing nicely. He had some nasty gashes in his side, but they're all healing. He can see again, although he still gets double vision. Come on, it's time we did the round. I'll introduce you to the boys — or anyway, to those who are awake.'

The man in the third bed was fast asleep, and as Rose looked down at him she suddenly wanted more than anything to touch his hand, to stroke his face, to make him look at her and smile.

But she left him sleeping. When she and the other nurse had done the round, had helped the men who needed it to take a bath and shave, she looked across the beds to him again.

'Do you let that officer sleep all day?' she asked Belinda.

'If that's what he wants.' Belinda shrugged. 'Sister Minton's always saying sleep is the great healer.'

Rose took a deep breath. 'I was wondering if *he* needs a bath?'

'Yes, he could do with one — he's been in those pyjamas all this week.' Belinda looked at Rose. 'I was just going to start the morning drinks. Do you need a hand, or can you manage?'

'I can manage.'

Rose collected towels and soap and then went over to the bed. The officer was still fast asleep. They all looked so young when they were sleeping, and Rose thought this one looked about fifteen. His long, dark lashes lay on his pale cheeks, and one arm was lying on his pillow, as if he were fending off an enemy. The back of his head was criss-crossed with long scars. She was glad he hadn't caught the blast full in the face.

She told herself she didn't like him. He drank too much, he had no social graces, and he ran after women. But what could one expect, she thought, when he came from a family like that?

'Lieutenant Denham?' she said, sharply.

'What?' Alex's dark eyes opened. He looked at Rose and blinked. 'Go away,' he muttered. 'I'm asleep.'

'No, Mr Denham,' Rose said firmly, 'you're very much awake. I want you out of bed and in the bath.'

'But why are *you* here?' Alex looked at Rose and frowned in puzzlement. 'You're in a nurse's uniform, but you can't be a nurse.'

'I *am* a nurse,' said Rose.

'You're not old enough, and you live in Dorset with your parents.' Alex turned over on his side. 'I'm going back to sleep.'

'You're going to have a bath, Lieutenant Denham.' Rose turned the blankets back. 'Come along, I haven't got all day.'

CHAPTER SEVEN

'Mr Denham's such a nice young man,' Belinda Cross said wistfully, as she and Rose sat in the sister's office writing up the day book, later that same week.

'Lieutenant Kelly and Captain Green are as nice as well,' said Rose.

'But Lieutenant Denham must be in a lot of pain. He had all that shrapnel in his head, and when I changed his dressing today his side was still a mess. But he always has a smile for me.'

'He drinks too much,' said Rose. 'Brandy, wine, champagne, you name it. Every time I pass his bed it's, "Sister, may I have a glass of brandy?" or "Sister, will you bring me some champagne?"'

'Rose, don't hold that against him,' said Belinda. 'They all drink too much. They've seen their friends get killed, and they've been wounded. They're dreading going back.'

'There's such a thing as moderation, and Alex Denham's liver must be pickled.'

'All the same, I like him.' Belinda closed the day book and then looked at her watch. 'It's time to do the bedtime drinks,' she said. 'God, my feet are killing me today. I've got new boots, and do they pinch!'

'I'll make the cocoa, then,' said Rose. 'You sit down and write those letters for Lieutenant Kelly.'

'Rose Courtenay, you're a brick.'

Anything to get out of the ward away from Alex, Rose thought gratefully. As she stirred the milk into a dozen cups of cocoa, she was annoyed to feel the colour creeping up her face. *He* had no right to make her blush.

When she'd led him over to the bath house that first morning, he had sat and watched her as she filled the wooden tub.

'I expect you can manage by yourself,' she'd told him briskly, as she checked the water to make sure it was hot.

'I don't think so, Sister.' He'd fumbled ineffectually with his dressing gown. 'I can't untie the belt on this.'

So she'd untied it for him.

He'd let the gown slide to the floor, then looked down helplessly at his pyjamas. 'I'm sorry, I can't manage buttons yet.'

She helped him take off his pyjama jacket.

He tugged at his pyjama trousers. 'The cord is in a knot.'

As Rose untied the cord, she felt her face begin to glow. She'd helped to bath hundreds of men, and they always hated it, resented being treated like helpless infants. Sometimes it was even worse than that, for some of them would be aroused, and then it was horribly embarrassing.

Also, nurses weren't supposed to be alone with patients. Unless they were very busy, baths were always done in pairs. 'I think you'll be fine now,' she said curtly.

'I'm still very unsteady on my feet.' As the sun poured through the dusty windows of the little bath house, Alex looked at her and smiled, and to her dismay her heart turned somersaults of pleasure. 'I think you'd better stay.'

He was most insistent he couldn't wash himself, so she had to do it, carefully dabbing at the half-healed shrapnel wounds that streaked down his left side, soaping him all over, then rinsing him with buckets of cool water from the pump outside. Then she wrapped him in a soft, white towel and rubbed him dry.

He smelled of cinnamon, she realised. Almost obliterated by the harsh, clean top notes of regulation issue army soap, there were intoxicating undertones of oriental spice and sun-warmed skin.

'Thank you, Sister.' As she dressed him in some clean pyjamas, then helped him put his dressing gown back on, he'd sighed contentedly. As she turned the collar back, she could feel his gaze upon her face.

'Rose, you're as red as anything,' he whispered. 'You have done this sort of thing before?'

'I beg your pardon, Mr Denham?'

'I said it's looking dark out there.' He grinned, and Rose was almost sure he winked. 'I think there's going to be a storm.'

* * *

She carried the tray of drinks into the ward. When she came to Alex's bed, she put his cup of cocoa on his locker, and then moved on without a word.

But as she walked back up the ward, he called her over. 'May I have a glass of brandy, please?' he asked politely.

'I think you've probably had enough today.' Rose was getting concerned about his drinking. He was always asking her for brandy, but he never seemed the worse for drink, and she'd been warned this was a danger sign.

He hadn't always been a hardened drinker, able to soak up brandy like a sponge and still seem stone cold sober. She had not forgotten the night he'd lurched across the ballroom at the Minster to ask her if she'd dance.

The smile he'd given her then had made her feel light-headed, as if *she* had drunk wine. 'Go on Sister, be a sport,' he said, and smiled again.

'But are you in pain?' she asked, concerned.

'In torment.' Alex's gaze was on her face. 'Sister, you can't imagine what it's like, I'm in such agony.'

'Dr Lloyd will be here soon,' said Rose. 'I'll ask if you can have a shot of morphine, so you won't need more alcohol tonight.'

* * *

The following morning, when Rose, Belinda and the orderlies took round the breakfast trays, they found the men were grinning and nodding knowingly at Rose.

'What's the matter with you all this morning?' she demanded, as she put Alex's tray down on his locker, then took the top off his boiled egg.

'Your notoriety has caught up with you.' Alex picked his spoon up and started on his egg. 'Where's my toast today?'

'The orderly is bringing it in a minute, don't be so impatient. What do you mean, my notoriety?'

'Your exploits in the field, Sister Courtenay,' Alex said. 'One of the chaps in Blenheim ward has a cousin or something on the trains, he had a letter from her yesterday. Apparently, you were famous for your pluck. Or should I say for your stupidity?'

'Mr Denham, if you speak to nursing staff like that, I shall report your insolence to Matron.'

'Carry on, report me to Field Marshall French himself,' said Alex, calmly. He reached across the tray to get some salt. 'Rose, you look so pretty when you're cross.'

* * *

Alex had meant it when he'd said he was in torment, but he was also happier than he'd ever been in all his life. The shrapnel wounds were healing very slowly, but they weren't particularly painful. The almost constant headaches made him nauseous and dizzy, but he could cope with that.

But he couldn't help playing up a bit, for when she changed his dressings Rose's cool fingers were so gentle. When she thought he really was in pain, she was concerned and kind.

As the weeks went by, she also let herself relax a little. On one or two occasions, she seemed to forget she was a nurse who wasn't allowed to get too friendly with her patients. She talked to him as if she was a real human being — and as if he was, too. She even brought him presents now and then.

'Look!' she said one morning, as she put his breakfast tray in front of him and whipped away his napkin with a flourish.

'Where did you get that?' he asked, amazed.

'We nursing staff were sent a dozen, and that one's mine, but I don't like them.' Rose picked up the orange. 'Shall I cut it up for you?'

'You ought to have it.'

'I told you, I don't like them.' Rose picked up his knife. 'How would you like it, in segments or in quarters, or shall I squeeze the juice into your glass?'

The next week, there was chocolate, which she said she didn't want, because it gave her spots. Then special fancy biscuits which a visiting colonel had left for all the nurses, but which the nurses shared all round the men.

When she had the time she sat and read to him, and sometimes they played cards, a round of rummy or two-handed whist.

'All four knaves,' she smiled, one heavy, sultry afternoon, as she put down her hand to show him that she'd won — again. 'See, four knaves, three sevens. What were you collecting?'

'I was waiting for the queen of hearts.'

Rose turned over the remaining cards. 'She's here, at the bottom of the deck. She's hiding from you, Alex.'

'No, Rose — she's sitting here beside me.'

'Mr Denham!' She tried to frown at him, but it was obvious she couldn't, because a smile was tugging at the corners of her mouth. 'You know you're not allowed to make improper observations to the nurses.'

'What do you mean, improper observations?' Alex frowned. 'I'm sorry, Sister Courtenay, but — what did I say?'

'You know full well. You're nothing but a knave yourself, and now I have to go and do a ward round.'

She fussed around him, bossily scooping up the cards and tucking all the blankets firmly round him, her mouth set in hard, straight line again.

But he could see the sparkle in her eyes, and was almost sure that if he grinned she'd start to smile again.

* * *

'I heard you were married,' she said one afternoon as she stripped away the bloodstained bandages, swabbed the wounds with saline, then pressed fresh gauze against his side.

'Yes,' he admitted, deadpan.

'Celia Easton said your wife was going to have a child.'

'The baby was stillborn,' he murmured. 'Chloe nearly died.'

'Oh, Alex — I'm so sorry!' Rose looked directly at him, and he saw the sympathy glowing in her soft, grey eyes. He had to grit his teeth and look away, or else he would have cried.

'I believe she's getting better now,' he managed, when he had regained his self-control.

'You *believe*?' Rose stared at him in horror. 'But didn't they let you have some leave?'

'We were undermanned along that section of the line,' lied Alex, glibly. 'I didn't like to ask for leave, and Chloe has her family around her, anyway. I write, of course.'

'Yes, of course,' said Rose.

* * *

'A telegram for you, Miss Courtenay.' The orderly who'd brought the evening post round handed the flimsy envelope to Rose. 'I hope it's not bad news.'

Everybody looked at Rose, and as she slit the envelope she was aware that the whole ward held its collective breath.

The message was short and to the point. *'Lady Courtenay very ill,'* it said. *'Suggest return to Dorset straight away.'*

'Rose?' began Belinda.

'My mother's ill,' said Rose. She pushed the telegram into her pocket. 'My father wants me to go home. I don't suppose it's anything very bad. Mummy has always been a drama queen.'

* * *

'When are you going?' asked Alex, who had almost managed to convince himself that this eternal summer was never going to end, that somehow he and Rose would be together for all time.

'As soon as I can get a lift to Rouen.' Rose had finished doing the morning's dressings, and now she was going from bed to bed, straightening the sheets and counterpanes before the sister did her round.

'When will that be?'

'Probably on Monday week, when the supplies come through.'

'Rose, I'm going to miss you.'

'I — I'll miss you, too. I'll miss all of you boys.'

Alex looked at Rose, she looked at him, and he felt a dreadful, yearning longing — he wanted to grab her hand and cry, don't leave me!

But of course he didn't. He picked up a new book he wasn't reading and opened it at random. 'You mustn't let me hold you up,' he said.

* * *

The journey back to England was long, involved and tedious, but for Rose it couldn't be long enough. She was dreading going home.

How would her parents greet her, and how should she behave? Would her old room be waiting for her, cosy, warm and comfortable as ever? Would Polly still be her maid?

As soon as she reached Charton, Rose saw everything had changed. As she walked into the Minster, she saw it was now a convalescent home for senior officers. All the Victorian clutter her mother loved was hidden away. The Persian carpets Boris liked to chew had been rolled up and stored. Instead of hot-house flowers, the whole place smelled of Lysol.

The matron who came up to greet her was a young, attractive Queen Alexandra nurse who introduced herself as Jessie Mason. 'Your parents are expecting you,' she smiled. 'You'll want to spend some time with them, I know. But do come up and see us here if you have an hour or two to spare. As you can imagine, we can always use an extra pair of willing hands!'

Sir Gerard, Lady Courtenay and Boris had moved into the Dower House, a tiny Queen Anne box a mile from the Minster. As Rose walked up the path to the front door, she took a few deep breaths. She feared she would be in for a hard time.

But Lady Courtenay didn't look fit enough to give her one. She was always pale, but now her cheeks were sunken, her blue eyes were dull and she had lost a lot of weight.

'So you've come home at last,' she said.

'Daddy said you were ill.' Rose felt the blush creep up her neck. 'I know you must have worried about me, but—'

'She knows I must have worried!' Frances Courtenay seemed to choke. 'Rose, you don't have children of your own. So don't insult me by presuming to imagine how I felt!'

She turned her head away. 'The doctor gave me chloral, but still I couldn't sleep. When I closed my eyes, I saw you as a little child. Your clothes would be on fire, or you'd be drowning. You'd cry to me to help you, but I couldn't. I was paralysed.'

'Mummy, please—'

'I don't know which was worse, dreaming about you when you were a baby, or waking up to know you'd disappeared, that absolutely anything might have happened, and I could do nothing.'

'Mummy, I'm so sorry.' Rose crouched at her mother's side and tried to take her hand.

Frances Courtenay snatched her hand away. She would not meet her daughter's gaze. 'Your father had the Dorset police out scouring the whole district,' she continued, tonelessly. 'He and Michael never stopped, they were out in all those autumn downpours, searching the estate and all the area round about.

'I know your father won't say anything to you. He won't reproach you, he's not that sort of man. But I saw him age a month for every single day you were away. He was too exhausted even to lift the telephone and call the chief inspector when you had the kindness to inform us where you'd gone.'

Boris loped in then. As Rose turned to greet him, he blinked and ambled over to her on arthritic feet, sniffing cautiously. She supposed he must have caught her old, familiar scent. But he was puzzled to find it overlaid with other, stranger smells.

She held out her hand to him. He nosed at it politely, but then ambled off again to settle down by her mother.

Rose's heart contracted as she imagined how he must have grieved. How he must have spent a hundred weary days and sleepless nights plodding and searching all around the Minster, looking for his mistress. He had aged, as well. She could see grey hairs on his black snout.

As she crouched there, feeling sick with guilt, it was as if the golden doors of childhood closed behind her, for she finally realised what a selfish, thoughtless monster she had been.

She took her mother's hand. 'Mummy, I'll make it up to you,' she promised. 'I won't go back to France. I've said I'll go and help up at the house, but I'll stay here and sit with you as often as you wish.'

Lady Courtenay shrugged indifferently. 'You father will be home at half past five.' She stroked the dog's soft muzzle. 'Perhaps you would be good enough to ring for Mrs Jackson, and remind her he will want some supper.'

* * *

'But what *is* wrong with her?' persisted Rose, when she went to see her mother's doctor and have a private talk with him.

'It's probably her heart.' Dr Weldon looked at Rose over his half-moon spectacles. 'She had a fever after you were born. I suspect the valves were damaged irreparably. Now she's getting on in years, the strain is bound to tell.'

'I never knew.'

'She didn't like to make a fuss.' The doctor shrugged. 'I told her it would be a risk to have another child. She said it didn't matter — you were perfect. My dear, she's very pleased to have you home.'

'Dr Weldon, is she going to die?'

'If she doesn't have a sudden shock or serious illness, she could maybe live to be a hundred.' The doctor looked at Rose severely. 'So, Miss Courtenay, don't upset her or go running off again.'

* * *

As the summer faded into autumn, Rose did her best to be a model daughter. Although she spent some time up at the Minster, helping out and getting to know Jessie Mason well, she took her mother shopping, visiting and paying calls. On sunny days, they went for drives in Lady Courtenay's little chaise.

She put up with the veiled comments and insinuations about her past behaviour made by Lady Easton and her crony Mrs Sefton. Lady Easton, Rose observed, was pregnant once again — although she must have been nearly fifty.

'Do you mean to stay in Dorset now?' asked Mrs Sefton, as Rose and Lady Courtenay sat and drank weak China tea in the drawing room at Easton Hall, and watched the youngest Easton children roll around the floor. Their latest nanny had just left, and Lady Easton was interviewing possible replacements in the dining room.

'I have no plans to go away.' Rose smiled at Mrs Sefton artlessly, then turned to see Michael's mother flounder in. 'Lady Easton, have you heard from Michael recently?'

'Yes indeed, he writes to me each week.' Lady Easton flopped into a chair. 'The dear boy's well and happy. He's doing his bit and being a stout fellow, I don't doubt.' She looked at Rose impressively. 'He always mentions you with great affection and respect.'

He must think there's still a chance I might get Daddy's money then, thought Rose. 'I must write soon,' she said. 'I hope he gets some leave now and again?'

'He was at home for Christmas, but the poor boy's been in France since then. Of course, we miss him terribly.'

'I'm sure you do.' After all, thought Rose, you only have another dozen children to keep you company.

'I heard Alex Denham has come home,' said Mrs Sefton, baring her large teeth. 'But his wife is not in Dorset. So I don't know what we should make of that.'

Rose made a mental note to keep away from Henry Denham's house, and off the footpaths on his land. Then she stood up. 'Mummy, if you're tired, I'll ring for Payne to bring the car.'

* * *

But she found she couldn't keep away. She started going for walks with Boris, dragging him along the cliff top, hoping she'd meet Alex going for a morning stroll.

One day, she did. As Boris wheezed and grunted, grumbling that he wanted to go home, she noticed Alex and another person coming down the track. If she turned off now, and if she went down to the beach, she could avoid them.

She stayed up on the cliff top.

She couldn't believe that Charlotte Stokeley had attached herself to Alex yet again. But this time they weren't laughing. Charlotte looked quite grim, and Alex was looking positively gloomy, tired and depressed.

'Good morning,' Rose said briskly.

'Good morning,' Charlotte murmured, and slipped her arm through Alex's. He didn't seem to have the strength or will to shake her off — or perhaps, thought Rose, he didn't *want* to shake her off?

'Lieutenant Denham.' Rose hoped her voice was neutral. 'We heard you were in Dorset, convalescing. I hope you're feeling better?'

'Thank you, I'm improving.' Alex shrugged, his eyes met Rose's, and they seemed to say, we can't talk here. In fact, we can't talk any more. Rose, we can never talk again.

'My parents would be delighted to see you and Mr Denham at the Dower House.' Rose knew she was sounding desperate now. 'My mother is at home most afternoons.'

'I'm not really fit for company.' Alex shook his head. 'But, even if I were, I couldn't accept their invitation. Soon, I'll be going back to France.'

Rose glanced at Charlotte Stokeley, and thought she could see triumph in her eyes. She said goodbye and walked back home.

* * *

Phoebe cowered in a corner, wondering if the blood would stain her dress. Daniel would be furious if it did. The turquoise satin had cost five guineas, and he'd had to pay a tailoress to make it up.

Also, would her dresser manage to cover all the cuts and bruises, especially the black eyes? If not, she wouldn't be able to go on and do her spot tonight. They'd have to find another girl, then Daniel would be even angrier, and he might well beat her up again.

'Whose is it?' he'd demanded, as he kicked her on the shin.

'Yours — I've told you half a million times!' Phoebe shrank away. She folded her arms across her bulging stomach. 'Dan, I wouldn't lie to you! I know how mad you get, when anybody lies.'

'My mother had fifteen.' Daniel glared at Phoebe in a fury. 'I know what size a woman ought to be when she's only six or seven months gone. You look damn near your time to me.'

'I'm carryin' lots of water,' Phoebe wept. 'The doctor says it might be twins.'

'My family don't have twins.' Daniel gave Phoebe one last kick. 'I was up in Liverpool three months, so you 'ad plenty of time to mess about. I've seen you lookin' at the soldiers. I've watched you smirk an' flap your drawers at them.'

'Dan, there's only you,' cried Phoebe, sobbing. 'There's only ever been you, I swear to God and all the saints.'

'You women are all liars,' muttered Daniel, unconvinced. 'Well, we'll soon find out. I'm dark, an' so's me Mum and Dad. So if this baby's fair, you're goin' to be in serious trouble.'

'Daniel, please!' begged Phoebe. 'New-born babies often has fair hair! I was fair myself 'til I was five. Ask anybody in the Green!'

'My family's kids are dark. So if this brat's a ginger nut or anything like that, I'm goin' to make you sorry you drew breath.'

* * *

'Breathe in, Mr Denham.' The doctor listened to Alex's chest. 'Now out again — that's excellent.' The doctor smiled, delighted. 'What about the headaches?'

'I don't get them any more.'

'You don't?' The doctor wrote on Alex's notes. 'It looks as if you're in the clear, my boy.'

'You mean I'm fit enough to go and get smashed up again?'

'We don't want to hear that sort of talk.' The doctor frowned. 'I know it's hard for you young officers, but this year ought to see the end of it. You chaps will be the heroes of the hour. Girls will be falling at your feet, old men will envy you.'

The doctor tapped his nose and grinned. 'You know your Shakespeare? "Gentlemen in England now abed," and all that sort of thing. Where are you going next?'

'To some place near Bethune.' Alex buttoned up his khaki shirt and found his tie. 'There are rumours of another push this autumn. My battalion will probably be in the thick of it.'

'Well, there you are, then. Jerry's going to get it in the neck, and you'll be home for Christmas.'

Christmas 1924, thought Alex. He pulled his gloves on then walked out of the doctor's stuffy office, feeling sick and tired, his everlasting headache worse than ever.

But at least he'd managed to put on something of an act. They'd finally passed him fit, and he was grateful, for the thought of going back to the trenches was all that kept him sane.

Perhaps this autumn they would finish it. Perhaps there'd be a real battle, somebody might win it, and the politicians would be forced to talk. Then he could go to India, as he'd planned. If he were half a world away from Rose, he might forget he'd ever seen her face.

* * *

He caught a train up to the railhead, then walked for miles along communication trenches looking for his company, which he finally found in the front line.

'Alex, my dear fellow, good to see you!' Captain Ford was evidently pleased to have him back. 'Just in time to have a pop at Jerry. We're going in next week, so we've been told and do believe. We're going to blow them up the Kaiser's arse.'

Michael Easton walked into the dugout. 'Hello, Denham,' he began. 'You're feeling better, I assume?'

'Yes, thank you, Easton.'

'Mr Easton, I told you to check the fire-steps, to see that they were properly revetted. The damned things looked as if they were going to crumble yesterday.' Captain Ford scowled angrily at Michael. 'But perhaps you've done it?'

'I'm just going now, sir.' Michael turned to leave.

'Lieutenant Easton, I didn't tell you to dismiss!'

'I'm sorry, sir. I thought—'

'You never think, man — that's your trouble. Anyway, you could say congratulations to Mr Denham here.'

'Sir?' frowned Michael.

'Alex's got himself another pip. The order came through yesterday. So when the time comes for the push, this company will be split into two. Captain Denham will be officer in charge of you and Lomax, heaven help him. All right, tell him you're delighted.'

'Well done, Captain Denham.' Michael held out his right hand and smiled, but Alex saw the hatred in his eyes.

CHAPTER EIGHT

Maria's letter came the day that Lady Courtenay was due to go to London for some tests. Sir Gerard had to be in court, but Rose could see he was relieved he wouldn't have to accompany her mother.

'Poor Gerard, he hates hospitals,' said Frances Courtenay, as she waved him off to deal with local poachers and to remand suspected German spies. 'I don't care for them myself. It's odd that you should have this strange desire to play at being a nurse.'

'We must be going.' Rose picked up Lady Courtenay's sable coat. 'Payne is here to take us to the station.'

* * *

They settled down in a first-class compartment. Lady Courtenay shook open *The Times* and began to read the obituaries, clucking as she scanned the lists of names.

'Peter Mallison, from the first battalion,' she frowned. 'Do you remember him? Mr Mallison was on the Bench, until that business with the chorus girl. I must write to Sylvia tonight. David Borden, Colin Graston-Smith, Alex—'

'Alex?'

'Burton-Powell, Royal Essex Rifles.' Lady Courtenay looked at Rose. 'Do we know him, darling?'

'No, I don't think we do.' Rose breathed again. Opening Maria's letter, she shut her ears to her mother's doleful litany.

'Now I have a favour to ask,' Maria wrote, three or four pages into long descriptions of even longer journeys through the French and Belgian countryside, during which the ambulance trains had been attacked and shelled by German planes. One of them had been derailed, killing two nurses and a hundred men.

> *'Rose, could you go and visit Phoebe? She hardly ever writes to me, unless she wants some money. But this month I've had three letters begging me to go and see her, which of course I can't. We're really busy over here. We ought to have four nurses to a train, but we're often down to two or three, and all leave is cancelled.*
>
> *'This October, our troops started using poison gas. But there are often mix-ups and it all blows back at them. The Germans bomb the trenches where they keep the cylinders, and these all explode. So now we're having to cope with men whose lungs are badly damaged, and most of them are going to die in the most awful way.*
>
> *'I shouldn't be writing this, I know. The censor will most probably strike it out, and all you'll see will be a mess of black. But will you go and see Phoebe? She's in lodgings at 15 Finker Street — that's in Bethnal Green. If she needs money, could you lend her some? I'll pay you back, upon my honour. I wouldn't trouble you, dear Rose, but there isn't anyone else to ask.*
>
> *'I hope your mother is better, and has forgiven you for running away. When I finally get some leave and can come back to England, I hope we'll meet again.*
>
> *'All my love, Maria.'*

Rose looked at the address Maria had given. She had never been to the East End. She supposed it must be full of costermongers selling oranges and lemons, cheerful Cockney flower girls and maybe even pearly kings and queens.

It would be an adventure to go to Bethnal Green, and see the place where Phoebe and Maria had grown up. She'd leave Lady Courtenay at the clinic, she decided, then get a cab to the East End. She would sort Phoebe out, then be back in time to take her mother home to Dorset on the evening train.

* * *

The train steamed into Paddington. They took a cab to Harley Street. 'Listen, Mummy,' Rose began, 'I'm going to leave you here with Sister Golding and the other nurses, and go to see a friend.'

'Very well, my darling.' Then Lady Courtenay smiled graciously at Sister Golding, who clearly knew her place and was deference itself to influential patients. 'Sister, when do you think we might be finished?'

'Well, Dr Firth will do some tests, then Mr Morris will examine you and have a little chat,' said Sister Golding. 'We don't know how long that's going to take, but Mr Morris likes to get away by four o'clock.'

'Off you go then, darling.' Lady Courtenay fluttered one white, fragile hand. 'Do remember to have luncheon. You could go to Bonner's in the Strand.'

Outside in the busy street, Rose flagged down a cab. She gave the driver the address. 'Where's that then, miss?' he frowned.

'Bethnal Green,' said Rose, whose imagination had conjured up a pretty park with winter trees.

'It's rough over that way, miss.' The driver shook his head. 'You don't want to be there after dark.'

'But it's not yet eleven,' Rose said crisply. 'So the sooner we set out, the sooner I'll get back.'

'On your head be it, miss,' the cabman said.

Rose watched the gracious buildings and smart shops of the West End give way to offices and banks, then to tenements and mouldy, peeling terraces. As the streets grew meaner and more narrow, the people crowding them grew less well-dressed and less well-fed.

She saw women with babies in their arms who looked even older than her mother. Little children had the pinched and wolfish faces of malevolent old men.

The streets grew shorter and more crowded. When the cab stopped for a brewer's wagon or a dray, the people lounging on the pavements or arguing outside the public houses took a good look at Rose.

In Dorset, peasants bobbed or pulled their forelocks to the gentry. But these Cockneys met her gaze with bold, hard stares or mirthless, knowing grins.

Market stalls piled high with second-hand clothes and shoes, or selling fruit and vegetables, lined almost every street. People pushing loaded barrows, old men touting patent medicines, baked-potato vendors and hurdy-gurdy men walked up the middle of the road. Ragged boys were fascinated by the motor car, touching it with sticky, dirty fingers and peering curiously inside, so the driver had to honk the horn to part the crowds and let the vehicle pass.

Rose saw buildings that had recently burnt down, and were in the process of being shored up or demolished. 'They have a lot of fires round here,' she said.

'It's them blasted Zeppelins tryin' to 'it the docks, but missin' by a mile or more.' The driver turned into a cobbled street of squalid tenements, grubby-looking old clothes shops and soot-stained terraces. 'This looks like the place you wanted, miss,' he added, grimly. 'What number was it, then?'

'Fifteen,' said Rose.

'It must be this one, by the pump.' The driver stopped, and Rose got out.

'I'll wait for you,' the driver said.

'There's no need, I might be here a while.' Rose took out her purse. 'How much do I owe you?'

'One and tenpence, miss — and you should put that purse away.'

Rose gave the cabman half a crown. As he drove away, she felt a sudden ripple of apprehension, and wished she'd kept him waiting. After what she'd seen in France, she had imagined nothing could surprise her — and she was still in London, after all. But this street in Bethnal Green was such an alien place she might just as well be on the moon.

She'd never seen such squalor, so many ragged people, such filthy, blackened buildings, such general decay. As for the smell — she'd thought she was inured to stench, that nothing could be more unpleasant than the smell of gangrene coming from a putrid wound. But this place stank far worse than that, of sewage and of drains, of tanneries and of slaughter houses, of centuries of grime.

Even in the smartest parts of London, the air rained soot from half a million chimneys. But here it was especially foetid, thick with fumes and smuts from workshops, sweatshops and a thousand factories that she later learned were rendering tallow, making matches, turning out shoddy furniture or cheap clothes.

She knocked on the door of the lodging house. As she stood there waiting, children came to look at her and point.

'You from the Board, miss?' asked shoeless boy.

'You one of them Sally Army people?' asked a girl who carried a tiny baby that was snivelling miserably.

'Where's yer tambourine?'

'You from the landlord, then?'

'Got a penny 'ave yer, miss?' The shoeless boy pawed hopefully at Rose's smart, black bag. 'Only me dad's off work this week, 'e's 'urt 'is back real bad.'

'Get off my nice clean step!' The door jerked open and the children scattered. 'Who are you and what do you want? This ain't a bleedin' knockin' shop,' declared the sour-faced woman who glared angrily at Rose.

'I'm looking for Phoebe Gower,' said Rose politely. 'I understand she lives here?'

'Well, she did,' the woman muttered. 'But she don't live 'ere no more.'

'Where is she now?' asked Rose.

'What's that to you, Miss Lah-di-dah?' The woman shooed Rose off her whitened step. 'If you're another of 'er mates from up the 'Aggerston Palace Music 'All, you can sling yer 'ook. This is a respectable 'ouse, an' I don't want no tarts an' so-called actresses round 'ere.'

'I only want to know where Phoebe's gone—'

'Try Rosenheim's.' The woman jerked her thumb. 'She might be lodgin' there.'

'Rosenheim's?' repeated Rose.

'You daft or somethin'?' barked the woman. 'Rosenheim's, the shop just up the road!'

* * *

The shop was dark and musty, and smelled of mice and damp. Rusting cans and faded cardboard packets filled the shelves, and sacks of flour and sugar sat on the floor.

'May I help you, miss?' A tiny, dark-haired woman dressed from head to foot in threadbare black emerged out of the shadows.

'Yes,' said Rose. 'I'm looking for—'

But then there was a scream of pain from somewhere in the building and the hairs stood up on Rose's head. 'Who was that?' she cried.

'My lodger, miss.' The shopkeeper shrugged helplessly. 'She's going to have a baby. I'm sorry, I must leave you for a minute.'

'Mrs Rosenheim? My name's Rose Courtenay, I'm Maria's friend. She asked me to come and visit Phoebe. I'm a nurse, so if there's anything I can do to help?'

'Oh, thank God, thank God!' Mrs Rosenheim's relief was almost tangible. 'Please, come in. She's in the parlour, we couldn't get her up the stairs.'

Rose followed Mrs Rosenheim into the gloomy parlour. Phoebe lay on a couch, her legs apart and panting hard. 'That you, Mrs R?' she gasped. 'You found Mrs Bloom?'

'Nathan's still out looking.' Mrs Rosenheim crouched down beside the labouring woman. 'Look, here's Maria's friend. She's a nurse, she'll help you.'

'Rose?' Phoebe gaped, astonished. 'What you doin' 'ere, 'ow'd you find me?'

'Maria sent me.' Rose dragged off her hat and coat and knelt by Phoebe's side. 'How long have you been in labour?'

'Bleedin' hours, Rose! It feels like days!' Phoebe's dark eyes filled and tears spilled over. 'Rose,' she sobbed, 'it's agony!'

'It's going to be all right, you'll see.' Rose took Phoebe's cold hand. 'We'll manage, you'll be fine.'

'I'm goin' to die.' Phoebe's huge brown eyes were dull with pain. 'How many babies you delivered, Rose?'

'Dozens,' Rose assured her, hoping Mrs Bloom would soon arrive.

* * *

'She's getting weaker.' It was half past one, and Rose had been sitting at Phoebe's side since twelve, watching her strength ebbing away and hearing her pathetic cries grow faint. 'This Mrs Bloom, is she a midwife?'

'Yes, and she could be anywhere in the Green.' Mrs Rosenheim looked worried sick. 'As I say, my Nathan's gone out looking.'

'What about getting a neighbour, or a friend?' suggested Rose. 'Someone who has children of her own, would she come and help us?'

'No one in the Green will get involved.' Mrs Rosenheim's dark eyes were like a frightened deer's. 'You won't understand, miss, and it would take me too long to explain, but they're all afraid of Daniel Hanson and what he might do. Dan is an important man round here.'

Daniel Hanson? Rose recalled the burly, scowling man she'd seen with Phoebe, that day in the West End restaurant. 'But you took her in,' she murmured. 'You can't be afraid?'

'Miss, I'm terrified.' Mrs Rosenheim twisted her thin hands, plaiting her fingers in anxiety. 'But Phoebe used to work for me. I knew her foster mother, may she rest in peace. When Phoebe came here, asking me for shelter, how could I turn Maisie's child away?'

'Rose!' Phoebe suddenly clutched at Rose's sleeve. 'Rose, I think it's coming!'

Rose looked, and saw a spreading stain darken the brocade of the old couch. She didn't know what to do, but there was nobody to ask. So she eased off Phoebe's drawers, knelt down between her patient's legs, and prayed.

She saw a pale disc which had to be the baby's head. 'Phoebe love, the baby's on its way,' she whispered, as the disc grew larger and the head emerged. She watched entranced as the small shoulders came. A moment later, the child had been born and lay on the green couch, a pale ghost.

'You need to cut the cord.' Mrs Rosenheim looked timidly over Rose's shoulder. 'You'll need some string. I'll go and get it.'

'Rose, don't go!' cried Phoebe.

'It's all right, I'm here.' Rose watched the blue-grey cord come slithering out, squirming as if it were a living thing. Where should she cut it? Why did Mrs Rosenheim want string?

Nothing in her training at St Benedict's or what she'd done in France had prepared her for the sheer astonishment and awe that had overwhelmed her as she'd watched Phoebe's baby being born.

She almost wept when she heard voices in the passage, and a plump and cheerful-looking woman came striding purposefully into the room.

'So, I'm too late,' she beamed. She knelt beside the patient. 'Excuse me, miss,' she said to Rose. 'Come on Phoebe, one more push, we need the afterbirth. Rachel, go and find a blanket, shawl or something warm to wrap the baby, otherwise she's going to die of cold.'

As Mrs Rosenheim scuttled off, Rose crouched beside the midwife, watching as her skilful hands completed what Rose had haphazardly begun.

'A lovely little girl.' Mrs Bloom had finished with Phoebe and was examining the tiny baby. 'Pretty as an angel, this one — going to be blonde, if I'm not very much mistaken. Let's wipe your face, my darling. Just look at those blue eyes! Miss, would you hold her for a minute?'

'Yeah, take 'er, Rose,' said Phoebe.

So Rose took the child, whose face was pale and whose great, blue eyes were wide with interest. Rose thought she had never seen anything so beautiful.

She offered her a finger, the baby grasped it firmly, and Rose fell in love.

* * *

'So make her rest and feed her up,' the midwife ordered, as she packed her basket, then plonked her black straw hat back on her head.

'But Phoebe isn't safe here, and you know it.' Rose could hear that Mrs Rosenheim was tired and scared. 'If my Joel and Simon had been here, it wouldn't matter — they could deal with Daniel. But there's only Nathan.'

'*Mamele*, don't worry.' Rose was cradling the child and hadn't noticed anyone come in, but now she turned to see a white-faced boy of Phoebe's age standing looking awkward and embarrassed by the parlour door.

He met Rose's gaze, and she thought how nice he looked, how sweet and calm and gentle. Then she saw he was crippled. His right leg was much shorter than his left, and on his foot he wore a built-up shoe.

She realised she would have to stay. At any rate, she couldn't go home to Dorset, leaving Phoebe weak from giving birth and Mrs Rosenheim afraid, and their only guardian a lame boy.

'Do you have a post office in Bethnal Green?' she asked, looking at Nathan.

'Yes, there's one in Old Ford Road.' Nathan smiled, and Rose saw his brown eyes were soft and kind. 'I thought I heard Phoebe call you Rose? So you must be Maria's friend?'

'Yes, that's right,' said Rose. 'I'm supposed to meet my mother later, but I think I ought to stay with Phoebe, at least until she's feeling stronger. So could you go and send some telegrams for me?'

'Of course. I'll do it now.' Nathan put his cap back on. 'If you write down what you want to say?'

Rose looked at her watch. It was only half past two, and so she hoped there would be time. But even if there wasn't, the clinic wouldn't put her mother out on to the street.

She gave the child to Nathan's mother, then wrote rapidly on the envelope of Maria's letter.

Nathan could send a message to the clinic asking them to keep her mother there until her husband came to fetch her, and another telegram to her father asking him to get the London train, then take Lady Courtenay home to Dorset. Sir Gerard would be puzzled, but Rose was sure he'd come. Explanations and apologies would have to wait.

'Rose?' Phoebe had been covered with a blanket and Rose thought she had gone to asleep. 'Rose, 'ow's the baby?'

'Fine.' Rose went to crouch at Phoebe's side. 'She's very pretty.'

'Mrs Bloom was sayin' she'd probably 'ave blonde 'air.'

'Yes, she's very pale, her skin's like cream. Do you want to hold her, Phoebe?'

'No, I don't — not yet.' Suddenly, Phoebe shuddered. 'I 'oped, I prayed,' she whispered. 'But it made no difference. She's goin' to be the dead spit of 'er dad.'

'Who *is* the baby's father?' Rose asked, gently. 'I'm sure he's going to want to see his daughter.'

'I bet 'e bloody won't!' Phoebe looked at Rose. 'You'll kill me,' she added wretchedly.

'Of course I won't.' Rose took her hand. 'Why should I want to hurt you?'

'That officer what you was with, when we saw you in that West End caff.' Phoebe shook her tousled head and sighed. 'I dunno 'ow 'e managed to track me down. But one night last winter, after I'd done me spot up at Palace, 'e was 'angin' about at the stage door, lookin' like 'e'd lost the family silver cos the 'orse 'ad broke its leg. Dan was out of town, an' I was lonely.'

Phoebe bit her lip. 'Rose, 'e's such a lovely-lookin' bloke. You 'ave to give 'im that.'

'Oh, Phoebe!' Rose was shocked.

'I suppose 'e's still your feller?'

'No — and he never was, you mustn't worry.' Rose stroked Phoebe's matted, tangled hair. 'He's just a neighbour, somebody I've known since I was little.'

'I don't believe you, Rose.' Phoebe's nose was running and her eyes were very bright. 'I seen the way 'e looked at you.'

'It's all right, Phoebe. Please don't cry.' Rose tried to smile. 'You just go to sleep.'

'Rose, you mustn't leave me!'

'I'm not going anywhere.'

* * *

'We're not getting anywhere,' said Freddie Lomax angrily and, although Alex couldn't agree in public, he and Captain Ford knew Freddie spoke for all of them.

That autumn, heavy rain and constant shelling by the Germans had turned the British trenches into muddy pits that stank of lyddite and latrines. Alex's company was down to half its total strength. Those who hadn't been killed or wounded had succumbed to frostbite or been gassed.

A month ago, a gas attack on German trenches opposite had been an awful, mortifying disaster. The Royal Dorsets had been told the gas would be discharged, and fifteen minutes later they'd go over to mop up any pockets of resistance, taking prisoner anyone who surrendered and bayoneting those who put up any fight.

But on the morning of the gas attack, the engineers couldn't find any spanners, and those the manufacturers had supplied were far too small. When all the cylinders had finally been opened and the gas discharged, the wind had changed and blown it back across the British lines. The Germans who had been supposed to perish sat safely in their trenches, burning oil-soaked cotton waste to keep the gas away.

In the weeks of skirmishing and easily-repulsed attacks that followed this debacle, Michael Easton, Freddie Lomax and their tired platoons had muddled through. But Alex got angry with himself whenever he lost men, even though Captain Ford assured him he was doing well.

'You still got half your buggers back,' he muttered, as he and Alex drowned their sorrows after yet another dismal show in which the battalion had lost more than fifty men. 'That's thirty more than Engelman or Maddox — and he's the only officer left alive in his poor sodding company.'

'This whole business is a waste of men.'

'That's dangerous talk, my boy.' Malcolm Ford looked gravely at the younger officer. 'Ours not to reason why, and all that skite. How's Easton shaping up these days?'

'He needs to look a bit more lively, or he might get shot by his own side.'

'You mean the windy bugger shits himself. I thought as much. You ought to send him out on night patrols.' Captain Ford gulped down his rum and poured himself some more. 'It's the only way. People like Easton find their feet or snuff it — take my word.'

'But I can't send him on his own, and I don't want to risk good men.'

'You can't do all the work yourself!' Captain Ford glared into Alex's eyes. 'You've been out every night this week, bringing in the wounded, taking prisoners, and you got that sniper yesterday. Let some other bugger have some fun.'

* * *

'You can go out tonight, Mike,' Alex said, as he and his lieutenants finished supper in their far from cosy dugout and lit their cigarettes. 'Go and get some badges, if you like. Two or three dead Germans have been lying near the wire since yesterday. We ought to know what regiment is opposite, so you could go and find out.'

'Rather Mike than me,' grinned Freddie Lomax, who Alex knew was brave enough. But Freddie also wanted to survive, so never volunteered for anything. Alex made a mental note to send him on patrol the following night.

Now he looked at Michael. 'I want those badges back by midnight — is that understood?'

'P-permission to take an NCO?' In the lamplight, Michael's face was green.

'Which one do you want?' Alex didn't want to lose a sergeant because Michael lost his nerve or gave an order which led him to his death.

'Corporal Brind,' said Michael.

'Yes, you may have Brind.' Like Freddie Lomax, the happy poacher was determined to survive, so if Michael told him to do anything absurd, he simply wouldn't hear him.

Brind would be all right.

* * *

Michael and Corporal Brind had crawled and slithered on their bellies across the stinking slime of no-man's-land, and now they were crouching in a crater six or seven feet away from the nearest of the German dead.

'Corporal Brind?' hissed Michael, as a flare went up and lit the sky, and the German gunner who had obviously seen them raked the ground with spurting fire.

'Sir?' Corporal Brind was hating this, for catching rats and rabbits was much more in his line. He'd never have volunteered for anything as daft and dangerous as a night patrol.

But it was all round the trench that Mr Bloody Easton had asked specially for him, and he was damning the lieutenant to the deepest pit of hell.

'Do something for me, Brind,' said Michael. 'I'll make it worth your while. Just keep your eye on Captain Denham.'

'I'm sorry, sir?'

'He's d-dangerous, Brind. He sends his men on pointless missions. Look at us tonight, stuck here in the middle of nowhere on a fool's errand. Denham isn't fit to run a laundry, let alone a troop of fighting men.'

Michael turned to stare wild-eyed at the astonished corporal. 'Did you know his mother was a whore?'

'It wouldn't surprise me, sir,' said Brind, who by now was seriously scared.

'She was a harlot, she went through dozens of men. Denham doesn't know his father, doesn't have a family—'

Corporal Brind had seen a dozen officers with the wind up. But Lieutenant Easton was literally gibbering with fear — and talking nonsense, too.

'Best get on,' he whispered, pointing to the nearest body. 'Look sir, Captain Denham don't expect us to do both these Jerry bastards, I'll be bound. So let's get this one's badges off of 'im, an' then we can go 'ome.'

CHAPTER NINE

The damp November evening closed in.

'Tell me about Maria,' invited Mrs Rosenheim. 'Where is she now, and what's she doing?'

'She's in France, she's working on the ambulance trains,' said Rose. 'The trains fetch wounded soldiers from the front and take them to the hospitals in Rouen and Boulogne.' They were sitting at the kitchen table, and Rose watched as Mrs Rosenheim cut up a wizened chicken. 'How did you meet Phoebe and Maria?' she asked.

'My neighbour Maisie Bowman fostered them.' Mrs Rosenheim dropped the chicken pieces into an iron pot. 'Maria was four and Phoebe was a baby when Maisie took them in. Maisie fostered dozens. Any child the Guardians offered her, she took it home and brought up right for just five shillin' a week.

'But those two little girls was always special. When Maria got her scholarship to grammar school, Maisie was so proud! She pawned her Sunday best to buy the books and uniform, and nothing was too good for her Maria.'

'Phoebe and Maria are very different,' said Rose.

'They both got loving, generous hearts. Those girls was good to Maisie. When she died, you should have seen the horses, all the silver harness, all the ostrich plumes! The big glass carriage, the flowers all piled up on the best mahogany coffin lined with purple satin. It was like the queen had passed away. Maria paid for that.'

'So now they haven't got a proper home?'

'They'll always have a home with me,' said Mrs Rosenheim. 'When I first came to England, I lodged with Maisie Bowman, may she rest in peace. A better woman never breathed. I can't begin to tell you what she did for me and mine.'

'If you have hot water on the stove, I'll go and help Phoebe wash,' said Rose. She wanted to know more about the sisters, but she didn't like to pry. 'Now she's had a sleep, a wash will make her feel much better.'

When Rose went into the parlour with a bowl of water and a sponge, she found the baby sleeping peacefully in a wooden vegetable crate, but Phoebe wasn't there.

'Phoebe?' Rose walked back into the passage. 'Phoebe!'

'Did you call?' asked Nathan, who'd just limped out of the shop.

'I wanted Phoebe,' Rose replied. 'I wonder, did she go upstairs?'

'I don't think so.' Nathan shrugged. 'It's cold up there, and all her things are down here in the parlour anyway.'

'Then where's her coat?' Rose was suddenly frightened. 'Where's her hat, where are her boots and gloves?'

'I don't know,' said Nathan, and now he looked at Rose. 'She must have gone out.'

'How could she go out?' cried Rose. 'She's just had a baby! She hasn't eaten for hours, she's far too weak—'

'She might have needed something.' Nathan stared down at his feet. 'God,' he muttered, 'I told her I would go and get it! Rose, you probably won't approve, but she—'

'She takes cocaine,' said Rose. 'I realised straight away. Soldiers take it, too. I've heard them talk about it on the wards, how it helps them stay awake and how it's good for pain. But Phoebe doesn't need to stay awake.'

'She still needs cocaine.' Nathan looked at Rose. 'That evil bastard Hanson beats her up, but she still has to go and do her spot, or he would beat her up again. I expect that's where she's gone tonight, to do her spot.'

'I've never heard anything like it in my life!' Rose was horrified. 'Why does she have anything to do with such a person?'

'Why does any woman like any man? Daniel is a *mensch* round here — or so he likes to think. He owns two music halls, he runs protection rackets, and he's well respected. It's something to be Daniel Hanson's woman.'

'But you're not afraid of him?'

'I don't think about it.'

'How many chemists are there in the district?'

'Two or three,' said Nathan.

'Let's go and find out if they've seen Phoebe.'

'We should check the Haggerston Palace first, to see if she's gone there.'

* * *

The Haggerston Palace Music Hall turned out to be a small, decaying place with peeling walls and dirty, littered steps that led to a malodorous interior of faded purple plush and tarnished gilt. It offered daily programmes of unknown singers singing popular songs, comedians with suggestive names, and a chorus line of local beauties.

'You seen Phoebe, Morrie?' Nathan asked the shrivelled gnome who was sweeping out the grubby foyer.

'Nah, she ain't come in.' Morrie sucked his cheeks reflectively. 'Daniel's 'oppin' mad — 'e's 'ad to get another tart to do 'er song an' dance. If she's got any sense, she'll keep out of 'is way.' Morrie grinned at Nathan. 'She dropped that nipper yet?'

'How would I know?' muttered Nathan, as he turned to go.

'I only asked!' called Morrie, as Rose followed Nathan down the steps. 'Old Daniel, 'e can't wait to be a father!'

They tried all the chemists' shops, but nobody remembered seeing Phoebe. Rose's feet were aching and she was faint with hunger, but she felt she couldn't complain when Nathan dragged himself along the cobbled pavements tirelessly.

Suddenly, he darted up a side street.

'What's up here?' asked Rose.

'A dairy.' Nathan shrugged. 'We need some milk.'

'What the 'ell do you want?' Nathan had knocked and called for several minutes before a sharp-faced woman with her head tied in a scarf opened an upstairs window and leaned out to glower at them. 'We're closed!' she screeched. 'So go away!'

'Mrs Simmons, please come down!' Nathan stepped back to let the angry woman see him in the moonlight. 'I'm sorry to disturb you. But we need some milk.'

'Look, if Rachel's makin' cheesecake in the middle of the night—'

'Mrs Simmons, it's important!'

'All right, I'm comin' down.' Mrs Simmons grinned. 'Tell me, rabbi — who's your lady friend?'

'Why did she call you rabbi?' Rose asked, as they waited in the freezing darkness for the woman to appear.

'I'm studying for the rabbinate,' said Nathan, but his tone suggested further questions were not welcome.

As Mrs Simmons handed Rose a can containing half a pint of milk, they heard a factory hooter blaring, then a second, then a third. Seconds later, a policeman cycled past. 'Get under cover, all of you!' he shouted, as he rode off into the night.

'God in heaven,' Mrs Simmons groaned. 'Bloody Zeps, what are they doin' over 'ere again? The docks is miles away.'

'What's going on?' asked Rose, alarmed.

'An air raid.' Nathan's already pale face was ashen.

'You'd better come in here,' said Mrs Simmons, stepping back.

'Thank you, Mrs Simmons, but my mother will be frightened.' Nathan turned and started to drag himself along the alley. 'I must get home.'

* * *

They found an anxious Mrs Rosenheim was looking out for them, defying police instructions to stay away from windows and go down to her cellar, if she had one.

'You didn't find her, then?' she asked.

'No, she's disappeared,' said Nathan.

'What shall we to do with this poor little thing?' The baby was crying pitifully, sucking at her fists and rooting for her mother's breast. 'I've tried to feed her, I gave her sugar water with a spoon and offered her some gruel. But what she really needs is milk.'

'We've got some.' Rose gave the can to Mrs Rosenheim, then took the tiny baby in her arms. She stroked her small pink hand, and gazed into her beautiful blue eyes. Again she felt the powerful tug of love. But now it was mixed with fear and dread.

They sat in the damp cellar all that night. They listened to the crump of falling bombs, and shuddered as they heard all the explosions.

Flakes of whitewash floated down and settled on their heads, as soft as snow. The baby whimpered, but sucked milk from the comforter Rose made from a corner of her handkerchief, and finally she slept.

The morning came at last. People crept out of their houses blinking and red-eyed, and fearful of the damage they might see. The bitter smell of burning brick and timber filled the cold air.

As Rose stared around, she saw most roofs in this particular street were missing half their tiles. A dozen chimney stacks lay broken on the road, and almost every window was blown out.

'Look at Mrs Taylor's house!' cried Nathan, horrified.

'Oh, my God.' Rose turned and saw a cottage had been hit and set on fire. A horse-drawn fire engine was standing in the street, and firemen were searching through the shell.

Rose gave the child to Mrs Rosenheim and ran up to the house. 'I'm a nurse,' she told the policeman who stood guard outside. 'If there's anything I can do—'

'There's nothing anyone can do for Mrs Taylor, miss.' The policeman blinked, as if he were trying not to cry. 'A woman and three kids, all burnt alive. What had they ever done to anybody?'

The devastation was repeated all along the road. The corner shop was standing, but every window had been broken. All the stock was ruined, and Mrs Rosenheim began to cry.

'I can't stand it any more!' she sobbed, butting her head against her son's thin chest. 'First they take your brothers, then your cousin Reuben, then they take our livelihood, our home!'

She looked down at the baby. 'What will I do with this one? How am I going to feed her, clothe her, when I don't have anything myself?'

Nathan hugged her, whispering soothing words in a language Rose had never heard until today. But Mrs Rosenheim would not be comforted. Rocking to and fro, she wailed like an animal in pain.

'Mrs Rosenheim?' Rose touched the little woman's bony shoulder. 'Let me have the baby. I'll take her home with me. I'll write to Maria and tell her Phoebe's missing. But I'll say she mustn't worry because you're looking out for her and we're sure she'll soon turn up again.'

'But Rose, how will you manage?' wept Mrs Rosenheim. 'A young girl like you, not married — how can you care for a new-born baby?'

'I live in the country,' Rose replied. 'My parents have a house in Dorset. If I take the baby there, you'll know she will be safe.'

Rose fished in her bag. 'I'll give you my address. When you see Phoebe, tell her where to find me, then she can come and get her daughter. Mrs Rosenheim, it's the only way,' she added, urgently. 'Maria is my friend. So let me help, and let me take the child.'

'*Mamele*?' whispered Nathan. 'Rose is right, you know. This is the best way.'

* * *

When Rose got to Paddington, she heard a train had been derailed near Reading. There were lots of casualties. The west-bound line was blocked, and all the trains to Cornwall, Devon and Dorset were having to be re-routed. The station heaved with anxious passengers and tired, disgruntled soldiers who were going home on leave.

Before the war, any well-dressed woman travelling alone and carrying a tiny baby would have excited curiosity. But nobody was interested today, even when the baby cried and Rose could not comfort it.

She'd hoped to get some milk when she was finally on the train, but there was no dining car or buffet, just carriage after carriage packed with soldiers.

The baby sobbed and wailed pathetically. As the train steamed out into the grimy London suburbs, Rose began to push her way past soldiers standing, sitting or slumped in all the corridors, smoking, playing cards or trying to sleep, until eventually she found the guard.

'I need some milk to feed the baby,' she informed him.

'Do you, miss?' The guard looked bored. 'Well, I ain't got a cow.'

'Please help me, she's so hungry.' Rose decided she hated this complacent, mean-eyed man whose polished buttons gleamed on his immaculate black jacket. 'You must have some milk on board. Perhaps the driver, or the fireman—'

'Sorry, miss.' The guard looked at his watch. 'If you'll excuse me, I got things to do.'

* * *

Rose arrived at Charton at five o'clock that evening. She'd been shunted all round rural Dorset, often standing in a draughty corridor with a baby who was now too weak and too exhausted to do anything but doze and whimper fitfully.

She stood on the station platform, breathing in the cold night air and trying to decide what she should do. She'd need to find a foster mother soon. But maybe that could wait. She'd go to the Dower House first, see her mother, and explain what she'd been doing in London. Lady Courtenay loved all babies, and was sure to make a fuss of this one.

* * *

'Hello, Polly!' Rose smiled gratefully at the maid who'd come to let her in. She hardly noticed Polly staring at the tiny baby, her eyes as round as marbles. 'What an awful journey! I expect my mother's in the sitting room?'

'Y-yes, Miss Courtenay.' Polly frowned. 'But she hasn't been very well today. I think she's asleep.'

'She won't mind if I wake her up.' Rose walked across the hallway. 'Polly, be an angel and make a pot of tea, and also warm some milk for this young lady. See if you can find a little spoon.'

'Yes, Miss Courtenay.' Polly shook her head, but then she did as she was told. She bustled down the passage to the kitchen, muttering to herself.

Rose hadn't meant to wake her mother until Polly brought the tea, but when she walked into the sitting room the baby woke. She looked at Rose with huge, blue eyes, and whimpered.

'Rose?' Lady Courtenay had been dozing on the sofa, but when she heard the baby she woke up. She blinked and stared. 'Oh, my God,' she whispered.

'Mummy, it's all right.' Rose smiled reassuringly. 'I'm sorry about what happened yesterday. But I knew they'd look after you at the clinic and I dare say Daddy got my telegram in time—'

'I think I'm going mad.' Frances Courtenay looked first at her daughter, then at the baby and then at Rose again. 'I thought you'd done everything you ever could to hurt me. But I see I was wrong.'

'What do you mean?' Rose was so exhausted and so thirsty she could hardly think. All she wanted was to sit down by the fire, drink her tea and feed the starving baby.

'You've no consideration for my feelings,' Lady Courtenay muttered. 'You have no dignity, no self-respect, no shame.'

At last, Rose understood. 'Mummy, it's not *my* baby!' she exclaimed. Almost laughing at the sheer absurdity of this, she went over to her mother, crouching down beside her and trying to take her hand.

'Don't touch me!' Frances Courtenay shrank away. 'My own daughter comes in here, grinning like a hoyden, behaving like a woman of the street, and then expects — God knows I prayed for children,' she went on, wretchedly. 'Your father wanted sons, of course. But when God sent you, I thanked him every hour of every day. Rose, how could you do this to us? How could you hurt us—'

'Mummy, don't be ridiculous!' Rose could not believe what she was hearing. She shook her head, as if to clear it. 'This is not *my* child! *I* wasn't pregnant, I—'

'You expect me to believe you?' Lady Courtenay turned her head away.

'Mummy, pregnant women are enormous, they have bulging stomachs, they—'

'Oh, there are ways and means. Rose, I'm not so ignorant and stupid I don't know that!' Frances Courtenay fidgeted and grimaced, twisting her white hands, pulling and tugging at her jewelled rings.

'When I was a girl, even respectable women used to lace themselves so tightly one never knew they were expecting until the baby came! As for women from the lower classes — we once had a parlour maid, she had her baby in the butler's pantry. She wouldn't let anybody in, we had to break the door down in the end, we—'

'Mummy, you're being silly. Please sit still and listen—'

'Why should I listen to you?' Lady Courtenay's eyes flashed sapphire fire. 'You lie and you deceive and you don't care how much you hurt me! I never did anything to you but love you, and — oh God in heaven!'

Rose watched in horror as her mother toppled forward, collapsing on the hearth rug. 'Mummy!' She knelt by Lady Courtenay, feeling for her pulse, but couldn't find one.

'Polly!' she shouted. 'Polly, come here — hurry! Where are my mother's tablets?' But Rose soon realised her mother was past the help of tablets. When Polly finally appeared, bringing the round red leather box upon a silver tray, it was too late to do anything.

'Oh, Miss Courtenay!' Polly dropped the tray and gasped. 'May God forgive you for the wicked thing you've done!'

'What's all the commotion?' Rose's father walked into the sitting room to find his wife lying lifeless on the hearth rug, the maid having hysterics and his daughter cradling a baby, while the tears poured unchecked down her face.

Sir Gerard looked at Rose, then at the child. His usually ruddy face was drained of all its colour.

'Daddy, let me talk to you,' cried Rose. 'Let me explain—'

'Get out of my sight.' Sir Gerard glared at Rose. 'You're not my daughter. I never want to see you in my house again.'

CHAPTER TEN

Still cradling the baby in her arms, Rose left the Dower House. Deep in shock, she didn't know how she walked along the path, let alone reached the road.

Before this evening, she had never seen her father angry, and this had been as frightening as Lady Courtenay dying. When she'd returned to Dorset, Sir Gerard had behaved as if she'd never been away. The tenants and servants took their tone from him and even Polly had concealed her curiosity.

The arrears of her allowance had mounted up, so she was rich. All her clothes hung clean and pressed in two capacious wardrobes, and her other belongings had been taken to the Dower House or stored. When she went to church or to the village, no one had commented or stared — at least, not openly.

* * *

She knew she couldn't go far tonight. It was as dark as pitch and threatening rain. A cold wind was gusting from the east, and she wasn't dressed or shod for walking miles across the fields or down the winding road back to the village. She'd already ricked her ankle coming along the drive to Charton Minster, and now it hurt to walk.

She had no choice. She set off down the footpath that would take her round the headland and to Easton Hall.

* * *

To Rose's great relief, Celia herself came to the door. She had evidently just come in, for she stood there in her outdoor clothes, one boot off, one on, and staring at the visitor in amazement.

'Oh, Celia!' Rose was almost fainting. 'I'm sorry, but you'll have to let me in.'

'Rose, what on earth—'

'I know I shouldn't have come here,' Rose continued. 'But there was nowhere else to go.'

'Rose Courtenay, you astonish me.' But Celia stood back to let the bedraggled visitor come inside.

Then she rang the bell. 'Hannah,' she said crisply to the goggling servant, 'please bring tea and sandwiches for us, and — warm milk for the baby, Rose?'

'Please,' said Rose, who was feeling sick and dizzy from hunger, cold and pain.

'Hurry along now, Hannah.' Celia turned back to Rose. 'Let's go into the parlour. There ought to be a decent fire in there.'

As they sat down, Celia glanced obliquely at the baby. 'I suppose it's Michael's child?'

'So the mother says.'

'Then it isn't yours?'

'Oh, Celia!' cried Rose, 'not you as well!'

'I'm sorry, but you must admit—'

'I know,' said Rose. 'I didn't mean to shout at you.'

'May I see?' Celia came to crouch by Rose's side. 'A boy or girl?'

'A girl.'

'Poor little thing.' Celia turned towards the open door. 'You may come in, Hannah! There's no need to stand there in the passage, listening.'

'I wasn't listening, miss.' But the maid looked sheepish as she carried in the laden tray.

'You may tell them in the kitchen that it's not Miss Courtenay's child,' Celia added curtly, as she poured. 'Then you may spread it all around the district.'

'Very good, Miss Easton.' The maid was blushing crimson. 'Miss, I know it's not my place to gossip about my betters.'

'It most certainly is not, but that has never stopped you,' said Celia genially.

The maid glanced furtively at Rose, then she scuttled out.

'Rose, don't cry,' said Celia, as Rose's grey eyes filled and tears rolled slowly down her cheeks. 'I'm not blind or stupid. I know what my precious brother does, how he behaves when he's away from Dorset. Believe me, he's not worth your grief.'

'I'm not crying for Michael.' Rose spooned up some milk then tried to feed the weak, exhausted baby, who was as pale as death. 'My mother thought—'

'Well, she would,' said Celia. 'She and Mrs Sefton—'

'You don't understand,' sobbed Rose. 'Celia, she's dead!'

* * *

The coal scuttle was empty and the room was growing cold. Celia stood up. 'We ought to go to bed,' she yawned. 'You'll have to sleep in Mike's room. I know it's not ideal, especially in the present circumstances. But otherwise we'll have to move a brat, and it's bound to go and wake my mother.'

'I don't mind where I sleep,' said Rose, who had forgotten Celia had a dozen brothers and sisters, and her mother and father must be somewhere in this great, decaying place.

But these days Celia was in charge. When Lady Easton came into the breakfast room that morning, all of a fluttering twitter and full of the news she'd just heard from her maid, Celia stayed quietly unperturbed.

'We must find the child a foster mother,' she said, briskly. 'Mummy, do please pass the marmalade. You could ring for Hannah, we're going to need more toast. Rose, there's the very person in the village. She's just had twins, but she's the sort of woman who could nurse a dozen, and what's more she's respectable and kind. You and I can visit often, and when Mike comes home—'

'We need to find her mother,' Rose reminded Celia.

'I think that might be awkward. I understand it's relatively easy to disappear in London?'

'Yes, perhaps.' Rose blushed. 'Let's hope she'll contact us.'

'If you write to Mrs Rubinstein, or whatever the woman's called, she could give this Phoebe person my name and address.'

Celia twinkled at the baby, who was lying in Rose's arms and doing her best to drink the milk Rose offered on a spoon. 'She's certainly getting the hang of that,' she smiled. 'What a clever girl! Rose, I meant to ask last night — what is the child's name?'

Rose had never given it a thought. This was not her baby, and she had no right to name her, but if she didn't, who would? 'What about Elizabeth, or Daisy?' she suggested.

'Daisy.' Celia smiled and nodded. 'Little Daisy — perfect.'

'What shall we tell the foster mother?' Rose asked anxiously.

'We tell the truth, of course.' Celia met Lady Easton's gaze. 'Rose was in an air raid. Daisy's mother is missing.'

'But what about her father?' Lady Easton asked.

'Let's not mention him.' Celia looked down at her finger nails. 'We'll have to see what Michael says, when he comes home again.'

'Michael?' Lady Easton frowned. 'Celia, my dear—'

'I'm sorry, Mummy.' Celia shrugged. 'It appears I'm now an aunt and you're a grandmamma. Rose, I'm due in Dorchester at twelve. I'm running a knitting bee for the Red Cross. Scarves and socks and all that sort of thing. But we have things to do.'

* * *

'What shall you do now?' asked Celia, as she and Rose walked down the path from Mrs Hobson's honey-coloured cottage, where Celia had introduced the baby, negotiated terms and said she'd visit often.

'I need somewhere to live.'

'You'd be very welcome at the Hall.'

'Perhaps I shouldn't stay there.' Rose glanced at Celia. 'I don't want your mother to be embarrassed. I'll go and see Miss Mason, at the house.'

At the Minster, Rose found the gossip and speculation had preceded her, but Jessie Mason wasn't interested in scandal. 'I know it's not my business,' she began, meeting Rose's tired gaze with candid, hazel eyes. 'But I would like to say that I have every faith in your respectability. I value your abilities as a nurse.'

'Then may I stay here?'

'Miss Courtenay, it's your home!' Jessie Mason spread her hands. 'Of course, Sir Gerard may decide to intervene. But as the matron of this place, I would be delighted if you'd stay.'

So Rose moved to the Minster, sleeping in an attic that had once belonged to Polly, and working all the hours she wasn't actually asleep or down in the village seeing Daisy. To her great relief, the child was thriving and contented. She had lost the pallor she'd once had, so Rose no longer feared she might die.

She was not invited to her mother's funeral. She was on duty when she heard them toll the knell, and doing a ward round when they brought the coffin to the family crypt, in the private chapel that adjoined the house.

As the mourners left the Minster and walked across the gravel sweep towards their waiting carriages, Rose forced herself to concentrate on a particularly awkward dressing. As the last carriage crunched across the gravel, she was sorting out a blockage in the drainage tube in Major Dyson's chest.

* * *

Rose wrote to Maria, explaining about Daisy but not mentioning her mother's death. Three or four times a week, she walked down to the honey-coloured cottage to see the child.

Whenever she sat in Mrs Hobson's warm and cluttered kitchen with Daisy on her lap, she knew how it must feel to be a mother. Gazing into Daisy's wide blue eyes, she felt a tugging at her heart and a sweet yearning that was almost pain.

She had to remind herself continually that this was Phoebe's baby. One day, Phoebe would come back and take her daughter home — wherever home might be.

Celia did her best to make sure everyone in Charton knew Daisy wasn't Rose's child. But people preferred to think the baby was a Courtenay bastard, for this was too delicious a piece of scandal for anyone to ignore.

When Rose was in the sluice room one December morning, she overheard some cleaning women gossiping and laughing. 'I don't care what that Miss Easton reckons,' said the first. 'It'll most likely be my lady's and some officer's.'

'Most probably 'e'll be a married man,' put in a second woman.

'That Miss Easton ain't no better than she should be.' The first cleaning woman snorted. 'These nobs, they covers up for one another, always has done, always will. You mark my words. If that nipper ain't Miss Courtenay's little indiscretion, I'm a Chinaman.'

'It's terrible about her ladyship.' The second cleaner sighed. 'Polly said they was at each other's throats before she dropped down dead. But when Miss Courtenay was a little girl, she was the apple of her mother's eye.'

'It's strange, how these rich women turn out bad. Do you remember Mrs Denham? She was a flighty piece. She took up with that artist chap, an' then when he got sick of her she came back 'ome to Dorset bold as brass, and brought her little boy. She expected poor old Mr Denham—'

Rose had heard enough. She swept out of the sluice, favoured the cleaners with a frosty stare, and asked if they had any work to do.

They scuttled off, but not without a parting shot. 'Some people seems to think they're better than the rest of us,' came floating down the corridor towards her, 'but I dunno 'ow they got the nerve.'

The situation soon became intolerable for Rose. As the gossip spread, as the story grew more lurid and sensational, even the convalescing officers smirked and nudged and murmured. Gentlemen or not, they gave Rose sly and knowing looks.

Sir Gerard was the only person who could put an end to it, so when she came off shift one evening Rose went over to the Dower House.

'I'm very sorry, miss.' Polly looked embarrassed and upset. 'Sir Gerard says he's not at home to you.'

'Oh, for God's sake, Polly!' Rose walked past the maid into the hallway. 'I'm not a casual caller, I'm his daughter.'

'Please, Miss Courtenay, don't go in!' Polly was almost crying. 'Sir Gerard said you weren't to come—'

'What's going on out here?' Sir Gerard came out of his smoking room. He scowled at Rose. 'What do *you* want? Polly, I thought I said—'

'It's not Polly's fault.' Although her father looked so angry that she feared he might quite literally throw her out, Rose faced up to him. 'I need to speak to you. It won't take very long.'

Sir Gerard looked from his daughter to his maid. 'Oh, very well,' he muttered. 'Polly, get on with your work. Rose, come in the sitting room. Shut the door behind you. You may have five minutes. What do you wish to say?'

'Just this — the child is not mine.'

'You expect me to believe you?' Sir Gerard's tone was mildness itself, but his eyes bulged dangerously, and Rose kept her distance. 'I have been on the Bench for thirty years, but you are the most impudent, bare-faced liar I have ever met. How you came to be my child, I shall never—'

'Daddy, you *saw* me!' interrupted Rose. 'I was living here, for heaven's sake! I can't believe you wouldn't have noticed if I had been carrying a child!'

'There are ways and means,' Sir Gerard muttered. 'I've heard of several cases where women of a certain class—'

'I give you my word.'

'You word is worth nothing.'

'Then how can I convince you?'

'You must convince a doctor first.' Sir Gerard looked down at his feet. 'If you wish to clear your name, make an appointment to see Dr Weldon.'

'You mean, let him examine me?'

Sir Gerard shrugged, then stared out of the window. 'Rose, *you* sought this interview — not I.'

For a few moments, Rose considered what Sir Gerard had said. He had a point, she realised — she could prove she wasn't lying, could become her father's child once more. She could prove she was an honest woman, as people used to say . . .

But then she found she couldn't — wouldn't — do it. 'I will not be examined by a doctor,' she told Sir Gerard, knowing her face must be on fire. 'If my own father chooses to believe the lies the local scandalmongers tell about his daughter, then so be it.'

'I have no daughter,' said Sir Gerard. Then he looked at the clock. 'I said five minutes, so it's time for you to leave.'

Rose walked out of the house. She strode along the path towards the Minster, and by the time she reached it she was breathing hard. She met the matron in the hall, and followed her into her office. 'I wish to go to France,' she said.

Jessie Mason looked at Rose and sighed. 'I know some people make it hard for you,' she murmured sympathetically. 'I know you've had some problems—'

'I'm sorry Matron, but the situation here's intolerable!' Rose choked back the tears that were welling up behind her eyes. 'Please, do this for me?'

'I'll make enquiries,' promised Jessie Mason. 'But Miss Courtenay, are you sure you wish to leave? Your father's had a dreadful shock. So won't he need to know his daughter's here, to help him cope?'

'He says he has no daughter,' Rose replied.

* * *

'A hospital for other ranks,' said Jessie Mason, four days later. 'It's mostly surgical, but some men have been gassed — not very pleasant. It sounds like quite hard work, as well. There are about three hundred men but only fifteen nurses, most of them volunteers.'

'I'll go,' said Rose.

'Do you feel fit enough? Miss Courtenay, you're still grieving. I'm sure your father needs you, whatever he may say.'

'I'll go to France,' insisted Rose.

* * *

'Miss Dennison, Miss Courtenay and Miss Troy!' intoned the station master, through his megaphone. 'Please join your party at the end of Platform 3!'

'Miss Courtenay?' Alex swallowed the last mouthful of bitter Red Cross coffee. He pushed his plate of greasy eggs away. 'Excuse me, David,' he muttered to Lieutenant Richardson, with whom he'd come to Rouen. 'I dare say you could find your own way back? There's someone I must see.'

It would not be Rose, he thought, as he pushed his way through all the crowds. There were hundreds of Miss Courtenays in England. There were probably a fair few of them in France.

He saw a gaggle of nurses at the far end of the station concourse and strode up to them. 'I beg your pardon, Sister.' He smiled politely at a middle-aged woman, who glared back at him. 'I'm sorry, could you let me through?'

Then at last he saw her, and knew there must be a God. 'Rose!' he shouted, waving.

She turned and stared at him. 'L-lieutenant Denham?' she said, frowning.

'He's a captain, idiot!' hissed another nurse, whose dark eyes twinkled as she grinned at him. 'Look, he's got three pips.'

Rose quelled her with a look. 'It's nice to see you're better, Captain Denham,' she said crisply. 'But how did you know I would be in Rouen?'

'I didn't know,' said Alex. 'I had a forty-eight hour pass, and I came here with another chap from my battalion. We're waiting for the train back to our sector. But then I heard the station master call you. Rose, I want to say—'

'Come over here,' she interrupted testily, and walked off down the platform. Alex followed her, and soon they were out of sight of all the nurses.

She stopped between two empty trains and then turned round to face him. 'Well?' she said.

'I owe you an apology,' said Alex.

'What do you mean?' frowned Rose.

'When I was in hospital, and you were so kind to me, I know that I annoyed you. When I said I couldn't bath myself that time, and I deliberately embarrassed you — I don't know why I did it, but I'm sorry. My behaviour was disgusting, and—'

'You think *your* behaviour was disgusting?' Rose laughed mirthlessly. 'Captain Denham, you don't know the meaning of the word.'

'What do you mean?'

'It doesn't matter.'

'Rose!'

'I ought not to tell you, but — what difference does it make? Men like him do as they please. If other people suffer, they don't care. Your dear friend and mine, your brother officer Lieutenant Easton — he asked me to marry him, you know.'

'I didn't know.'

'Of course, he wants my father's money. I'm well aware of that. But after he asked me to be his wife, he was still chasing other women. Poor little Phoebe, she's the sort of girl who probably thinks she knows it all. But really she knows nothing. She'd trust a perfect stranger with her last half crown. She trusted Michael Easton, and he left her helpless and afraid.'

Rose's voice was shrill and rising, and her face was flushed. 'How *could* he?' she demanded. 'How could he use her and abuse her, how could he just walk away and leave her? How—'

'Rose, calm down,' said Alex. 'Please, don't get so upset.'

'Why shouldn't I be upset?' Rose glared at him. 'You men, you're all the same! Everyone in Dorset knows you got poor Mrs Denham pregnant long before you married her, so how did you entice *her* into bed? By saying that if she'd let you sleep with her, she'd get a diamond ring?'

'You've said enough,' scowled Alex.

'I've hardly even started! What were you doing with Charlotte Stokeley on the cliff top, when you were in Dorset recently?'

'I — what do you mean?' Alex was genuinely astonished. 'Rose, the girl attached herself to me. Whenever I'm in Dorset, she comes hanging round the house. I can't avoid her, she—'

'She isn't one of your many women, then?'

'God, Rose, she's a child! You're being quite ridiculous.'

'I don't think so. I—'

'This is a pointless conversation.' Alex turned on his heel to walk away. 'Well, goodbye, Rose.'

'You come back here and listen to me!' Rose caught him by the sleeve and spun him round, then carried on berating him.

Alex didn't know how to stop her ranting. If she'd been a man he would have hit her, knocked her down. So should he slap her hard, to bring her to her senses before she had a fit and fell down foaming at the mouth?

But he couldn't bring himself to slap her, so he put his hands upon her shoulders, drew her to him — then he kissed her fiercely on the lips.

She struggled for a moment, and he thought she'd break away. She'd scream for the police, and he'd be a lieutenant or cashiered or in a military prison before the day was done.

But she didn't scream. She gradually stopped struggling, although she was still tense. Finally, however, she relaxed.

He kissed her very lingeringly and very gently this time, tasting her and opening her reluctant mouth with his. He held her very close to him, feeling the lovely warmth of her and breathing her delicious scent, and kissing her again, again, again.

CHAPTER ELEVEN

The sudden striking of the station clock brought Rose back to reality.

'Why did you do that?' she cried, horrified by what she'd done herself, and furiously pushing him away.

'I don't know.' Alex shrugged, but Rose could see his eyes were black and burning. 'Actually, I do,' he said. 'It was because I had to kiss you, or lie down and die.'

'You do talk nonsense.'

'It's not nonsense, Rose. I've wanted to kiss you since I was fourteen.'

'Then why didn't you?'

'You'd have slapped my face! Your father would have had me branded, put me in the stocks. Everyone in Dorset knows you're going to marry Michael Easton, although I didn't know he had proposed until today.'

'You think I *want* to marry him?'

'I suppose you do.' Alex shrugged again. 'I know you like him, and he certainly likes you.'

'You take too much for granted, Captain Denham. No power on earth would make me marry Michael.'

'What?' A sudden smile lit Alex's face. 'Rose, what do you mean?'

'I don't mean anything.' Rose stared down at her feet. 'I know what they think of me in Dorset. But I'm not a whore. I don't steal other women's men.'

'I never said you did.' As Rose began to hurry along the platform, Alex caught her arm. 'You say I take too much for granted,' he continued urgently. 'Well, perhaps I do. But when I kissed you, it was plain you liked it.'

'I must go, and you must never talk like this again.'

'You don't mean that.' Alex's fingers bit into her flesh, and Rose knew she couldn't get away. He'd let her scream the station down before he let her go.

'Listen, Rose,' he went on feverishly. 'There isn't time to court you. In a different place and in a different situation, I'd have bought you flowers, I'd have watched you flirt with other men and waste my time. But we don't have time.'

'What are you trying to say?'

'I want you,' he replied. 'I want you so much it hurts. I've never felt such pain.'

She thought of slapping him, of screaming, of all the other options open to outraged virginity. But she also knew she must be honest, or she would hate herself.

'Alex, I know it hurts,' she whispered sadly, 'because it hurts me, too.'

* * *

'Miss Courtenay!' cried a strident voice, and Rose looked to see two nurses sprinting down the platform.

'There you are at last!' exclaimed Miss Troy, a fierce-looking spinster who wore two hectic spots of rouge high on her bony cheekbones. 'Miss Dennison and I have been distraught! It's ten past four, and time we're entrained.' They took Rose into custody, and then began to frogmarch her away.

'I'm going to Auchonville!' Rose looked back at Alex, and the smile he gave her made her feel like dancing. 'To the hospital for other ranks. I don't know the address, but write to me!'

'Of course I'll write!' Recovering from his surprise, Alex started running and soon caught up with them. As he drew level, he leaned across Miss Dennison to kiss Rose on the cheek. Then he ran on, leaving them behind.

'What a strange young man,' said Elsie Dennison.

'I dare say he's been drinking,' said Miss Troy.

* * *

'When could you get some leave?' he wrote, after he had said he longed to see her, that being away from her was torture. *'I'm due a week or more, but I don't think I'm going to get it. My CO has jaundice, half the other officers are sick, and all the men have coughs and colds. I'm very healthy, but this means I'm doing all the work.'*

'I'm not due any leave at all,' Rose wrote despondently. *'I haven't been here long enough. But we're not very busy, and in an emergency we're allowed a twenty-four hour pass. I could say it was a family matter.'*

'I'll come by rail to Belancourt,' wrote Alex. *'Then I'll walk to Auchonville. If I promise to find a case or two of decent brandy, I expect they'll let me have three days.'*

A part of Rose was almost willing fate to stop her meeting Alex, but a transparent fib about a cousin in hospital in Tournonville secured the precious twenty-four hour pass. A promise to work two of Elsie's shifts for one of hers ensured she wouldn't be missed if she was late the following day.

She almost hoped he wouldn't come, but she found him waiting for her in the market place at Auchonville, and to her astonishment he was sitting in a car.

'Where did you get that?' she cried, amazed.

'It's my CO's,' said Alex, grinning. 'He has an arrangement with a woman in Harfoix, she keeps it in her garage. I promised Malcolm that if he'd lend me this old bus today, I'd bring back half a dozen crates of Armagnac tomorrow.'

They drove out of the town, and soon were in the leafless but as yet undamaged countryside of pretty little villages and ancient Norman churches. Before they'd gone five miles, however, Rose touched Alex's sleeve.

'Stop the car,' she said.

He brought the vehicle to a shuddering halt. 'I didn't mean to take that bend so fast,' he said, and grinned a wry apology. 'Sorry if I shook you up a bit. Do you feel sick?'

'It's not your driving.' Rose looked down at her hands. 'Alex, this is wrong. You have a wife.'

'But I don't love her, and she doesn't love me.'

'How do you know she doesn't love you?'

'Last September, when I was in Dorset convalescing, she didn't come and see me. She was staying with her aunt, and said she couldn't get away. She only writes to me when she wants money, but I don't know what she does with it. Henry gives her an allowance, and she gets half my pay.'

'I see.' Rose looked at him. 'Everyone in Dorset thinks I'm wicked, cruel, ungrateful. I'm a liar, as well. Alex, do you want to kiss a liar?'

'More than anything in all the world.'

* * *

The proprietor of the small hotel, which was tucked away along a back street in the little town of Richelcourt, glowered morosely at the woman and the British officer.

Rose didn't care. He was old, she told herself, he'd seen it all before, he wasn't going to judge. When Alex asked him for a room, he muttered an enormous sum in francs, and then produced a tarnished key.

Alex locked the bedroom door behind them, then took Rose in his arms. She didn't know what to do. Familiarity with young men's bodies hadn't taught her how to be a lover, and she was as innocent of passion as she'd been when she was still a child.

Alex kissed her hairline, and she shuddered. Then he pushed her cloak back from her shoulders, and she froze. 'It's all right,' he murmured, soothingly. 'We won't do anything you don't want to do. There's no need to be frightened.'

'I — I'm not frightened.' Battening down her terror and trying to stop shaking, Rose looked up at him, into his eyes. 'I want to go to bed.'

'You're sure?'

'Why else do you think I came here?' she demanded, in a high-pitched voice unlike her own.

'Rose, you mustn't think I want—'

'You mean you've changed your mind?'

'That's *your* privilege.' Alex let his hands slide down her shoulders, electrifying her and making her feel weak with longing. He took her hands in his. 'All right, we'll go to bed.'

The huge, sagging bed had musty curtains, and when Alex drew them it was like being in a scarlet cave. There was no other world outside. Alex had no wife, Rose wasn't playing truant and wasn't about to give herself to a man she knew she couldn't marry. There was no war, no duty and no time.

She hadn't thought about the actual process, about the loss of her virginity. She only knew she wanted Alex. She wanted to be naked next to him, as she'd wanted that day in the bath house, when the dappled light had filtered through the net-screened doorway and made him looked so beautiful that she had almost wept, when the sun had stroked his smooth brown nutmeg-scented skin.

He was very careful, caressing and reassuring her as if she were a nervous mare whom he was too considerate to frighten. 'I promise I'll be gentle,' he said softly, as he took off her clothes, as he kissed her face, her neck, her hair, and as he found the tender, sensitive places she hadn't known were there before today.

As he kissed her, the material of his jacket grazed her skin, and made her shudder. 'At least take off your coat,' she whispered, suddenly embarrassed and ashamed.

'You do it for me.'

When they were both naked, Alex traced a line from Rose's throat down to her navel, then he slid one hand between her legs. She gasped and trembled, but she let him part her thighs, then find a place she hadn't known existed until this afternoon.

'Rose, try to relax,' he whispered, as he kissed behind her ear and made her shiver with delicious pleasure. 'I promise I won't hurt you. There's no need to be afraid.'

But Rose found she wanted pain, and when Alex finally came inside her and it hurt like hell, she sighed with satisfaction.

* * *

'Did I hurt you?' Alex asked, as he let his weight down on her body, as he took her in his arms and planted rows of kisses in her hair.

'Yes, you hurt me.'

'I didn't mean to be so rough. I'm sorry.'

'You're not to be sorry, because I was in heaven.'

'So was I.' Alex rolled over on his back and then pulled Rose on top of him, so her hair came tumbling round her face. 'This is the first time I've seen it loose,' he said, as he played with a long, curling strand.

'It might well be the last. I hate my hair, it's so unruly, I think it makes me look like some old witch.' Rose grasped two great handfuls, pushing it behind her ears then starting on a plait.

'Leave it.' Alex pulled her hands away. 'Your hair is beautiful, and so are you. Rose, are you hungry?'

'I suppose I must be. I didn't get a chance to eat this morning.'

'Let's go and feed you, then.'

They dressed, then went to eat at an estaminet in the town. Alex asked for brandy and told the waiter he could leave the bottle on the table.

They sat in silence until the food arrived. Then Rose made her confession. 'I told them I was visiting my cousin who's in hospital in Tournonville.' She looked up from her plate. 'You must think that's awful, when there are so many people actually getting hurt.'

'It's not awful, Rose,' said Alex, gravely. 'But I'm amazed to find that you are such an accomplished liar nowadays.'

'It frightens *me*,' admitted Rose. 'I never used to think I could be wicked, but I suppose I must be. Alex, I thought the French were meant to be accomplished cooks. This ragout is disgusting.'

'It does look rather ghastly.' Alex hadn't eaten anything, and now he drained his brandy. 'Let's go back to bed.'

* * *

'That night you wouldn't dance with me,' said Alex, winding a skein of Rose's hair around his index finger, then letting go and watching it spring back into a curl. 'I've never been so hurt in all my life.'

'Did you ask me to dance?' teased Rose. She kissed him. 'I don't remember that.'

'You must — I asked you twice!'

'But when you asked me first, you didn't really think I would. "Miss Courtenay, if you mean to dance?" What sort of invitation's that?'

'Well, I was nervous.' Alex grinned. 'I was also trying not to notice that revolting dress.'

'It was a lovely dress!'

'Rose, it was hideous. It was a horrid shade of piglet pink, and you looked quite ridiculous, hung with all those awful beads and sequins, like a walking Christmas tree.'

'I hate you, Alex Denham!' Rose jumped up. 'I'm going back to Auchonville this minute.'

'You'll have a nice long walk. So wrap up well, it's going to freeze tonight.' Alex lay back against the pillows, watching Rose pull on her thick black woollen stockings. 'Rose, don't be offended. Most women look much better without clothes.'

'You should know.' Rose groped for her chemise. 'You'll have seen so many of them naked, after all.'

'Only ten or twenty — certainly no more.' Alex yawned and stretched luxuriously. 'William had his half a dozen favourites, and drew and painted them most of the time.'

'I was forgetting.' Rose sat down again and looked at Alex. 'You know everything about my life, but yours is a mystery to me.'

'I'd have thought what happened was common knowledge?'

'Everybody talked, of course,' said Rose. 'But they all clammed up and pursed their lips whenever children were about. I knew your mother often went away, and people wondered if she would come back.'

'Rose, come here.' Alex pulled her into his embrace and let her lean against him. 'My mother and William Rayner met when she was seventeen. He had come to paint her sister's portrait, at their house.

'A few months later she was pregnant, probably with William's child, but there's a possibility she had other lovers, too. William wouldn't marry her, and so she married Henry. He was very much in love and would have taken her on any terms.'

'What happened then?'

'Three or four years later, she saw William at a party. She went away with him. But they didn't always get on well, her parents had disowned her, so she travelled back and forth to Dorset, dragging me.'

'You must have been so puzzled and confused?'

'I don't remember.' Alex shrugged. 'Mrs Sefton called me the encumbrance, and wouldn't have me in her house. But Henry was always very kind to me.'

'Poor Mr Denham.'

'Yes, he should have had a better wife. He certainly deserved one.'

'It's strange I don't remember Mrs Denham. You and Mr Denham used to call at Charton Minster, but your mother never came.'

'She was not invited. Rose, your family is respectable, and so *my* mother would have been as welcome as the plague.'

'Alex, did you love your mother?'

'I loved her very much. She was the sort of person one couldn't help but love. While she was dying, William was distraught. I thought he would go mad with grief.'

'But he's still alive?'

'I think so.' Alex shrugged again. 'Although he'll have another mistress now. I don't suppose he thinks about my mother any more.'

'What a horrid person he must be.'

'No, he's a charming man. I always liked him.'

'You're so forgiving, Alex. I don't think *I* would be.' Rose twisted round to look at him. 'Do you see much of Michael?'

'Yes, because he's in my company.'

'Do you get on well?'

'We rub along.' Alex didn't tell her Michael was a liability, whose only talent was shooting those unwary Germans who happened to stick their heads above the parapet. Thanks to Michael, Freddie Lomax and the other officers all knew Alex's personal history. Michael had made a special pet of odious Corporal Brind, and Brind had spread Lieutenant Easton's stories all around the men.

But there were compensations. It had been particularly pleasant to hear Sergeant Norris tell the happy poacher to keep his filthy slander to himself, that in the sergeant's frank opinion it didn't matter if Mr Denham's mother was a whore or Queen of Timbuctoo. The captain was no more incompetent than any other useless officer, and Corporal Brind's own parents must have been a pair of dirty-minded, mad baboons.

Alex wrapped a quilt round Rose's shoulders. 'Easton's been telling everyone he's going to marry you.'

'He just wants Daddy's money. If I were a pauper, Michael wouldn't look at me.'

'*I* think he's very proud. You nurses are doing splendid work in France.'

'If he knew what splendid work I'd done this afternoon—'

'Rose, do you regret it?'

'No, and I never shall — even if I live to be a hundred.' Rose rubbed her eyes and yawned. 'Oh Alex, I'm so tired!'

'Then go to sleep.' Alex pulled the quilts and blankets round them, then snuffed out the light.

* * *

'Rose?' It was nearly dawn and Alex knew he had to leave. Otherwise, he would be on a charge.

'Let me sleep,' moaned Rose.

'Darling, I must go. I have to find the Armagnac, then take that wretched car back to Harfoix.'

'Go on, leave me then.' Rose looked at him with drowsy, sated eyes. 'But how will I get back to Auchonville?'

'There's a train to Belancourt at ten, then you can walk.' He stroked her hip. 'The exercise will do you good.'

'You're such a beast.'

'I know.' He smiled. 'I love you.'

'Do you honestly?'

'I love you and I'll always love you. Rose, I promise you.'

'A morning promise. One made to be broken before it's afternoon?'

'One to be kept until the sun stops rising in the sky.'

'But *I'm* supposed to be the liar.'

'So don't say you love me.' Alex kissed her on the mouth. 'Go back to sleep instead.'

* * *

'It was very quiet last night,' said Elsie, as Rose pulled off her gloves. 'In fact, I put my feet up on the stove and went to sleep. But this afternoon it will be bedlam. They're bringing thirty patients from Harfoix, all of them gassed.'

'That's all right,' smiled Rose. 'I'll get them settled. You and Nancy Harris can still go into town.'

'How is your cousin?' asked Miss Troy, who'd just walked in.

'He's in excellent spirits,' Rose replied. 'He was thrilled to see me.'

'I'm sure he must have been,' said Elsie, wryly. 'Rose, your new collar must be rubbing. You have a sore patch on your neck.'

* * *

Rose broke all the rules but didn't care. She worried about being caught, but only because if she were caught she'd be sent back to England.

Nurses were forbidden to go anywhere alone, unless they had permission from their matron and a pass. They were not allowed to go out walking with officers or men. They couldn't even go for walks themselves unless they went in pairs.

But whenever Alex managed to arrange an errand to the riding school in Belancourt, or to the training camp nearby, whenever he could snatch a couple of hours and get a lift to Auchonville, Rose would beg Miss Troy or Elsie Dennison to cover up for her, sweeten them with cigarettes and chocolate, then slip out on her own.

'I suppose it's that peculiar young man we saw in Rouen?' Elsie said one evening, as Rose came panting in and flung herself down on the camp bed in the spartan wooden hut they shared.

'He's not peculiar, he's lovely!'

'I hope he's worth the mess you'll both be in when Matron or the military police catch up with you.'

'Matron never notices a thing, and the police are busy chasing soldiers who have cut and run.' Rose smiled at her friend. 'Elsie, will you do my Wednesday morning? Then I'll do both your Friday nights.'

'Yes, all right.' Elsie glanced up from the letter she was writing to her fiancé in the Dardanelles. 'I don't know where you get the energy.'

But Rose was never tired. She fizzed and buzzed with restless energy, her grey eyes sparkled and her complexion glowed.

Although she was forever swapping shifts, trading one night off for two on duty, so that when she wasn't with Alex she was almost always on the wards, she found she needed hardly any rest.

The hospital was full, but the nurses weren't rushed off their feet. Apart from men who had been gassed and needed special nursing, most patients at this time of year were sick, not gassed or wounded. A few were injured, but most were getting over colds, croup, frostbite or trench foot.

'It's always quiet in winter,' muttered Alex, when they met for half an hour in Auchonville the following Saturday. 'The next big push will be in spring or summer. Then you'll learn what war is all about.'

It wasn't spring or summer yet. Rose refused to think about the awful implications of a push, as Alex called the great attack everybody knew was coming soon and ought to end the war.

What would happen then? Alex had signed on for twenty years or more, so when this dismal business was all over, where would he go next?

'God only knows,' he said, as he and Rose sat in the market square, enjoying the December sunshine on an unusually bright, clear day. 'Let's hope it's India or Burma.'

'Why?' asked Rose.

'It's easier to get promoted there.' Alex lit a cigarette, then let a perfect smoke ring rise high into the sky. 'I want to be a colonel and make Henry proud of me.'

Rose looked at the smoke ring, floating higher and higher, losing substance, shape and form. Alex had said he loved her, promised he always would, but if he went to India, what would she do then? Tag along behind the baggage wagons with the other riff-raff, in a motley crew of money-lenders, cooks and whores?

'What are you thinking, Rose?' asked Alex.

'I — nothing important.' Rose looked at him and saw he was dishevelled, grimed and filthy. He hadn't shaved for days.

He hadn't even combed his hair. His boots were clogged and dirty, and his trousers caked with dried-on mud.

Several buttons were missing from his jacket, which was scuffed and torn. He smelled of trenches — of lice-repellent, smoke and dank latrines, of mouldy clothes and slime.

How could he bear to live like that? How could he and millions like him crouch in sordid holes, ever fearful of a gas attack, a bombing raid?

When he *did* escape, when he snatched an hour of peace and spent it sitting in a village square, smoking cheap French cigarettes and staring at the bright blue cloudless sky, how did he find the courage to go back?

'Captain Denham, sir?' A lorry trundled up to them, and a cheerful corporal grinned and waved. 'You said one o'clock, sir — but I managed to get all this lot loaded up by ten. So we've time to drop the parcels off at Nelanville.'

'Good show, Corporal Ross.' Alex threw his cigarette away. 'I have to go,' he murmured, as Rose realised with a sinking heart they would not be having lunch together.

He wouldn't even kiss her in front of odious, over-zealous, grinning Corporal Ross.

* * *

The nurses held a raffle to decide which two should be off shift on Christmas Day.

'I've won!' squealed Rose, delighted.

'So have I,' said Elsie Dennison.

'What shall you do, Elsie?' Rose asked, beaming.

'Sleep,' said Elsie, rubbing her red eyes. 'I'll come and watch the boys open their presents, then I'll go back to bed.'

'What about you, Rose?' enquired Miss Troy.

'I'll give a hand with breakfast, help take round the parcels, and then I'll have a rest,' Rose answered, glibly. 'I've got a stack of books I haven't read.'

* * *

She wrote to him immediately to tell him the good news. She hardly dared to hope he'd get away. But it seemed he might. *'It's my turn,'* he said. *'I spent last Christmas in this stinking midden. My darling, say your prayers.'*

Rose knew there was no need to pray, for nothing could go wrong. Even when Miss Troy came down with raging tonsillitis, she knew she could escape just after two, when Elsie would fill in.

One of the QA nurses at the hospital had happened to remark that when she got some leave, she and another sister liked to go to a hotel a mile or two from Auchonville, and rent a room just for the afternoon. There, they'd have a long, luxurious bath, eat cakes and read the latest novelettes, pretending they were having a quiet Sunday back in England.

'I've booked a room,' wrote Rose. *'So if you don't come, I'll sit and stuff myself with food, and drink a bottle of brandy. Then cry all on my own.'*

But Alex came. 'My darling, you're so clever,' he exclaimed, as he came out of the steamy bathroom, looking like a Roman senator, swathed in snow-white towels.

'So where's my Christmas present, then?' asked Rose.

'I *have* got you something.' Alex grinned. 'But if you could have anything you liked, what would it be?'

'Just you,' said Rose. 'I've missed you so much,' she told him, as she kissed him, as she inhaled the scent of warm, clean skin, as she held Alex tight.

* * *

'The manager knows what's going on, but doesn't give a damn.' Rose shrugged like a Frenchman. 'These English nurses, just so many prostitutes and harlots, thank God our lovely French girls don't behave like English whores.'

'If any Frenchman spoke like that in front of me, I'd knock him down,' said Alex. 'God, I hate the French! The British army's trying to defend their stinking country, but all they do is grumble, charge us ten times what their filthy goods and rotten services are worth, and water down the beer.'

'So if we'd let the Germans march through Belgium unmolested, the British wouldn't be in France and the French might actually prefer it?'

'I'd put a bet on that,' said Alex. 'But this summer ought to see the end. It can't go on much longer, after all. There won't be anybody left to fight, and men are going to mutiny if they have to spend another winter up to their necks in slime.'

'I don't know how you stand it.' Rose didn't want to think about what he was going back to, and she didn't want him to think about it either, so she kissed him, then she tickled him until he caught her wrists and forced her back against the pillows.

'Alex,' she continued, 'I knew there was something strange about you. I've just realised what. You don't smell of alcohol today.'

'I'm on the wagon.' Alex wound his fingers in her hair. 'I used to drink because it gave me courage, even though it made me careless, too. I would go on a bombing raid and make lots of mistakes, but I would somehow muddle through. But now I want to stay alive.'

'You mind you do,' said Rose. 'I couldn't bear it if you died.'

'I won't die, I promise. But I don't know what we're going to do when this is over.' Rose saw Alex's eyes grow dark with longing. 'Chloe's given me no grounds for a divorce. Other men will want to marry you, so I may have to let you go.'

'I don't want to go!'

'But Rose, your reputation, your good name—'

'What good name? Everyone in Dorset thinks I must be Daisy's mother, that I'll go with anyone. It doesn't matter. The only thing I care about is you, and if you die—'

'I told you, I'm not going to die. They've tried to kill me — twice they've even buried me, but I came out alive.'

'You might still be hurt, and you know some lives aren't worth living.' Rose looked up at Alex anxiously. 'We're being wicked, and we'll be made to pay.'

'Who is going to punish us?' asked Alex. 'Rose, you're spoiling Christmas.'

'I'm sorry.'

'So you should be.' Alex groped across the bed until he found his jacket. 'I didn't get a chance to go to Bond Street, but I've got you something.'

Rose's eyes lit up. 'I thought you were joking!'

'You might hate it and think it's very old-fashioned, but I think it's pretty.' Alex handed Rose a velvet box. 'It was my mother's.'

'It's beautiful.' Rose took the silver locket from its nest. 'But are you sure you want to give it to me?'

'Yes, Rose, I'm sure.' Alex clipped the locket round her neck.

'I don't have anything for you,' said Rose.

'No?' Alex smiled. 'Rose, I thought you'd given me your heart?'

CHAPTER TWELVE

As he limped along the narrow alley, Nathan stopped occasionally to listen for stealthy footsteps following him.

But there was no sound. He reached the dingy house at the end, and then tapped lightly on the peeling door. 'Phoebe?' he whispered. 'Open up, it's me.'

Nothing broke the silence.

'Phoebe!' Nathan rapped more urgently. 'Come on, it's freezing out here in the street!'

'You got no bloody patience.' As the door creaked open, Nathan saw a wraith with wild, parti-coloured hair and staring, troubled eyes. 'Come in, then,' it said sharply, grabbing his cuff and dragging him inside. 'I 'ope nobody followed you?'

'They didn't, I made sure of that.'

'You got some stuff for me?'

'Yes, but what you need is food, not drugs. Phoebe, when did you last sleep?'

'I can't sleep, you know that.'

'If you don't sleep, you'll die.'

'It'll be a merciful release.'

'I've brought you some *cholent*.' Nathan put the bowl down on the table. 'God, it's cold in here!'

'I don't feel it.' Phoebe grimaced. 'But if you're staying, you could try to start a fire. Them coals is damp, the rain comes down the chimney. But I can't ask Morrie for no more. He's already takin' far too many risks for me.'

Fishing in his pocket, Nathan found a box of matches. He tore up the newspaper in which Mrs Rosenheim had wrapped the bowl of *cholent*, then he stuffed it down between the coals.

He struck a lucifer, knelt to blow gently on the flames, and prayed. The paper flared and, after he'd added a few dry sticks of wood, the damp coals kindled. Soon, there was a blaze.

* * *

Nathan hadn't meant to lumber Morrie with this burden. But three days after Rose had gone to Dorset, taking Phoebe's baby, Phoebe came back to the shop. Frozen, scared and starving, she'd begged them to hide her from Daniel and his friends.

Nathan knew he couldn't ask his mother to take Phoebe in. After the raid, she'd raved and gibbered like a lunatic. Nathan's brothers were dead, her home was ruined. She was half-crazed with grief and fear.

But Morrie Feinman, stage-door keeper at the Haggerston Palace Music Hall, lived in a dilapidated ruin of a house at the far end of a stinking alley where no one ever went.

Everybody knew he hated women. He hated Daniel too and dared to say as much in public, calling him a villain to his face. Nathan supposed he got away with it because their mothers had been related.

'I'll pay you seven shillings a week,' said Nathan.

'You're a fool,' said Morrie.

'If you say so.' Nathan had struggled grimly to his feet. 'I'll look elsewhere.'

'Don't be so hasty, boy. I never said I wouldn't help you and your pretty *shiksa*.' Morrie had bared his blackened stumps of teeth and held out one gnarled hand. 'A fortnight in advance.'

'You won't breathe a word to anybody?'

'You think I'm crazy?' Morrie grinned again. 'I don't want her filthy *goyisch* blood on my clean floor.'

'How is Morrie treating you?' asked Nathan, as he put the dish upon the trivet.

'I 'ardly ever sees him.' Phoebe shivered, rubbed her arms and then ran shaking fingers through her matted, straw-like hair. 'You 'eard from Maria?'

'No, not a thing,' said Nathan. 'But you could write to her yourself.'

'I can't, I'm too ashamed. Anyway, it's better if she don't know where I've gone. I don't suppose she'll want to see me, not now I've disgraced meself.'

'You know Maria's not like that. I think you ought—'

'Well, I ain't goin' to bloody write, an' that's the end of it!'

'Calm down, Phoebe.' Nathan stirred the *cholent* with a blackened, buckled spoon. The appetising smell of peas and barley filled the fusty room.

'Come over here and eat,' urged Nathan gently. 'You need to get your strength back.'

'Do I?' Phoebe looked at him with sad, dull eyes. 'So tell me why?'

'You're young, you're beautiful. You have your life ahead of you.' Nathan smiled, and stirred the food again. 'Come and sit here by the fire, and let me give you some of this *cholent*. It's my mother's speciality. It keeps out the cold.'

* * *

Although it was the coldest, wettest January on record, Rose was never cold. Although she was working double shifts, and sometimes didn't go to bed for three days in succession, merely dozing with her feet up on the big, black stoves that warmed the wards, she was never tired.

Earlier that month, there'd been a gas attack on British trenches to the north of Auchonville, and a ward was allocated to the ten worst cases. Though Rose was seeing terrible, distressing things, and was filled with pity for the choking, gasping, dying men for whom she could do nothing but try to ease their suffering as their lungs dissolved and were coughed up in bloodstained gobbets, she could not be sad.

It was as if she walked with angels, for nothing could upset her, nothing could pierce the armour that was light as thistledown, and which she had worn since that first day she'd realised she was loved.

Their visits to hotels were getting fewer for, as the days were lengthening, the build-up of supplies and ammunition for the great attack meant Alex was kept busy. Miles and miles more trenches spread tentacles across the ruined countryside. Ammunition dumps proliferated, and riding schools and training camps sprang up where there had once been fields.

At the beginning of a dull, damp February, Alex caught a cold that turned into a raging fever. He spent a week in hospital, then was given a few days leave and told to get his strength back before returning to his company.

Rose was delighted when he wrote to tell her he was staying at a guest house near Harfoix, and had asked the owner if his *femme* could come and stay.

'You're as big a liar as me,' said Rose, who had for once arranged legitimate leave.

'I didn't lie, I said you were my *femme*.'

'Your wife — or woman.' Rose was somehow disappointed that the word meant both, that it had not been necessary to lie. 'I couldn't get a ring,' she added. 'So Madame Minot will suspect I'm not your wife.'

'As if it matters.' Alex had been lying on his back staring at the cracks which spread across the dirty ceiling. Now he rolled on to his side and took Rose in his arms. 'She'll get her rotten money, and that's all she cares about. Rose, if I scarpered, I wonder if they'd catch me?'

'Oh, Alex, you're not thinking of deserting?'

'Of course not, I'd be shot. But if I thought I'd get away with it, perhaps I'd walk and keep on walking.'

'Why?' asked Rose, ready to sympathise about the cold and filth and squalor, about the threat of death and injury.

'Because it's all so pointless,' muttered Alex. 'We don't have enough equipment, ammunition, arms — enough of anything.'

'But all those ammunition dumps—'

'For every one of ours, the Germans have a hundred.'

'You're telling me you're afraid?'

'I'm terrified.' Alex looked at Rose. 'I didn't use to be. I thought the men who shirked and cried were cowards, who should be put against the wall. But that was in another life, before I dared to hope. Rose, when I had no hope, I had no fear.'

'I know it must be horrible.' Rose took his hand and stroked the scarred, bruised knuckles. 'I know *I* would be scared.'

'Rose, you don't understand. I'm not exactly scared — most of the time I just get on with it. Sometimes I enjoy it.'

'*Do* you?'

'Yes, because it's all a game, and I'm quite good at it. But soldiers are supposed to fight, and what we're doing these days isn't fighting.'

'What is it, then?'

'We're murdering each other, and it's not the same. Rose, I know I shall get hurt again. One day it will be my turn to die. Once, I accepted it, but now, I *want* my life!'

'I know.' Rose didn't know what else to say. 'Alex, do you hate the Germans?'

'Only when they pinch our food.'

'I'm sorry?'

'They're partial to our bully beef, and they're always mounting raids to steal from our supplies. But the poor sods are stuck in the same filthy holes as us, wondering what their idiot generals are planning next, and wanting to go home.

'They make more effort in their trenches, though. One we captured a few weeks ago had oak-panelled dugouts, with armchairs and a carpet on the floor. It was a real home from home.'

'So did you occupy it?'

'No, we bombed it.' Alex's grin was humourless. 'We can't have *our* chaps getting soft.'

* * *

'Miss Courtenay?' Rose was already fifteen minutes late, and as she panted down the corridor, trying her apron strings and breathing hard, the matron came out of her office. 'I know you're due on Harley Ward, but this won't take a minute, so will you step inside?'

Rose suddenly felt sick. She'd been found out. Someone had seen her on a night time ramble or sitting with Alex in a village square, and now she was about to be sent home.

But the matron didn't look annoyed. She smiled and motioned Rose towards an easy chair. 'You're happy here, Miss Courtenay?' she asked pleasantly.

'Yes, of course,' said Rose.

'You were on the ambulance trains when you first came to France?'

'Yes, that's right.'

'It seems they want you back.'

The matron glanced down at the letter lying on her desk. 'I shall be extremely sad to lose you. I've noticed you often volunteer for extra shifts, and I must admit I've seldom known such a devoted, selfless worker. But you'll be seeing old friends, and I'm sure you'll soon settle down again.'

Rose stared at the matron, horrified. 'Why do they want me?' she cried.

'I believe a certain Staff Nurse Gower asked for you.'

'I see.' Rose cursed Maria. 'Do I have to go?'

'Yes, I'm afraid you do.' The matron spread her hands. 'I know you've got on splendidly with us, and you're very popular with all the staff and men. But the trains need nurses, and you have the necessary skills. Miss Courtenay, you might be a volunteer, but you're an army nurse. So if the army sends for you, you go.'

* * *

'God, it's so unfair!' wailed Rose. 'Why don't I have any say? Matron said how well I'd got on here!'

'It will be exciting.' Elsie put her arm round Rose's shoulders. 'Why don't you want to go?'

'Elsie, you know why!'

'He might get posted to a different sector.' Elsie offered Rose her handkerchief and said to have a good, hard blow. 'The army's always moving them around. How long has he been near Auchonville?'

'Only since last autumn.'

'Then it's time he moved again.'

'Elsie, you're so hard!'

'Rose, I'm realistic.' Elsie smiled in sympathy. 'I'm going to miss you terribly,' she added ruefully. 'I'm not cut out to be a nurse, I don't have your strength and stamina, but you've pulled me through. I'll never get Norah Troy to do my shifts.'

'You'll be all right,' sniffed Rose. 'But Elsie, why *did* you decide to be a nurse?'

'My father's a lieutenant-colonel. My brothers are in Flanders, they're both in the front line. My fiancé's in the army, too. I couldn't sit at home in Kent and *knit*.'

* * *

'It will be an opportunity. You'll be travelling round again, you'll see a bit of France.'

When Alex took this philosophical attitude as well, Rose felt the first stirrings of unease, as if her stomach were full of snakes. They were lying in bed in Madame Minot's sordid guest house, Rose feared for the last time. She looked at Alex, although she knew his face as well or even better than her own.

Since autumn, he had changed. The sullen, sulky boy had disappeared, and although he sometimes scowled or grimaced, he was more often happy and contented.

Or was he complacent?

He had Rose where he wanted her, he knew how much she loved him, so would he move on to some other challenge now? There were scores and scores of pretty nurses, and they would all like Alex, all be enchanted by his lovely smile and fathomless dark eyes.

'I don't want to leave you.' There, she'd said it and he could scoff and grin.

'I don't want you to go. But I'll write every day.'

'It won't be the same.'

'Of course it won't.' He shrugged, and Rose thought bitterly that his awful childhood must have made him stoical — had taught him to accept, not to rebel. 'When I get some leave, I'll come and see you.'

'I won't be able to get away, because those trains are prisons. We live on them, and we're not allowed to leave unless we go in pairs. I'd never be able to slip away and slip back on again — the damned thing would move off and leave me stranded.'

'We'll find a way,' said Alex.

'*You* might find someone else.' Rose felt the tears well up behind her eyes and threaten to spill over. 'I sometimes think all this must be a dream.'

'Then we're both asleep,' said Alex, softly. 'Rose, there'll never be anyone but you, and so you must be careful. I don't want to hear about you falling off a foot-board, or getting squashed between two moving trains.'

'I'll be careful. Alex?'

'Yes?'

'I–I'll write to you.'

'I know you will, and I'll write back. Rose, what's the matter?'

‘Nothing.’ Rose reached for her clothes. ‘I must be going. Elsie can’t manage by herself and Norah’s sick again, so I’m on shift at eight.’

* * *

‘Rose!’ The train was waiting at Amiens, and Maria had obviously been looking out for her, for now she hopped down nimbly. ‘It’s wonderful to see you! How did you get here? By rail from Belancourt, or did you find a lift?’

‘I got a lift.’ Rose blinked back the tears that were threatening to spill over. As she’d watched Alex drive away in the battered vehicle that belonged to his CO, she’d thought her heart would break in little pieces.

‘Come on board, I’ll show you round.’ Maria was relaxed and cheerful, in the highest spirits. ‘This is the best ambulance train we’ve got,’ she went on, proudly. ‘You can’t imagine how much things have changed! We’ve got proper bunks for all the men, the nurses have a bedroom each. The kitchen is all modern, and we’ve got ample room to stow supplies, so we’re not always falling over boxes.

‘We leave at ten o’clock tonight. I think we’re going north. There hasn’t been a battle, but I believe they’re taking lots of punishment up there.’

‘I see,’ said Rose, who didn’t care where she went.

‘Rose?’ Maria finally noticed she was quiet. ‘You don’t have much to say for yourself.’

‘I’m tired.’

‘Poor Rose. Well, Judith and Fiona will soon be back from town, and then we’ll have some supper. You’ll like them, Judith is a scream, she can mimic anybody. You should hear her take off Sister Glossop! Rose, what *is* the matter?’

‘Nothing.’

‘Then why are you so gloomy?’ Maria looked at Rose and frowned. ‘It — it isn’t Phoebe?’

‘It’s not Phoebe.’

'Then who is it — a man?'

Rose nodded miserably.

'There are problems?'

'Yes.'

'He's married?'

'Yes.'

'But you're fond of him?'

'It's more than that, Maria.' Rose began to cry. 'I l-love him more than anything!'

'Then I hope you're being very careful,' said Maria.

'I've been reckless from the start. But it doesn't matter, because I *want* his child.'

'Oh, Rose!' Maria shook her head. 'What does he say about it?'

'I haven't told him yet.'

'You idiot, he'll have to know! You can't cope on your own, and you—'

There was a clatter of boots and suddenly two bright-eyed nurses jumped on to the running board outside the kitchen window. They started making faces through the glass.

'You got that kettle on, Maria?' mouthed a pretty redhead.

'You better have!' went on a tall brunette. 'I'm as dry as the Sahara desert, and my flipping feet are killing me!'

* * *

Alex was trying to stick a plaster on a brand new gash on his right hand when Michael Easton came into the dugout, looking as if he'd eaten bitter aloes.

'Sir?' he muttered, and Alex could see how much it cost the baronet's heir to call the bastard *sir*, 'Major Gethyn says he'd like an urgent word with you.'

'Alex, my dear fellow, you're our man for night patrols.' The major was scowling at a sheet of orders. 'Those machine gun placements opposite — awful nuisance, doing frightful damage to morale. We need you and your chaps to take them out.'

'This evening, sir?' asked Alex, who'd meant to write to Rose, whom he was missing like a body part — which he supposed was not surprising, since she'd made off with his heart and soul.

'If it's not too bright.' The major sniffed. 'I know there's a full moon, but the forecast reckons there'll be cloud. I leave it up to you, but don't wait until the cows come home. I want those buggers sorted out.'

After stand to arms, the cloud banked up. Alex thought he might as well go out, and so he chose a sergeant and another officer, told them to bring as many grenades and bombs as they could carry, then set off.

The gunners weren't exactly opposite. Finding a position from which they could lob their bombs, then hope to make it back to the British lines, involved a half mile slither across a stinking swamp, cutting through a section of the wire, then skulking past some bombed-out houses, which Alex knew might well be occupied by German snipers.

'Almost there, sir,' Sergeant Norris murmured, as they picked their way in freezing darkness past a house, then crouched behind a garden wall.

'Sergeant, you stay here,' said Alex. He had skirted round the wall and could now see their target. 'David, we'll go in and get them panicking. Norris, when you hear the first explosions, throw the heavy ones for all you're worth, then get off home to bed.'

Leaving the sergeant and the bombs, Alex and Lieutenant Richardson slithered on their stomachs through the mud, grenades hung around their waists and slung on bandoliers from their shoulders.

They got so close that they could hear the Germans talking. Alex turned to his companion, signalled he should wait, and then inched forward, pulling out the pin of a grenade.

As he threw it, orange fire lit the night behind him. He turned to see a sheet of flame enveloping Lieutenant Richardson, and Sergeant Norris running like a crab towards the stricken officer. Machine gun bullets threw up sprays of mud and splintered ice.

'Get the bombs off him!' Alex rolled Lieutenant Richardson in the stinking mire, pulling at his belt and tugging at his bandoliers, trying to get them off before the grenades he carried all exploded.

David Richardson was badly burnt. His clothes were charred black shreds, his hair was gone, and strips of skin hung from his back and face.

Alex dragged his own jacket off and wrapped it round the shivering lieutenant. 'David, I'll be back,' he promised. 'Come on, Sergeant Norris. We're going to blow those sods back to their mothers in Berlin.'

* * *

Alex hadn't written for three whole weeks, and now Rose feared the worst. She'd offered God all sorts of deals. Alex could have found another woman, could have even had some sort of grand reunion with Chloe, if he wasn't wounded, wasn't dead.

Then, one morning, she had a premonition of disaster. 'It's all so pointless,' he had muttered. When she'd asked if he was frightened, he had said — what *had* he said? She could not remember.

But if he'd climbed out of a trench one day, walked off and kept on walking, when they caught him he'd be shot.

A fortnight later, she finally had some post. She realised he must have written several dozen letters, but they'd all gone astray. She didn't recognise the writing on the bulky packet, but supposed it was some army clerk's. So where was he, in hospital? Or in some army prison and awaiting execution?

It was even worse than that.

The cutting was from *The Times*. 'Captain Alexander Stephen Denham, 3rd Battalion, Royal Dorset Regiment, died of wounds on February 26,' she read.

Rose stared down at the letters. *'I'll probably get some leave next week,'* he'd written on one he hadn't finished, *'so I'll get a lift to Amiens and hope I can see you.'*

Henry Denham wrote that he'd received all Alex's things, and found Rose's letters in his pack. *'I'm sorry to be the bearer of bad tidings,'* he continued. *'I didn't know you and Alex were so close. My dear, please come and visit me when you are back in England. I'd like to give you some of my boy's things.'*

Henry had sent her all the letters she had written to Alex. Creased and folded and refolded, stained with damp and tattered at the corners, read and read again, they all smelled of dirt and mould and blood.

When Maria came to look for her, Rose was in so much pain she couldn't speak. She couldn't hear, she couldn't see, for a mist has risen and she couldn't grope her way out of the shrouding horror.

'Let's get you to bed.' Rose was aware of somebody undressing her, of tying back her hair, of tucking her between the sheets. Somebody was giving her a drink of something bitter, making her swallow small, reluctant sips.

When she woke again, Maria was sitting on her bed. The train was due to leave at six, and Rose knew she couldn't stay there, taking up a nurse's precious quarters. If she couldn't function, she would have to let them find someone to take her place.

What would she do then? How would she survive the night, all alone and feeling as if she'd been stabbed through the heart?

'Rose?' Maria had brought black coffee. 'I've arranged for you to spend the night in Rouen.'

'I'm staying here with you.'

'Rose, you're in no fit state—'

'Don't you understand, I *need* to work!' Rose met Maria's startled gaze. 'It's either that or lose my mind.'

Rose got up and dressed, plaited her long, dark hair and twisted it into a chignon, and then she went on duty with the rest.

'I'm not the only one,' she told herself, as she moved on down the rocking train, charging carrel tubes, adjusting splints, applying poultices and fomentations.

As she cut off muddied, bloodied uniforms with enormous shears, as she helped the doctor clean then stitch a jagged wound or staunch a flow of blood, she smiled and soothed and murmured words of comfort.

Cheerful, diligent, efficient, that night someone else was occupying Rose's body. She was in another place and in another time, and far away.

CHAPTER THIRTEEN

'You're only one of thousands,' Rose told herself repeatedly, as she tried to batten down the pain. 'Every minute of every day, some poor woman gets a telegram. They loved their men as much as you loved him.'

'They couldn't have done,' her other self replied.

She worked every shift she could, but sometimes she was forced to take some rest. Then, as she lay sleepless, the bad thoughts came crowding in.

'It's your fault he's dead,' they whispered. 'You knew it was wrong, and that you'd both be punished. You killed Alex Denham as surely as if you'd stabbed him through the heart. Why don't you kill yourself, and make an end of it?'

But she knew she couldn't kill herself. If she did, she'd be a murderess, as well as all the other awful things. This new life inside her was her inheritance, her last precious gift from him and, although she didn't know how she'd cope alone and friendless, she was determined she would find a way.

She thought of Alex's mother, who had done her blundering best for him. But she would not rely on men. She'd go back to England soon, and find herself a job. She'd say she was a widow. She would have the baby, and then work for them both. They would be a little family.

* * *

The trains went back and forth, thundering through the night at breakneck speed towards another scene from hell, then trundling slowly back to bases in the towns or on the coast with yet more loads of pain and misery.

Rose started to get heartburn, backache, morning sickness that went on all day. The sweet, rotting smell of wounds made her feel nauseous, and often she would have to go and vomit secretly in buckets already full of bloodstained dressings.

The buttons on her dress began to strain to meet around her middle, her breasts were swollen and her ankles puffy, so her boots were much too tight.

One March evening, as they sped east towards another casualty clearing station to collect another crisis load, Maria found her sitting in the kitchen, staring through the glass at the black night.

'Rose?' Maria touched her shoulder. 'Sister Glossop's just been told there's been a raid near Albert. There are lots of casualties, so we'll be very busy coming back. I think you ought to go to bed.'

'Why?' asked Rose.

'If you don't rest, you're going to have a breakdown.'

'Who would care?'

'Rose, you're my friend, and *I* would care!' Maria sat down too. 'But I care about the men, as well. You're exhausted, and exhausted people make mistakes. You won't notice someone's bleeding, that a carrel tube is blocked. You'll make errors that will cost men's lives.'

Maria took Rose's cold hands and rubbed warmth into them. 'Do you still feel sick?' she asked.

'A bit, but that's the train.'

'When will it begin to show?'

'It won't,' said Rose. She bit her lip and looked away. She was determined not to cry. 'I got the curse this morning, and I've been bleeding like a pig all day. Maria, I've lost everything.'

'Oh, sweetheart!' cried Maria.

'I know you're going to say it's for the best.'

'I wouldn't be so cruel.' Maria put her arm round Rose's shoulders. 'I'll help you get through this, I promise. You did so much for Phoebe.'

'Have you heard from Phoebe?'

'No.' Maria shrugged. 'I've written care of Mrs Rosenheim, but there's no news, they don't know where she's gone, if she's alive or dead. Rose, do you write to Mrs Hobson?

'Yes, and she wrote back last week. Daisy's doing well. I meant to tell you.' Rose looked at Maria with haunted eyes. 'Do you think I'm useless, then? Should I go back to England?'

'No, but you should try to rest, and remember everyone needs sleep. You're a splendid nurse. You work so hard, you're always kind and gentle with the men, and Sister Glossop thinks the world of you.'

'I'm a whore. A wicked, worthless liar. A stupid, greedy harlot who took someone else's man.'

* * *

Nathan was beginning to think there must be someone looking after him. Otherwise he wouldn't have managed to crawl the length of this foul, reeking alley.

But there was no God. If there were, he wouldn't let scum like Hanson walk the earth, much less do the things that Hanson's friends had done tonight.

He didn't dare go home. His mother would have a heart attack if she saw him in this state, bruised and bleeding with a broken nose, split lips and half his teeth knocked out.

He knew he must be dripping blood and leaving a thin trail of it along the grimy pavements. After the men had finished kicking him, a dog ran up to lick his bleeding face. As he crawled painfully away, it followed him down the street. As he groped his way along the alley, rats came from their holes to look at him.

He kept going, inching forward on his knees along the bumpy cobbles, and finally he reached the house where Phoebe was in hiding. He tapped with bleeding knuckles on the door.

Phoebe gasped in horror when she saw him. 'It's all right,' he managed to croak, before collapsing like a sack of offal on the threshold. 'No one followed me.'

She dragged him in and laid him on the couch. Then she washed his face, clucking in dismay as all the damage was revealed. 'I think your nose is broken,' she began, and winced as much as he did as she dabbed it with a sponge.

'I dare say you're right.' He could feel broken bone and gristle loose inside the jelly of his face. 'It's a shame I couldn't find my teeth. I've heard that if you stick them back in time, they root again.'

'Oh, Nathan!' Phoebe's brown eyes filled. 'Why did they hurt you?'

'You know why.' Nathan shrugged, then winced again. 'But I didn't tell them anything.'

'You should have done!' cried Phoebe. 'I never expected you to run such risks! I never wanted you to take such punishment for me!' Phoebe started crying. 'I n-never knew you were so brave.'

'Phoebe, I'm not brave. They didn't offer me a choice, they didn't ask if I was scared. Even if I'd told them where you were, they'd still have beaten me.'

'They know you're not afraid of him, and that makes you braver than anybody else in Bethnal Green.'

Phoebe looked at Nathan's battered face, into his blackened eyes. 'Daniel is a vicious, evil man. Everyone in the Green is scared of him and all his friends, but I don't think you've ever been afraid. It must be because you're so religious. You believe in God.'

'I believe in God?' Nathan would have laughed if he had not had broken ribs and even breathing had not been so painful. 'I go to the study house to please my mother.'

'But you're going to be a rabbi?'

'I don't think so, Phoebe.' Nathan's split lip twisted bitterly. 'You know my father died in Russia, killed by Cossacks as he tried to stop the sons of Satan from burning down his home. My brothers have been killed in France, in a useless war in which the Russians are our allies — may their evil names be blotted out! Even here in England, death comes falling from the sky.'

He coughed, and spat out bits of tooth and clots of bright red blood. 'How could I stand up in a synagogue, and tell the people to believe in a just God, when I don't believe in one myself?'

'Then how do you manage to be so brave?'

'I told you, I'm not brave.' Nathan looked at Phoebe. 'But I want to live, and what's the point of living if you're afraid? Phoebe, I think you should get out of London.'

'But where else could I go?'

'My mother has some relatives in Leeds. I'll write them, I'm sure they'll take you in.'

'Nathan, why are you doin' this for me?'

'You know,' said Nathan. 'I think you've always known.'

* * *

Later, Phoebe watched him sleep. Morrie made a song and dance when he returned from bullying the chorus girls, sweeping out the Palace and probably giving Daniel Hanson lip.

But when he realised the blood that stained the horsehair couch was Nathan's, as opposed to Phoebe's gentile gore, he quietened down again.

'I'll go and tell old mother Rosenheim her precious Nathan's stayin' 'ere tonight,' he muttered sourly. 'It won't do 'er any good to see 'im in that mess.'

'You mustn't tell 'er I'm 'ere, too!' cried Phoebe. 'She don't know where I am — an' anyway, she wouldn't like to think that me and Nathan was alone.'

'She knows her boy's been sweet on you since you was four years old.' Morrie sucked his stumps of teeth and grinned. 'What 'appened to that nipper you was 'avin'?' he demanded.

'It — it died.' Phoebe turned away to look at Nathan, who seemed fast asleep.

'Just as well, I reckon.' Morrie chewed the insides of his cheeks. 'A girl like you ain't fit to be a mother, ain't cut out to fetch up kids. I meant to ask you — 'ow's your stuck-up sister gettin' on? The one what learned to talk like Lady Muck an' went to be a nurse?'

'Maria went to France.'

'Oh, did she?' Morrie shook his grizzled head. 'A dirty lot, them French. You mark my words — one day we'll see 'er an' 'er belly come waddlin' up the Green.'

* * *

March turned into April, covering the land with green and hiding some of what the shells had done the previous winter.

The spring gave way to a warm May, and in spite of grief that dragged her down, Rose sometimes felt her broken spirits lifting. This year, she thought, would see the end of it. This summer would be when the Allies gained the upper hand.

She read the newspapers and knew that back in England more than half a million conscripts were learning how to fire a rifle, lob grenades and use a bayonet. Bank clerks, farming lads and civil servants were being turned into soldiers.

Factories were making bombs and shells by the ten million. This June or July, the Allies would overwhelm the German army and send it packing to Berlin.

One balmy afternoon the train was in a siding outside Amiens. The engine driver had a nap while the nurses waited for a lorry to bring down fresh supplies of dressings, food and medicine.

'You asleep?' Maria asked, as she flopped down by Rose who was sitting on the running board.

'Just dozing.' Rose said, stretching. 'When will we be off?'

'Oh, we've got an hour or two, don't worry.' Maria turned her face towards the sun. 'Sister Glossop said we're waiting for a dozen troop trains to go through.'

'So this is it,' said Rose.

'Yes, I reckon this is where we're going to make the breakthrough, in the valley of the Somme. Rose, you look quite well today. You actually have some colour in your cheeks. How do you feel?'

'I'm fine.'

'You're not exactly fine. You still cry at night, and some mornings you look terrible. But today, you seem much better, so you're coping, getting stronger.'

Rose supposed Maria must be right. Sitting here in the warm sunshine, she was not in pain. The awful, sickening, churning misery, the debilitating grief that threatened to destroy her sanity, overwhelmed her only now and then.

On a day like this, she could be philosophical. She could think about him without crying. Even God could not change history, and she blessed the day they'd met in Rouen, when he'd told her what she'd known since that appalling party.

They'd wasted so much time. But the months they'd had together had been worth a lifetime of regret.

'Letters, Sisters!' An orderly came striding down the track, carrying the canvas bag he'd taken off the lorry that had just pulled up beside the line. 'Here you are, Miss Courtenay, three for you.'

Rose glanced through them. One from Celia Easton, one from Elsie, one from — no, it couldn't be, after what had happened. But all the same, he'd written.

So perhaps he'd changed his mind?

CHAPTER FOURTEEN

Then she realised he must be dead, that this was something found among his things, to be sent to the daughter he'd disowned. It would a legacy of blame, saying she was responsible for Lady Courtenay's death, and she'd also driven her father to an early grave.

She wondered who would inherit Charton Minster, but couldn't summon up the strength to care. Opening the letter, she saw there were several pages, covered with Sir Gerard Courtenay's bold, Victorian script.

'My dear Rose,' he'd written, which was the first surprise.

'I hope you are in good health, and doing well in France.

'When you were last in Dorset, we parted on bad terms. You may have regretted certain hasty things you said to me. You have always been inclined to speak first and think later. We are father and daughter still, however, and although a less forgiving parent might have been more harsh with you, I am prepared to overlook your faults and lay no blame.

'Michael Easton had some leave a couple of weeks ago, and came to see me. Michael is an excellent young man, who is bravely doing his duty to his king and country. In spite of

all the hardships that our gallant officers are suffering in this present crisis, he was bearing up remarkably.

'He still respects and honours you. Last autumn, he could have withdrawn his offer of marriage, and I would not have blamed him. But it seems this fine young man is still in love with you, and still wishes you to be his wife.

'I urge you to think about this very seriously. It is what your mother would have wanted and would give me tremendous pleasure, too. Michael knows you are my heir, but he has expectations of his own, and I feel he is a generous man who would love a beggar maid if her mind and character were pure.

'I should be so pleased to see you settled with a husband who could guide you and protect you, and form your opinions, for the rest of what I hope will be a useful life.'

'It's good news, I hope?' enquired Maria.

'Well, it isn't bad.' Rose put the letter in her apron pocket, and looked at Maria thoughtfully. 'I didn't know my father was a such a gullible old man.'

She stood up and stretched. 'Come on, let's help the men with those supplies.'

* * *

As Rose laid out dressings on the trays and made up quarts of sterilising fluid, she thought of Michael Easton, the fine young man who fathered children then abandoned them, and who was interested in Rose because one day she'd have some money.

Then Michael wrote himself, to say he still had one day's leave, and he'd like to meet her for a chat. Maybe he could take her out to tea, the next time she was due in Rouen?

She thought perhaps she ought to go and meet him. If she didn't, Michael would probably tell her father she was being difficult. Sir Gerard would write again, and so it would go on.

She couldn't pretend she wasn't allowed to see him by herself. These days, all the rules and regulations that had governed nurses' conduct since the beginning of the war were very much relaxed. In the early summer of 1916, it was common to see sisters arm in arm with officers, sitting in cafés with their beaux and flirting decorously.

Three weeks later, Michael was waiting on the station platform as the train pulled in. She saw him from the window, and realised she'd forgotten he was so handsome, so broad-shouldered and so tall. In his smart, clean uniform and highly-polished boots, he looked every inch the gallant British officer and perfect gentleman.

'Hello, Rose,' he said. He turned to the lieutenant at his side. 'This is Freddie Lomax, he's in my company.'

'Good afternoon, Miss Courtenay. I've heard so much about you.' Freddie Lomax smiled. He shook hands with Rose, then turned to Michael. 'Miss Courtenay's even prettier than you said.'

Maria and Fiona had been too tired to go walking, but Rose persuaded Judith to go with her into Rouen. When the cathedral was in sight, Michael's friend took Judith off towards the nearest shops, while Michael led Rose down a narrow alley. 'It's a short cut,' he said.

When they were half way down, he stopped and penned her up against a wall, his hands on either side of her so she could not escape.

'I thought you were taking me to tea,' she said, hoping he wasn't going to try to kiss her or anything like that.

'First of all we need to clear the air,' said Michael gravely.

'What do you mean?'

'Rose, that little girl is *not* my child!' Michael's large, blue eyes were wide and candid. 'Celia told me what you did, how you went to London, and how you brought the baby back to Dorset. It was jolly decent of you to care, and now things have settled down, everyone agrees it was a splendid thing to do.

'But whatever Phoebe may have told you, she and I — Rose, I know I'm fallible. But I have more integrity than that.'

'You're saying you never went to bed with Phoebe?'

'No, upon my honour.'

Rose looked at him and wondered who was lying — him or Phoebe? But she was far too tired to argue. She didn't have any proof that he had ever slept with Phoebe, anyway. So she decided she'd back down — at least for now.

'You must be very angry with me, then,' she said. 'I'm sorry, Michael, I didn't even think about the consequences for you. But when Phoebe told me—'

'There's no need to apologise,' smiled Michael. 'It's turned out for the best. The baby has a proper home, and Celia has an interest in life. Of course, we can't keep Daisy down in Dorset. When the war is over, we'll have to look for Phoebe. Then we can reunite her with the child.'

'You're being very reasonable about it.' Rose hoped Michael couldn't hear the insincerity in her voice.

'I don't see the need to make a fuss.' Michael stroked a strand of Rose's hair back from her forehead. She felt as if a spider's web had brushed against her face, and needed all her self-control not to shudder.

'Do you have an answer to the question I asked you, long before this wretched business started?' Michael smiled again. 'I said I wouldn't rush you, and I won't. But I went to see your father when I was on leave. Poor man, he's lost so much.'

'I know.'

'He'd be thrilled if you and I got married.'

Rose looked up at Michael. She wondered if it might work out. She wanted children, Michael would need an heir to his estate and, if she married him, she'd have a home, security, a spotless reputation. Nobody in Charton, even Mrs Sefton, would dare disparage Michael Easton's wife.

One day, she'd be Lady Easton. Could she love Sir Michael? Maybe not, but it would not be hard to be his wife. If she closed her eyes, she could imagine — but that would not be fair. 'Let me have a week or two?' she asked him.

'I don't want to hurry you. I know you'd like to see some more of life before you finally settle down. You nurses are doing splendid work in France. So just tell me when the answer's yes.'

'You're being very understanding.' Rose felt she was being stifled. It was as if a soft but heavy pillow were being pressed against her face. Ducking under Michael's arm, she walked off down the alley.

He soon caught up. 'I suppose you heard about poor Denham?'

'I — yes,' she managed to say at last, glad they were no longer face to face.

'Old Henry's terribly cut up. Alex wasn't his son, of course, but the poor chap treated him like one. He must feel the loss.'

'You went to see him, then?'

'Celia and I drove over there one morning. I thought it might buck him up a bit. He asked what happened and, when I explained, he cried.'

'What did happen, then?' asked Rose, wanting to know but dreading it.

'He'd gone out on patrol with two more men. They were carrying grenades, and when he got hit they all exploded. Some Irish Guards out mending wire found him, burnt to death.'

'How horrible.' Rose felt Michael's gaze upon her, but she couldn't look at him.

'At least they got the body back,' said Michael. 'They found his papers in his pockets, badly singed but legible. Paper doesn't always burn, you see. Especially if it's damp. So even if they're in a shocking state, bodies can often be identified.'

'W-where is he buried?' faltered Rose.

'In a cemetery near St Etienne.' Michael was still looking at her, and now his voice was sharp. 'Why do you ask?'

'I was just making conversation.' Rose dug her nails into her palms, determined she would not betray her lover, that she would not cry.

'I understand the body was in an awful mess,' continued Michael. 'It wouldn't have survived the trip back home. It could have been much worse, though. Those two other chaps weren't ever found. A bit rough on their families, and—'

'Michael, I don't want to know all this.' Rose's throat had closed. The tang of roasted flesh was in her nostrils, and she felt light-headed.

But Michael carried on. 'Denham was always reckless,' he continued. 'Always out on night patrol, or on hare-brained escapades that didn't ever amount to anything. Some of the chaps said he was brave, but Denham wasn't brave. He was over-confident and took too many risks, usually with other people's lives.

'Ah, here it is — the Golden Bell. I hope you're hungry, Rose? I must say I could eat a horse.'

* * *

'I'm fine,' said Rose when she and Judith got back on the train.

'Well, you don't *look* fine.' Maria frowned. 'You've had more colour lately, but tonight you're pale as death.'

'I'm tired, like all of us,' said Rose. 'I'll be all right, don't make a fuss. Maria, where exactly is St Etienne?'

'Twenty or thirty miles away, I think.' Maria shrugged. 'It's just a tiny place. A couple of streets, a baker's shop, a church, some little farms. There's an army hospital a mile or two outside.'

'Does it have cemetery?'

'Yes, I think it does.'

Then Maria understood.

* * *

The trains went back and forth, sometimes with heavy loads of wounded after raids or skirmishes, sometimes just half full, for there had been no battles or disasters that warm, pleasant summer. In the valley of the Somme there was a slow but steady build-up of artillery, and increasing restlessness among officers and men.

Then the guns began to roar, and by the end of June everyone in the district was half deafened, for the barrage carried on and on, night and day and day and night, remorseless and unending.

'There can't be any Germans left alive along this stretch of front,' observed Maria, as the guns continued to pound a countryside in which Rose thought nothing could survive.

Then, as suddenly as they'd started, all the guns fell silent.

'Ladies, we've attacked!' As Rose and Maria stood in the sluice making up some demi-johns of Dakin's antiseptic, Sister Glossop bustled down the corridor, the streamers on her head-dress flying and her sharp glance darting everywhere, as she checked for smuts or specks of grime that might have dared pollute her pristine train.

Rose felt the thud and shudder as the engine coupled with the carriages behind it, and soon the train was racing eastwards through the glorious summer afternoon.

'We're probably going to have to treat a lot of wounded Germans,' Sister Glossop told them. 'So although we must be fair, of course our soldiers must take precedence.'

'Do we keep the Germans and our boys apart?' Maria asked.

'Yes, it might be best.' The sister smiled complacently. 'But there shouldn't be many of our own chaps needing treatment. This must have been a splendid day for them!'

The orderlies and nurses didn't rush to make up bunks or set out trays of dressings. There wasn't any need, if they would be returning with an almost empty train.

* * *

'How many?' called Maria, as the carriages shuddered to a halt and a man in khaki came running up the railway line.

'It'll be thousands, Sister!' Rose could see the man looked grey. 'Our lads are being massacred over there! It's not a battle, it's a slaughter!'

'But we thought this was going to be the end?' Rose could hear the rumble of what she feared must be German guns. She could see the flashes as shells burst overhead, although the day was bright. 'A great attack, they told us. The Germans would be finished. Our guns have been firing at them for a week or more, so surely almost everyone is dead?'

'We might have wounded one or two.' The soldier wiped his hand across his eyes. 'The barrage didn't even cut the wire, let alone kill Germans. When our lads went over, the Jerries came out of their dugouts, and then they gunned them down.'

'But what about the British guns? Our men surely didn't go over without our guns supporting them?'

'I don't know what happened, Sister, but it was a balls-up.' The soldier turned to stare along the track. 'You'd better roll your sleeves up. Here they come.'

Rose watched aghast as stretcher after stretcher case was loaded, as the bunks were filled and men were dumped down on the floor, in all the corridors and even in the sluice.

'We can't take any more,' cried Sister Glossop, as stretcher bearers clambered over bodies, looking for spaces underneath the bunks, shoving two wounded men together so they could squash a third, a fourth in somehow, somewhere, anywhere. 'We won't have room to move.'

'Major Leighton's orders, Sister,' said a stretcher bearer who was carrying a slim, blond boy, and who looked like some appalling mummer from a ghastly carnival. Ribbons of soiled dressings hung like summer fairings round his neck, his cheeks were striped with gore, and his khaki overall was streaked and splashed with blood. 'You must take eighty more, and pack them in.'

'We can't,' repeated Sister Glossop, looking as if she'd cry.

'I'm sorry, Sister, but the major says you must.' The stretcher bearer gently moved the sister to one side, then lugged the pale, blond boy on to the train.

Eventually the train moved off, clanking and swaying as it chugged away from Armageddon. The orderlies and nurses began to cut off filthy, muddied uniforms and tried to staunch the flow of blood from men whose bodies looked like human sieves.

As one man was treated, Rose was horribly aware that the one in the next bunk was dying. She worked with desperate haste, and soon her apron, sleeves and cuffs were wringing wet with blood.

The floor was ankle deep in blood, dripping from men who lay like leaking wineskins on the bunks, the shelves, the floor. Everywhere she looked, Rose saw scenes from some appalling nightmare. She slopped and squelched her way down corridors awash with blood, swirling and foaming with the jolting movement of the train, like some devil's wash day.

The long summer twilight ended. A host of stars lit up the purple sky, and less than half the casualties had been seen. Rose worked on doggedly. The fumes of chloroform the doctor used on men who needed an immediate amputation made her feel light-headed. As she passed a table where an orderly was trying to get a sergeant to go under anaesthetic, she tripped and nearly fell.

'All right, Sister?' asked the blood-boltered orderly who'd caught her, as the chloroform-soaked pad he wielded hit her squarely in the face.

'I'm fine,' she said, and swayed on down the train. But now the soldiers all merged into one amorphous mass. They swam together in a shoal of khaki, then retreated in a blood-stained haze.

'Go and get some air, or you'll pass out!' Grabbing Rose and dragging her towards an open window, Maria pushed Rose's head right out and told her to inhale.

'Come on, Rose!' she cried. 'Some nice deep breaths! Great lungfuls — breathe in — out — and in again! Feeling better now?'

'Yes, thank you.' Shuddering and gasping, Rose came back inside. 'My m-mother always told me it was very dangerous to lean out of a train,' she gulped, as she wiped a blood-stained hand across her streaming eyes.

'Did she, now?' Maria somehow managed a faint smile. 'Try not to look so worried, Rose,' she said. 'You're doing very well.'

'But we'll never see to all of them before we get to Rouen. What will happen to the ones we haven't got round to treating?'

'Do what you can, be glad we're saving some.' Maria shrugged. 'But most of them will die.'

Rose went on down the train. In one carriage there were half a dozen dark-haired officers, all with dreadful wounds. They all had Alex's face. Those who still had faces, anyway.

As Rose cut away the shirt of one, she was almost glad Alex had died. He wouldn't have wanted to have been a human gargoyle with half a mangled body or a nightmare of a face. He was better off dead.

* * *

The days became a blur of blood and bone-weary fatigue. The trains went backwards, forwards, racing to the railhead at Vecquement-sur-Somme, loading up with broken bodies and slowly trundling west to Rouen with their freight of suffering and death.

Sometimes, Rose looked up at the sky and saw how blue it was, how beautiful. Just as it should be in July, she thought, when these conscripted shop assistants, clerks and office boys ought to have been walking in the parks and showing off to girls, taking Sunday trips to Margate or Southend, but instead were being murdered and mutilated on the Somme.

'What were our generals thinking of?' As they cleared up at the end of yet another gruelling journey, Maria's tone was light and conversational, but her eyes were hard as tempered steel. 'When the wretched Germans saw our men come out and walk towards their blasted guns, I don't suppose they could believe their luck.'

'What do you mean?' asked Judith, yawning.

'Surely you've heard what the men are saying? That first day, they were supposed to take possession of German trenches full of German dead. But they walked into a hail of fire. It was like a shooting gallery, I heard one man say. The Germans sat in their machine gun nests, and cut our soldiers down.'

* * *

It remained a shooting gallery. The optimism of that first summer morning died with all the murdered men. But still the Allied troops were sent to try to take a wood, a trench, a village, and still they were cut down.

'When we've unloaded, shall we go and get something to eat?' Maria asked Rose, as the train came trundling into Rouen with its dreadful cargo, one evening in the middle of July.

Tonight, thought Rose, Maria looked like a butcher's boy, in an apron striped and smeared with blood, in boots slick and encrusted with the blood that dripped on to the floor as young men died.

As she washed her hands and face, dyeing the water orange-red, Rose thought she would always smell the blood, would always have that sweet, metallic tang inside her nostrils. She rolled down her sleeves and shook her head. 'I'm not really hungry,' she replied.

'Rose, nobody's hungry, but we have to eat, or we'll collapse. Judith, you come too. We're only going to the Red Cross café in the square, just to have some toast or something, otherwise we'll die.'

As they ate their toast and drank their tepid, bitter coffee, Sister Glossop came into the café. When Rose had met her first, she'd been a spruce, determined woman who looked like a busy, speckled hen.

Now she was bedraggled and looked ill. She was a veteran of the Boer War, an army nurse who Rose could see had always managed to take control of things, and put wounds and sickness in their place.

But she couldn't cope with wholesale murder. 'We have to leave again in half an hour,' she murmured, as she sat down heavily. 'My dear Miss Courtenay, when did you last sleep? You look terrible.'

Rose didn't have the nerve to tell the sister she looked dreadful, too.

The train sped back to Vecquement, pulling into a siding where electric lights were trained on wires, and where the wounded waited, sitting, lying or wandering aimlessly about.

The stretcher bearers carried in the worst ones, laying them down on bunks still stained and bloodied from the men who'd bled in them before. Rose picked up her shears and started work.

Leaning over one unconscious man whose legs were mangled and would probably be amputated as the train sped west, she had a sudden sense of déjà-vu.

Looking at the shoulder flashes on his bloodstained jacket, she saw he was from the Royal Dorsets, that he was broad-shouldered and well-made, and that his hair was dark.

She suddenly felt nauseous, and the world began to swim. She held on to the bunk to keep her balance. But of course it wasn't Alex. This man was the officer who'd been with Michael Easton, when they'd met for tea that day in Rouen.

Lieutenant Lennox? No, Lieutenant Lomax, Freddie Lomax. She felt his pulse and grimaced. He wasn't going to live. He'd lost far too much blood, and his face already had the grey-green otherworldly look that meant only a miracle could save him.

As she cut away his shirt and saw the bullet wounds that made a ghastly pattern on his chest, his dark eyes flickered open.

'Freddie?' she said gently. 'You're very badly wounded, but we'll do our best for you.'

Freddie Lomax looked at her, but couldn't seem to focus. As she began to clean him up, he closed his eyes and died.

She left him, moved on down the train, surrounded by the dreadful sights of broken, tortured men, some of them boys years younger than herself, whose suffering could not be eased because there was no time to give them pain-relieving morphine.

As their wounds were probed and cleaned, they tried not to cry out. They didn't want to be a nuisance even as they died.

As Judith passed her, carrying a kidney bowl and knuckling her eyes, Rose was glad she didn't have a heart, that it was safely buried with Alex in the army cemetery at St Etienne.

The machine that these days pumped her blood around her body did a splendid job, and now she was a mere automaton. She wasn't even hungry. She found she could keep going for hours, for days, on coffee and dry toast.

It was only when she had to deal with someone who'd been burnt, who'd been blown up or set on fire, when she had to look into a young man's ruined face, that she wanted to sit down and cry.

* * *

They got back in the early hours to find some letters waiting. So, after all the casualties had been carried off the train and taken to the hospital ships tied up along the river, Maria made some coffee, and the nurses sat down in the kitchen.

'These must be from some of the boys we've nursed.' Maria fanned her letters out. 'It's always nice to hear from them.'

'But have you heard from Phoebe?' Rose enquired.

'No.' Maria shrugged. 'So what have you got — anything exciting?'

'I don't think so.' Rose smiled wearily. 'I'm too tired to read them anyway.'

CHAPTER FIFTEEN

'You left them in the kitchen,' said Maria, as she handed Rose her letters later that same morning. 'Go on, open them.'

So Rose scanned the first.

'He had a septic finger,' Celia said.

'Just a little cut. But he must have got some dirt in it, because his whole hand swelled up horribly. He couldn't hold a rifle, so he missed the great attack. We are so relieved! You will be, too. Apparently, Michael is the sole survivor of the 3rd Battalion. The rest of them are dead.

'Daisy is very well. Her hair is curling into ringlets and she has two new teeth. She is a sweet, contented child and a great favourite with Mrs Hobson. I hope to have her picture taken soon, and I shall send you a print. I've not heard from her mother. But if she is a low, loose-living woman, I suppose we shouldn't be surprised.

'My knitting circle goes from strength to strength. We've made a splendid effort this July — four thousand pairs of socks and fifteen hundred balaclavas are on their way to France.'

Rose went to help the others make up bunks. 'Daisy's very well,' she told Maria, who she knew was saving up her leave and hoped to go to England soon. 'If we could get some leave together, we could go and see her, maybe.'

'You mean go to Dorset?' frowned Maria. 'I'm not sure I'd be welcome.'

'Yes, you would,' insisted Rose. She suddenly had a brainwave. 'We could stay at Henry Denham's house. He asked me to go and see him, and I'm sure he'd put us up.'

Rose pushed her other letters into her pocket. She'd seen there was another from her father, in which he'd be asking why she hadn't given the gallant Michael her consent to be his wife. She was getting sick and tired of being badgered.

The bunks were almost done, the trays were laid. Glancing at her watch, she decided she could snatch ten minutes. She'd write to Sir Gerard now, and tell him she wasn't going to marry Michael Easton. Then she'd write to Michael, saying she hoped they'd always be good friends, but she couldn't be his wife.

As she walked back to her own couchette, she opened the third letter. This was written on cheap blue Forces paper, much stamped and franked and creased. Misdirected, it had followed her around, and finally caught up with her in Rouen.

It would be from a soldier she had nursed, thanking her for what she'd done, telling her he was fit again and ready to go back.

Hearing this invariably depressed her, for it seemed a futile waste of time to mend a man only to send him back to be blown up again or killed.

She took out the single sheet inside.

'My dearest Rose,' she read. *'Since I'm not yet able to hold a pen myself, a sister is kindly writing this for me.'* She scanned the rest in mounting disbelief.

'Maria!' Rose ran down the empty train. Laughing and crying all at once, she blundered into empty bunks and scraped her knees and shins, but didn't notice, didn't care.

She finally found Maria in the sluice, washing a stack of kidney bowls. 'Maria, look!' she cried. 'Maria, it's a miracle! He's alive!'

'Miss Courtenay?' Before Maria could ask Rose what was going on and why she was hysterical, Sister Glossop bustled in. 'A little more decorum, if you please.'

'Oh, Sister Glossop!' Thrusting the letter at Maria, Rose beamed at the sister, knuckling her tears away and gulping like a goldfish out of water. She made an effort to calm down. 'May I have some leave?'

'I beg your pardon?' Sister Glossop frowned, and shadows like raw liver deepened underneath her eyes. 'Miss Courtenay, there's a battle going on. I'm sure you must have noticed?'

'Just twelve hours, Sister Glossop, please!' Rose was jigging up and down, a sprat upon a griddle. 'I'll do extra shifts, I'll work a twenty-four hour day, I'll cover sickness, everything. But please let me have a pass tonight!'

Sister Glossop looked at Rose. 'I've never heard you laugh before, Miss Courtenay. I didn't think you could. But no, you can't have leave.'

'I'll cover Rose's shifts.' Maria looked earnestly at Sister Glossop. 'I know she'll do mine for me.'

Sister Glossop frowned. 'This is a family matter, I assume?'

'Rose's cousin,' said Maria glibly.

'Really?' Sister Glossop raised one eyebrow. 'Oh — very well, Miss Courtenay. You'll have to work tonight, but if you'll make the time up later, you may have tomorrow off.' The sister smiled grimly. 'That's provided Dr Wood agrees.'

Maria grinned at Rose. They knew it was unlikely young Dr Wood, the officer nominally in charge, would dare to challenge Sister Glossop.

* * *

Rose went by train to Egreville, a small town near the Belgian border. Then she hitched a lift to Valoucourt, a tiny village. Asking for directions in her halting schoolgirl French, she walked for miles down muddy tracks until she came to Forges les Eaux.

Left empty by the family that owned it because it was so close to the front line, the manor house had been taken over by the British army. As its roof and turrets loomed between the summer trees, she slowed her pace. She was trying to remember what Michael had said about the night patrol. She wished she'd questioned him more closely.

There had been two other men with Alex, she did remember that. All three had presumably been carrying grenades. If they'd been hit, they'd probably have gone up like Roman candles.

He had said he couldn't hold a pen. She shuddered as she realised his strong brown hands would now be stiff red claws, that couldn't manage anything as subtle as a pen. As for his face — she didn't want to think about his face.

She had heard there was a special hospital in London that was making marvellous lifelike masks, based on army photographs, for men with damaged faces. Perhaps they could help Alex. Maybe in due course he would be able to face the world again.

Rose squared her shoulders. Whatever Alex looked like now, whatever awful damage the flames had done to him, to Rose he'd always be the slim, brown boy who had bewitched her with his lovely smile and great dark eyes.

What if those eyes were blind?

It didn't matter. She would love him still. She would leave the VAD, and take him home to Dorset. She'd find a house and get a job. She would look after him.

She walked up to the gatehouse.

'Good morning, Sister,' said the orderly on duty. He took in Rose's filthy boots and grass-stained, mud-streaked skirt. 'You must have walked a tidy way.'

'I'm sure the exercise has done me good.' Rose smiled at him. 'I've come to visit Captain Denham.'

* * *

'I understand he was quite badly hurt?' As Rose followed a blue-skirted nurse along a polished corridor, she raked her fingers through her messy hair.

She knew she looked a sight. They'd made her leave her muddy boots outside, and the nurse had stared astonished at her dirty dress.

'Quite badly, yes.' The nurse turned back to smile. 'But he's getting stronger every day. Now he can remember things that happened before the raid, he's looking brighter.' She opened the door into a sunny ward. 'Here we are, Miss Courtenay. Please come in.'

Rose took a deep breath, then followed the nurse into the ward. She hoped she'd see him first. She knew what fire could do to human flesh, but she still felt the need to be prepared, then she wouldn't look shocked or horrified. She wouldn't upset *him*.

'Where is he?' she whispered.

'Over in the corner, by the window.'

Rose looked, and saw the man she'd always known. He was a little thinner in the face, but apart from that he hadn't changed. Dressed in the usual loose, hospital blues, he was sitting reading, and hadn't noticed anyone come in.

Relief and gratitude to somebody or something made her feel light-headed, and she was afraid she might pass out. But she drew a deep, relaxing breath, then walked up to him on stealthy, stockinged feet.

'Alex?' she said softly, crouching down beside his chair.

'Rose?' At first he looked as if he'd seen a ghost, but then the smile he gave her made her want to sing.

* * *

'At first, I couldn't believe it.' Rose wanted desperately to touch him, make sure he was real and would not disappear. 'I thought it was some horrible, cruel joke.'

'I'm sorry, Rose.' Alex looked so stricken she longed to kiss the frown away, to make him smile again. But she couldn't even touch him, not with all the nurses and other patients staring, and with doctors hovering about.

'What happened?' she asked, gently.

'I'd gone out with two other chaps. One of us got hit and set on fire. I wrapped David in my jacket, which had all my papers in the pockets. Then I must have got blown up myself. When they found me I was crawling round a crater, miles away from our position. God know how I got there. I suppose I was trying to get home.'

'Then you and the other soldier got mixed up.' Rose shook her head at him. 'Why don't you men wear chains around your necks, with your names and numbers on metal discs? Those silly little cardboard things are useless. More than half the men I see have lost them, and no wonder when you tie them round your necks with bits of string.'

'So we should have necklaces and lockets?'

'Maybe,' Rose replied. 'Who exactly found you, then?'

'Some chaps who'd been out mending wire.'

'You said you couldn't hold a pen.'

'I can't.' He looked down at his hands, and Rose saw the burns were at a stage when any movement would be painful. But they were going to heal. Of course he'd have some scars, the skin would always pucker and those angry weals would never fade, but in a couple of months he would be able to use his hands again.

'Where else were you hurt?' asked Rose.

'Something must have hit me on the head. I remember waking up in this place, but everything before it was a blank. I didn't have any papers and I didn't know my name.

'They tried to trace my regiment, of course. But thousands of poor chaps are missing, and a lot of them must look like me.' Alex shrugged. 'People have even come out here from England, hoping I might be their son.'

'What happened next?'

'A week or two ago, one of the sisters came in humming a tune they used to play at dances, in the summer before the war. Suddenly I saw a woman in a long pink dress, and it was you.

'I grabbed the sister's arm and made her hum the tune again, over and over. She humoured me, but God — she looked so frightened! She must have thought I'd really lost my mind. Then, everything started coming back to me.'

* * *

'Captain Denham, it's a lovely day.' The nurse in blue smiled down at them. 'If Miss Courtenay helps you to the terrace, I'll bring you both some coffee.' She held out Rose's boots, which had been cleaned.

So Rose took Alex through the double doors. They sat down on a lichen-clad stone bench, and turned their faces to the sun.

Still she couldn't touch him. She didn't dare, for she was afraid that if she did she'd feel Maria shaking her and saying she'd overslept.

Then she looked at Alex, at the little creases at the corners of his eyes, at a thin white scar that snaked along his forehead, then disappeared into his raven hair. This mundane appraisal could not be the stuff of dreams.

'When I heard from Henry,' she began, 'when he sent my letters back and told me you'd been killed, I thought I'd die of grief.'

'Poor Rose.' Alex carefully brushed a strand of hair back from her face. 'Poor darling, I can see you haven't slept.'

'When I first got Henry's letter, I didn't think I'd ever sleep again.'

'I couldn't wait to see you.' Alex stroked the coil of hair with one stiff, awkward hand. 'Actually, I wondered if you'd come. I thought you might have found somebody else.'

'Alex, don't be absurd.' Rose took his hands in hers and worked the fingers, smoothing and massaging them. 'When you didn't write,' she whispered, 'and I didn't know about the raid, I wondered if you'd changed your mind. I thought perhaps you had gone back to Chloe, and—'

'You idiot, how could you think that?' Then Alex took Rose in his arms and kissed her with such fervour she forgot she was on public view, that other men were walking on the terrace.

She came back to reality only when she heard the nurse suggesting they ought to drink their coffee before it was stone cold.

* * *

'The great attack, I missed it,' muttered Alex. 'I wasn't there, I let them down.'

'Oh, don't be silly.' Rose took his cup and put it on the tray. 'If you'd been there, you would have died with them.'

'I might have thought of something. I might have kept a few of us alive. I'm being sent home, you know.'

'For good?' asked Rose, delighted.

'I hope not!' Alex grimaced. 'They say I need to see a specialist. I've been hit on the head so many times they want to do some tests. They're going to send me to a hospital in London, to let some psychiatrist look at me.'

'It might be for the best.'

'What's that supposed to mean? Rose, I might have lost my memory, but I'm not insane.'

'Of course you're not. But you've been badly hurt. You need a rest.'

'I won't get one in Dorset.' Alex looked earnestly at Rose. 'I'm going to ask Henry if he'll talk to Chloe. She might be persuaded to divorce me. She can have any terms she wants. Of course, I might take far too much granted. Maybe you wouldn't want to marry me?'

'I don't care about being married. So do as you think fit, as long as you're in this world, not the next.'

* * *

It was late September when they finally let him go and he left Forges les Eaux for the last time. He paced the deck of a big troop ship full of wounded soldiers who had copped their Blighty ones, watching for the first sight of England rising from the sea.

Henry was there to meet him as arranged, but his heart sank like a stone in water when he saw Chloe was also in the car.

'Hello,' she said, as he got in beside her and noticed she was looking extraordinarily well. Rose had been so thin and drawn and haggard, he'd felt shoulder blades as sharp as bayonets when he'd hugged her, but Chloe looked prosperous, plump, relaxed. In a new black musquash coat and tiny matching hat, complete with a flirtatious little veil, it was clear the widow had gone to lots of trouble to choose attractive weeds.

'You've come back from the dead,' she murmured, as she offered him her well-rouged cheek.

'I'm not good enough to die.' Alex kissed the air beside her head.

'Off we go, Macnaughten.' As the chauffeur drove out of the station, Henry Denham turned to beam at Alex. 'It's splendid to have you back again,' he said, and Alex saw the old man's eyes were bright. 'But we're going to have to feed you up — don't you think so, Chloe?'

'Yes, he needs a few square meals,' said Chloe, distantly.

Henry's house was still the ruinous pile Alex remembered from his wandering childhood. Since the war began, it had been very hard to find good servants, and the house was far too large for Henry's two elderly, arthritic maids. So although the army had been thrilled when Sir Gerard offered it the splendour of the Minster, the requisition board turned Henry Denham's offer down.

Chloe had occupied the best, south-facing bedroom. When she retired for the night, she told Alex pointedly that she'd had a maid make up the bed in his old room.

* * *

The following morning, Henry bumbled off to see his bailiff, leaving Chloe and Alex sitting at the breakfast table.

'How have you been managing for money?' he enquired.

'I haven't been extravagant, if that's what you're suggesting.' Chloe looked defensive. 'I bought a house in Weymouth in the spring. Of course, it isn't paid for yet. But there are tenants, and they pay off the loan with some to spare. I don't waste my allowance.'

'No.' He looked at her and saw she wasn't clinging, weak and helpless, as he had arrogantly supposed. She didn't need his pity. If he hadn't married her, she wouldn't have had the baby in the workhouse. Of course her parents would have ranted, said she was a fool, but they would not have thrown her out.

'How are your parents?' he enquired politely.

'They're both well.' Chloe shrugged. 'Of course, my father didn't go to France. They kept the older sergeants at the depot. My mother is hoping it will all be over before my brother Jack is seventeen.'

'I hope so, too.' Alex met her pale, blue-glazed gaze. 'Chloe, will you divorce me?'

'I was wondering when we'd come to that.' Chloe's blank expression didn't change. 'I know about you and that woman. Henry and Mrs Sefton were discussing it, they must have thought I was out in the garden or stone deaf. She had a baby, did you know? Everybody talks about her, they all think it's scandalous, the way she has the nerve to walk round Charton as if she owns the place. But I suppose these spoiled, rich women think—'

'Chloe, that's enough.'

'I beg your pardon?'

'I don't wish to hear the local slander.'

'You're telling me the baby's not her child?'

'I'm telling you that none of it is any of your business.'

'There's no need to shout at me!' Chloe's blue eyes brimmed. 'I tried to be a proper wife,' she sniffed. 'I know you never loved me.'

'I don't think you loved *me*. You panicked, and I made the wrong decision. Chloe, I know we made our bed, but we don't have to lie on it. You'll always be provided for, I promise.'

'Your promises are worthless,' Chloe wept. 'You made a promise before the registrar, you said you'd spend your life with me. No, I won't divorce you. It's a disgrace to be divorced. My friends would sneer and point at me.'

'You shouldn't care for people as mean-spirited as that.'

'It's all right for you to talk.' Chloe stared around the breakfast room. 'You were brought up in a different world. I know about your mother. I know what she did. You live in a world where such behaviour is allowed.'

'You know nothing at all about my mother.'

'How long has it been going on?' asked Chloe. 'I mean between you and that Courtenay woman, when did it all start?'

'I've loved Rose since I was twelve years old.' Alex got up and walked out of the room.

The hospital which specialised in head wounds was near Charing Cross, but instead of getting a cab Alex thought he'd walk from Paddington and savour the delights of being home.

He loved London, dirty, stinking, fog-stained London, where his mother and he had lived in basement flats and tenements with a wide variety of men. But he'd always known he was cherished. A lover might be occupying her bed, but he was always in her heart, and she had loved him best.

He had to see two specialists today — a psychiatrist first, who asked him lots of questions about his family, most of which he parried or evaded.

Then things got more personal.

'Did you love your mother, Captain Denham?' asked the doctor.

'Yes, I did.'

'But maybe you were jealous of your father?'

'I'm sorry, I can't answer that.'

'We'll leave it for the moment.' The doctor looked at him. 'Do you find it hard to form relationships with women?'

'Why do you want to know?'

'Captain Denham, please don't be obstructive.'

'I thought I'd come here to be medically examined, not be grilled about my private life?'

'We're trying to help you in the best way we know how.' The psychiatrist smiled professionally. 'Your recent loss of memory suggests you are repressing something that could be important. But you should be aware it's no disgrace to feel afraid. If you've been in actions in which you didn't acquit yourself with honour, there's no need to be ashamed.'

'I lost my memory when something heavy hit me on the head.' Alex scowled at him. 'When I'm in a front line trench, I'm constantly afraid. So is everyone else with any sense. I'm not ashamed of it.'

'You missed the great attack this summer.' The doctor wrote down something on his pad. 'You must have lost some friends?'

'I don't wish to talk about it.' Alex put his hat on and stood up. 'Good morning, Dr Searle.'

The other doctor merely poked and prodded him, shone lights into his eyes and made him walk along a line. As he buttoned up his shirt, the doctor frowned at him. 'You need to put some weight on,' he said, tartly, 'but otherwise, you're in good shape for someone who's been in it from the start.'

'So I'll soon be going back to France?'

'Of course you won't, your hands aren't better yet. They'll need another month at least, and lots of exercising to increase their flexibility. I'll give you a chart.' The doctor leaned back in his chair. 'In any case, I think you've done your bit.'

'You mean I'm going to be downgraded?'

'I mean you could be useful here in England, on the Staff.'

'I want to go to France.'

'Well, you must spend the winter here in England. In my frank opinion, you won't be fit again until the spring.' The doctor scribbled something on his notes. 'By then, this ghastly business might be over. Let's hope so, anyway.'

Alex left the hospital planning his escape from Dorset, wondering if he could get a job instructing new recruits at one of the big training camps in France, or in a riding school, or even at a desk. There must be a doctor somewhere who would pass him fit.

He couldn't last the winter without Rose. He had to see her, or he'd die.

* * *

Rose read the letter from Michael, asking if they could meet again in Rouen. She supposed they should. She ought to tell him, anyway.

'Let's go and have some coffee,' he began, as he led her past the shops and down the wide main street. There were evidently to be no mutterings in alleys, not today.

He was smiling, and looked extremely fit and well. She saw his hand had healed, and all that remained was a tiny, white-rimmed scar, but it had saved his life. He was in much better shape than Alex, who'd looked older, thinner, much more careworn and permanently tired.

'I don't want to go into a café.' Leaving the pavement, Rose sat down upon a bench beneath some chestnut trees, giving Michael no real option but to sit down too. She took a slow, deep breath. 'Michael, I can't marry you.'

'You can't or won't?'

'I cannot, will not — it's impossible. I don't want to hurt your feelings. We've always been good friends, and I hope we can continue friends. But I—'

'It's Denham, isn't it?' Michael stared into the middle distance. 'I heard you went rushing off to see him when he turned up in that hospital.'

'Whoever told you that?'

'The girl you brought along the time we went out with poor Lomax.'

'You've been seeing Judith?'

'I don't see why I shouldn't.' Michael's cold, blue eyes were hard as flints. 'Mrs Sefton told my mother you and Denham have been writing volumes to each other. Letters every day or twice a day. She reckons it's been going on for years.'

'She's wrong, as always.'

'You're carrying a torch for Denham.' Michael turned to Rose. 'All right, don't marry me. But don't get involved with sodding Denham!'

'I've heard enough,' said Rose, and got up to go.

'Well, that's too bad.' Michael caught her arm and pulled her down. 'He's married, but look how he treats his wife. If you throw in your lot with Denham, what makes you think he might be kind to you?'

'I don't wish to discuss it.'

'He might be breathing hearts and flowers at present, but one day he'll lose interest. You'll start to bore him, then he'll abandon you.'

Michael scowled at Rose. 'If you'd agreed to marry me, it would have been forever. If I'd strayed, it would be with a woman who understood I couldn't leave my wife. Rose, you're a lady, or you used to be. There are ladies, there are women, and I know the difference. But Denham never did, and his sort—'

'I don't want to hear this.' Leaving Michael sitting on the bench, Rose walked back to the station.

CHAPTER SIXTEEN

By the time she got back to the station, Rose was feeling sick. At first, she thought it must be guilt. After all, she had been harsh with Michael, but as she stood in the sluice, making up the gallons of antiseptic they'd probably need that night, she found she had a hammering headache, her mouth was dry as sandpaper, and she was shivering.

'I think you must be going down with something,' said Maria. 'I dare say it's that wretched bug poor Judith had last week. Listen, Rose, if we're called out this evening, you don't have to come. Stay at Madame Gaultier's in town. I'll tell Sister Glossop you're not well.'

'She'll think I'm shirking,' muttered Rose.

'Of course she won't.' Maria turned to a couple of orderlies who had just walked in. 'Harry, Leonard, doesn't Rose look out of sorts tonight?'

'She looks washed out,' said Leonard. 'Come on, Sister Courtenay. Let's get you round to Madame Gaultier's. You need a good night's sleep.'

* * *

Rose had been in bed only an hour when she heard someone banging on the door of Madame Gaultier's guest house. Then Madame Gaultier herself came running up the stairs. 'Sister Courtenay?' she cried. 'You're wanted straight away!'

'I'm coming down.' Rose got out of bed. She steadied herself against the washstand, then began to dress. She pulled her boots on, grabbed her bag and hurried down the stairs, where she found an RAMC orderly was pacing up and down.

'I'm sorry, Sister Courtenay,' he began. 'They said you weren't too grand, but a sister from my train has had to go to England, where her mother's dying. Now we've been called out to a CCS. We need another nurse to help us out.'

Rose pulled on her coat, and left the house.

The engine was coupled to the train and ready to depart. 'Miss Courtenay?' smiled a QA nurse. 'I'm so glad Peter found you! We're already one nurse short, and from the sound of it there'll be an awful lot to do. But are you all right? You look quite pale.'

'I've just woken up.' Rose rubbed her eyes. 'Where shall I put my bag?'

'I'll show you,' said nurse, and led Rose down the train. 'You can have Sister Allingham's couchette. Come along, we need to make up lots of antiseptic, then set out the trays.'

Rose didn't know how she managed to work that night. She ached all over and wanted to be sick. When they reached the railhead, there were several hundred men on stretchers waiting for the train.

She helped load up, then set to work. Although today had probably been as horrible as any on the Somme, she was relieved to see most of the men had already had some treatment, or at least first aid. Their wounds were dressed, their broken bones were splinted. All the nursing staff would need to do was keep an eye on them, making sure no drainage tubes got blocked, checking vital signs, and giving them whatever drugs the doctor might prescribe.

They got the patients settled in the bunks. The train drew out of Vecquement and chugged into the darkness.

They heard the planes before they saw them, buzzing like giant mosquitoes in the smoky autumn night. They felt the sudden shudder as the driver pulled the brakes.

The lights were always dimmed throughout the night, but now they were extinguished altogether. The train ground to a halt. It lay like an enormous metal snake along the line.

'What's happening, Sister?' A soldier with both legs in splints looked fearfully at Rose, his face a pale mask in the moonlit night.

'I think there must be German planes about.' Rose crouched down beside him. 'I don't think we need worry. They're probably after troop trains. I'm sure they can't be interested in us.'

'They might be.' The boy's thin face was ashen. 'Sister, if they bomb us—'

'They won't,' soothed Rose, although she knew they might. The great, long silver snake must be a tempting target, and she knew the ambulance trains were frequently attacked, though so far she'd been lucky.

But people's luck ran out.

* * *

The planes came closer. Rose could see an orderly at the far end of the carriage, holding the hand of an absurdly young redheaded boy. The orderly smiled and gave her the thumbs up. Suddenly she felt better, sure it would be all right.

There was silence now, apart from the sound of laboured breathing and occasional groans. Rose cursed the moon, a beautiful harvest orb in the black sky, which lit the night as clear as day. She prayed the German planes would just fly over them. The men on this train had already suffered, they had done their bit.

There were a couple of red flashes, and the carriage rocked. Rose lost her balance and fell heavily to the floor, then rolled against a bunk because the carriage was on its side. She could hear the thin, reluctant screams of men who couldn't help it, and knew she had to get to them.

Then there was another flash. The stricken carriage shuddered, there was a sudden roaring in her ears, and she found herself in total darkness. The carriage filled with smoke. She couldn't breathe, and there was something wet and heavy pressing clammily against her side.

* * *

'No one here has any consideration for my feelings,' Chloe grumbled, as she ate her breakfast one bright morning. 'I hate living in the country. It's so quiet, and it's so dark at night.' She pulled her musquash coat around her shoulders. 'God, it's freezing in this horrid place.'

Alex didn't comment, for Henry's house had always been a cold, damp mausoleum and he was used to it. 'Why don't you go and see your mother?' he suggested, as he scanned Henry's copy of *The Times*. 'She and your father are still living at the depot. You could stay in Dorchester all winter, if you wish.'

'You'd like that, wouldn't you?' Chloe speared some bacon. She began to chew it angrily. 'If I wasn't here, you could moon around the place and dream about your trollop. I wouldn't be in your way.'

'I beg your pardon?'

'Nothing.' Chloe turned up the collar of her coat. 'What's the matter, Alex? You've gone very pale. Where are you going now?'

'What's that to you?'

Alex ran out of the breakfast room, then sprinted to the village, where he sent a dozen telegrams. He had to know exactly what had happened. It could not be helped if what he'd written would soon be common knowledge all round Charton.

* * *

'Why didn't you let me know?' demanded Alex angrily, as he sat down next to Rose's bed in the London hospital. 'Of course, I didn't expect your father to come dashing round to Henry's house with news of you. But you could have asked a nurse to write!'

'I didn't think you'd hear about it yet,' said Rose, and bit her lower lip.

'It was reported in *The Times*, but of course they didn't give your names.' He was slightly mollified, but still upset she hadn't written. She hadn't seemed to realise he would worry. 'I had to ask an awful lot of people before I found out where the train had come from, and which particular nurses were involved.'

'I was going to ask someone to write to you,' said Rose, 'but I didn't want you to see me looking such a fright.'

'Rose, you're such an idiot.' Now Alex didn't know if he should laugh or cry. 'You could never look anything but beautiful to me.'

'I've got all these cuts across my face — *and* two black eyes.'

'You have the loveliest eyes in all the world.'

'My wrist is broken. They've taken out my spleen, and I have this great gash across my stomach. Alex, I'm a wreck.'

'You're going to mend. Listen, I'm booked into a place in Aldgate. I'll come and see you every day. When they let you out of here, I'll drive you home to Dorset.' Alex took her hand. 'Rose, I'm sorry I shouted, I didn't mean to make you cry.'

Rose turned her head away. 'I heard the nurses whispering last night,' she murmured, and her voice was wretched. 'They say — they say I can't have children now!'

'Oh, darling!' Alex held her while she sobbed her heart out, while she cried and cried and cried.

* * *

Boris plodded along the shingle beach, sniffing Alex crossly and doing his best to get between them. Entanglements of rusting wire disfigured the small beach, and these prevented him from running down into the water. He would not be tempted by the ginger biscuits Rose had brought especially for him.

The waves sucked at the pebbles, dragging them down then pushing them up again, indifferent to the concerns of dogs and men. The autumn storms had littered the beach with driftwood and other flotsam and jetsam lately washed ashore from France, wedging these bits of rubbish in the wire, but Boris was too annoyed with Rose to go and look at it.

She linked her arm through Alex's. 'How much longer will you be on sick leave?' she enquired.

'I have to stay in England until spring. Then I'll go back to France.'

'I was wondering if they'd offer you a staff job.'

'They did, but I refused it.'

'Why?' asked Rose.

'I have unfinished business over there.'

'You mean your friends have all been killed while you've been left alive. But why should you die, too?'

'I have to go,' said Alex, and Rose could see the sulky, mulish child he used to be, 'but I don't mean to die.'

'You will if you persist in being so reckless.'

'I'm not reckless, Rose. I used to be, but that was in the early days, when I felt I had to prove myself. I was scared that if I didn't do lots of stupid things, the other men would think I was a coward.'

'Then it's a miracle you've survived.'

'I'll go on surviving, too,' said Alex. 'Rose, men don't trust an officer who's reckless. They won't follow him. They need to know that if he leads them into trouble, he can lead them out of it again. Anyway, you'll be going back to France.'

'It's not the same.'

'Rose, they nearly killed you!'

'I don't go courting death.'

'I don't, either. So we'll both come through.' Alex pulled her close and slid his hands inside her coat. He kissed her very tenderly at first, but then with passion, and she felt herself begin to glow.

'If it was summer, and there wasn't any wire, we could swim round to the cove,' she whispered, as he kissed her neck. 'Nobody would find us there, and we could—'

'Yes, we could — but where can we go in winter?' Alex's hands ran up and down her spine.

'Nowhere's safe from Mrs Sefton.'

'God, this is a nightmare.' Alex groaned into her hair. 'I want you so much it's killing me!'

'Why don't we go to bed, then?'

'Where, exactly? You can't come to Henry's house, and your father wouldn't welcome me! What would I say to him? Good evening, sir, your daughter is expecting me. May I go upstairs? In any case, your wrist is not healed yet, and you must still be bruised inside.'

'I'm feeling better these days.' Rose smiled up at him. 'Listen, we'll go to Charmouth or Lyme Regis. We'll book into a small hotel or guest house, and stay there for a week.'

'What will Sir Gerard say?'

'That I'm a harlot, that I have the morals of a guttersnipe, that I'm not his child.' Rose kissed Alex on the mouth. 'But I honestly don't care. I've heard it all before.'

Boris decided he had had enough. He lunged at Rose and shoved himself between them, whining for attention.

* * *

'Where are you going?' asked Sir Gerard, who had changed. While Rose was growing up, he'd always been a kindly father, generous and indulgent, but reserved. Now he was querulous and always asking questions, like an irritating child.

Rose had told him she would not be marrying Michael Easton, but he didn't believe it, and kept asking when he should put the announcement in *The Times*.

Why did Rose not respect her mother's wishes, he demanded. When would she leave the VAD? She was always out — where did she go? He'd seen her suitcase in the hall — where was she going today?

'To spend a week in Lyme,' she told him. 'I'll be back on Sunday.'

'I would prefer it if you stayed at home with me.'

'Daddy, Polly will look after you.'

'You're a wicked, cruel girl. You drove your mother to an early grave.'

* * *

'My father thinks I'm wicked.' Muffled up in greatcoats, Rose and Alex sat on the sea wall, their backs to Lyme, staring out across the wind-whipped waves. 'I suppose I must be.'

'You're not wicked, Rose.' Alex put his arm around her waist and pulled her close to him. 'He wants you to leave the VAD and marry Easton, then settle down at Charton and start producing heirs. You're not going to do it. So there's no solution.'

'I wish my mother hadn't died.' Rose laid her head on Alex's shoulder. 'I'll never forgive myself for that.'

'You shouldn't have run away that time, but Lady Courtenay brought most of her troubles on herself. Rose, she smothered you. I don't know how you stood it for so long.'

The tide was out, and Alex jumped Rose down on to the sand. 'Come on, you need some exercise. You see the fishing boat that's hauled up by the bathing huts? I'll give you a race.'

'Your legs are longer, so you're bound to win.'

'You have a minute's start.' Alex grinned. 'Well, go on. Go on!'

* * *

'God, Alex, you're so slow!' Flushed and breathing heavily, Rose turned round to laugh at him as he came panting up, holding his side.

'I let you win,' he gasped.

'No you jolly well didn't! I beat you fair and square!'

'Rose, you look so beautiful, scarlet in the face and with your hair all coming down.'

'You're so horrid and sarcastic that I can't think why I put up with you.'

'It's because you love me. Oh, my God!' Alex collapsed against the fishing boat, where he lay groaning.

'What's the matter?' cried Rose, alarmed.

'I can't stand it any more.' Laughing, Alex pulled her down on top of him, then began to kiss her greedily. 'Rose, I know it's only half past three, but we have got to go to bed.'

* * *

'I hope you had a pleasant stay in Lyme,' said Celia Easton, who'd called at the Dower House with a bag of khaki wool and some knitting needles, so Rose could learn to knit, and profitably occupy her time. 'I must say, you're looking well. You have some colour in your cheeks.'

'I've been out for a walk.' Rose had just seen Alex off to London, where he had another appointment with an army doctor — not with the psychiatrist, whom he had refused to see again, but with one he thought might let him go back to France before the spring.

'I'm going to call on Mrs Hobson,' said Celia briskly. 'Daisy had a cough last week, but I think she must be better now. Why don't you come with me?'

Rose jumped up at once. 'I've been meaning to pop over,' she told Celia, as she rang for Polly to bring her hat and coat.

'Really?' Celia grimaced. 'I thought *you* had other fish to fry.'

* * *

Mrs Hobson's kitchen was a mass of babies and small children, all dressed in cotton pinafores and staring at the visitors with round, defensive eyes. As Rose smiled at a little fair-haired boy, the child began to cry.

'Hush now, Donald,' Celia said crisply, and Donald hushed at once. 'Good morning, Mrs Hobson. How is everyone today?'

'We're right as rain, Miss Easton.' A large, untidy woman, Mrs Hobson scooped a tiny baby from a cradle by the fire. 'Mary-Anne, my youngest,' she said proudly.

'She's extremely sweet.' Celia looked round the cottage kitchen. 'Miss Courtenay was hoping to meet Daisy.'

'She's over by the range with Bob and Nancy. I reckon she'll be walking any day.'

Rose turned to see a blonde-haired child, gazing at the visitors and sucking two fat fingers.

'Come on, Daisy love,' urged Mrs Hobson. 'Show these nice ladies how well you can crawl!'

The child stared at them with wide, blue eyes. But then she crawled across the flagstones. When she reached Mrs Hobson, she hauled herself up on unsteady feet. She hid her face against her foster mother's apron.

'Hello, Daisy.' Rose crouched beside the child, and saw the little scrap she'd brought from London just a year ago now had chubby legs and flaxen curls. Daisy was going to be a little milkmaid, pink and cream and gold.

Still clinging to her foster mother's apron, Daisy turned to look at Rose, who smiled encouragingly. The child thought about it for a moment, then smiled back, displaying a row of pearly little teeth.

'Do you think she'd come to me?' asked Rose.

'I expect so.' Mrs Hobson took the baby's hand. 'If you sit in the rocking chair, she might sit on your knee.'

Encouraged by Mrs Hobson, Daisy sat on Rose's lap. She looked at Rose's buttons, stroked a lock of hair that had come loose, then found the locket round her neck.

Rose watched her play with it, enjoying the sensation of the roly-poly little body sitting warmly on her lap. So was she

Michael's child? She had Michael's colouring, but so did half the children in the kingdom. All the same, there was a look of him. Daisy had his eyes, his face, his smile.

Then Rose felt how much she wanted babies, little sloe-eyed replicas of Alex, with his smooth brown skin and thick dark hair, and she mourned the baby she had lost.

'We must be going.' Celia had given Mrs Hobson wool and needles, and was pulling on her gloves.

'Goodbye, Daisy.' Rose let the child slide off her knee. She watched her crawl across the floor towards her foster brother and sister playing with wooden bricks beside the fire. 'I'll come again.'

They walked back through the village. 'Michael assured me Daisy's not his daughter,' Rose told Celia. 'She's not your responsibility. I'm the one who brought her here, so I should pay her keep.'

'I don't think we need believe all my dear brother says.' Celia shrugged and turned to Rose. 'I'm fond of her, you know. She's such a charming little thing. I don't suppose you'll marry Mike?'

'You mean you know about Alex?'

'I know you're seeing him. Well, if you go swanning off to Lyme in the company of a married man, you surely don't expect the village crones will fail to notice?'

'All the same—'

'Rose, you must be careful. Alex is very nice and very handsome, but he's already got a wife.'

* * *

They parted in the village, and Rose took the winding lane back to the Dower House. She saw the woman in a black fur coat, and supposed she was a nursing sister at the Minster who couldn't bear to be without her fur, even though she should have worn the regulation dark blue overcoat.

'Good afternoon,' said Rose, and would have walked on quickly, for it was cold and she was tired.

'Good afternoon, Miss Courtenay.' The woman stopped and stared at Rose with prominent blue eyes. 'I understand you know my husband?'

'You must be Mrs Denham.' Rose realised she was being scrutinised and probably found wanting. This woman looked so smart and elegant in her fur and patent leather boots, with fashionably bobbed hair and a discreet amount of rouge stroked high along her cheekbones. 'I'm so sorry, but—'

'*You're* sorry!' Chloe spat. 'I know all about you and my husband! But whatever Alex may have told you, I don't mean to let him go.'

Rose saw Chloe's eyes were hard with hatred. 'I'll let him have his fun with you,' she muttered. 'There's no way I can stop him, after all. When the bit's between his teeth, he's like most men, he needs to have his way. So make the most of it, Miss Courtenay. Enjoy your assignations in disreputable hotels. But remember I'm his wife and he'll be coming back to me. I'm the one he loves.'

Rose watched Chloe walk off down the lane. She must have lain in wait, she thought, because this track led to the Dower House then to the Minster. The road to Henry Denham's house was half a mile away.

* * *

When Rose met Alex from the London train, she saw at once he was in a temper.

'I can't go back until next March,' he said, through gritted teeth.

'Well, nor can I,' said Rose. She wished he wouldn't scowl like that, it made him look so grim. 'I'll have forgotten everything I know.'

'Why don't you go and work for Sister Mason at the house?'

'I don't think so, Alex. Nowadays I have a rather dubious reputation. Mrs Sefton and her friends have been quite busy lately.'

‘I hate that wretched woman.’ Alex’s scowl deepened. ‘She’s made friends with Chloe, did you know? My wife goes over to her house. I don’t know what they talk about, but I can guess.’

‘Alex, you mustn’t make it hard for Chloe. She knows she’s lost you, and she doesn’t know what to do. Maybe you didn’t break her heart, but you did hurt her pride.’

* * *

‘I’m going to live with Mrs Thorne in Weymouth.’

When Alex walked back into Henry’s house, he found Chloe had packed her boxes and made Macnaughten lug them down the stairs.

‘I met that woman yesterday,’ she added. ‘I don’t know what you see in her, I’m sure. She’s supposed to be a famous beauty, but she looks like a witch with all that straggling black hair. She’s got horrid scabs all down her face, she’s scrawny and she’s ugly. But I suppose she’s rich, and—’

‘I’ll make sure your allowance is sent to Weymouth,’ interrupted Alex.

‘Let’s call it conscience money, shall we?’ Chloe sneered.

‘I’ll drive you to the station.’

‘There’s no need.’ Chloe hitched her fur around her shoulders. ‘Henry said Macnaughten would be very glad to take me. He knows you have other things to do.’

* * *

‘Alex, it doesn’t matter,’ Rose said softly, as they walked along the beach towards the jutting headland, skirting a fresh landslip which had recently revealed a whole new batch of fossils, ancient bones and smooth, round rocks. ‘Everybody knows, or thinks they know. If they want to gossip, we can’t stop them.’

‘I hate them all.’ Alex pushed his hands into his pockets and kicked an ammonite along the beach. ‘God, there’s no escape,’ he groaned. ‘Look who’s coming down the cliff path now.’

'Good afternoon, Miss Courtenay — Captain Denham.' Mrs Sefton carried a little hammer and a bag. Now her mouth stretched wide, a comic rictus of a grin, and her three old basset hounds looked almost as delighted.

She pottered on to search for geological trophies, but suddenly she seemed to change her mind, and scurried off along the windswept beach.

'There, our fate is sealed.' Rose took Alex's arm. 'By the time I get back to the house, it will be all round Charton that she found us *in flagrante* on the sands.'

'This country stinks.' Alex gave the ammonite a kick and sent it bouncing through the waves. 'The English are a nation of narrow-minded, scandal-mongering spinsters like that Easton girl, and interfering cows like Mrs Sefton.'

'Darling, do calm down. Celia's my friend, and when Mrs Sefton sees us walking on the beach, it makes her day.'

'You'll be saying next you like the bitch.'

'Well, I don't hate everyone, like you.'

'You're one of them, that's why. I'm a nobody, but *you're* Miss Courtenay of Charton Minster. Whatever you do, you'll always be the squire's precious daughter. Mrs Sefton—'

'That's enough of Mrs Sefton! I don't care what she and all her village cronies think or say!' Rose spun Alex round and met his sullen, angry gaze. 'My darling, listen to me. I love you.'

'So you say.'

'What's that supposed to mean?'

'Oh, nothing.' Alex shook her arm away. 'It's freezing on this beach. I'm going home.'

* * *

It seemed that Mrs Sefton had lost no time in doing her worst, for when Rose walked into the Dower House, Sir Gerard was waiting for her, looking grim.

'I understand you're carrying on an affair with Alex Denham,' he began, without preamble. He turned to stare out of the window. 'I don't know how your mother and I produced a child like you. A daughter who has shamed us, hurt us, who has dragged the Courtenay name through so much muck and filth that it will never be clean again.'

'Daddy, you're exaggerating—'

'Do you deny you're seeing this man?' Sir Gerard rounded on her in a fury. 'I expect you do! But I have no wish to hear the lies and fabrications you've no doubt prepared for me today.'

'I don't deny I'm seeing Alex,' Rose said quietly. 'But—'

'He's married, girl!' Sir Gerard glared. 'He has a wife, she had his child! He's a ne'er-do-well, a wastrel, Mrs Sefton says—'

'Mrs Sefton!' Rose glared back at him. 'Since when did Gerard Courtenay listen to the likes of Mrs Sefton? To nonsense churned out by a malicious, ignorant old woman who does nothing useful with her rotten, empty life? Who roams the district spying on her neighbours, then runs back to Charton to spread slander?'

'What you're doing is a scandal!' cried Sir Gerard. 'You must give up this man.'

'I won't.'

'I'll disinherit you!' Sir Gerard's eyes were bulging. 'Listen to me, child. I don't make idle threats. I'll leave this whole estate to charity—'

'Do as you think fit.' Rose turned to go.

'Come back here, you wicked girl!'

But Rose kept walking, out of the sitting room, out of the Dower House and off down the path, where she met Polly coming home.

Polly's eyes were cold. 'What have you done now, miss?' she began.

'I beg your pardon, Polly?'

'It's not my place to tell my betters how they should behave.' Polly sniffed and brushed past Rose. 'But if I was you, Miss Courtenay, if I had *your* conscience, I wouldn't sleep at night.'

CHAPTER SEVENTEEN

She didn't know how he'd managed to arrange it, but Rose found Alex waiting for her on the starboard deck of the *Medusa*. Standing side by side, they watched the coast of England fade away.

'I think we're both insane,' said Rose. 'I should be working in some cottage hospital in Dorset. You ought to be in Whitehall, pushing papers round a desk.'

'Then I *would* go mad,' said Alex. 'Rose, you'd better go and find your friends. You'll need your orders, and now the ship is moving you can't stay on deck with me.'

But Rose leaned against the rail and smiled up at him, delighted to be with Alex and be going back to France. She'd taken off her hat to let the wind rake through her hair. It had been bobbed the week before, and now it framed her face with curls.

'There'll be a QA sister here somewhere,' she told Alex. 'She's bound to have my orders. If I don't turn up, I expect she'll come and look for me.'

'I'd hate to be responsible for you,' said Alex grimly. 'If I were your commanding officer, you'd be on punishment duty all the time.'

'You mean if I didn't bend, you'd break me?'

'I've never broken anyone,' said Alex, staring out across the foam-flecked waves. 'As for breaking you — I know I couldn't do it. I'd pity anyone who had to try.'

* * *

'Miss Courtenay, there you are at last.' Rose found Sister Marshall sitting in the first-class lounge, with half a dozen other Queen Alexandra nurses and some timid-looking volunteers. 'I understand you've been on sick leave. I trust you're fit again?'

'Yes thank you, Sister,' Rose replied demurely.

'You're going to a village near Bailleul. The hospital takes casualties from all the clearing stations south of Ypres, so your experience will be very welcome.' The sister fixed Rose with a hard, blue stare. 'Miss Courtenay, I'd appreciate it if you'd stay with us, and not go wandering round the decks again.'

So Rose didn't see Alex until the ship docked at Boulogne, and even then it was only for a moment as she and the other nurses were marched off in single file, like a flock of geese.

He noticed her at last, and nodded briefly. Then he turned away and started talking to a sergeant major. Instead of lovers, it was as if they were acquaintances or casual friends.

She knew he couldn't come and say goodbye, but as he was swept away by a vast, undulating tide of khaki, she felt cold fingers grasp her heart. Now he was sure of her and knew how much she loved him, had he become complacent? Maybe she was boring him?

All that year he'd been so restless, badgering the army to let him go back earlier than planned. A couple of short stints as an instructor at a training camp in Yorkshire during January and February had probably kept him sane.

She thought of Chloe, of the other woman's baffled anger. She knew it could not be easy to be Alex Denham wife.

* * *

The hospital in Flanders turned out to be a cluster of long wooden huts and large marquees, surrounded by a township of flapping two-man tents in which the nurses lived.

After getting a lift into Bailleul, Rose had trudged through devastated countryside in which there was hardly any green. No cowslip, primrose or even wood anemone had come up to greet the spring. She couldn't help comparing this bleak and wasted land with the golden glory that was Charton, where the rain fell sweetly on a million daffodils beneath the leafless trees.

She strode along the lines of canvas, looking for the tent in which she would be shivering for the next few weeks, until the warmer weather came.

She finally tracked it down and went inside. 'Elsie!' she exclaimed, staring in astonishment at her friend from Auchonville who was sitting cross-legged on her bed, brushing her hair.

'Rose Courtenay!' Elsie dropped her brush. Jumping up, she hugged Rose in delight. 'I thought you must be dead. We heard you were on that train they bombed.'

'But they didn't get me.' Rose dumped her suitcase on the sagging canvas bed. 'Elsie, it's so good to see you! I never thought you'd stick it out.'

'I didn't want anyone to say I was a slacker.' Elsie blushed. 'I couldn't have faced my father or my brothers if I'd shirked.'

'You're hardly shirking here. We're only twenty miles from the front line.'

'Actually, it's more like ten,' said Elsie, shuddering. 'The noise is awful sometimes, and the sky is all lit up at night. They keep telling us we're going to move. Last week, we were ordered to pack up and get the men away. But then they brought another convoy in, and said we had to stay. So here we sit, and hope we don't get bombed.'

'The Germans don't bomb hospitals,' said Rose. 'It's a well known fact. We can all rest easy in our beds.'

She started to unpack.

* * *

In spite of a persistent rumour doing the rounds of pubs in Charton, Lyme and Dorchester, where he'd been feted as a sole survivor, Alex found the original third battalion of the Royal Dorsets hadn't been wiped out. By the time he reached the salient that made a semi-circle round the ruined town of Ypres, he'd seen a dozen people he knew.

Michael Easton had survived the autumn on the Somme, and as Alex slogged along the last few miles of trenches, he heard a familiar voice.

'Captain Denham, sir!' Corporal Brind looked prosperous and happy, even though his uniform was filthy and he was bent double beneath his pack. He was carrying a sandbag that Alex knew would probably be full of things he'd pinched.

'Just a few comforts for the troops,' he added, grinning as he stroked the canvas sack. 'A nice bit of fruit cake, a couple of hundred Woodbines and the *Daily Sketch*, so that our boys can have—'

The rest of what he said was lost as a dozen shells exploded in the purple sky. A burst of answering artillery made the churned-up mud shake like a jelly, and clods of earth came raining from above.

'Come on, sir,' mouthed Brind. 'It's always pretty hot down this here alley. Jerry keeps it covered night and day.'

The noise intensified. A hundred yards in front of them a shrapnel shell exploded, and a piece of metal sliced through Alex's greatcoat sleeve before embedding itself in the trench wall.

'They get you, sir?' husked Brind.

'I don't think so.' Alex knew he wouldn't feel any pain. That would come much later, when he had recovered from the shock of being hit. But he couldn't feel any ominous trickling dampness either, so he hoped he was unscathed.

* * *

He and Brind got home at stand to arms. After a day of sleeping, writing letters, cleaning weapons and picking lice out of their dirty clothes, the men would work all night, shoring up the trenches, burying their dead, going on patrol in no-man's-land and bringing down supplies.

Although the shelling never stopped and men were being killed, everybody seemed in quite good spirits. Alex could see why. They had the bombs and shells to do the job. The ammunition dumps he'd passed as he came down the line had been immense, so huge it was hard to believe that just two years ago the army had been almost out of shells, and many attacks which had been going well had been aborted, because there was no artillery support to see them through.

Things were getting done. There was an end in sight, and men were saying that maybe by *this* Christmas it would all be over and they'd be going home.

As Alex found his way around the sector, he saw the engineers had tunnelled deep beneath the German lines, sapping forward underneath the enemy emplacements, laying mines and high explosive ready for some giant firework party to be held in summer.

Or so rumour said.

* * *

'The fellow you've replaced went mad,' said Major Whelan, who was Alex's senior officer and also the battalion commander. 'He was a drunkard, too. Some chaps can't function sober, I'll admit. But Henderson was useless drunk or sober, night or day.'

'Once he led a whole platoon into a German trench,' said Harry Langham, who was Major Whelan's aide. 'He got them all blown up, then came back singing *Tipperary*, with not a mark on him. They had to send him to the funny farm. Do you drink much, Captain Denham?'

'I don't drink at all,' said Alex.

'What's that supposed to mean?' The major frowned. 'I hope you're not a Presbyterian? I don't like holy officers. They aggravate the men.'

'I'm not holy, sir.'

'I'm glad to hear it.' Major Whelan grinned. 'Who do you know from when you were out last?'

'Lieutenant Easton, Corporal Brind—'

'Oh yes, young Easton. He's never had a single scratch. I don't know what to make of him. I'd say he was windy. He makes a mess of all his night patrols, hangs back, never volunteers. He sets a bad example to his men.'

'But he's a damned fine shot,' said Harry Langham. 'He must be the best in the battalion. If you want something hit, Lieutenant Easton is your man.'

* * *

Alex soon got used to being back, to being cold, to wearing filthy clothes and getting shot at night and day. He had enough to keep him occupied, for when Major Whelan was away he took command of the battalion. This meant doing endless paperwork, as well as looking after all the men.

He knew he wasn't fit. Some days he could hardly stay awake. He had a nagging headache that never went away. When he could snatch an hour to himself, he didn't want to drink *vin blanc*, play cards or walk around the sector looking nonchalant and setting a good example to the men.

After hours of filling in forms, of writing letters of condolence to the relatives of dead or wounded men, he couldn't find the energy to write a private letter, even one to Rose. He just lay down and slept.

Sleep became his quest, his holy grail — he longed for it. If he could sleep, even the ominous scrape and scrabble of German sappers mining underneath the British trenches, where they'd be planting high explosive and planning to blow the company to glory, didn't worry him.

'You're due three days leave,' said Major Whelan, looking at the roster in the dugout. 'What are you going to do with it?'

'I hadn't really thought about it, sir.'

'You need some relaxation,' said the major. 'Go and find yourself a girl and have a bit of fun. Alex, you're a conscientious officer, but you're so damned serious all the time. Eat, drink and be merry with a pretty mademoiselle — that's my advice to you.'

So Alex wrote to Rose, suggesting they might meet. If he could find a guest house in St Omer, would she come and stay?

'I can't get away,' she told him. *'We're extremely busy, wounded men are coming down from the salient all the time. Matron is a stickler for filling in our time sheets, and signing in and out. She notices if anyone misses breakfast, and she wants to know the reason why. So I'm sorry. It'll have to be some other time.'*

He felt as if she'd punched him in the face.

* * *

In June, the ridge above Messines was blown. Thousands of startled Germans were taken prisoner, and many thousands more entombed alive. In reserve that week, Alex watched through field-glasses as Allied forces walked through Armageddon, pushing forward to a new front line.

Then everybody went on holiday. Alex had assumed this breakthrough would be followed by a mass attack, that the whole German army would be pushed back to Berlin. But nothing happened.

The men and officers grew restless, muttering they'd wasted the only decent chance they'd ever had to have a bash at Jerry. They went out on patrol and took more German prisoners, they bombed the enemy's trenches and they cut the enemy's wire. They drilled and went out skirmishing, but still no order to move forward came.

* * *

'What do those halfwits at headquarters think they're doing?' Major Whelan stared through the field periscope trained on the German lines. 'If those idiots on the Staff don't get a blasted move on, the summer will be over. It's jolly wet in Flanders in the autumn, and I don't fancy trying to take those ridges in the rain.'

But Alex didn't care what happened in the Ypres salient. He was fretting about Rose. She hardly ever wrote to him, and when she did her letters told him everything and nothing. She talked about her work, her friends, she said she'd been to Hazebrouck and Saint Omer for the afternoon.

She'd finally got some leave, but it seemed she'd spent it in Boulogne, with some girl called Elsie. She never talked about their future, so perhaps they didn't have one any more?

You take too much for granted, Captain Denham. Oh, don't be silly. I don't care about being married. Everything she'd said to him was branded on his brain.

He took his tone from her and answered her infrequent letters briefly and dispassionately. He now decided that the girl who'd kissed him with such fervour on a windswept beach, who had defied her family and friends to be with him, was just a mirage, an illusion.

Reality was the cold, disdainful beauty in the horrible pink gown — the heiress who had snubbed him when he'd asked her if she'd dance. She'd marry Michael Easton and break Alex Denham's heart.

He had very little to do with Michael, who kept out of his way. But he couldn't help noticing that when Michael looked at him it was with utter loathing — and there was madness in those pale blue eyes.

July was hot and sunny, leave came round again, and Alex wondered if he might see Rose. She hadn't written for at least a fortnight, so he told himself she must be busy, and it might be difficult for her to get away.

He thought about it for a week or more. Should he come straight out with it, should he confess and tell her he had to see her or go mad? But in the end he wasn't brave enough, and went back home to Dorset.

He stayed with Henry, who was glad to see him. He went for long, exhausting walks around the cliffs and headlands, never stopping to admire the glorious panorama rolling out in front of him, never resting on a fragrant cushion of wild thyme, never gazing at the green and gold and blue of summer landscape, sea and sky.

He merely walked, head down, and found exhaustion helped to numb the pain.

* * *

In the third week of July, the British guns began to fire again, pounding enemy trenches and churning up the ground that Allied troops would have to cross if there should be a battle.

Alex could see it would be difficult to get men, guns and tanks across such horrible terrain. He shrugged and went to check the saps, where his men were mining.

'At long last.' Later on that day, Major Whelan came back from brigade headquarters bringing with him maps and battle plans.

'It's going to be next week,' he told his captains as he handed round the maps. 'A surprise attack, with twelve divisions, huge offensives on all fronts — those ought to get the buggers moving.'

The major grinned, then glanced at Alex. '*You* don't look very offensive, Mr Denham.'

'Sir?' Alex had been thinking about Rose, deciding he would not prolong the agony. If he could find the courage, he'd write to her that evening, to say he would let her go.

'Your lot's going over first, with Mr Langham's chaps.' Major Whelan glared. 'Alex, are you listening? Look lively, man! We'll expect your boys to cut the wire and occupy that farmhouse on the right by ten o'clock. You'll have to work out how you're going to do it.'

* * *

The week before the great assault, the weather changed and it rained every day. The trenches flooded. Latrines and sump holes overflowed, and men had to wade through stinking sewage as they squelched their way into position, ready for the surprise attack on the last day of a hot July that had turned autumnal and depressing overnight.

Alex's four lieutenants led their men into the front line trenches. At three o'clock the Allied barrage lifted and the first wave of infantry set off across the swamp.

Alex's men got over without taking casualties. The four platoons went forward, moving through the shrouding mist and darkness.

When they'd rehearsed it, this manoeuvre had looked quite straightforward, and he was confident they'd reach the farmhouse, where a hundred Germans were supposed to be dug in. They would flush them out and take them prisoner. Or if they resisted shoot them, finishing them off with bayonets.

The driving rain made staying in the rehearsed formation hard. They couldn't see each other, and Alex was afraid that if the weather didn't improve they'd lose their way.

They should be going due east, which sounded simple, but it was difficult trying to find their way in this dense fog, or make sense of the destroyed terrain.

Burdened by their sodden packs and clothes that soaked up water like so many sponges, the men slogged through the greasy mud that came up to their ankles, then to their knees, then to their thighs.

The German guns had opened up. Men were falling all around and others coming up behind them couldn't help treading them into the mud. Men who'd been blown up and landed on the German wire flapped like ghastly washing as machine gun bullets peppered them.

* * *

The company was well spread out and hopefully still making for the farmhouse. But the mist was even denser now, and all Alex saw were looming shapes. The noise of battle, the relentless rat-tat-tat of gunfire, the whining of the shells flying overhead was deafening, drowning out the screams of men who fell. So he thought he had imagined the sharp yell of panic on his left.

He knew he shouldn't stop. It was up to stretcher bearers coming up behind him to rescue wounded men. Then he heard the scream again.

He squelched a few feet back into the mist, then almost walked into the crater into which the man had either fallen or been blown.

The second wave of infantry was coming over now, and Alex knew a man trapped in the mud would certainly be trampled, trodden down by his own side. There was just a minute, maybe less, before the two of them were overwhelmed.

He held out his right hand. The soldier grabbed it, but the sucking mud refused to let its victim go.

'I can't get out,' he gasped, and the sheer dead weight of him threatened to pull Alex in as well.

He knew the voice. He recognised the face beneath the mud. 'You've got to help yourself!' He glared at Michael Easton. 'Push your feet against the side and try to walk up, can't you?'

Michael floundered helplessly, and Alex thought he'd have to let him drown, but then he managed to brace himself against the marginally more solid rim, and Alex hauled him out.

'You'll be all right,' yelled Alex, as Michael dripped and shivered. 'Come on, we've got to catch up with the others, they'll be miles ahead by now.'

Michael didn't move, so Alex slapped him. 'Come *on*!' he shouted. 'Listen, Easton! If you don't shift yourself, I'll shove you back into the hole and watch you drown!'

'Bastard.' There was too much noise to hear, but Alex saw him mouth the word, and a second later Michael took a swing at him.

Alex parried it, then punched him hard. A thin streak of blood gleamed red on Michael's muddy cheekbone, but he gulped and gasped as if it were a mortal wound. He fell at Alex's feet and lay there shuddering and whimpering like a child.

Alex heard the second wave of infantry approaching. If he stayed here, he would be mown down. He pulled Michael upright, then heaved his wet, dead weight on to his shoulders in a fireman's lift.

He began to stagger across the swamp towards the ruined farmhouse, doubting if he'd reach it and telling himself that he must be the biggest fool alive.

CHAPTER EIGHTEEN

'I suppose it's raining?' muttered Elsie, from the relative comfort of her camp bed.

'Yes, I'm afraid it's tipping down. I'd stay in bed if I were you. You're not on shift until this afternoon.' Rose pulled on her galoshes, slung her mackintosh cape around her shoulders, then sloshed across the fields towards the wooden huts that loomed out of the mist and rain.

The summer had been warm and sunny, and wounded men had sat outside the huts or big marquees, their faces turned towards the healing sun. The more adventurous had gone for walks around the ruined countryside. But now torrential autumn rains had turned the whole of Belgium into one vast sea of mud.

Rose walked into the hut shaking the rain out of her hair, and found the ward sister sticking pins and tape into a map of Flanders that was hung up in the office, marking the front line. 'We're doing well,' she smiled.

'That's good,' said Rose, who couldn't help but think about the cost in young men's lives. They were coming down in thousands from the Ypres salient. Their injuries were horrible and stank of putrefaction, for in the mud of Flanders even trivial wounds became infected. Even a small cut could mean an otherwise healthy limb developed gangrene, and the only way to deal with that was amputation.

It rained and rained, and filthy water swirled around the huts. In spite of off-duty sappers digging trenches to drain off the surplus water, the wards were often deep in muck and slime.

'This winter's going to be foul,' said Elsie, as she and Rose slopped home again at the end of yet another shift.

'Ghastly,' Rose agreed, despondently. Living in a flooded tent and working in a flooded hospital, she almost wished herself back on the trains.

Then she thought of Alex and what he must be suffering in the east, and was ashamed. She must write tonight, she thought, a bright and breezy letter telling him about her trip with several other nurses to the coast, where they'd had a freezing swim, their first and last that year.

But it was hard to write to Alex, and getting harder all the time. She suspected — no, she knew — he must have someone else. They hadn't seen each other since they'd returned to France, and although he'd written in June suggesting they might meet, she had not dared to ask for any leave. The hospital was full to overflowing. A few snatched hours in a café in St Omer and that day trip to Boulogne with Elsie was all the holiday she would have that year.

Celia had written a month ago, and mentioned that he'd been to visit Henry in the summer. Mrs Sefton and a friend had spotted him out walking with the bailiff's eldest daughter.

'She is by all accounts a rather forward sort of person, who always has an eye to the main chance,' continued Celia. *'My mother wouldn't be at all surprised to find she's angling after Alex Denham, even though he's married. She's that sort of girl.'*

Rose shook her head. The bailiff's daughter had a pretty face and neat, trim figure. Seventeen or eighteen now, she was in the bloom of youth and beauty. But Rose was a haggard twenty-one, who felt she must look more like forty-five.

Although the German bombs had failed to kill her, they had put their mark on her for life. She had long red weals across her stomach that would never fade, and her face was scarred by flying glass. Once white and soft, her hands were red and ruined. The nails were cracked, the knuckles raw.

She might have been attractive once, but she was not a beauty now.

* * *

When she came off shift one evening later that week, she met Elsie trudging through the mud, looking even gloomier than Rose felt. 'What's the matter, Elsie?' she began.

'I've had a letter from my father. God knows how he got it past the censor, but he did. Rose, I feel so tired! I don't know how I'll stay awake tonight.'

'You'll be all right,' said Rose. 'What did your father have to say?'

'The Germans are moving troops out of the east. The new Russian government has made peace with Germany, so Jerry will soon make mincemeat out of us.'

'How does your father know?'

'He's been on the Staff since last July. It might be just a rumour, I suppose. But my mother wants me back in Kent.'

'When will you be leaving?'

'I'm not going home! Both my brothers are still in Flanders, and I won't have James and Matthew saying I got the wind up.' Elsie looked at Rose. 'But I don't know how we're going to beat them. Where will we find the men?'

'I don't know.' Rose would never have believed the mighty Allied army could be defeated by a bunch of Prussians. But it seemed it might.

The rumour that the German government had made peace with Russia was all round the wards by eight o'clock the following morning. Two days later, rumour turned out to be fact.

'We're bound to be evacuated soon,' said Elsie hopefully, as she wrung out the hem of her blue dress. 'They can't leave us here like sitting ducks, waiting for the Germans to arrive. A nice, warm chateau near the coast. That's where I'd like to be.'

December came, then January. All leave was cancelled, nurses who were sick or couldn't cope went home to England, and although the hospital was ready to pack up and leave, the order never came. Rose hoped it never would. It would be a nightmare, trying to evacuate a thousand wounded men through the January mud and slime.

'You mustn't worry, Sister,' said a burly sergeant, as Rose changed the dressing on his leg one freezing day. 'If the Jerries come, me and the lads will make it quick for you. We'll shoot you nurses dead.'

* * *

'Letters for you, Sister Courtenay.' The ward orderly handed Rose a bundle, and when she saw Alex's handwriting her heart began to sing, because if he could write, he was alive.

She slit the envelope. The letter was very short and to the point. *'We have to meet,'* he said. *'We need to talk.'*

After begging, pleading and finally inventing a sick brother in hospital in Boulogne, Rose managed to get leave. Alex said he'd be in Steenvoorde the next Saturday.

She found him waiting at the railhead. Their eyes met briefly and he nodded. Then he looked away.

She tried to smile, but her face was frozen. She longed to hug him, kiss him, but she didn't dare — he might push her away. 'H-how are things?' she faltered.

'Looking bad for us,' he said.

'You mean we're going to lose the war?'

'I don't see how we're going to win.'

'I thought the Americans were coming?'

'Where are they, then?' said Alex. 'We haven't seen any in our sector, and it's the busiest part of the whole line.'

Rose didn't want to talk about the war or the Americans. 'You look tired,' she told him.

'So do you.' He looked at her and scowled. 'You're far too thin. I wish you hadn't cut your hair.'

'I do, too. My neck's been cold all winter. But I'm letting it grow again, and I—'

'You're dangerously close to the front line,' said Alex, suddenly interrupting. 'Why don't you go home?'

'You mean go back to England?' Rose felt hollow and afraid. She looked at him, but now Alex wouldn't meet her gaze. 'I d-don't think I could. We're so short of nurses.'

'But if the Germans come—'

'I'd be a match for any German.' Rose tried to meet his eyes again, but failed. 'In any case, they couldn't do anything terrible to me. I'm a British nurse, and I'm protected.'

'Rose, all prisoners are protected, too. But they get shot — and worse.'

'I'll be all right,' insisted Rose. 'I'm miles and miles behind the line. Alex, it's so nice to see you. Let's go and find a café and have something to eat.'

She led him down a narrow street of bombed-out Flemish houses. As they walked, she tucked her arm though his and laid her hand upon his sleeve. There was nobody about, and he could have kissed her if he'd wished.

But he didn't seem to wish, so when she let him go to stoop and tie her bootlace, she didn't take his arm again.

They failed to find a café, and soon they were walking back towards the railhead. 'I have to go,' said Alex. 'Rose, listen to me. I want you to go home.'

'I can't, I'm needed here.'

'You won't be any use to anybody if you're dead.'

'They won't get me,' said Rose.

'You never listen to reason, do you?' Alex glared at her, his dark eyes burning. 'Rose, your trouble is you're spoiled, and much too fond of your own way. You never think anyone else might have a point — much less be right.'

'If we're told to leave, of course I'll go.' Rose looked at him and screwed her courage to the sticking point. 'Alex, I must ask you—'

'I came here to tell you to go home, not be asked a lot of questions!' Alex glowered at Rose. 'I don't know why I bothered. This afternoon has been a waste of time.'

As the train came puffing down the line, he turned and walked away, leaving Rose to stare in disbelief.

She wouldn't cry. There was no point in crying for Alex Denham. She'd known all along it was hopeless, that he would break her heart.

* * *

'They've broken through!' cried Elsie, running into the tent they shared and shaking Rose awake.

It was a cold March morning. Rose had done a twenty-four hour shift and was exhausted. 'What's happened?' she demanded, as she grabbed her clothes and started scrambling into them.

'The Germans have come through near Albert, thousands of them, our boys couldn't stop them. They've retaken Passchendaele, they'll recapture all the Ypres salient—'

'But Elsie, how—'

'Rose, get your flipping boots on! It doesn't matter about your cap. The Germans are less than fifteen miles from here, and we have to get the men away.'

The lorries — not enough of them — drew up outside the huts. Orderlies carried stretcher cases into them. Nurses helped the walking wounded climb into the wagons commandeered from neighbouring towns and villages.

When all the men were loaded, there was no room for nurses, so they started walking west. Columns of marching soldiers overtook them, and sometimes they got lifts in cars or lorries. Then they would be dumped beside the road.

'I'm sorry, Sisters,' a harassed-looking officer would say. 'We have to dig in here and wait for Jerry. You keep going west. If any of our convoys come this way, I'll ask them to watch out for you.'

No convoys came, so Rose and Elsie and a couple of dozen other nurses walked for three whole days, begging food from villagers who had hardly anything themselves, sleeping in barns and stables, and washing and drinking from the troughs and wells in stableyards.

All along the route they heard the same appalling stories. The British army was retreating. Millions of prisoners had been taken, and nothing could stop the Germans winning now.

* * *

The attack had been a sudden storm, a typhoon of terror that had scattered Alex's company and left small huddles of survivors sheltering in ditches, ruined barns or up against brick walls.

Some of his men were wounded and some been taken prisoner, but most of them were dead. The whole division was falling back in disarray, leaving behind it ammunition dumps and tanks that would soon be turned against the British, whom he could see were beaten anyway.

He was so afraid for Rose that he had no fear to spare for anybody else, even himself. Finding he was the senior officer in a raggle-taggle of men from half a dozen regiments, he realised they could run, surrender — or dig in and fight.

'We'll dig in here,' he told the men. He had regrouped them in a battered village square, ten miles or more behind last week's original British line. The houses had been flattened by the hurricane bombardment, and dead men and horses lay in grotesque attitudes everywhere. The village stood on a low rise from which they could survey the Ypres salient. They could see the enemy approaching, a grey mass of infantry and lumbering German tanks, following in the wake of the most deafening and terrifying bombardment Alex had ever known.

'They'll have to bring their lorries and heavy armoured cars along this road,' he said to the men, who looked at him like sheep, or dogs expecting to be fed. 'If we get the cobbles up and dig a row of trenches, we can hold them up for hours, or maybe even days.'

Stripping off his jacket, he picked up an entrenching tool someone had left lying in the road, and started hacking at the cobbles.

A sergeant found a spade and began hacking at the pavement next to him, and two minutes later the men had all found tools of some sort and begun to dig.

'I reckon we could mount an ambush,' said a sergeant major, who was digging hard by Alex's side. 'If we booby-trap these holes—'

'With what?' demanded Alex, testily. 'We don't have any shells, trench mortars—'

'But we've got grenades. The lads have their Lee Enfields, and you have your revolver. We can't blow their convoy up, but we could make it hot for them.'

'We'll all be killed,' said Alex, who was himself resigned to dying, but always hated losing men.

'I dare say we will,' agreed the sergeant major calmly. 'But if they take us prisoner, they'll probably bayonet us anyway. Sir, there are hospitals five miles from here. If we can make things difficult for Jerry, the nurses might have time to get some wounded blokes away — and to escape themselves.'

'We'll do it,' said Alex grimly, and dug on.

* * *

Rose's boots disintegrated on the cobbled roads of Flanders, and she walked the last few miles to freedom wearing wooden pattens given her by a farmer's wife. By the time she reached Boulogne, she had weeping sores the size of florins on her insteps. But these were nothing compared with the soreness in her heart.

As she and her friends had walked, they'd heard appalling, frightening stories. Hospitals had been shelled and nurses killed. Lorry loads of wounded had been bombed, and the survivors shot or bayoneted in cold blood.

In Boulogne, the nurses who had walked from Rose's hospital had two days to recuperate, then were needed on the wards again. Rose and Elsie found themselves in a converted chateau, doing dressings underneath enormous chandeliers and the disapproving gaze of nymphs who stared down outraged from elaborate painted ceilings.

As Rose was doing a ward round one May morning, Elsie came in grinning. 'We've beaten off the Hun!' she cried.

'What do you mean?' asked Rose, who was concentrating on a very awkward dressing.

'We've turned the tide!' Elsie was beaming like a summer beacon. 'The Jerries have overreached themselves, our boys have got them on the run. Rose, we're going to win this war!'

'Good,' said Rose, without expression.

'Rose, what's the matter with you today? Don't you realise it's a blooming miracle?'

'Elsie, could you move out of my light?' Rose frowned down at her work. 'I'm sorry, Captain Russell. This next bit's going to be a bit uncomfortable for you.'

Where was Alex, wondered Rose, as she picked some bits of shrapnel from the wound in Captain Russell's shoulder. Somewhere east of Ypres? Somewhere in the valley of the Somme? A prisoner, wounded, dead?

She wrote to him to wish him well, hoping the letter would catch up with him, wherever he might be. Then she wrote a letter to Maria, saying she was safe.

She didn't hear from Alex, but she did get a letter from Maria. *'I was so relieved to hear from you,'* Maria said. *'I was very anxious. But, my dear Rose, I have great faith in your resourcefulness, and I was almost sure you'd be all right.*

'I have a favour to ask you — yes, another one. I've been saving up my leave, and hope to get a chance to go to England. I want to look for Phoebe. I was wondering if you'd come?'

'Of course I'll come, if I can get some leave,' wrote Rose that evening. She was curious about Phoebe, who had disappeared into the aether — and she owed Maria so much.

After swapping shifts and begging favours, she managed to get three days — not much, but just enough to make it worth her while going to England, if she could get a passage.

She had arranged to meet Maria at the station in Boulogne, but as she was about to leave she was summoned to the matron's office. There was a stack of letters on her desk.

'Please sit down, Miss Courtenay,' said the matron. 'I'm sorry to say I have bad news for you.'

CHAPTER NINETEEN

The pile of letters told Rose everything. 'W-what happened to him?' she asked, determined not to cry.

'I beg your pardon?' The matron frowned, not understanding. 'My dear, are you engaged? I'm sorry, I didn't know.'

'I'm not engaged, but who—'

'A lady. She has made you her executor. Miss Courtenay, I'm so sorry,' said the matron. 'The Germans bombed a train three days ago. Your friend Miss Gower was killed.'

'Maria?' Rose stared, incredulous. 'I don't believe you. Maria can't be dead!'

* * *

'Go and have half an hour by yourself,' the matron added kindly, as she took the brandy glass from Rose's shaking hand. 'Walk in the gardens, if you wish. The air will do you good.'

Rose went to her room to weep. Sitting by the window, she gazed through a mist of tears at the summer flowers growing wild and straggling in untended beds.

She wondered if she was going to lose the only other person whom she loved. Or maybe she'd lost him already.

She hadn't heard from him for weeks. She knew he wouldn't have time to write long letters, but he could have sent a Forces postcard, scribbled a line or two to tell her he was still alive.

'Rose, try not to worry,' said Elsie, who had come off shift and made Rose tell her everything. 'I'm really sorry about your friend. But Captain Denham's going to be all right.'

'How do *you* know?' Rose demanded fretfully. 'Elsie, you don't have a crystal ball, you're not a seer.'

'I'm willing it, like I will my George to live. We have to live in hope, or we would all die in despair.'

'You sound just like that ghastly woman in the *Daily Mail*.'

'Sorry. Rose, where are you going now?'

'Back on the ward.' Rose tied her apron. 'There's no point in sitting wailing, is there? It won't bring poor Maria back, and I expect you want to go to bed.'

* * *

The hospital was full to overflowing. The fighting in the east meant convoys came in every day. The nurses all worked double shifts, but still they never finished. There were always more men coming in.

As well as the wounded, every day they took in more men who were sick or dying from a horrible new form of grippe or influenza that turned their bodies into putrid jelly. For these men the nurses could do nothing but give fluids and try to keep them comfortable. Most of them still died.

'Sister Crowley's got it too,' said Elsie. 'She's in isolation, and they say she's very ill. Rose, you don't look too good — not sickening, are you?'

'No, I'm fine,' said Rose, who had long since realised that death came first for those who wanted desperately to live — not for those who didn't care if they died.

In the middle of August Rose at last received a letter, but she was too tired to open it. She'd just worked round the clock, her mind and body were exhausted. She dropped it on her locker and then fell into bed.

She woke up four hours later, only minimally refreshed but due to go on shift again. As she dressed, she saw the letter and wondered about throwing it away. If she didn't know what was inside, it couldn't give her pain. But curiosity got the better of her and she slit it open. She steeled herself and read.

'We're giving them a hammering,' wrote Alex. *'We've broken through all their defences, taken thousands of them prisoner, captured all their guns.'*

He described a battle he'd fought in east of Amiens. The third battalion of the Royal Dorsets had taken seven hundred men and forty German officers prisoner, but had not had a single casualty.

Best of all he ended with, *'Look after yourself, my darling Rose,'* and sent her all his love.

'Sister Temple reckons things are looking up,' said Elsie, who'd just walked in yawning.

'She's absolutely right,' smiled Rose.

* * *

Alex supposed it was elation that had made him write to Rose so freely and unguardedly, sending her his love and laying himself wide open to her scorn. He hardly dared to hope she would reply.

But she wrote back at once. *'I've asked for leave,'* she said. *'It's difficult at present, with so many people sick and lots of nurses going down with influenza, too. I was due three days I didn't take, so I've asked Sister Temple if I can have them now.'*

As Alex's train pulled into Rouen, he saw her waiting on the station platform. He had a chance to look at her before she noticed him.

She was still so pretty it almost took his breath away. But she wasn't the girl he'd asked to dance, that evening in a long-forgotten spring. Then, she had been coltish, gawky, awkward. Now she was confident and self-assured. She was far too thin, of course, but almost all the nurses looked half-starved. He'd never seen a chubby one in France.

He watched her as she scanned the coaches, chewing her lower lip and — looking anxiously for him? She frowned — in disappointment? — as a captain from the Royal Sussex touched her arm then spoke to her, as she pointed to the Red Cross café, as the captain nodded, walked away.

He saw he had been right to take the risk. But, he told himself, he was a fool! Why had he ever doubted her? Why had he ever thought she didn't love him?

Then she saw him, and the most glorious smile lit her face. In his haste to get to her he almost fell out of the carriage, but he managed to right himself in time. He caught her in his arms and spun her round, knocking off her hat and making everybody stare at him.

'Do — do you remember Elsie Dennison?' she gasped, when he finally let her go and she had got her breath back.

'Of course I do,' said Alex, holding out his hand. 'Good afternoon, Miss Dennison.'

'We came down together, but Elsie's going shopping.'

'I need some writing paper.' Elsie blushed and dimpled and seemed inclined to linger, but then to his relief she walked away.

* * *

'You look well,' said Rose. 'You've put on weight, they must be feeding you again. What's this new ribbon on your tunic?'

'Oh, nothing important.' Alex shrugged. 'It isn't the Victoria Cross, or anything like that.'

'Let me see — blue and red — the DSO?'

'That's it, but Rose—'

'Why didn't you tell me when you wrote?'

'I'm not exactly proud of it,' said Alex. 'Actually, I thought I'd be court-martialled.'

‘Why, what did you do?’

‘I pulled a man out of a flooded crater, and carried him to safety. But we were in the middle of a battle, I was responsible for other people, and I should have left him to his fate. I don’t want to talk about it. We could find a café, if you like.’

‘Why don’t we go down here, then? It should bring us out on the main square.’

They walked along a narrow street that snaked between the high, blind walls of shops and warehouses. When they were half way down it, Alex stopped. ‘I don’t know how to say this,’ he began, ‘but I’m so very sorry—’

‘It can’t be helped.’ Rose had decided she’d be brave, that there was no reason why they should not stay friends, that she would not be bitter. ‘Come on, let’s find that café. You can tell me about it on the way.’

‘Rose, for heaven’s sake!’ He caught her arm. ‘I know I’ve been an idiot—’

‘We don’t arrange these things,’ said Rose. ‘Alex, it was lovely while it lasted. But—’

‘Oh, my God — you didn’t think that?’ Alex stared at her, his face a picture of amazement. ‘Rose, there’s no one else! There never was, there never will be!’ Now he held her by the shoulders, gripping her so tightly that she winced. ‘You must believe me!’

‘But—’

‘I’ve never lied to you. I’ve never been unfaithful to you, even in my dreams. Oh, Rose, my love — I’ve missed you!’

Rose looked hard at him and she could see he wasn’t lying — he was the sort of person whose every thought and feeling was written on his face, and he couldn’t have lied convincingly, even to save his life. ‘I’ve missed you, too,’ she said.

Then he kissed her with such sweetness and such tenderness that she couldn’t believe she’d ever doubted him, and she knew everything would be all right.

‘I must be going soon,’ she told him, as they drank their coffee. ‘I’m on duty again at eight tonight.’

'I have to go, as well. We need horses now, so I offered to fetch some from the depot here in Rouen. Otherwise I'd have never got away.'

'So you'll be doing cavalry charges, will you?'

'No, of course not, Rose. I'm in the infantry. But now we've left the trenches, everything is moving much more quickly. We company commanders have to get around our sectors, and to do that we need horses.'

'You're looking forward to going back.' Rose could see the sparkle in his eyes, and didn't fool herself that this was just because they'd reached a better understanding. 'The soldiers in this town all look like you — as if they've won some sort of prize. But, Alex — how *did* we turn the tide?'

'The Germans did it for us. They staked it all on one big push, and failed — but only just. If they'd held on a few more days, it would have been all up for us.'

'But now they're beaten?'

'Maybe.' Alex grimaced. 'It's up to us to finish it, so if we make a mess of this campaign, the whole damned business will grind on for yet another winter — or winters, possibly. I don't want to think about it.'

'It's time I went to look for Elsie.'

'I don't want you to go.'

'You have a job to do.' Rose smiled at him. 'So go and do it. Find your horses, catch your train back to the front, and try to stay alive.'

* * *

Alex meant to live. After years of skulking in a muddy, stinking ditch, he was more than ready for the proper battles in which he'd always longed to fight.

Today was going to be another Blenheim. He stood up on his stirrups and watched a khaki flood of Yorkshire infantry pour like cream into a breach, surround the German guns, then put a mass of bucket-helmeted, field-grey troops to flight. The Dorsets followed in a second wave, sinuously curving round a bluff and cutting off the enemy's retreat.

As they completed this manoeuvre, trapping a thousand German infantry and forcing their surrender, Alex was afraid he'd start to cry. He'd drilled these men, rehearsed them, led them, and they'd done him proud.

Like so many sheepdogs, they crouched with guns trained on their captured enemies who sat disarmed and desolate. Grinning and smoking Woodbines, they looked very pleased with life.

But some men weren't enjoying this at all. Some, including Michael Easton, were near breaking point. Every time a shell exploded, Michael winced and cowered, and the men in his platoon had long since ceased to take much heed of him, following their sergeant while their lieutenant dithered in the rear.

The following day the Dorsets took a village. They occupied the ruined houses, then checked these for booby traps and any Germans stragglers who might still be holding on and felt like dying hard.

Alex sent Michael's men to check some barns. He watched as they approached. The men went forward cautiously, Lee Enfields at the ready and using walls for cover. But Michael Easton wandered aimlessly, as if he couldn't give a damn — or was too scared to think.

'What do you make of Mr Easton?' Alex asked his company sergeant major, who crouched down beside him, watching the platoon advance.

'He's a liability, sir. You should get rid of him.' The company sergeant major shook his head. 'You should have done it months ago.'

'I didn't want to lose him. I think of all those snipers he's picked off, and all those men he's hit.'

'Yes, but we're not in the trenches these days. We're not potting snipers now. This is something different, and he's useless. Sir, just look at him. If there's any Jerries in those barns, any minute now they're going to turn him into carrion. Sergeant Black's in charge of that platoon, not Mr Easton.'

Fortunately for Michael, except for starving cats and mournful dogs to which the men fed bully beef and biscuits, the village proved to be deserted. So Alex told his officers and NCOs to post sufficient sentries, then get the company settled for the night. He sent for Michael, who took his time to come.

'Sit down, Mike.' Alex had set up company headquarters in a ruined cottage, but for the moment the two men were by themselves. 'Listen, I've been watching you today, and I've decided you'd be better out of it. So I'm going to send you down the line.'

'You have no authority,' said Michael. 'It's up to Major Whelan to decide.'

'I make recommendations, all the same.' Alex was tired, he had a lot to do before tomorrow, and he didn't want an argument. 'I'm not saying it's your fault. Some men don't adjust as well as others to battle situations, and nobody's to blame.' Alex stood up, stretching. 'Mike, I know we've had our differences—'

'You keep away from me!' As Alex's shadow fell upon him, Michael shrank away. 'God, I hate you! You've always taken everything that's mine, you've always spoiled it all for me, you bastard, son of a filthy whore—'

Then he was suddenly on his feet, and as Alex came towards him, Michael raised his fist as if to strike.

'I wouldn't hit a senior officer, Mike,' said Alex softly. 'If you do, you know you'll be court-martialled, and then they'll lock you up. In any case, if you hit me, I'll damned well hit you back, and twice as hard.'

Michael dropped his fist, but he glared at Alex with such mad, wild eyes that Alex shuddered, for he'd never seen such hatred, even in the eyes of men he'd wounded, even in the gaze of men he'd killed.

'Sit,' he rapped, as if he were talking to a disobedient dog.

Michael sat down on the broken chair.

'Stay there for at least an hour, do you hear me? If you move an inch, I'll throw the book at you, I swear.'

Alex went outside. He took a few deep breaths, then went to find an NCO.

'Lieutenant Easton is unwell,' he told the corporal he found brewing up some coffee in a can. 'I've left him resting in that cottage. Go and get a couple of your mates, and then take turns to stay outside.'

'You mean he's under arrest, sir?' asked the puzzled NCO.

'I don't mean anything of the sort.' Alex met the corporal's curious gaze. 'He needs a bit of peace and quiet, that's all.'

'Then, sir, if you will pardon me, he ought not to be here.'

'I know,' said Alex testily.

* * *

'Lieutenant Easton, sir.' Alex had not wanted to involve his senior officer, but he had no choice. 'He's lost his nerve, he should be out of it.'

'You think so?' Major Whelan sniffed 'Why, has he started shitting himself or something? Or frightening the horses, and setting a bad example to the men?'

'Michael Easton's scared of his own shadow. He should be on the general staff, or in a training camp — at any rate, somewhere behind the lines. Sir, you know he's never been a very effective officer.'

'He's no worse than any civilian halfwit playing soldiers,' said the major curtly. 'You regular army men expect too much of some poor chaps.'

'Sir, Lieutenant Easton is a danger to himself, and to his men — or he would be, if they heeded him.'

'You mean it, don't you?' Major Whelan tossed his pen across the grimy table. 'All right, Alex,' he conceded, sighing. 'Send him in to see me.'

* * *

'I interviewed young Easton.' Major Whelan shook his head. 'The chap seems rational enough to me. I agree he's always been a windy blighter, but he's not alone in that. Actually, I used to know his father — Tom Easton was a prefect in my house, a thoroughly decent sort.'

'Maybe, but with respect I think his son should see a doctor.'

'I don't know if it's necessary.' Major Whelan fiddled with a pencil. 'He's been through quite a lot. Been in it from the first, I understand.'

'Yes, but now he's done his bit and ought to be sent home.'

'He seemed quite sound to me.' The major frowned. 'I've noticed there's a bit of friction between young Mike Easton and yourself. A clash of personalities, or whatever those trick cyclist fellows call it these days.'

'That's beside the point.' Alex would not back down. 'Easton's ill, he ought to be discharged. I'd like you to put that down in writing, and I'll sign it.'

'You're making something out of nothing, man! Alex, you're a splendid officer. But you've had a damned long war yourself. You've been badly wounded several times, and I know about that business with your memory, when you got yourself hit on the head. It might be you who needs to be discharged.'

'I don't think so, sir.'

'Easton's the best marksman in your company, in the whole brigade. Perhaps you're slightly jealous? When you pulled him out of that damned crater, maybe he didn't thank you properly? Look, if he really bothers you, I'll transfer him to another company, will that be all right?'

Nobody will want him Alex thought, but didn't say.

'Actually,' the major said, 'this little problem ought to solve itself. The third battalion's moving soon. The orders came this morning. We're all going to Russia.'

Russia, thought Alex — why should they go to Russia?

CHAPTER TWENTY

'I beg your pardon, sir?' frowned Alex.

'You heard me, Mr Denham. Our government's keen to keep in with the Russians. Well, *some* of the Russians. Of course we don't support the Reds. They made peace with the Hun.'

'So we're going to fight the Bolsheviks?'

'I don't know about fight. There's civil war in Russia, as you know. I reckon we're being sent to make it clear to Comrade Lenin that the British Government supports the other side.'

The major scratched his chin. 'There are big ammunition dumps in Archangel, left there by our boys before this revolution business started. The Reds apparently help themselves, and Lloyd George isn't having it.'

Alex could hardly believe what he was hearing. 'You mean a crack battalion of seasoned fighting men is being sent to Russia to guard a heap of shells?'

'Yes, you could say that.'

'But we have unfinished business here.'

'Listen, Alex — other chaps are capable of dealing with the Germans. We're well out of it, if you ask me. This Russian stunt should be a cushy number, the men will be delighted, but don't go telling everyone just yet. It's all hush-hush for now.'

'I think the men should know at once.'

'I dare say they'll find out. They always do. You don't look very happy, man. I thought you'd be pleased?'

'Oh, I am, sir,' Alex told him, deadpan. 'I'm absolutely thrilled.'

* * *

He rode back to the ruined village where the third battalion was dug in. The British field artillery was pounding German strongholds a couple of miles away, and when the barrage lifted the battalion would attack.

Alex didn't want to go to Russia. He'd meant to stay in France, to see the Germans finally defeated, not hear about it in some distant land.

As he went downstairs into the cellar that served as company headquarters, his servant Private Arrowsmith appeared. 'I hear we're off to fight the Ruskies, sir?'

'How do *you* know, Arrowsmith?'

'Chinese whispers, sir.' Private Arrowsmith tapped his nose and grinned. 'A bloke from the King's Own Yorkshires mentioned it to me last Saturday. Good news, ain't it sir? All the lads is fit to bust with joy!'

Indeed, the men seemed jubilant and very keen to go. Alex supposed this was because although the Germans might look almost beaten, and there were rumours of an armistice, there were also rumours of a whole new battle plan involving tanks and aerial bombardment, to get under way the following spring.

Alex couldn't see the Germans holding out that long, but the enemy might have reserves. The Americans might pull out and go back home. Men who'd done it once would do almost anything, go almost anywhere, to escape a winter in the trenches.

A lot of them were going to escape it anyway, he decided. Dozens were ill with some sort of infection that made them sweat and shiver and eventually collapse. He'd sent five to the CCS that morning and, as the company formed up in readiness to attack, he could see that several others didn't look very fit.

* * *

A fortnight later he had three days leave, and met Rose in Amiens. He had hardly begun to tell her he was going to Russia before she informed him that she knew.

'But how did you find out?' he frowned, wondering what other secret plans were common knowledge.

'Elsie's father is on the Staff, he tells her everything.' Rose looked at him and smiled artlessly. 'Maybe I could come along?'

'I never heard anything so ridiculous. Rose, this won't be a parish outing.'

'It will be less dangerous than staying here in France. Especially if the Germans rally, like they did before.'

'They won't do that, they're spent, exhausted.'

'All the same, I'd like a change, to get away from all this mess and chaos.' They were in a bombed-out café that had just re-opened, drinking bitter coffee made from chicory and acorns, and eating yellow, rubbery *brioche*. 'They're bound to send some nurses, so I'm going to volunteer.'

'You can't go to Archangel.'

'Of course I can. Alex, you're such a spoilsport. You don't like me having any fun.' Rose looked at him from underneath her lashes. 'I'm never going to get another chance to go to Russia, after all.'

'I hope they keep you here in France. Russia's a ghastly place by all accounts, and the Russians are a vicious race. The Reds and Whites are equally sadistic. Both lots skin their enemies alive.'

'I'm sure they don't,' said Rose. 'Darling, sometimes you're so miserable. You don't like anyone or anything.'

Alex watched Rose cut into her cake and pop it piece by piece into her mouth. They wouldn't accept her, he decided, even though she had the skills and training.

Of course they'd send some nurses. But only about a dozen at most, and probably — hopefully — those would all be regular QA.

* * *

But Rose got what she wanted, then talked Elsie Dennison into volunteering too, although Elsie didn't need much persuading.

'It'll be so exciting!' she exclaimed. 'I can't wait to see the Northern Lights! Rose, do you think we might meet Eskimos? Will there be polar bears?'

'I hope so.' Rose stuffed clothes into a case. 'Elsie, I'm so glad you're coming, but I was surprised you volunteered. I thought you might have had enough of nursing. They reckon the Germans can't hold out much longer, and aren't you dying to go home?'

'Yes,' admitted Elsie. 'But this is my last chance to have adventures, so I want to go to Russia, too. When I get home, I'll have to settle down. I'll be a country doctor's wife, I won't go anywhere, do anything. If George comes back, of course.'

'I'm sure he will.'

'But even if he doesn't, my mother will want me back at Haddeston Manor. It'll be like it was before the war — paying calls and making soup for charity, playing tennis, knitting socks and gloves. My whole life was so trivial and dull, you can't imagine.'

'I can.' Rose thought of her mother and her life at Charton Minster. 'Mine was just the same.'

* * *

Elsie, Rose and twelve other nurses crossed the English Channel in a fog, then caught the evening sleeper train to Cardiff. The following morning they had a hurried breakfast in a Forces cafeteria, then stood watching from the quay as tugs and a flotilla of small boats brought the former P&O liner into Cardiff Bay.

'*What's* it called?' frowned Elsie, peering at the ship shortsightedly.

'The *Kalyan*,' Rose replied.

'What sort of a name is that?'

'They can't all be the *Galahad* or *Invincible*!' Rose laughed at Elsie's frown. 'Come on, let's go and get a better look.'

An hour later the two doctors, fourteen nurses and a dozen orderlies were allowed on board.

'This is wonderful!' cried Elsie as they walked the decks, exploring wards and operating theatres, all newly installed, all gleaming white. 'Look at this place! Look at all the lights, the tables, trolleys, all this new equipment. We've got running water. The last time *I* was in an operating theatre, we were in a horrible old tent and all the water was in buckets!'

The ship had been well-insulated, too. Radiators everywhere gave off almost suffocating heat. 'We won't be cold *this* winter!' Rose exclaimed.

'Miss Dennison and Miss Courtenay, do calm down.' The middle-aged QA sister in charge of all the nursing staff looked pained and disapproving.

'But it *is* exciting, Sister Harrison,' said a staff nurse. She turned to Rose and smiled. 'This is an adventure for us all.'

'It might be for you younger girls, but I've served in South Africa and Malta. So you must excuse me if I don't get worked up about a bit of ice and snow.'

Sister Harrison pursed her lips. 'Miss Courtenay and Miss Dennison, you may be volunteers, but don't forget you're still on active service. I should not need to tell you that you must behave with proper dignity and decorum at all times.'

Then Sister Harrison swept off — probably, thought Rose, to discipline the captain and the crew.

* * *

Rose and Elsie chose a cabin on the larboard side, so they could look out for whales and icebergs.

'When did Captain Denham leave?' asked Elsie.

'Last Thursday,' Rose replied. 'I didn't come because of him, you know. I probably won't see him, anyway.'

'Oh, you might,' said Elsie. 'I hope he doesn't get hurt, of course. But maybe we could get up concert parties now and then, if Sister Harrison agrees. Does Captain Denham sing?'

'I honestly don't know. So you think that old dragon plans to let us have some fun?'

'You never know. Staff Nurse Pelham says she might look like the wrath of God, but she's quite a sweetheart underneath.'

'I'll bet she wears an iron vest,' said Rose.

* * *

The ship took on supplies of food and fuel, and finally left Cardiff on the third day of November, escorted by a British battleship and three French destroyers.

They were off the coast of Lapland and Elsie had just spotted her first iceberg when the captain sent a message to ask the crew and passengers to meet him on the bridge.

'Ladies and gentlemen,' he began, 'I have just received a radio message. This morning, at eleven o'clock, Germany and all her allies formally surrendered. So the war is over.'

'Over?' whispered Rose. She suddenly felt cold. Although she'd been expecting this, although she'd dreamed and longed for peace for years, she felt somehow bereaved. She found she couldn't move. She couldn't say another word. She almost heard the silence ticking by. It was as if the crew and passengers had all been turned to stone.

Then Sister Harrison sighed and shook her head. She brushed her eyes, and Rose saw she was crying. Dr Miller bit his lip, and several other nurses started weeping, or blinking rapidly.

'We should be happy,' whispered Elsie.

'Yes, we should.' But Rose's eyes had filled. 'You'll see your fiancé soon.'

'I don't know about that.' Rose saw Elsie's eyes were very bright. 'George is still in Africa, and one of the crew was saying yesterday the ice is building up. We won't be going home until the spring.'

* * *

Twelve days after leaving Cardiff, the liner left the open waters of the cold White Sea and steamed into the estuary of the River Dvina.

Now, they were so near the Arctic Circle that the autumn days were barely light. But through her cabin window Rose could just make out the iron-grey hulks of British warships, which had come — to stop the Bolshevik Revolution? To safeguard British interests in Russia?

To make sure the Reds were hammered, as Alex might have put it, to support a noble cause, to help the Whites prevail? Or just to guard a heap of rusting shells, and in doing so waste more British lives?

Where might he be, she wondered, as she gazed across the snowy landscape at the deep, dark forest that must go on forever, at the wooden houses lurking among the slender silver birches, firs and pines.

'It looks like something from a fairy story,' whispered Elsie. 'I keep expecting to see elves and witches.'

'I can see some people.' Rose had acquired a pair of field-glasses, and now she pointed to the headland on which the town of Archangel was built, to the huddled clusters of grey-brown wooden houses among the winter trees. A scattering of more substantial buildings — a post office, a hospital, a city hall, perhaps — loomed in the gloaming near the centre of the town, and they could see the gilded onion domes of a small wooden church.

Smoke coiled lazily from the crooked chimneys. In the scrubby gardens, people bundled up against the cold seemed to be pulling roots. Or maybe they were feeding pigs or chickens.

'Let's go up on deck,' suggested Rose.

'All right, said Elsie, looking doubtful. 'If you think it's safe?'

'Why shouldn't it be safe?'

'I don't know.' Elsie shuddered, although the cabin was — as always — stifling. 'Rose, I don't like this place. Look at those awful woods.'

'They're only trees, for heaven's sake,' said Rose.

Muffled up in sheepskin greatcoats, thick serge skirts and sheepskin hats with ear flaps, Rose and Elsie leaned over the rail, watching as the crew dropped ropes and chains to men below. They gazed across the snowy landscape at the silver birches, at the forest — full of wolves and Bolsheviks?

They should be safe enough in Archangel, thought Rose. The docks and harbour had become an army camp, with tents and dozens of prefabricated wooden huts, with sentries stationed everywhere. The perimeter wasn't fenced or wired, she noticed, but perhaps there wasn't any need. The natural boundary was the forest.

* * *

Sister Harrison called a meeting of the nurses. 'You may leave the ship in pairs,' she said. 'You may walk around the army camp. But you may not leave it, and the town itself is out of bounds. This whole district is alive with Reds.'

'Why did we come here?' whispered Elsie.

'You may play hockey, if you wish,' the sister went on crisply. 'I'd recommend it, because the exercise will do you good. The men have marked out several pitches, and the brigadier tells me we may use them. Of course, there must be no contact with the men.'

'I'm sure you'll find a way to see him,' murmured Elsie. 'I expect he'll come and look for you.'

'Miss Dennison, did you wish to address the meeting?' snapped Sister Harrison.

'No, Sister Harrison,' Elsie said.

'Then have the goodness to attend when I am speaking, and stop whispering to your insubordinate friend.'

* * *

The weeks went by and Rose saw hardly anything of the army — just the men on sentry duty who stamped their dreary way round the perimeter of the camp, and the ones she treated on board ship.

From these few casualties, she learned patrols went deep into the frozen forest, staying there for weeks, looking for Reds. The actual front, where the White Russians and the remains of the Imperial Army were making their last stand against the Reds, was several hundred miles away.

There was lots of skirmishing in the forests. The beleaguered Whites were taking plenty of punishment from the Reds, the wounded soldiers said. The ammunition dumps were strongly guarded by British and Canadians, but still the Bolsheviks found ways to help their devious selves.

As time went on, a steady stream of wounded came out of the woods. Most of the men had gunshot wounds or frostbite. The wards for men and officers filled up. Lurid tales of what the Bolsheviks did to men they captured made Rose shudder.

'I'm sure they make it up,' she said, as Elsie shook and shivered. 'You know how soldiers gossip. They all exaggerate, and most of them tell lies.'

But as more casualties came in, floated on great wooden barges down a channel in the River Dvina or brought overland on fur-lined sleighs, Rose began to understand why people feared the Reds, and why the local peasants who brought wood and game into the camp had terror in their eyes.

The nurses were used to seeing awful sights and dreadful wounds, but now they started seeing things they'd never seen before — men who had been deliberately mutilated, men who had been captured by the Bolsheviks and rescued, but only after they'd been tortured.

Several nurses started having nightmares, and hardened veterans of the Somme and of the Ypres Salient refused to leave the safety of the ship.

'Did you hear about that poor young chap in Henley Ward?' Elsie asked Rose, shuddering, as they sat down to supper one December evening.

'You mean the one the Reds took hostage?' Rose didn't want to talk about it. 'Yes, I heard,' she said. 'Elsie, would you pass the gravy, please?'

'Staff Nurse Pelham told me Captain Miller's patched him up. But after what they did to him, I don't think he'll be able — I mean, he won't have children. He won't be a man.'

'I'm amazed the Russians are so cruel. They're far worse than the Germans.' Rose gave up trying to eat her supper. She sat back and lit a cigarette, hoping it would calm her fraying nerves.

Christmas came and went without the usual concert parties, dressing up or any other festive mirth. The war was over, they had cause to celebrate, but nobody was in the mood for fun. They wanted to go home, to leave this ghastly country, get away.

But the seas had frozen. They were trapped until the spring.

* * *

Rose tried to find out where the Royal Dorsets had been sent. She finally discovered they and the Canadians had gone deep into the forest. As well as the ammunition dumps, they were guarding fords and levees on the River Dvina, shooting wolves and Reds, and living like wolves themselves on what they hunted, beast or man.

She wished she'd never asked for details. 'They're *not* eating Bolsheviks,' she said, as she changed the dressing on a sergeant major's arm. 'Wolves and bears, perhaps. But British people don't eat other human beings.'

'If there's nothing else, they do.' The sergeant major shrugged. 'A Red tastes just like pork, without the crackling. Of course, you don't get apple sauce out there.'

* * *

One afternoon in January, as the sullen light was slowly dying, Staff Nurse Pelham came into the rest room where nurses not on duty read or sewed. 'Miss Courtenay, Sister Marlow, Miss Devine?' Rose saw she looked flustered and upset. 'You're needed down on Walton Ward. The Bolsheviks attacked a dump last night. The Canadians had the worst of it, but they got a few of our boys, too.'

As Rose and the other nurses hurried into the ward, an orderly was ticking off some names. As she passed him, she glanced at the list.

Lieutenant Fraser, KOYLI. Captain Morris, Berks and Bucks. Captain Denham, Second Lieutenant Lawson, Royal Dorsets.

It was as much as she could do to stand, for suddenly she was trembling and her legs were threatening to give way. What had they done to him, the murderous, filthy Bolsheviks? She grabbed the rail of a bunk, and held it while she swayed and tried to swallow rising bile.

'Miss Courtenay, come along!' Sister Harrison swept past, carrying swabs and dressings on a tray. 'You and Sister Marlow can deal with Captain Morris and Lieutenant Fraser, while Miss Devine and I prepare the other two for theatre. What's the matter, child?'

'N-nothing, Sister Harrison.' Behind the sister, Rose could see two bodies dressed in filthy, bloodstained khaki. Both lay motionless and silent. So were they unconscious, were they dead?

She forced herself to look away. She and the other nurse began to cut the tattered uniforms off the other soldiers, bracing themselves for horrors they might see.

'I saw the name!' Rose cried an hour later, as Elsie tried to reassure her, to suggest it might be someone else. But, failing that, to convince Rose it would be all right.

'Very well, he's wounded.' Elsie put her arm round Rose's shoulders. 'But they got him out of it, he's in theatre now, and Dr Miller is a brilliant surgeon. If anyone can do it, he'll pull Captain Denham through.'

'But will he have a life worth living?' Rose glared at Elsie savagely. 'You've seen what they do, those filthy butchers!'

'Rose, don't let yourself get carried away. Let's wait and see, all right?'

* * *

Alex knew he had been blinded. The darkness was so dense, so black, it couldn't be just night, not even this enshrouding Arctic night.

They were unwrapping him, as if he were a parcel. He lay there and let them, didn't murmur, didn't cry out when they hurt him, for what would be the point? If he'd lost his sight it didn't matter, nothing mattered any more.

It was a strange existence, being a soldier. One minute, you were out there on the battlefield, armed and powerful, killing people — or doing your best not to be killed. The next, you were lying on your back while people poked and prodded you, and you couldn't do anything to stop them.

They unwrapped the dressings round his head. A male voice was murmuring something, but he couldn't catch what he was saying, there was a roaring in his ears. Now he could see whiteness, brightness, and what he thought must be the sun, or an electric light.

'Call me if you need me, Nurse,' the male voice said crisply. 'Captain Denham, can you hear me? Your chaps got you out of it, you're going to be all right. You've got a head wound and concussion. Your vision will be blurred for several days, but in a week or so you should see normally again. The bullet wound in your leg looks rather nasty, but will heal.'

Then he was aware that someone in a nurse's uniform was leaning over him. Someone who smelled of soap and Lysol, but whose human, personal scent he knew. He thought he must be dreaming. He stared and tried to focus, but in vain.

'Alex, can you speak?' asked Rose.

'Yes, I can speak.' He would have given anything in the world to see her face, but it was still a blank, white shape. 'Rose, this is a vile country, full of vile people!'

'Yes, I know,' she said. 'But don't worry about it now. Just go to sleep.'

'I can't sleep!' He thought he'd never sleep again. 'That poor sod they caught, they crucified. We found him hanging from a tree.'

Then he felt a needle stab his arm, and everything dissolved into a mist.

* * *

Rose wasn't usually on Walton Ward, but four days after Alex had come in, she got herself transferred.

'You're looking better now,' she told him, as she changed the dressing on his leg one dull, grey morning. 'How's your vision these days?'

'It's almost back to normal, except that I see two of everything.'

'How many fingers am I holding up?'

'God, I don't know.' He frowned, then grinned. 'But there are two of you. Two Roses, twins — now there's a ghastly thought.'

'I see they're giving you too much morphine.' Rose put the used dressing in the bucket. 'Captain Miller says you're very lucky. They didn't crack your skull, and the bullet in your leg just missed the bone. I was afraid of gangrene, but although your calf is quite a mess, the wound looks pink and healthy.'

'So I won't lose my leg?'

'Of course you won't.' Rose reached for a bottle. 'Now, Captain Denham,' she said softly, as she swabbed the wound with Lysol, 'tell me you're sorry I came.'

'I wish you were anywhere but here in stinking Russia. What's that stuff you're putting on my leg? Jesus Christ, it stings!'

'Captain Denham, please don't use offensive language in the hearing of the nursing staff.'

'I'm very sorry, Sister.' She felt him watching her as she bound up the wound, and it was like being bathed in sunshine. 'You will come back and see me?'

'Yes, of course.' She walked off down the ward, her heart as light as gossamer. Alex might be sick, but he was safe.

* * *

Three weeks later, he was almost better. He could see properly again, and get about on crutches. Weak and obviously in pain, he still needed morphine. But he didn't have the greenish pallor he'd had when first brought in, bleeding from a head wound and shot through the leg, when he and his company had been ambushed by Reds.

There was hardly any contact with the outside world. Letters from England came infrequently, brought by the Royal Navy ice-breakers that patrolled the frozen Barents Sea.

'They've still got that awful influenza back at home.' Rose was helping Alex dress, and noticing how thin he was, how wasted. It would, she thought with satisfaction, be several months before he was passed fit, and by then they all might be in England once again. 'Celia's been quite ill, apparently.'

'So has Chloe,' said Alex.

'How do you know?'

'Henry wrote to me before we left.'

'I hope she'll be all right.' Rose met Alex's gaze. 'I don't want to hear of anybody sick or dying. There's already been too much of that.'

Alex shrugged and fumbled with his buttons. 'But some people seem to have charmed lives. Celia's bloody brother's still unscathed.'

'Yes, he's become quite famous.' Rose helped Alex step into his shoes. 'I was on a men's ward yesterday, and they were discussing Mr Easton, how he's come through the war without a scratch, and now it seems the Bolsheviks can't touch him.'

* * *

As Alex gained more strength, he started fretting and talking about going out again.

Convalescing men were sent to walk around the decks, and get some gentle exercise, but Alex paced the decks all day. One afternoon Rose found him sitting muffled in a coat, watching the sky. 'I'm going to ask to be discharged tomorrow,' he began.

'But Captain Miller says it will be weeks before you're fit again.'

'I want to get the buggers who crucified poor Arrowsmith.'

'You think you could find them?'

'They're holed up in a village near the river.' Alex's dark eyes narrowed. 'I know exactly where it is, and I'd only need a dozen men, a few grenades.'

The following day he was more restless still. 'It's so stuffy in this place,' he grumbled. 'The air's like cotton wadding. I can hardly breathe. Why can't we have the portholes open?'

'It's freezing hard out there, and if we let the cold air in, the radiators burst. Why don't you go on deck and walk around?'

'I'm sick of traipsing round the deck.'

'I'll be off shift in twenty minutes.' Rose glanced through a porthole. 'It's almost dark, but it's not snowing. If you wear your boots and hat and greatcoat, I'll take you for a stroll around the camp. You're right, it's very stuffy in the wards. I could do with some fresh air myself.'

* * *

Half an hour later, Rose and Alex left the ship to take their walk around the army camp.

There was nobody about, for all the men on duty were in the forests on patrol. The others were no doubt staying in their huts, playing cards and drinking potent local vodka, stoking the enormous cast-iron stoves with wood bought from the peasants, and getting up a comfortable fug.

Although it was mid-afternoon, the Arctic night had chased away the feeble Arctic day, and the purple sky was full of stars. Lights from the ship cast eerie shadows on the crisp white snow, so it was bright enough to see.

'It's beautiful,' said Alex, staring up into twinkling sky, then gazing at the forest. 'The world without the human race. What a delightful prospect that would be.'

'You don't mean that,' said Rose.

'All right, the world without the human race except for you and me.'

They were both well wrapped up against the cold, in fur-lined boots and greatcoats, sheepskin gloves and fur-lined Russian hats with flaps and peaks.

After they'd been walking for five minutes, Alex took Rose's arm, and leaned against her for support. He was still quite weak, she thought. They shouldn't stay out long.

They passed one of the pitches where the troops played hockey on the ice, but nobody was playing there today. Perhaps, thought Rose, they were afraid some Bolsheviks would come out of the forest, and take them away.

Only the previous week the Reds had captured seven British soldiers, hung them up from birches and tortured them to death, then left the bodies where they would be found.

'How far do you want to walk?' she asked.

'Just a little way, towards that clump of silver birches.' Alex let her go. 'I can stand up by myself,' he added. 'You go and run around a bit, get your circulation going, eh?'

'You won't collapse or anything?'

'Of course not, I'll be fine.'

So Rose went on ahead of him. Soon she was several hundred yards away. Although it was so cold, the air was fresh and clear and crisp.

Delighted to be getting exercise, and feeling almost *too* warm in her sheepskin coat and boots, she ran on through the freshly-fallen snow, scooping it up and throwing snowballs at the naked birches, almost forgetting she was in an alien, hostile land, and enjoying being a child again.

* * *

'Rose, come back!' Alex's voice cut sharply through the air.

She saw the shadows first, and thought they might be wolves or bears — or Bolsheviks. She didn't stop to check, but started sprinting back to Alex, afraid not for herself, but absolutely terrified for him.

Then, another English voice, this one with a familiar rural burr, rang out into the night. 'It's all right, Sister! We're a platoon of Dorsets — not a bunch of murdering Reds!'

Michael Easton and a dozen men, all muffled up in coats and boots and carrying heavy packs, came out of the shadows of the forest. Rose stopped and gasped in sheer relief.

She saw that Michael Easton's eyes were cold, and sharp as knives of ice. She wondered what he and his men had seen while they'd been in the forest — and what they might have done.

Michael stopped within a yard of Rose. 'March the men back to the huts,' he muttered to his sergeant. 'I need to have a word with Sister Courtenay here.'

'I'm going back to the ship,' said Rose.

'You're not going anywhere just yet.'

Michael's men trudged off into the darkness. 'So, Rose,' he whispered, and his vodka-tainted breath was sour on her face, 'I think we have something to discuss. When you ran away from me that day we met in Rouen, it wasn't very lady-like behaviour. I feel you should apologise.'

Rose stared up at him. She assumed he hadn't noticed Alex, or maybe he had chosen to ignore him, which was probably just as well. She didn't want Michael starting anything.

'Go back to your hut,' she said. 'We haven't anything to say to one another, least of all out here.'

'I want to know why you won't marry me.'

'Mike, I just — I don't—'

'You want me to beat it out of you?' hissed Michael.

'All right then, you're a liar and a coward!' Rose glared back at him. 'You seduced poor Phoebe, you deny the child is yours, but anyone only has to look at her to see your face! You might be a soldier, but you're only half a man!'

'You bitch,' said Michael, softly. 'You're not content to spread malicious rumours all round Dorset. You've even turned my family against me with your lies and gossip. Celia is besotted with that brat. She wants to have it living at our house. But I'm not having that, especially as I reckon it must be yours and Denham's.'

He grabbed her arm and held it, and suddenly she felt the touch of metal, hard against her face. The revolver steady in his hand, he held the muzzle to her head.

'You needn't think I ever wanted you,' he muttered, coldly.

'Let me go!' Rose kicked him hard, scraped her heel down his shin and hacked against his leg, but he was too muffled up to feel the impact.

'I don't let any woman make a fool of me,' Michael went on, bitterly. 'If I can't have you, no one can.'

'What the hell do you think you're doing, Easton?' At the sound of Alex's voice piercing the frozen darkness, Michael jumped and Rose groaned inwardly. Why hadn't Alex gone back to the ship? He was unarmed, unfit — he couldn't tackle Michael, who would trample him into the snow.

'Ah, the bastard.' Michael grinned. 'I wondered why your harlot was wandering around outside, but now of course it's obvious. You've been playing games out in the snow, and you've just played your last.' Still holding on to Rose, Michael took careful aim at Alex's chest.

CHAPTER TWENTY-ONE

Someone has to come, thought Rose, despairing. This camp must hold at least a thousand men. There must be working parties somewhere out there in the darkness. There are dozens of sentries in the forest, stamping up and down the tracks and looking out for Reds.

She could scream for help. But if she screamed, would anybody hear her in this waste of ice and snow, where every sound was muffled, and even the crack of gunfire sounded like a gentle tap on wood?

She shook her head. This must be a nightmare, she decided. I shall wake up soon. But if I *am* awake, it can't be Alex Michael wants to kill. Mike wants to pay me back for hurting him, and Alex is in the way.

She twisted round to look at him, to talk to him, to reason with him if she could, but at that very moment Michael fired. The shot went wide, startling some ravens lurking in the winter trees.

She heard Michael swear.

Alex was about ten yards away. 'All right, Easton,' he calmly, holding out one hand. 'You've had your bit of fun. Let go of Rose and throw the gun to me.'

'Go and fuck yourself,' spat Michael, giving Rose's arm a vicious twist. 'God, if you only knew I how much I hate you! All my life you've been there. Getting in my way, and poaching after everything that's mine!'

'Mike, I don't want anything of yours. I never did.'

'Don't come any closer!' Michael's grip had tightened. Rose could hear the panic in his voice, and now she was afraid — for him, for Alex, for herself. She knew most soldiers could be casually cruel, and frightened men did awful, dreadful things.

She'd heard them talking on the wards, about the times when fear had made them kill their wounded prisoners, or shoot down enemies who'd surrendered in cold blood. She could actually smell the fear on Michael, damp and rank as a dog fox.

The fear also gave him strength, for suddenly he jerked her arm so viciously she felt something crack. 'If you come any nearer, I'll kill you then I'll kill your whore!' he cried. 'I mean it, Denham! Don't play games with me!'

Rose knew her arm was broken, probably at the point where she had broken it before. Now, flames of pain seared past her shoulder blades, then licked across her collar bone. She couldn't flex her fingers or articulate her hand. She hoped she wouldn't faint.

She didn't know what to do. If she tried to hook her leg round Michael's, would he fall? Or would he fire again at Alex, and at such close range how could he miss? If she made one more effort to escape and somehow managed to get away, what could she do then?

Alex didn't know he was in danger, that was plain. He'd had a shot of morphine an hour or two ago. As well as dulling pain, morphine made men over-confident, and made them think they could do anything.

'Michael, let me go,' she whispered softly.

'Shut up, bitch.' Michael aimed his Webley. 'Come one step closer, Denham, and you're dead.'

But Alex took that step and, as he did so, Michael fired.

Alex fell, and Rose began to scream. She jerked away from Michael, finally breaking free, then rounding on him with a violent fury that evidently astonished him, for he stood stock still and let her kick him.

Trying to grab the gun, she hacked at him and fought him, cursing because her right arm wouldn't work and she was clumsy with her left.

He soon recovered from his surprise. He caught Rose round the waist and held her tight, her face pressed to his chest.

Rose wriggled free and screamed again with all her might, squirming and trying to claw at Michael's face. A second shot rang out, and Rose screamed louder and more desperately.

Then there was a third shot. Michael's gun flew from his hand. A spray of blood curved like a scarlet rainbow and fell pattering on the snow.

Yelping, Michael spun away from Rose. Then he sagged and crumpled, like a broken marionette.

* * *

The sound of gunfire and Rose's anguished screams finally brought men running from the huts.

They found a nursing sister, one arm trailing like a broken wing, crouching by a fallen man, desperately feeling for a pulse and calling out his Christian name.

'What's happened?' asked a sergeant, who was pulling on his greatcoat and staring at the scene with big, round eyes.

'Lieutenant Easton has gone mad!' Rose was trying to get Alex to sit up. 'This officer is bleeding from the forearm, and Lieutenant Easton's hurt as well.'

'Yeah, and he looks quite bad.' A corporal had gone to see to Michael, who was sitting on the ground and sobbing. 'It's his right hand — there ain't much left of it.'

The sergeant hunkered down by Alex. 'It's Captain Denham, isn't it?' he asked.

'Yes,' said Alex tersely. 'Where is Sister Courtenay?'

'She's here, sir,' said the sergeant.

'She's hurt?'

'Yes, sir, she's hurt. Sir, what shall we do with the lieutenant?'

'Take him to the guard room and tell Sergeant Blake to lock him up.'

'But Corporal Taylor says he's wounded.'

'Sergeant, do as you are told.' Alex struggled to his feet. 'Or *you'll* be on a charge.'

* * *

'What will happen to Mike?' asked Rose, as she watched three men march him away.

Alex shrugged. 'He'll probably be court-martialled, but I doubt if he'll be punished. I sent in a report before we left, saying I thought he shouldn't come to Russia, that he was mentally unfit, and that he should have gone home years ago. Rose, what did he do to you?'

'It's just my arm.'

'It's broken?'

'Yes, I think so.' Rose suddenly felt ill. The trees were moving, crowding in on them.

'Sergeant!' Alex caught her as she swayed. 'For God's sake, man — don't stand there gawking! Help me get Miss Courtenay to the ship.'

As she stumbled through the snow, supported by a sergeant and a corporal, Rose turned to look at Alex. 'I didn't know you had your Webley,' she said, frowning. 'You're not supposed to have a gun when you're in hospital.'

'Rose, I wouldn't have left the ship without one.' Alex grinned and dabbed at his left sleeve, which was now dark with blood. 'I wouldn't have brought *you* out here unarmed, with a million Bolsheviks and other scum about.'

* * *

Rose knew there would be gossip, that all the nursing staff would be agog. She hoped the fuss would die down quickly, but to her distress she soon became a cause célèbre. She'd saved the life of Captain Denham, who was everybody's favourite patient. But who now turned out to be in love with her — *and* was a married man.

Sister Harrison was scandalised. 'I shall be making a report at once,' she said severely. 'If this had happened in France, you would be on the boat back home. You might be an effective nurse, Miss Courtenay, but your personal conduct has made you a disgrace to the profession. I will not have nursing staff conducting love affairs on board my ship.'

'But the others all think it's romantic,' smiled Elsie, when she came to the sick bay to see Rose. 'Although there's a bit of envy, too. Staff Nurse Pelham's positively green that you should have a couple of officers fighting over you!'

'It wasn't like that at all.' Rose eased her plastered arm, then fiddled with the knots that held the sling. 'Elsie, how is Alex, do you know?'

'The bullet merely grazed him.' Elsie grinned. 'The wound just needed dressing. He'll be better in a week.'

'What will happen to him now?'

'Well, of course the boys are ragging him. But they all say he has good taste in nurses. After all, he nabbed the prettiest one.'

'He won't be court-martialled, or anything like that?'

'I don't think so. Why?'

'Sister Harrison's furious with me. She says I've brought the nursing service into disrepute, that I'll never be allowed to nurse a man or officer again. I'm a disgrace, and ought to hang my head in shame.'

'She's just a miserable old bat. I don't suppose she's ever had a man, or even been in love.'

'She's absolutely right, though.' Rose's grey eyes filled, then overflowed. 'He's married to another woman. I should never have got involved with him. He'll be the death of me!'

'We don't choose whom we love,' said Elsie. 'I was supposed to marry George's brother. He's the eldest son with all the money, and my mother had it all worked out.'

'But you fell in love with George?'

'Yes, I did,' said Elsie, and she blushed. 'Rose, you can't imagine all the ructions, all the carrying on! Everybody thought I must be pregnant. Or insane. My sister said I should be locked away.'

'You're a dark horse, Elsie Dennison. Why didn't you tell me this before?'

'You never asked. Anyway, when we first met, I was doing my hopeless best to be a proper nurse, and you'd begun a passionate affair with Captain Denham.'

'God, the risks I took!' Rose shook her head. 'You must have thought I was a lunatic.'

'No, I could see you were in love.' Elsie shrugged. 'That first stage doesn't last very long. Rose, you don't *have* to kiss him nowadays. You don't *need* to hear him say he loves you.'

'No, but of course I'd like to kiss him.'

'I'd give anything to spend an hour or two with George.'

'We can wait.' Rose grimaced ruefully. 'I'll have no choice. Thanks to Sister Harrison, I'm as good as under guard. If this ship had a dungeon, I'd be in it.'

* * *

Rose's arm took several weeks to mend, and February had turned into March before she could be any use again, this time well away from patients whom she might contaminate, or fascinate like a modern day Salome with her wanton ways.

The scarlet woman of the *Kalyan* spent her time in sluices, scrubbing bed pans, disinfecting urine bottles, sterilising kidney bowls and bleaching all the sinks.

She heard that Alex had returned to service, but she refused to think about him out there in the snowy wastes, or about the dangers he'd be facing in the forest.

The British army was shoring up a lost cause, anyway — or so Elsie said. The Whites were losing, all the men assured her, and back in Britain there was no support for British interference in Russian home affairs. The men were all demoralised and longing to go home.

So when Elsie came to find Rose one bright day in March, when it was still light at three o'clock and the Arctic spring was finally challenging the Arctic winter and the silver birches were showing tips of green, Rose was thrilled to hear they would soon be pulling out.

'When?' she asked, excitedly.

'After they've blown up all those ammunition dumps, of course.'

'Why can't we just leave the wretched dumps?' Rose turned back to her kidney bowls. 'If they start blowing things up, there'll be more injuries, more deaths.'

'I'm sure he'll be careful.'

'It's not just him!' cried Rose. 'I'm not that selfish! I care about the other men, as well!'

She began to scrub with angry fury. 'I don't want any more killing, maiming, dying. There's been enough these past four years to last the human race a century.'

* * *

The ammunition dumps were all blown up, mistakes were made, and more men died. The sound of tons of shells, grenades and high explosive going up made the black earth tremble. In the harbour at Archangel, the fleet of Allied ships rocked on the waves.

In April, heavy ice-breakers got through. They led the British warships through narrow channels cut in the still frozen Barents Sea.

'We'll see the spring in England,' Elsie said, as she and Rose stood on the deck, gazing hopefully towards the promised land, knowing they wouldn't see it for at least another week.

Rose thought about spring at Charton Minster, how it was the loveliest time of year, a dream of blue and gold. She'd done her travelling, and was looking forward to being home again, to seeing Celia, Daisy — even her father, if he would let his wayward, prodigal daughter visit him.

She was returning in disgrace. Sister Harrison had told her she would not be getting a campaign medal. As soon as she stepped off the *Kalyan*, she'd no longer be an army nurse — or any other kind, if Sister Harrison had her way. She had embroiled the nursing service in shame and ignominy.

'What will you do now?' asked Elsie, as their ship steamed into Liverpool.

'I don't know,' said Rose.

'Do you have any money?'

'Yes, a little.'

'I think you should go home and see your father.'

'I might not be welcome. He said he was going to change his will and disinherit me.'

'Go to Dorset anyway, and if there are any problems, come and stay with me.' Elsie handed Rose an envelope, and Rose knew by the feel of it that it was full of money.

'Elsie Dennison, you're a brick,' she whispered.

'You're my friend,' said Elsie, and she smiled. 'It'll work out, you'll see. You and Captain Denham, I mean. You're going to be all right.'

'Elsie, I don't even know if he's alive or dead.' Rose put the envelope in her bag, telling herself she'd get some sort of job without delay. Elsie would have her money back before the year was out.

She caught a train to Dorchester, and then took the branch line down to Charton. She walked along the private gravelled road which served the Courtenay family estate, then cut across the fields.

She stood on a small bluff from which she could see the little Dower House and the great golden Minster, then the distant headland and behind it a blue curl of sunlit sea.

She'd never seen a sight so gloriously beautiful, never felt such passionate love for this green, rolling country. It broke her heart to know she had no right to be here, that if her father wanted he could have his steward or his bailiff turn her off his land.

As she stood and gazed, she realised she had not come home. She would be a wanderer now, and Charton would never be her home again.

CHAPTER TWENTY-TWO

'Rose! Rose, wait for me!'

She turned to see Alex running up the path that branched off from the village. In a pair of moleskin trousers and an old tweed jacket, he looked more like a gipsy than a soldier.

Then she saw the smile that had enchanted her so many years ago. She dropped her case and ran to meet him.

They stood there hesitating for a moment.

Then Alex took Rose in his arms and kissed her, tenderly at first, and then with mounting passion, and she forgot her earlier dejection, for now she knew that in the truest, most important sense she had indeed come home.

'I knew we would be leaving two or three days before the *Kalyan* sailed, but I didn't dare get in touch with you,' he told her, as he held her tight. 'I didn't want to get you into any further trouble.'

'You couldn't have done that.' Rose shook her head. 'I've been dismissed. I left the service in disgrace. I'm not to be invited to any of the reunions they're planning. I won't get any medals. I shan't be taking part in any victory parades.'

'It's all because of me,' said Alex. 'If you hadn't got involved with me, you'd be a matron now. You'd have whole rows of medals.'

'I don't know about medals, but I might still be a nurse, if not a very good one.'

'Rose, don't be ridiculous. You did your bit, and more. Whatever anyone else might say, I'm very proud of you.'

'That's something, I suppose.'

'Do you have a smile for me, my darling?'

'I'm sorry, Alex. It's wonderful to see you, but I'm tired.'

'So let's get you to bed.' Alex picked up her case. 'I suppose you're going to the Dower House?'

'Yes, I was going to see my father. But I don't know if he'll let me in.'

'Come and stay with me and Henry, then.' Alex took her hand, and led her in the opposite direction to the Dower House.

'But — but where's Chloe?' faltered Rose.

'She's staying with her parents at the depot. I don't suppose she's coming back to me.' Alex shrugged. 'The house is grim in winter, I'll admit. But it's almost bearable in spring.'

So Rose went back to Henry Denham's house. She went straight up to Alex's room, undressed and went to bed.

She slept all day, and when she finally woke up she saw Alex sitting by the window, his feet up on the sill, and he was staring out across the fields.

'Alex?' Yawning and stretching like a cat, she smiled at him. 'What are you doing over there?'

'Just making plans and wondering if they'll come to anything.'

'So tell me, then?'

'Do you want to spend your life with me?' Alex came over to the bed and sat down next to Rose. 'I don't think I can live without you, but when I think about all the time I've wasted, and how badly I've behaved, I feel you'd be much better off without me.'

'Then I'd die,' said Rose. 'Last year, when I thought you didn't love me, the only thing that kept me going was having a job to do. I was just pretending I was living. I was as good as dead inside.'

'Oh, Rose, I'm sorry!'

'So you should be.' Rose poked Alex in the chest, and grinned at him. 'Where did you get this ghastly outfit?'

'These are Henry's clothes. The roof above this bedroom leaks, and last winter all my stuff got soaked. Everything is mildewed and decayed.'

'Well, you look like a poacher, as if you should be up before the Bench. So get undressed and come to bed.'

* * *

'What happened to Michael?' Rose asked Alex, as he and she lay tangled up in sheets and eiderdowns, several hours later. 'I couldn't find out anything. The nurses were forbidden to discuss the men with me.'

'They had a surgeon look at him, and take off his right hand. Then he was invalided home to Dorset, suffering from neurasthenia. That was the official diagnosis, anyway.'

'So there was no court martial, after all?'

'No.' Alex shrugged his shoulders. 'They don't court martial madmen. Of course, since he came home, there's been some muttering in the village — why hasn't Mike won any medals, why is he hiding up at Easton Hall, why doesn't he want to show his face in church, and all that kind of thing. You know how soldiers gossip, there's been a lot of speculation back at barracks about what went on in Russia, and it's spreading round the village, too. But Lady Easton's going to give a party to welcome him back home. I don't believe the Denhams are invited.'

'If they were, I don't suppose they'd go.'

'Well, Henry might, if Mrs Sefton called for him, and drove him in her trap.' Alex lay back against the crumpled pillows and took Rose in his arms. 'You still have the locket I gave you.'

'Did you think I'd lose it?'

'I thought you might decide you didn't want to wear it any more.'

'Alex, listen to me,' said Rose, 'and listen carefully. Do you see this old quilt? You'll notice that it's leaking.' She pulled out a big handful of soft down. 'If I hear another word of nonsense, I shall push this stuffing down your throat!'

* * *

They stayed in bed for three whole days, occasionally going down to the decrepit kitchens to forage in the stone and marble larders, and having cold collations of whatever they found there back in Alex's bed.

They plundered Henry's cellar, and drank his pre-war burgundy straight from the dusty bottles. Alex lost all his English inhibitions and became a savage, wanton lover, his smooth, brown body coiling like a snake, possessing and devouring Rose.

She was drunk with love. So much kissing meant her mouth was swollen, and her neck and breasts were blotched and bruised from too much loving, of which she knew she'd never have enough.

'What must Henry think of us?' she whispered the fourth morning, after another glorious, sleepless night.

'He's probably delighted we're so happy. Come on, let's get up. I have to go to work today.'

'Why, what are you doing?'

'I'm still in the army, don't forget, so I have to do a stint in barracks now and then.'

'In Dorchester?'

'Of course.' Alex shrugged his shoulders. 'But there isn't much to do, so I get home quite often.'

'Good.' Rose bit her lip. 'I suppose I ought to go and see my father.'

'Yes, you should.' Alex grinned and shook his head. 'I'm sure the village hags have been their usual busy selves, so Sir Gerard's bound to know you're back.'

* * *

Rose left it a few days, then she found she couldn't leave it any more. She took the path that led her past the Minster.

The convalescent officers were long gone, and the great, golden house was full of workmen, cleaning, painting and re-polishing the scuffed and pitted floors.

No one challenged her, so she walked upstairs to her old bedroom, where once she'd schemed and dreamed — it seemed like half a century ago. She stood and gazed towards the distant headland, towards the sunlit Channel.

'May I help you, madam?' said a woman's voice that held the warm, familiar Dorset burr.

'Polly?' Rose spun round to see her former maid, who carried a pile of dust sheets and was frowning. The frown soon turned to recognition, and Polly's face took on a look that Rose could not interpret.

Then she realised that thanks to Henry's servants, her amatory exploits must be common knowledge in the village, and Polly's expression must be one of scorn.

'I was on my way to see my father,' Rose said, lightly, 'but I thought I'd look in here first.'

'The poor old Minster, it's not a pretty sight.' Polly laid the dust sheets on the bed. 'Those soldiers were a very grubby lot. The nurses weren't much better. Miss, you should have seen the bathrooms. I've never been so disgusted in my life! It'll be years before we're straight again.'

'Where's Sir Gerard, Polly?'

'He's still living at the Dower House, miss. He hasn't got the heart to move back here, where he and your mother — well, you know.'

'I hope he's well?'

'He had a couple of colds last winter, but now summer's coming I hope he'll be all right.' Rose saw Polly looked embarrassed now. She was pink and blushing, and her hands were twisting nervously. 'M-miss Courtenay?'

'Yes?'

'I don't want you to hear this in the village, so I'll tell you myself.' Polly looked past Rose's head. 'Miss, I hope I've always known my place?'

'Polly, of course you have. But nowadays—'

'It's just that — well, your father is a very lonely man. After you went to be a nurse, and poor Lady Courtenay passed away, he — he had nobody.'

'I'm back now, Polly,' Rose said softly. 'I'll make it up to him, I promise.'

'Miss, it isn't that, and whatever Mrs Sefton says, I'm not a fallen woman! I don't want his money, or to come between him and his daughter. I love you both too much for that. But Miss Courtenay, poor Sir Gerard—'

Polly was bright scarlet. 'Them awful, spiteful things I said to you, Miss Courtenay — I've thought about them often, and I'm so ashamed.'

'It's all right, Polly.' Rose finally understood. 'I don't mind,' she added, remembering Elsie's words. 'I know as well as anyone that we don't choose whom we love.'

When Rose called at the Dower House, her father wasn't there. Or he wouldn't see her, but she didn't force the issue with the nervous-looking maid.

By the time she returned to Henry's house, she found that Alex had gone out, but not to work, apparently.

'He had a phone call, and then he went off somewhere in my car.' Henry was bumbling round his rotting orangery, tending his collection of dusty-looking cacti and other spiny, predatory plants. 'I'm just about to have a spot of luncheon, if you'd care to join me?'

* * *

'You're looking well,' said Alex, as Chloe leaned her powdered cheek towards him and he kissed the air obediently.

'*You* look awful.' Chloe stared at him. 'I used to think you were so handsome. But you're not handsome now.'

Alex was determined not to let Chloe rile him. He ushered her from the street into the inn where he had booked a private dining room.

He ordered all three courses to be brought and left in chafing dishes. Then he sent the man away, saying he and Mrs Denham would serve themselves.

'Why did you want to see me?' Alex asked, as Chloe started on her soup. Then, when Chloe didn't reply, he added, 'Chloe, I've been thinking. If you could see a way to let me go—'

'So you can marry the harlot?' Chloe sniffed and shuddered. She stroked the collar of her new and clearly very expensive jacket with one smooth, white hand.

'I think it would be best for all concerned if you and I admitted we're not suited,' persisted Alex.

'*You* can admit whatever you choose,' said Chloe. '*I've* done nothing wrong.' She glared at him, her pale eyes narrowed. 'You do admit desertion, adultery and cruelty?'

Alex shrugged.

'Very well, if you agree you're in the wrong, I'll go and see my solicitor tomorrow.'

Alex stared, astonished. What solicitor? Why was Chloe being so decent? Why was she agreeing to let him go? Carefully, go carefully, he told himself. 'The fault will all be on my side,' he murmured.

'Well, I should hope so, too.' Chloe's eyes were slits. 'I don't suppose any woman had a husband worse than you!'

'How will you manage?' Alex asked, aware that he was holding a box of live grenades which threatened to go off all at once. 'I mean financially?'

'You'll have to make a settlement on me.' Chloe's blue eyes glittered. 'My lawyer's already given me some good advice on settlements.'

'Chloe, who *is* your lawyer?'

'Mr Reade of Reade and Makepeace, not that it's any concern of yours, I'm sure.'

'That's the Easton family's firm,' said Alex, and the smell of rats was suddenly so strong and all-pervasive that it overpowered Chloe's expensive scent of roses.

'So now they're *my* solicitors, as well.' Chloe's eyes were icicles of malice. 'You and that woman — you're going to be so poor, you know. So very, very poor.'

Alex sat there silent, not knowing what to think — let alone to say. Chloe couldn't afford the services of Reade and Makepeace. She couldn't afford expensive clothes. What was Michael Easton up to now, and how was he involved in this?

He pushed his soup aside, got up and left the inn.

* * *

'Let them do their worst,' said Rose. 'They can't take your money, because you don't have any money. They can't destroy your reputation. Michael has no influence in the army, and even if he tried to do you down, your commanding officers would all stick up for you. What else is there to fear?'

'The worst thing — losing you.'

'Well, I'm afraid you're stuck with me.' Rose stroked his hair back from his forehead. 'Please stop frowning, it makes you look so grim.'

'I want to marry you, and make a decent life for both of us, but if Chloe ruins me financially, how are we going to live?'

'You'll think of something, Alex. You always do.' Rose shrugged her shoulders. 'I could take in washing.'

'It might come to that.'

'I don't care, as long as I have you.'

* * *

A few days later, Alex told Rose he had to go to London for a week.

'Why?' asked Rose, and followed him upstairs into their room.

'I have some things to do, people to see.'

'May I come, too?'

'It's only boring army business, darling.' Alex threw his shaving things into a battered case. 'It wouldn't interest you.'

'But why are you going to London? I thought you were based in Dorchester?'

'London's where I'll find this chap I need to go and see. I'll soon be home again, don't worry.' Alex grinned at Rose. 'You haven't seen the last of me.'

Rose saw Alex off at Charton station. Then, mainly to distract her from her fretting, she started cleaning Henry Denham's house, chivvying the elderly female servants and geriatric butler into taking down the curtains for an airing, cleaning all the filthy, fogged-up windows, and beating all the grime-encrusted carpets on a line.

Two days later, when she'd finished and Henry hadn't even seemed to notice, let alone be pleased, she wondered why she'd bothered. She looked around for something else to do.

Eventually, she decided she couldn't put off seeing Sir Gerard any longer. She walked up to the Dower House, prepared to insist on seeing her father, pushing past all his servants if this proved necessary.

But she was admitted straight away and shown into Sir Gerard's drawing room, where he sat in an ancient dressing gown, drinking his morning coffee.

'Sit down, Rose,' he said.

She sat, and saw he looked much better than when she'd seen him last. Polly must be doing him good, she thought.

'You've come to your senses, then?' he asked.

'I beg your pardon, Daddy?'

'You've come back home, and you've decided you will do your duty?'

'My duty?'

'You're going to marry that young man who always did *his* duty, and who loves you still.'

'I haven't seen Mike since I got back,' said Rose.

'Then I suggest you do, before he decides to make any alternative arrangements.'

Sir Gerard stirred his cooling coffee with a silver spoon. Rose looked at the carpet and wondered what to say — should she tell her father what had happened, how Michael had behaved in Russia, tell him the village gossip was all true?

She didn't think he'd believe her — or the village.

'I saw our Mr Heatherley on Tuesday,' said Sir Gerard.

Rose looked up at once, wondering why he'd seen the family's lawyer, and suddenly afraid her father must be ill, or even dying.

'I've settled all my affairs,' he said. 'Rose, you know that Charton has been in our family for a thousand years, or thereabouts?'

'Yes, of course, but I—'

'I have no male heir, so I have had to make some hard decisions.' Sir Gerard shrugged. 'You've proved yourself to be the usual kind of female flibbertigibbet, so I've made sure you'll have some proper guidance when I'm gone.

'Rose,' he continued earnestly, 'forget this man you're seeing! Marry someone worthy of you! Marry a man who'll care for you, look after you?'

Rose didn't trust herself to speak.

'I'm gifting the whole estate to Michael Easton,' said Sir Gerard. 'I have no plans to marry again, and in default of any male succession, it appears I can do this.'

So Michael Easton would inherit Charton. Rose felt as if her father had punched her in the stomach, or hit her with a hammer. But she wouldn't beg, she wouldn't plead, she wouldn't grovel, and she certainly wouldn't marry Michael Easton.

'In that case, Daddy,' she said stiffly, 'I'd better tell you now. I'm going to marry Alex.'

Sir Gerard shrugged. 'If you marry a man who's been divorced, I won't be able to see you any more.'

Rose could see he meant it. The choice was Michael, misery, wealth and comfort, or Alex, happiness and poverty.

There was no choice.

She stood up, kissed her father on the brow and left the room. As she left the Dower House, she knew she couldn't blame him, for he was a product of his class, of prejudice, of narrow-mindedness handed down the Courtenay generations for a thousand years.

In shock, but knowing deep down that she'd expected something like it, she went into the village to see Daisy.

* * *

After several visits to the cottage, Daisy got used to Rose, and even started looking out for her, so Rose began to take the little girl for walks or outings in Sir Gerard's ancient gig.

Rose and Mrs Hobson got on well. By June, she was no longer stiff *Miss Courtenay*, the landlord's well-born daughter, but plain and simple Rose.

She often took Daisy to the shingle beach, where they had impromptu sandy picnics, and looked for whelks and fossils.

'She's such a little poppet,' Rose said wistfully, as she returned the sleepy infant to her foster mother at the end of yet another lazy, lovely day spent watching fishing boats go out, and paddling in the surf.

'She's my little precious.' Mrs Hobson took the dozing child. 'She ain't my blood, I know. But I loves this baby like my own.'

* * *

It was as if the war had never happened. Alex was still based in Dorchester, where he was adjutant to the colonel, doing paperwork all day and grumbling he'd have joined the Civil Service if he'd wanted to be a clerk.

When he was on leave, he joined in Rose's and Daisy's expeditions, and Daisy got to know him, squealing with delight whenever Alex picked her up and swung her round, and fishing in his pockets for sweets or little toys.

'She's such a flirt,' said Rose, as Daisy whispered into Alex's ear, or smiled from underneath her long, soft lashes, coyly looking up at him. When Alex smiled at her or spoke, she blushed and hid her face, then peered round Rose's skirts and beamed, her lovely blue eyes bright.

She was her father's child in looks. Everybody in the village said so, and for once the gossip was well-founded, for she had Michael's eyes, his mouth, his nose, his corn-gold hair. All she had of Phoebe was her heart-shaped face and charming smile, her sweet, flirtatious air. Michael might be able to deny his daughter now, but one day he was going to have to face it.

Daisy Hobson was his child.

* * *

'A letter for you, my dear,' said Henry, one hot July morning. 'The fellow brought it from the Dower House.'

When Maria died, Rose had written to Phoebe Gower care of Mrs Rosenheim, but not had a reply. Now she realised why. The letter had come from Leeds, and Phoebe's scrawled directions were all wrong, so the letter had been sent all over Dorset.

She wrote back at once, inviting Phoebe to come down to Charton and stay at Henry's house.

Phoebe got down from the train at Charton looking scared. She stared around aghast, as if she'd never seen green fields or rolling hills before. She sniffed suspiciously, as if she'd never breathed sweet, country air.

'Rose, thank God you're 'ere!' She fell on Rose's neck and hugged her tight. 'Them people in the carriage, they've been giving me such looks! As if I was from Afriker, or somethin'. What's wrong with me 'at, I'd like to know?'

'Your hat's divine, and you look lovely — that's why people stared.' Rose took the visitor's arms from round her neck. 'Phoebe, this is Daisy.'

''Ello, sweetheart!' Phoebe crouched to smile at the child, but Daisy went all shy and hid her face.

'She'll come round,' said Rose. 'Where's your luggage? Just this case? We'll carry that between us.'

They walked out of the station and through Charton village, then took the road that led them past the Minster.

'I used to live there once,' said Rose, and pointed to the honey-coloured house.

'You never did!' Phoebe stared, amazed and open-mouthed. 'Your old man a duke or somethin'?'

'No, he's just a country gentleman. The Minster's been our family home for centuries, but I'm not welcome now.'

'Where you stayin', then?'

'At a friend's house. You'll be staying there, too.'

'You mean with your feller, Daisy's dad?' Phoebe's huge, dark eyes were suddenly scared. 'Rose, I don't really think I want to see—'

'Phoebe, I've told you half a dozen times! Michael's not my feller, as you put it, never has been, never will be!' Rose scooped Daisy up. 'Let's get a move on, then we'll be in time for tea.'

They got back to Henry's house just as one of the ancient maids was staggering through the double doors and out on to the terrace with the tea tray, where Henry was sitting in a wicker chair.

'Ah, Rose and young Miss Daisy and a friend.' Dressed like a vagrant in his mildewed, ragged tweeds, Henry scrambled up and bowed to Phoebe, who stared at him, astonished. 'How do you do, Miss—'

'Gower, Phoebe Gower. Phoebe, this is Mr Henry Denham.' Rose and Daisy sat down on a bench, and Rose motioned Phoebe towards the other wicker chair. 'Thank you, Eliza, you may go. I shall pour out the tea.'

Phoebe stared around as if amazed. Although the house was crumbling and decrepit, the terrace looked very beautiful in summer, with its riot of scarlet pelargoniums in the weathered troughs and great stone urns, with its formal paving of lichened, golden stone, and its view of headlands, fields and sea.

Rose blessed Henry Denham, who put Phoebe at her ease, asking her about her journey, smiling and looking interested in everything she said.

He drank his tea and then excused himself, saying he ought to go and see his roses. Daisy toddled after him.

'I'll be sorry to see Daisy go,' said Rose, as they watched the little girl take Henry's wrinkled hand. He offered her a biscuit from his pocket, and she scattered crumbs for his little flock of tame white doves. 'She's such a lovely child.'

'Yeah, she's a peach.' Phoebe gazed across the heat-hazed garden. 'Looks just like 'er dad, though. Rose, when you brought 'er 'ere, did you 'ave any trouble?'

'You mean, did people wonder whose she was?' Rose shrugged. 'Well, as you say, it's obvious she's Michael's. I imagine all the village biddies thought she must be mine. But as for actual trouble — well, not really, no.'

* * *

Leaving Henry to look after Daisy, Rose took Phoebe to her room, ready to apologise for all the mushrooms growing on the walls and the air of general decay.

But Phoebe was enchanted. 'Look at that enormous bed!' she cried. 'All them velvet curtains! Rose, it's like in a film! Milady's boudoir, eh? I'll feel like I'm the queen tonight!'

'Phoebe, it's just a big, old-fashioned bed.' Rose put Phoebe's little cardboard suitcase on the chest of drawers. 'Let's go and find Daisy now.'

Rose had arranged with Mrs Hobson to keep the little girl at Henry's house, so she and Phoebe could get to know each other before they went away.

But as the days went by and Phoebe's pale skin tanned a golden brown, Rose saw Phoebe took very little interest in the child. She spoke to her and played with her, but never sat her on her lap or cuddled her. If Daisy wanted reassurance or affection, she always went to Rose.

'You don't need to be afraid of Daisy,' Rose told Phoebe one cool evening, after they'd put the little girl to bed. 'I know she's small, but children are quite tough.'

'Yeah, I suppose they must be.' Phoebe shrugged. 'Rose, do you play cribbage? Henry was tellin' me 'e 'ad a board.'

* * *

Alex had been away from home, but now he had some leave and was in Dorset for a week. 'Alex, this is Phoebe Gower,' said Rose. 'She's come to visit Daisy.'

'Good afternoon, Miss Gower.' Alex held out his hand and Phoebe smirked, preening herself and patting her neat chignon of dark hair, a flirt just like her daughter.

Although he was polite and pleasant, Alex seemed proof against all Phoebe's charms. After they'd had tea and cake and talked about the weather for a while, he took Rose indoors, leaving Daisy looking at her mother.

They went straight upstairs. Afterwards, Alex lay back on the pillows. 'The third battalion's marked for India,' he said, and stared up at the ceiling.

'When did you find out?'

'There was a rumour several weeks ago.'

'That's why you went to London, wasn't it?'

'Yes, to see a man who'd just got back.'

'When do you go?' asked Rose.

'September or October. I've been bumped up to major. So I'll have a decent bungalow, some money, all the servants I could need. In India, I'll be living in a style I could only dream about in Britain.' He turned to her at last. 'Rose, how would you like to be a *mem*?'

'You mean you'd take me with you?'

'I'd be going for twenty years! I'm certainly not leaving you behind!'

'But we won't be married before you leave, there isn't time.'

'That's what I went to see this chap about. He was in a similar situation. Rose, I know it's not ideal, but Kendall says that if we don't rock any boats, there shouldn't be any problems. You'll be Mrs Denham, you'll be treated as my wife, and shown the same respect. As soon as the divorce comes through, we'll marry. So are you coming?'

'Alex, you'll be marrying a pauper,' Rose reminded him. 'Daddy won't change his mind.'

'Let Easton inherit the whole of Dorset,' Alex said, so softly that Rose could hardly hear the words. 'My darling, I have *you*.'

'What about Chloe's settlement?'

'Henry says he's going to pay her off.' Alex shrugged. 'I'll pay him back. I'll make my fortune out in India, and I'll pay him back, I've promised him.'

* * *

The following morning, Phoebe seemed subdued, or even tearful.

''E's very nice, your Alex,' she began, as she and Rose sat in the breakfast room, eating toast and watching Daisy follow the ducks that came up from the lake each morning hoping to find crusts, and were now waddling round the sunny terrace. ''E's got nice manners, too — not like some people I could mention, what don't live a million miles away.'

'I'm glad you like him. I love him very much.' Rose took Phoebe's hand. 'Phoebe, about Daisy—'

'Rose, you know I can't take 'er!' Phoebe's mouth was working and she looked as if she might start to cry. 'These past few days, I've tried an' tried! I like 'er well enough. She's very sweet an' everythin'—'

Phoebe rummaged in her pocket, searching for a handkerchief. 'But she don't know me. She don't feel like my child.'

'But Phoebe, she's your daughter,' Rose said, gently. 'You must feel—'

'I'm sorry, Rose, I don't.' Phoebe glanced towards open the door. 'Look out, 'ere comes your feller.'

Alex walked into the breakfast room and sat down at the table. 'You're very quiet, ladies,' he began.

'We was thinkin',' Phoebe told him.

'About what?' Alex looked Rose. 'Darling, what's the matter?'

'Nothing, Alex.'

'Rose, it's everythin'!' Phoebe looked anxiously at Alex. 'Rose might 'ave said I'm goin' with a Jewish feller, yeah?'

'She didn't, but go on.'

'I'm goin' to convert. I'm 'avin' lessons with the local rabbi, and I'm doin' all right.' Phoebe turned to Rose. 'Nathan's done so much for me!' she cried. ''Idin' me when Dan was after me, then takin' me to Leeds an' lodgin' me with his relations there. But there's nothin' for us 'ere in Britain. So now the war is over, we're goin' to New York, to start again.'

Phoebe looked earnestly at Rose. 'We're takin' Mrs R, of course. She's been like a mother, what that woman 'asn't done for me ain't nobody's business. But as for little Daisy — money's tight already. I can't ask Nathan to do this for me, as well.'

'Phoebe, love, Maria left some money. You could have—'

'Oh, for God's sake, Rose!' wailed Phoebe, bursting into tears.

'Phoebe, don't upset yourself,' said Alex. 'If you feel you can't take Daisy to New York with you, we shall have to think of something else. Rose, is there any coffee?'

* * *

Henry shuffled in just then, and Rose began to talk of eggs and bacon. Phoebe's sobbing turned to furtive sniffing. Later, she and Henry went off arm in arm to feed the doves.

'Henry's such a lovely man,' said Rose. 'So good, so generous, so kind.'

'Yes, I'm going to miss the dear old chap.'

'Alex, what exactly did you mean when you said we'd have to think of something else for Daisy?'

'Of course, it's really up to you.' Alex buttered a slice of bread, then cut it into fingers. 'She doesn't have a proper home. She needs one, and she could have one with us.'

Rose stared at him, astonished. 'You — you mean we could adopt her?'

'I don't see why not.'

'Alex, Michael would have killed you! He's going to inherit what should be yours and mine. But you'd still take his child?'

'We still don't know if Daisy *is* his daughter, and anyway she needs a family.' Alex watched Daisy toddle across flagstones, clapping her podgy little hands, and scattering all the ducks. 'Daisy?'

Daisy stopped. She turned to him and beamed. She came inside and climbed on to his lap, then helped herself to fingers of his bread.

'Sins of the fathers,' Alex murmured, as he stroked her silky, golden curls. 'Rose, the child is always innocent, but always suffers most.'

Then Rose understood. Alex was remembering his own appalling childhood, and — loving little Daisy as he did — he didn't have any choice.

'Daisy?' Rose reached out to stroke one soft, pink hand. 'We're going on a ship to India.'

Daisy twisted round to frown at Alex.

'Don't look so worried, sweetheart.' Alex smiled reassuringly. 'It's going to be a very big adventure for us all.'

At the end of yet another golden afternoon, when Daisy was asleep on Henry's lap and Phoebe had gone upstairs to do her packing, Rose took Alex for a walk.

They followed the winding path around the headland and watched the tide race in. 'You've gone very quiet again,' said Alex, taking Rose's hand. 'You're happy to take Daisy?'

'More than happy,' Rose assured him.

'It's just that I was thinking — if we can't have children of our own — Daisy is so lovely.'

'Yes, she's gorgeous,' Rose agreed.

'So what's the problem?'

'There's no problem.' Rose smiled up at him. 'There's something I must to tell you.'

'What?'

'I didn't want to say until I was certain. But now I'm almost sure. Alex, it's like a miracle, and I never thought it would happen. But I'm going to have a child.'

'You're what?' Alex stared at her in disbelief. 'But when you were in hospital, you said—'

'I know I did. But I've been getting fatter, every morning I feel slightly sick, and there are all the other signs as well. Alex, are you pleased?'

'You need to ask me if I'm pleased?' Alex picked her up and swung her round. 'Rose, I'm delighted. We're going to have the perfect family.'

THE END

ACKNOWLEDGEMENTS

If it hadn't been for the eternally inspiring and totally wonderful RNA, I'd never have become a novelist, so a big collective hug to the entire organisation in its Golden Anniversary year.

Thanks to everyone at Choc Lit for all their help and support. They've been brilliant in every way.

ABOUT THE AUTHOR

Margaret James was born and brought up in Hereford. She studied English at London University, and has written many short stories, articles and serials for magazines. She is the author of fifteen published novels.

Margaret is a long-standing contributor to *Writing Magazine* for which she writes the Fiction Focus column and an author interview for each issue. She's also a creative writing tutor for the London School of Journalism.

An active member of the Romantic Novelists' Association, she contributed to the 50th anniversary anthology *Loves Me, Loves Me Not*. Margaret's short story is *The Service of My Lady*.

For more information on Margaret visit:
www.twitter.com/majanovelist

THE CHOC LIT STORY

Established in 2009, Choc Lit is an independent, award-winning publisher dedicated to creating a delicious selection of quality women's fiction.

We have won 18 awards, including Publisher of the Year and the Romantic Novel of the Year, and have been shortlisted for countless others. In 2023, we were shortlisted for Publisher of the Year by the Romantic Novelists' Association.

All our novels are selected by genuine readers. We are proud to publish talented first-time authors, as well as established writers whose books we love introducing to a new generation of readers.

In 2023, we became a Joffe Books company. Best known for publishing a wide range of commercial fiction, Joffe Books has its roots in women's fiction. Today it is one of the largest independent publishers in the UK.

We love to hear from you, so please email us about absolutely anything bookish at choc-lit@joffebooks.com.

If you want to receive free books every Friday and hear about all our new releases, join our mailing list here: www.joffebooks.com/freebooks.

Printed in Great Britain
by Amazon

62985242R00170